TO WEAVE THE WIND

ARTS OF SUBSTANCE - NOVEL 2

SHARON ROSE

ETERNAROSE PUBLISHING

DEDICATION

To Jade,
May you find the unique gifts within yourself,
and always treasure them.

CONTENTS

CHAPTER 1

Some ambassador she was! On the cusp of her destiny, and all Fanteal wanted was to summon a gale to carry her away.

Instead, she asked the breeze to sweep the wildflower fragrance up the hill to her. She climbed the tilted steps, letting the delicate scents waft over her. For the last time.

If only she could savor this without the taint of loss. Just like yesterday, dancing beneath two full moons, all too aware that it was the last time. A thought that had betrayed her to tears. Fanteal adjusted for the broken step beneath her foot, as wobbly as her emotions. At least her partner had seemed to believe the excuse that she'd gotten something in her eye. Her mother had not.

She could almost hear the echo of her mother's delicately whispered reproof. "Tears at a celebration? Because you'll dance in a different home come the next New Year? You are being honored tonight. Act like it."

As though tears and smiles were kept in little boxes to be taken out at the appropriate moment.

Typical of her mother. She'd even arranged a farewell event for Fanteal's siblings before the arrival of Dirklan's prime minister. This was her mother's royal version of kindness—that her children would have a day with no duties except to enjoy one another. Or perhaps it was a method to get the official parting over with, lest tears rise when Fanteal should be smiling.

Cresting the long flight of steps, Fanteal absorbed the pressure of hilltop wind. Maybe such events had worked for her mother when she'd left her home to become Ambassador of Dirklan. In fact, her separation had been harder in some ways. Younger than Fanteal and destined for the added weight of a queen's crown. She had never met the man she would marry within days of arrival. None of this changed the fact that she'd had no substance gift to lose.

How could a mother who hated wind and loved a roof overhead possibly know what her wind-weaving daughter was giving up?

A chipmunk skittered into hiding as Fanteal picked her way across the overgrown tiles of the pavilion. Or so the ruin was called. Whatever the structure had been, only columns and one pediment remained standing. Two statues guarded the final approach. Worn faceless by centuries of wind, rain, and occasional snow. Some kind of seated animal—they could have been anything from lions to dogs. She rested a hand against one. "Or are you a pair of giant chipmunks?"

She snorted. Rock. Supposedly enduring and stable. Yet it wore away to nothing, while air still blanketed the hilltop no matter how the currents flowed. She had woven the wind here many a time, practicing her gift with creation's most elusive and vibrant substance. The invisible breath in their lungs. Though it couldn't be grasped in one's hand, it was more real than all other forms of matter. Not that anyone but a wind weaver would agree.

Among humans, that was. An enormous ocean eagle sailed by, resting upon the air as it angled toward its harborside nest. They understood.

Fanteal reached out to sample the swirl high overhead. A little drier than usual, for she had bidden the water vapor to depart when she set the circular pattern in motion earlier. Rain was never invited when the harbor's passage to Dirklan needed to be opened.

She leaned against one of the columns. Cold and rough. As unyielding as the covenant signed all those generations ago. An endless succession of ambassadors must be exchanged between the royal house of Welcia and its belowground province of Dirklan. So she, Princess Fanteal Nirundale de Noviam, must leave her palace home under the wide blue sky and become Ambassador Fanteal in the caverns below. A place without royal titles, where family names mattered little, and where the open sky did not exist.

Fanteal slapped her palm against the column, which hurt her without moving or acknowledging her existence. "Yes," she snarled, "you are exactly like that decree."

Ever since her substance gift had manifested, it had warred with her assumed destiny. The ambassador role did feel right, and her studies of government, economy, negotiation, and such still fascinated her. If only she could serve aboveground where her wind weaving gift also had a purpose. Surely some other member of the royal family would be a more suitable ambassador to Dirklan than she.

Never once had another stepped forward. Never once had her esteemed grandfather hinted that another might be preferred. If he, the prime minister of Dirklan, raised no issue over her gift, then no one else would object. All he ever did was praise her knowledge and skill.

Last year, he'd expounded on the tour he planned to give her through the cavernous domains of Dirklan Province. Such a delight it would be for him to introduce her belowground. Why would he think otherwise? He'd sent his own daughter aboveground to marry the king. In his eyes, he was bringing Fanteal to her rightful home. Where she must pretend that she wasn't hopelessly out of place.

Uhf. How to get her mind off this moaning? Fanteal strode from the column, her gown dragging over weed clumps. She would know one person, a grandfather who loved her. That was more acquaintance than her mother had possessed in her new home, and she'd succeeded.

A stumbling footstep and mumbled complaint intruded. Someone ascended the broken steps that led up from the valley.

She returned to the head of the stairs and looked down. Lord Yaeger. Did he need something? More likely acting on his belief that being a quarter hour early counted as being late. She understood his time obsession no better now than at her twelfth birthday celebration, when he'd been appointed to oversee her education as ambassador. How thrilled she'd been, how grown up she'd felt. Fanteal smirked. Twice that age now, but she was still considered young for her role.

Lord Yaeger caught sight of her and halted, motioning her to come down. She nodded but gave the sun's low position a pointed glance. She was not late. Perhaps she should check the harbor in case anything was going amiss.

She extended her weaving senses. The wind still obeyed. The water, she couldn't sense, but if something was wrong, her father would be tending it, and she would have felt his presence.

Lord Yaeger motioned with more vigor, so she bade the air lift his words to her ear. "Come down from there," he called. "You will be late."

She hid a smile, remembering his parting gift. An elegant bracelet. She'd nearly laughed aloud when she realized the jeweled oval was the face of a watch. Thoughtful in his way, for she would need it in Dirklan, so she'd promised to think fondly of him when she wore it belowground. But neither affection nor respect for him would make her give up her final moments of freedom within the sky.

Fanteal summoned the wind. It embraced her, supporting her as she leaned forward. It spread the silk chiffon of her gown into a rippling train. She jumped from the top step and cleared a dozen stairs. With one foot, she touched the landing enough to launch herself again, angling away from the long staircase. Her descent was more like a deer's than a woman's. She savored every instant of free flight as she sailed from boulder to hummock, from crumbling wall to smooth rock.

She was neither heated nor breathless when she reached the paved walk that led to the palace enclosure. Ascending to the top of the wall was just as easy, for the wind hastened to bear her weight. When she stepped within the colonnade, she let gratitude flavor her internal murmur of *enough now*. The gust stilled instantly.

She eased into a normal pace as she followed the colonnade to the chapel that adjoined it. If her father wanted her sooner, he would be there.

Still empty, but he would come, and together they would use their gifts. She pushed away the internal taunt of *for the last time*. In truth, the last time would be tomorrow, when the haste of departure would grant no leisure to mourn. One final day for some miracle to save her from a lifetime in the caverns.

Maybe a few minutes in this little open-air chapel was what she needed. It had been built for private worship, after all, when members of the royal family needed peace or answers. She crossed the oval floor's intricate mosaic. A salty breeze from the harbor swept between the front columns, which supported the domed roof. The altar nestled in the curve overlooking the harbor. Fire gems glowed in the brazier. A wall enclosed the chapel's rear half-circle to protect its mysterious treasure—four etched golden pillars, cloaked in shadow, barely visible.

Fanteal approached the altar. Bowls of flowers surround the brazier. Irises, water lilies, and willow blossoms represented the substance gifts, and an array of vine roses represented the varied life gifts. She searched within as she considered her choices. Willow blossoms and roses to embody the silent prayers of her conflicted gifts. Of what use could wind weaving be to an ambassador dwelling in caverns?

She placed the flowers in a bowl of fragrance oil and stirred them with her fingers while the oil absorbed their scents. The fire gems in the brazier flickered with colored light, an occasional flame licking around one and then another. They sprang to life as she spread the flowers across the gems. The oil sizzled and released its fragrance. It gathered in a cloud around her. The breeze detoured past the chapel, lingering to whisper in the bushes outside.

Fanteal wiped her scented fingers through her hair. She stood with her eyes closed, her lips moving silently. Trying to plead her case to Ellincreo, and yet avoid any hint that she objected to his will. All the while, hoping it wasn't what everyone planned for her.

No answer came, no stirring to change her designated course. Though one should never seek a vision upon the golden statues, she peered into their alcove. Would a plain column take on form and motion? Show her what she should do?

Nothing.

Her father's long stride approached along the colonnade. He halted between the columns of the chapel. "Ah, a final offering at your favorite altar. May I ask what you blended?"

"Willow blossoms for the wind weaver in me and roses for the ambassador." She couldn't hold his gaze. "They weren't blended, though. Separate sides of the burner, for my time has come to leave one of them in order to embrace the other."

He drew near and rested his hands against her shoulders. She looked up from his sumptuously embroidered tunic, focusing on each detail of his face, soon to be only memories. The lines framing his mouth, the gray that mixed with brown in his thick eyebrows, the steady gaze of his dark blue eyes.

"You've decided, then?" Half statement, half question.

"Shall we say rather that I've admitted to the decision that has already been made for me."

He squeezed her shoulders. "Do not say that, Fanteal. You *do* have a choice."

She smiled and tried for a bantering tone. "Alas, you have raised me honorably. I am faced with only two options. One selfish. The other worthy, and according to my mother, wholly delightful. What's a girl to do?"

His eyebrows nudged closer. "What has she been saying now?"

"It's not that. It's what she *doesn't* say. Cannot say. She thinks I grieve for home and family, and that is true. But she doesn't understand that I am..." Her throat constricted. "...losing the sky."

"I know." He paused. "The best I can imagine is living in a desert for the rest of my life. To never again see a stream, much less the ocean. But there would still be water somewhere, and perhaps as a streamer, I could help desert dwellers conserve or find more of the water we take for granted. There is plenty of air in the caverns. You'll use your gift differently, but you will still use it."

"For what? The voice-lifting trick?"

A hint of reproof lurked in his eyes. "Words are crucial, but worthless if they are not heard. Do not underestimate the importance of being the royal ambassador. From what your grandfather said last year, the need is great."

She understood his emphasis. Ore shipments had fallen way off—for no reason that any abovegrounder could discern. "I don't see how I'm supposed to fix inadequate trade payments if Grandfather allows them. He is prime minister, after all. Re-elected so many times that the people obviously trust him. He's the one with actual authority."

"Focus on the hidden causes. Find out why the people have lost faith in the crown. Why they feel justified in not paying for all the food we send. Work on that."

She'd seen the other side of this issue, for her mother actively represented Dirklan. But belowground, Fanteal worried she'd just be seen as young and unknown. They wouldn't even trust her to stay until she married one of them. Another worry, marriage, though her grandfather promised she wouldn't be pressured. A year seemed plenty long enough to find a husband...and not nearly long enough. But they'd been through all of this, and indeed, her decision had been made—regardless of who made it. She knew what she had to do.

An inaudible voice brought her thoughts to a halt. A voice she had never before discerned. Harsh. Grating. Her eyes flew to her father's. "Is that the former belowground?"

"Indeed. Your gift is truly amazing."

"No more than yours. You can sense the formers working too."

"True, but I've never known a wind weaver to perceive the command of a former." He took her hand and led her from the chapel onto the harborside colonnade. "That was the chief former of Dirklan. He gives the dome over Passage Lake that nudge to let me know he is prepared for the opening. It is time to lower the whirlpool."

They followed the curving walkway along the cliff's edge, stopping before it met a sheltered flight of steps. From here, they could view the natural harbor and the retractable palace dock, which had been drawn back from its anchor where the cliff gave way to shoreline.

Fanteal sat on the colonnade's low wall. The harbor spread out below her. Sunlight frosted ominous waves that hid the dome within the seabed. The city of Regissa wrapped around the harbor's near side. Rigid port docks stood empty, for the ships remained at sea when counter tides transformed the harbor from safe to treacherous. Seaweed lay in sodden heaps on exposed rock. The current circled, skewed backwards as only occurred when the two moons synchronized at the half year and new year.

She sensed her father's silent command. The water's energy compressed toward the midst of the harbor. Waves slowed near the piers but picked up speed in the center. This, she felt through the air, where it rested on the water.

She sent her gentle call to the wind, commanding it to match the water's motion. Faster and faster, she urged the spiral. A vortex formed and dipped its tip into the water. So persuadable, it was, so ready to lend its energy to the sea. The whirlpool sank quickly. It beat against the rock panels of the dome below, twisting them open. And there within the panels, she sensed the former who had command of them.

How strange that her gift would reveal a new aspect on this of all days. No time to think of that now, for the whirlpool must lift—from the lake beneath the dome—a vessel holding precious cargo, her grandfather and his aides.

CHAPTER 2

Intent though he was, calm satisfaction filled her father's voice. "The vessel is within the whirlpool's grip." He commanded the water to draw it up.

Fanteal sensed the object only when it reached the surface and pressed against the air that she held within her awareness. She squinted across the sparkling blue waters. There it was—its red and white top a flashing blur as it spun. More like a domed saucer than a boat. Time to unwind the whirlpool.

Her father was already ordering the swirl to still, but with the entire harbor circling, momentum fought him. The wind was quicker to obey, for it had plenty of space above and less demand from gravity. Fanteal bade it draw energy up from the water. Fine mist rose along with the twining wind, and she dispersed the stray moisture through the airways.

As the harbor calmed, the spinning vessel slowed. She could now discern the vertical red and white stripes on its broad, domed top. Within it, the four twirling seats would now be slowing. A wild ride that she would soon experience. Her mother had endured it, but Fanteal intended to *enjoy* the thrill.

The king turned to her. "Well done, Fanteal. Such proficiency is unusual indeed. It's been a long time since we've had a wind weaver as gifted as you."

Pleasure welled up and almost brought tears to her eyes. He never let his partiality bias his judgment. "Thank you, Father."

He touched her cheek. No words could contain the rest of what they felt. In a moment he was gone, descending the steps to the dock.

Fanteal stayed where she was. Her part would come later. Her grandfather always went first to visit with his daughter, then came time to visit with his grandchildren. But today would be different. Today she would be presented as Royal Ambassador of Welcia.

The vessel in the harbor followed an arced current toward shore, guided now by one of the harbor streamers. Dockhands released the withdrawn dock, and it slid out on its track. They readied hooks and ropes. Her father came into sight, Lord Yaeger and a few other nobles following him. They paused on the shore. Dockhands snagged the vessel and rotated it to bring the hatch within the curved recess of the dock. They tied off ropes, flipped heavy latches, and jerked the hatch open.

Fanteal set the air currents to detour around the dock area, for belowgrounders disliked strong wind. A couple of black-haired aides climbed out of the vessel. She waited for her grandfather's snowy head to appear. Instead, the men looked around, then crossed the dock toward shore.

Why weren't the prime minister's aides assisting him? Why did they approach the king without him? What were they saying? Then, her father turned and looked up at her. Even from this height, she could see his frown. The aides followed his gaze. She didn't recognize either of them. Dockhands steadied someone else who swayed as he emerged from the vessel. Still not the one she sought.

Air thickened in her chest. She jumped up, raced along the colonnade, and descended the sheltered steps in flying leaps. Remembering propriety in time, she slowed to a dignified pace before reaching the bottom. The wind greeted her as she stepped out onto the slope that led to the dock. It became her trainbearer, spreading her full skirts to flow behind her.

The younger of the two men watched her approach, his smile growing.

When she reached the king, he took her hand and lifted it formally. "Allow me to present Royal Ambassador of Welcia, Princess Fanteal de Noviam."

Though the introduction had barely begun, the younger man murmured, "Exquisite!"

Idiot. Fanteal granted him no answer. Turning to the king, she asked, "Where is my grandfather?"

He withdrew his narrowed gaze from the stranger. His expression softened as he took both of her hands. "I'm sorry to grieve you at this moment, my dear, but they bring sad news. Prime Minister Nirundale has left this life."

She averted her face from the strangers, certain now of who they must be. Her world quaked. The older man was uttering a speech of condolence while her lungs clamped. She didn't answer. Couldn't. Her father's grasp tightened on her fingertips. She blinked her wet eyes hard. This was not the moment for tears. Nor for breathless shock. She focused on practiced formality and turned, letting her father lift her hand again on his open palm.

He slightly extended it toward the elder of the two men. "Fanteal, I must introduce to you Prime Minister Sened Mikkael."

Fanteal transferred her hand from her father's to his, and the prime minister received it respectfully on the back of his hand. "It will be a delight to welcome you to Dirklan, Lady Fanteal."

Using her belowground title already. She uttered prepared words. "I look forward to extending the ancient bond between our peoples."

He inclined his head, then shifted her hand toward the younger man. "May I present my son, Jaikon Mikkael."

Jaikon clasped her fingers with unearned familiarity. Did he not know better? Or not care? He smiled down at her, moving closer. "I could not have asked for a more beautiful bride."

She gasped and jerked her hand away. His appreciative look warped into something far different.

"You have *not* asked for that honor," the king said between his teeth. "Nor have you been granted what you assume."

Oh, the expressions that chased over Jaikon's face. And those of the two men who had come up behind him from the vessel. Even the prime minister looked irritated, though he had better control.

"Before any further discussion," Sir Mikkael said to the king, "I would like to speak with *our* ambassador. Will you please introduce me to Queen Ambassador Trissina?"

"Certainly." The king turned to ascend the walkway to the palace.

Ah, a chance to escape, for this first meeting was not hers. Fanteal hurried back to the stairs.

The wind swirled after her, allowing the breeze to rush over the group behind her.

J aikon stared after her. Was he not insulted enough? Must she run away from him too?

His father whispered a word into his ear. "Remember!"

He almost ground his teeth. His father had warned him, and the moment they were alone, he'd have to listen to the same old rebuke. Deserved, too, which made it no easier to bear. The two envoys who'd accompanied them had already pushed past him, close on the prime minister's heels. Tomorrow, they would spread word belowground of his blunder. The rumors would be all over Dirklan.

Jaikon looked up to the cliff-top colonnade. A lone figure drew out of sight behind the column where he'd first caught a glimpse of the ambassador.

It must be her. Was she alone? If so, could he somehow smooth over his premature words? He tensed his jaw. Everyone knew they were expected to wed, and he'd only meant to compliment her. In any case, she couldn't reject him any worse than she already had. The party he should have joined was several paces away, apparently unaware that he wasn't following. He couldn't let this chance slip away.

Jaikon trod the path she had taken and found the stairs to the colonnade. But when he reached the spot where he'd seen her, it was deserted. He hesitated. The breeze was stronger here than by the dock. It forced air at his nostrils, making it hard to breathe. He shielded his face with a hand. How could these people stand it?

Ahead of him, the colonnade passed through a structure, one portion overlooking the harbor and the rest jutting into a garden where flowers bloomed around a fir tree. He'd search that far.

Pausing in the welcome shade between two of the columns, he found Fanteal standing within the curve that overlooked the harbor. Her head was bowed, her long hair falling forward to hide her face. She gripped the rail that edged a surface. White showed on her knuckles.

Was this a good idea? Regardless, if she'd heard his approach, he could not now turn back. "Please forgive me for intruding."

Her back went straight as a column, and her face hard as marble. Though she was a foot shorter than he, she seemed to be staring down at him.

"I came to apologize." He shifted. "From what your father said, I gather my words were misconstrued."

"There are times when it's wise to allow emotions to cool before offering an apology."

"Considering how...presumptuous I must have sounded, I'd rather admit my error at once."

"You do not, in fact, find me exquisite?"

He returned the challenge in her eyes. The princess chose to be difficult, did she? For now, he must humor her, but perhaps it was she who blundered this time. "I'm not apologizing for stating you're beautiful. That is a simple fact. When you ran down the slope, with your train streaming out behind, you were as graceful as a dancer. But though the sight was enchanting, it doesn't excuse me for expressing myself so poorly. For that, I do apologize."

Halfway through his answer, her expression of indignation transformed to arrested attention. She turned to lean against the railing, a puzzled crease between her brows.

"Did I say something...strange?" he asked.

"No. I'm just wondering what, exactly, you saw."

"I beg your pardon?"

"I didn't run down the slope."

What was this? Was she trying to throw him off-balance because she couldn't reasonably reject his apology? Did her manners extend no further than one formal sentence prepared for the prime minister? What sort of ambassador was being sent to them? Easily offended? Capricious? He guarded his expression as earlier worries resurfaced. Was she a spoiled princess who thought that royal rank excused her from common courtesy? She would find otherwise. No matter how much he needed to humor her, he wasn't about to follow her through pointless ramblings.

He stepped closer to the nearby brazier and changed the subject. "I never imagined this purpose for the gems we trade to you. What's the point of setting them amid fire?"

"We burn our offerings here."

"Is this a...what do you call it...a chapel?" She nodded, and he looked more closely at his surroundings. "Where are the idols?"

"There are no idols. If you mean the statues, they're in the back."

He peered into the darker area. "Why are they kept in the shadows?"

"Because they are hard to see."

"Do you always speak in riddles?"

A hint of chill returned to her voice. "It's hard to discuss things that you clearly don't understand."

"Then enlighten me. What, exactly, are the statues?"

"I cannot even begin to explain them to you."

Evasive, but he wasn't giving up. "Fine. If the statues are too much, then tell me of the offering."

He endured her solemn gaze before she gestured to the bowls of flowers and oil. "Items are selected that have significance to oneself or the situation. Flowers are often soaked in this oil to draw out their fragrance. Then they're spread on the brazier to burn during worship."

"How are the flowers significant?"

"They represent different things. For instance, irises represent the earth because they grow from buried tubers. Water lilies stand for water, of course, and willow blossoms for the wind. But it needn't be flowers that are offered. Just anything that will burn."

"Is it permitted that I make such an offering?"

Her mouth softened. "Anyone may do so."

Ah, that reached her. Though unsure why, he'd take the chance to show her there was more to him than one verbal misstep. He looked at the flowers. No. She'd referred to the substance gifts, and he wasn't following that lead! Jaikon took a few steps out to the garden. Direct sunlight intensified the heat and hurried his choice. He broke off a sprig from the fir tree, with a green cone nestled in its needles. A bush bore clumps of berries, like miniature grape clusters. He plucked one of these and scooped up a handful of earth.

Fanteal still waited by the altar when he returned. At least she hadn't run away.

"What now?" he asked.

"Spread them on the brazier. You may soak them in oil first if you like, but it's not necessary."

"The unnecessary doesn't interest me." He placed his items on the firelit gems, explaining their significance. "In Dirklan, the evergreen represents Ellincreo, the only one worthy of worship. This earth represents Dirklan itself, and the fruit represents the food we need from aboveground." The fir sprig flared in a sudden burst and disintegrated, while flames licked around the berries. Already, this seemed silly, but he must search for meaning. "It does seem fitting to offer this on the gems that we trade for food."

Fanteal held her silence, and he waited. His father had warned him to keep an open mind. What was supposed to happen? The only difference was the stillness. The wind gave him a brief respite, no longer pushing and pulling the air past his face. Smoke hung above the brazier, soured with the scent of unripe fruit, while dirt congealed over a few diamonds.

He still didn't get it. "Where is the worship in this act? Is there something beyond the tradition?"

"Worship is in the heart. The offering only sets the ambiance."

Yi! The ambiance stunk. Remembering to guard his tongue, he sought inoffensive words. "Belowground, we start worship with song. I look forward to escorting you to the sacred chamber." He turned away from the stench, only to gasp at the sight before him. "What is that?"

Fanteal nearly choked. She couldn't blame him for his disgust. One of the statues was revealed, taking on the form of a man stark against a hazy glow. She had never seen anything so hideous. "It's…the one that represents formers." She couldn't force herself to explain more. After all her days of longing for a vision, why must she see this?

Jaikon moved toward it, a look of fascinated revulsion marring his face. He mustn't touch, but did he know that? She longed to run but stayed just near enough to grab his arm if he reached for the transformed gold. How dreadful that she must witness his humiliating revelation.

As if to emphasize the grotesqueness of his vision, the wind weaver statue began to glow with a gentle beauty. Fanteal released a shaky breath. A vision of her own! That proved the other could have nothing to do with her. She gravitated toward her own statue, but try as she would, she could not drag her eyes from the earthen figure.

It stood with feet planted and chest thrust forward. From head to foot, it was covered with filth. Not soil—rotting filth. A rancid smell emanated from it. A network of fibrous fungi draped from the decaying matter on its eyebrows, obscuring its view. Bits of debris adhered to the sludge around its nose and mouth. Powdery dust floated toward it, became entrapped, and solidified the crust that nearly sealed its nose. Its parted lips sneered despite the stiffening mire that held their corners shut. How could such arrogance exist within such filth?

Jaikon's nostrils pinched—from disgust at the odor or the vision? Yet he stared into that haughty face.

Fanteal's stomach heaved, and she forced her eyes down. A glimmer snagged her attention. A chunk of filth had fallen from the statue's calf, revealing the luster of pure gold. How strange.

She stepped back to bring her own statue within her field of view, longing to see its serene face turning away from this beastly creature. No such comfort was granted her.

The mosaic floor appeared to swirl like water as the wind statue seemed to move like a living woman! Within the vision, she extended her arms beyond her head and leaned forward to dive. Fanteal could almost feel air rushing past in her leap. The hands parted the waters. That determined face plunged beneath the waves.

Fanteal shuddered, swaying when the statues became rigid pillars again. Why, oh why, had that beast been revealed to her if not to warn her away? Why did she still have to pass through the waters?

The light in the alcove faded, and she stumbled to the altar rail. She needed time to think, but Jaikon's voice intruded.

"How can you worship such a hideous thing?"

"No, we don't. The statues are rarely revealed. I've never even seen one, much less worshipped it."

He huffed. "Now that you know what's hidden in the shadows, do you still wish to persist in this so-called worship?"

She clung to the railing. "You mustn't speak of this. You truly do not understand what you're saying."

He leaned against the far end of the altar rail, his arms folded across his chest as he studied her. After a few minutes, he said, "Do you realize that there are no statues, no altars, and certainly no chapels for personal visions beneath the waters?"

"Yes, of course."

"Are you intending to give up your faith or planning to bring some remnant of this with you?"

She pressed a hand to her temple. How could he jump to such conclusions? "You overrate what you see here. These are merely *things*. My faith is within me; I need no object to sustain it."

"Then why do you look so mournful?"

"I..." How could she tell him that she had just seen his true self? He thought their marriage was certain. And with a new prime minister, he wouldn't be the only one to believe that. No! A promise had been made, and she wouldn't let it go. "My grandfather..." Her throat closed with a squeak.

"Ah! I am sorry." His brow creased. "I keep forgetting how recent his death must seem to you."

She allowed him to misunderstand her. Better to let her parents tell the prime minister of her grandfather's promise. Instead, she asked, "When did he die?"

"Eleven months ago. Not long after his last visit here. Were you fond of him?"

His voice had softened. Gentleness? It seemed so contradictory it almost dizzied her. She needed to get alone and think. And remember that she was an ambassador. She pulled that invisible mantle around her mind and steadied her voice. "Yes, very fond of him."

Jaikon reached toward her just as Lord Yaeger's voice made them both jump.

CHAPTER 3

The straight-backed man stared at Jaikon, chin raised. "Who granted you permission to approach the princess?"

Whoa. Jaikon tensed. He needed *permission*? What had he messed up this time? Who was this gray-haired man? Had he been with the king at the dock?

"I did, Lord Yaeger," Lady Fanteal said, sparing Jaikon the need to answer. "What brings you here?"

At her calm words, the man edged his chin lower. "The queen summons you, my lady." He extended his hand to her, palm down. "I came to escort you."

"I will go to her, but will accept the escort of our guest, the prime minister's son."

Giving him status now? Whatever this all meant, Jaikon took the cue and stepped toward her, offering his arm.

She looked at it. "Thank you, but the occasion requires more formality."

Now what was he supposed to do?

"Lord Yaeger, please demonstrate our custom." She rested her hand on the back of the man's, which he held at her shoulder height while standing a yard away. He turned to lead her from the chapel, but she took only one step before lifting her hand and looking to Jaikon.

Fine, he could play a part if he must. He took her hand at the desired height, but she didn't move with him.

"Palm up is appropriate only for a father or a husband."

"Ah." He rotated his hand so she could clasp its back. Was there no end to this?

Finally, they stepped onto the colonnade opposite where he had entered the chapel, Lord Yaeger following at a respectful distance. Jaikon squinted at his first clear view of the palace. The vast structure of fair stone gleamed against a blue sky. Belowground, light shafts gave them full daylight but never at this intensity. Nor the heat. At least the wind didn't blow as it had on the far side of the chapel. Elaborate carvings and balconies lent fitting grandeur to the palace, but the turrets and peaks were a bit much.

As they walked away from the harbor, he glimpsed a bit of the city. All roofs were peaked. Why? More space separated the buildings than seemed necessary, and if he wasn't mistaken, trees grew between some. There were supposed to be vast fields up here, though they must be farther away. No sign of Mount Estelle either. Would he be able to see it from the palace grounds?

"Does the view match your expectation?" Fanteal asked.

Was she pointing out that belowgrounders had no idea what the capital city of Regissa looked like? "It is certainly different than what I'm used to. Don't you get tired, holding your arm out in this fashion?"

"Not at all." Her voice lilted. "You're supporting it. If the strain is too much for you, take heart. You only need to keep it up until we're inside the palace."

He hoped her tone indicated jest rather than insult. "I can stand it as long as we don't have to turn ninety degrees and sidestep through doorways."

She coughed, and her lips quivered before she cleared her throat. At least she had some sense of humor. "I have found that bending elbows can bring two people quite near. In doorways, for instance, or on the dancefloor."

"A great relief." He matched her ironic tone. "Why are we performing this little parade?"

"To improve the first impression you made," she replied. "Scores of eyes are no doubt watching our every move. It is in your best interests to show me respect, at least in public."

She still smiled, so he tried more banter. "Should I be thanking you for deigning to rest your hand on mine?"

She cleared her throat again. "You may consider this *my* apology. Having come down to the dock, where I didn't belong, I should not have rushed off again. The dock workers have ears and tongues, so putting your words and my behavior together, the rumors won't sound good."

"Is that why Lord Yaeger despised me before we were even introduced?"

She tilted her head. "He was there, after all. Though he'll never let a feeling show, he is quite fond of me. Be careless toward me, and you will offend him."

Odd, for the man appeared older than her father. "Is he a relation?"

"No, but he's my mentor. There is not a soul in Welcia who has a better understanding of government and provincial relations."

What was she talking about? "Your mentor?"

She regarded him. "The education of an ambassador goes well beyond the basics."

"I suppose so."

She angled her head toward another paved walk. "We turn here."

He shortened his steps as she swept around the outside of the turn. Her graceful movement was lovely. The wind angled into his face again. "Ugh!" He jerked his free hand up to shield his nose and mouth. "This awful wind. How do you breathe?" Shock flitted over her face, gone as quickly as the wind. He lowered his hand, though a swaying tree suggested another gust was on the way. "I suppose you're used to it."

"Indeed!" Such an odd intonation...gone with her next words. "I'm curious. Did you know Prime Minister Nirundale well?"

"Not really. I was in company with him several times when my father brought me to some of the larger events, but I never exchanged more than a few words with Sir Nirundale."

They climbed a few steps between flower-laden bushes. Their scents were pleasant enough, but the gardens reminded him of a broken flask of perfume. Was everything up here a touch too extreme?

"Which domain did your father govern before he was elected prime minister?" she asked.

"He wasn't governor. He was chief of staff to Governor Brakentel of Northeshur."

She raised her brows. "Oh? Is it not still the governors who stand for election as prime minister?"

"Typically," he said, "but only because they're well known. In the case of Northeshur, it wasn't advisable. Our concerns over failing imports affect the entire province, and they must now be represented at the highest level. In order to give his advantage to my father, Governor Brakentel chose not to stand for election."

"I...don't understand. Why wouldn't the governor represent Northeshur himself?"

"Because his only son is married and is forty-three besides." Jaikon switched back to a humorous tone. "Hardly a suitable match for our new ambassador."

She didn't return his smile. "Were the citizens of Dirklan electing a prime minister or a husband for the ambassador?"

He laughed. "That's putting it a little strong. Let's just say, they knew a suitable match needed to be available to you. In all other issues, they were choosing who would be the best prime minister."

"I see."

Why did she draw the words out with such disfavor? What did she expect? "Lady Fanteal, we have waited eleven years for the crown's new ambassador to reaffirm the bond between Welcia above and Welcia below. Sir Nirundale announced last year that he would bring you to us on his next visit."

"*That*, I fully understand."

He held back his response, for servants stood outside the double doors they approached. Fanteal's demeanor was a portrait of regal calm. The servants grasped ornate handles and swung the doors wide. Beyond them, more people paused their activities to bow. She maintained her effortless pace across the hall and up the curved staircase. He barely had time to admire the murals of seascapes, embellished with sapphires, aquamarines, and diamonds from the mines of Dirklan.

Queen Trissina, Ambassador of Dirklan and daughter of the late Prime Minister Nirundale, awaited them in the reception salon, attended only by Jaikon's father. She sat in the center of the room on a couch, which was half buried in yards of emerald silk flowing from her shoulders and waist. Her thick, black hair was twisted into a complex knot, and she bore a strong resemblance to her deceased father in all but height. An attractively mature woman, but when her ethereal daughter sat to embrace her, she appeared only plain and solid.

The contrasts between the two couldn't have been greater. Fanteal's free blond locks gleamed next to her mother's black coiffure. The princess's white gown shimmered with richness, but it seemed to float next to the heavy green silk. The queen wore large gems in heavy, gold settings; her daughter wore pearls. Fanteal was graceful motion. The queen was erect dignity. It seemed that Fanteal had inherited nothing from her mother except her scant height.

Though the princess was nothing like what Jaikon had expected, the queen was. Even in sharing grief with Fanteal over Sir Nirundale's passing, an unshakable presence emanated from the grand lady. Perhaps there was hope for her daughter.

Jaikon waited for them to finish consoling one another. Finally, his father introduced him, and he stated his practiced greetings to the queen ambassador.

She looked him over. "It's unfortunate that you could not be adequately welcomed at your arrival."

What to make of that? What had she heard? He may as well make use of what Fanteal had said. "Your daughter calls me a guest and allowed me to escort her. It's more than adequate welcome, considering the sad news we brought."

As they spoke, King Darinneth entered and looked Jaikon up and down.

"I heard that you parted on unpleasant terms," the queen said. "How is it that you accompanied her here?"

Jaikon swallowed. "The misunderstanding troubled me, so I went in search of her to apologize."

With a hopeful lilt, the queen asked her daughter, "Did you accept his apology, my dear?"

Fanteal shrugged. "Of course. It was only for expressing himself poorly. Speaking one's mind is no great fault, and it provides me with a clear understanding. I am now certain that the word *ambassador* means *wife* to him. Perhaps to many of our belowground citizens as well."

What now—a polite shrew? Her father narrowed his eyes, and her mother also looked displeased. "Then I will speak plainly again," Jaikon said. "Why is it a surprise that the royal ambassador is expected to marry the prime minister's offspring? Hasn't it been so since the covenant was ratified? Didn't your last ambassador, Melthindi De Noviam, marry the prime minister's daughter?"

The king spoke low and even. "Such marriages have occurred, but so have others. Why should we expect her to marry you, when your very existence is a surprise? Sir Nirundale did not intend that Ambassador Fanteal would marry into his family, though he had a grandson of similar age. He planned to introduce her to suitable bachelors, but she was to choose whom to marry."

The ramifications of giving a naive princess a choice between the political figures of Dirklan played through Jaikon's mind. The hair at the nape of his neck stood up. Before he could think of anything to say, his father replied.

"The circumstances have changed. We understand that we've brought you sad, even shocking, news. Yet the foundation of our relationship is not based on circumstances or individuals. It is based on a covenant, ratified by Dirklan Province and by royal decree. A covenant that contains no provision for cancellation. For this very reason, the ruling families of Welcia and Dirklan remain united. Does the crown of Welcia still acknowledge its responsibilities?"

"Be assured that it does," the king replied.

"And if it were you who had died, instead of Sir Nirundale, what answer would I be given?"

"Be assured that it does," Fanteal repeated.

Sir Mikkael's brow twitched, and the king offered an explanation. "Princess Fanteal is my eldest child and therefore heir to the crown. When she takes her position as ambassador, her brother, Telamien, will become my successor. He would give you the same answer, though he is yet an adolescent."

Jaikon's father nodded. "I'm relieved to hear this. Some in Dirklan doubt your commitment. We have matters to discuss other than marriage. Perhaps our children should take the opportunity to become better acquainted while we discuss trade concerns."

Queen Trissina glanced to her daughter. "You could show him the chapel, my dear. Jaikon, the aboveground approach to worship is quite different from ours and is widely misunderstood in Dirklan. I'd like you to have the chance to see that it is indeed worship of Ellincreo."

Fanteal hurried into speech "I was in the chapel when Jaikon found me. I explained how we begin worship, and he has already made an offering of his own."

The queen looked up at him. "And…?"

Again, Fanteal answered before he could. "He seemed to expect something from the offering itself. I think it distracted him from worship. Perhaps he'd like to see the art gallery." She rose as she spoke and moved toward Jaikon and the door.

"Later." The queen fixed her eyes on him. "I would like you to understand this, or you'll cause my daughter distress. Now that you know the offering is only a beginning, perhaps you could try again."

"Madam, it is not the offering that distracts me, but the thought of worshiping near that grotesque, revolting statue."

Gasps and stunned silence followed his words. The clock ticked off seconds before the door burst open.

A crying child ran to the queen and threw herself into her lap. "Mama, I wanted to see Granfadder!"

"Oh, I know. So did I," she crooned, gathering the child in her arms and rising to her feet.

Fanteal fled from the room. Neither parent tried to detain her.

The queen stopped before Sir Mikkael. "My daughter has spent her life studying Dirklan—its lands, its economy, its government, its customs. How much time has your son spent on the study of Welcia above?"

"You know that hasn't been possible. To wed the ambassador became his destiny only months ago. Nor is there anyone to teach him. Is it not better for us to learn directly from your ambassador, rather than from Dirklians who have never been aboveground?"

"There are some basic points that you should have bothered to learn before your arrival," the queen said. "And one in particular—the statues are *never* discussed. Never!"

She swept from the room amid a furious rustling of silk, her child cradled against her shoulder.

The king addressed Lord Yaeger, who had opened the door for the queen. "Summon the nobles and the other Dirklians to the delegation chamber." He, too, left the room.

Just beyond the doorway, Lord Yaeger addressed someone outside.

Jaikon's father leaned near him and spoke through barely parted lips. "Regardless of your delight in speaking your mind, I believe the Welcians can survive without your opinions."

Jaikon inclined his head, lips closed on the words that wanted out.

"Also, do not embarrass me again by going off without a word to anyone."

"Yes, sir." He cleared his tight throat. "What has become of Deltum and Tershel?"

"Deltum could barely manage the stairs due to dizziness. Tershel didn't heed the warning about wind and was gasping by the time we reached the palace. A medic took them aside to rest. I gather that the wind did not trouble you?"

"Only when I searched for Fanteal. After that, it was mostly still."

Footsteps and Deltum's voice reached them, approaching the open doorway.

"Come with us and listen," Jaikon's father said. "It is time for the envoys to speak, not you."

Lord Yaeger escorted the four Dirklians to the chamber. As they arrived in the room full of strangers, the king and queen entered through another door.

"The order of business has changed," King Darinneth said. "Since we are welcoming a new prime minister, I have requested that our queen, the Ambassador of Dirklan, begin with introductions."

Queen Ambassador Trissina took over, escorting the foursome through the crowd and presenting lords and ladies from the aboveground provinces. Servants passed among them with trays of light food and drink. Much appreciated, since Jaikon had avoided breakfast. He couldn't name the varied mixtures served on crisp wafers or the tart beverage, but they were delicious.

Finally, attendees began taking places at the tables. Jaikon hoped he would not need to address anyone by name, but at least someone had set placards on each table, indicating the province represented. That helped.

The king also sat at a table, making no show of his royalty beyond his rich clothing. Surprisingly, the queen escorted the Dirklians to their table and sat beside Jaikon's father. Why? Because she was the Dirklian ambassador? It still seemed odd. Extra chairs were arranged against the walls, for aids perhaps. Determined to stay out of trouble, Jaikon backstepped from his own group and took a chair between two of the windows. Four of them graced one wall, reaching all the way to the high ceiling. They stood open to let in the sunshine and an annoying breeze.

What of Ambassador Fanteal? Shouldn't she be here?

CHAPTER 4

Fanteal watched in the mirror of her dressing table as a maid entwined an emerald silk ribbon into a braid that circled her head. The maid picked up the matching ambassador's sash, but Fanteal held her hand out for it. "Thank you. I can finish."

The young woman curtsied and left the room.

Alone. No need to hide her confused feelings.

Fanteal draped the sash over her shoulder, took the clasp from her bare dresser, and walked to the full-length mirror. Her hands shook as she gathered the silk into the clasp and pinned it at her shoulder. No one must see her trembling. She tied the sash's tapered ends through the side loop in her skirt, then turned to make sure they flowed gracefully. This was how she should have been dressed for the formal greeting of the prime minister—in the symbolic green of a life gift, which now took precedence over her substance gift.

She mustn't stay in her suite much longer. An ambassador did not hide, no matter how awful the situation. She ought to be out there building rapport. How was she supposed to do that among lords and ladies of the realm when Jaikon insisted on shouting his ignorance?

She stepped onto her balcony for a touch of the breeze. Her mother would be the primary spokesperson while Dirklians visited, but Fanteal needed to show her value as quickly as possible. Before they relegated her to token status—nothing but surety held in a marriage bond. Which they'd already done, apparently, but she wasn't giving in. Not after spending her life preparing for an ambassadorship.

She looked down to the walkway and spotted the top of her brother's fair hair. He lingered outside the delegation chamber windows, for he'd gained their father's permission to listen even though he couldn't join them until next year. He could fill her in if she'd missed anything big.

Fanteal slipped through her suite, down a corridor and staircase, then out onto the walkway. Ahead, Telamien braced himself against the railing, his arms crossed. His height made him look older than he was—his glower, not so much.

She stepped close enough to whisper, "What are they talking about? Did I miss anything important?"

"No. Mother sent for hors d'oeuvres and introduced every single attendee to the newcomers. They've barely started the meeting."

"What's gotten you so angry, then?"

"Can't you guess? I know well enough that the oaf claimed you as his bride the instant he saw you. Then I heard with my own ears when he announced that he's grotesque and revolting."

"Hush." She might have known Telamien would hear. "He didn't mean that—didn't understand at all."

"*We* understand."

She couldn't deny that. "Have you forgotten that it is not to be spoken of?"

"You'd already heard his words. I won't shame either of us by spreading it." Telamien gripped her arm. "Please tell me you're not going with them. How will you avoid the marriage once you're down there? You'll be miserable."

"I..." *Uhf*, he was making this harder. "I can refuse to marry him, but I can *not* refuse to go below."

"I can't bear to think of you with him. This changes everything about our goodbyes." He pulled her into a boyish hug even though he dwarfed her.

And here she was, fighting tears again. "Well, maybe when you're king, you can ask them to bring me aboveground during the annual visits. Not customary for the ambassador, but it's worth a try."

"There'll be no trying. I'll demand it. I won't forget you."

She drew back from the hug and forced a smile. "Then I have that to look forward to. I must join them."

Fanteal entered the delegation chamber through an anteroom that connected it to the walkway. She turned the handle quietly, not wanting to interrupt whoever might be speaking. Ah, Sir Mikkael, giving a prepared speech, by the sound of it. She should join her father since she represented the crown, but he was seated too far away to reach without creating a stir. Well, it wasn't critical to sit beside him. It wasn't as though she could represent the king while he was present, anyway.

Jaikon must not be directly participating either, for he sat between the windows. She cringed inwardly. Had he heard Telamien and her? A vacant chair sat near him. If she took that place, he would acknowledge her and maybe she could read the answer in his manner.

When she reached him, his polite nod could have meant anything. Oh, well. It probably looked good to others that she sat with him. The four people who'd heard his awful remark would not repeat it, so no one else present would understand if she avoided Jaikon.

The meeting was already vastly different from her grandfather's visits. His aides always came with stacks of papers and left with other stacks after hours of meeting with the nobles and officials. As prime minister, Sir Nirundale had initiated those meetings but left his knowledgeable staff to hash through problems and determine solutions. His role was relational. The family time of the past was forever gone, yet it was all the more important that the royal family share some private conversation with the Mikkaels.

Perhaps the formal nature of the prime minister's speech was not surprising. He'd never been here, after all. The subject was trade, of course. Seed arrived too damaged to plant. Husked grain was too shattered for dry storage. Often damp as well, and it had to be baked at once, with mediocre results. Dirklians went without bread half the winter months. Fruit arrived battered. If it could be eaten at all, it could not be processed for winter storage. Textiles, paper, and a host of other imports fared about the same. He detailed the damage to every product.

She'd heard similar complaints before but never to this extent. How had it become so much worse in one year?

Lord Perkel of Narsun Province looked startled at first, frowning deeper as the list of grievances wound on. Dirklan's import cataract was under his jurisdiction. She felt for him, knowing how vigorously he monitored the work, even performing surprise inspections himself.

When his turn came to speak, he expressed his concern and his desire to discuss solutions with the prime minister's aides.

No greater offense, it seemed, could have been stated or taken.

Deltum and Tershel weren't aides but envoys of Dirklan's exporting domains, entitled to speak on behalf of their governors. Speak, they did, vaunting themselves as experts on all matters of trade. They'd come for accusation not solutions. Their raised voices and elaborate gestures ceased only when they hyperventilated. Doubtless, that frustration worsened their anger. Her grandfather's aides never had this much trouble. Had they prepared better? Known some technique to compensate for the richer air aboveground? Why hadn't they passed it on as required?

During a moment when both envoys fell into gasps, Fanteal's mother sent her a pointed look. Her silent request wouldn't be easy. Fanteal worked with vast currents, but she was the only wind weaver in the room. She isolated an air pocket surrounding the Dirklian group while her mother instructed them to breathe slower.

That was the one time they listened to anyone. Probably because they couldn't speak. They sneered at the Welcian claims, spoke over lords and ladies, and even interrupted the queen ambassador when she spoke on Dirklan's behalf.

Countless times, Fanteal straightened fingers that had curled tight. She fought the anger that plagued everyone, though her own burned hottest over the disrespect shown to her mother. How could these two envoys be such fools? Was she not Queen of Welcia in addition to being Ambassador of Dirklan? Sir Mikkael didn't directly insult the queen, but he did nothing to restrain the two men.

What did this mean for her role of Royal Ambassador to Dirklan?

The door of his bedroom gave Jaikon privacy, but the transom window above it forced him to listen to Deltum and Tershel arguing in the shared parlor of the visitors' suite. His father had intended to send the two envoys down through the passage in the small vessel tonight, but it was packed with Fanteal's luggage. According to the local streamers, it could not all be transferred to the large vessel—something to do with weight distribution. But since there were only four seats in the large vessel, at least one of the envoys had to go down tonight with half of her luggage. Both wanted the honor of joining the select dinner, hosted by the king and queen. What a surprise.

Jaikon changed into his formalwear as slowly as possible, then looked over his shoulder into the full-length mirror to check the extended tails of his cutaway shirt. Did they still wear this style aboveground? The circular timepiece in his room told him nothing. He'd only seen one in his life, and that had been broken. Better to join bickering envoys than be late.

He stepped into the parlor, thankful that the look on his father's face wasn't directed at him.

"Enough," Sir Mikkael said. "Neither of you will join us for dinner, so you cannot claim I am showing preference. Tershel, you will go through the passage during tonight's opening because the rich air troubles you the most. Deltum, you will remain in this suite until it is time to board the large vessel tomorrow." He strode from the room.

Jaikon hurried after his father. A servant waited near the corridor's turn and escorted them downstairs to a large drawing room. Jaikon checked for an instant on the threshold. Was this a mistake? The king and queen were surrounded by all five of their children. The only noble present was Lord Yaeger.

No mistake, for the queen ambassador began introductions. Prince Telamien first, heir to the throne. He was almost as tall as Jaikon, but his face, patchy with the hint of a coming beard, revealed his youth. Then the children, two girls and a boy, who offered polite responses with their curtsies and bow.

"You may return to your game," the queen said.

The children's quaint propriety vanished as they played some sort of hide-and-search game, while the adults talked. Fanteal watched them. Realizing these were her last few hours with them, Jaikon didn't try to converse with her.

Soon, the youngest sat on a footstool, clutching her doll and refusing to join in. Fanteal rose from her mother's side and claimed a turn to hide the next object. This she did, making much noise around the room to provide false clues. When the children uncovered their eyes, Fanteal stood near the youngest and pointed in a direction the other two couldn't see. The doll lay forgotten during the next round of searching, and the youngest girl won for the first time. The boy narrowed his eyes but didn't raise a fuss. Instead, he made use of a distraction to shove the doll behind a cushion. That was doubtless outside of the rules, but Jaikon turned his gaze back to the adults.

A servant entered and announced that dinner awaited them.

As the queen stood, everyone rose. To the three children, she said, "Time to go upstairs now, my dears."

The middle girl took her little sister's hand and led her to one door as the adult party followed the king and queen toward another.

"My doll." The little girl ran to the footstool where she'd left it and wailed, "She's gone!"

From somewhere beneath the queen's regal calm, a worn look surfaced. Jaikon glanced back. The boy gazed innocently at the ceiling.

Jaikon walked to the couch. "Perhaps she is hiding. I wonder if she's here." He lifted the cushion. The girl beamed but then ducked her head. He squatted and presented the doll to her.

"Thank you," she whispered, clutching it to her chest, then ran back to her sister.

As Jaikon returned to the stalled procession, Telamien narrowed his eyes at him. "How did you know?"

Was he actually suspicious? "I saw your brother hide it there."

"That explains his angelic look," the king said, continuing into the dining room.

Jaikon was seated between Fanteal and her mother, who sat at one end opposite the king.

Fanteal actually smiled at him and arched an eyebrow. "I gather you have brothers and sisters."

"No, but my friends did. Teasing siblings seems to be a universal trait."

"I suppose. Thank you for averting a scene. She's not the whiny sort, but she's had a rough day."

"Happy to spare you at least one scene." He meant it in jest, but her eyebrows flicked.

After a tiny pause, she asked, "Are Deltum and Tershel feeling unwell?"

"My father is sparing you that scene."

"Ah."

Servants placed salads before each person. No other food on the table. How strange, but he was too hungry to care. He ate every bite, though Fanteal left half of hers. The plates were removed, and soon another was set before him. Meat he didn't recognize, with sauce drizzled over it, and a border of...were those colored vegetables? Why were they cut to resemble flowers?

Fanteal sliced off a dainty piece of her meat. "This is quail. I understand you don't have them belowground."

He stopped staring and picked up his knife and fork. "True. What is a quail?"

"A small ground bird."

At least it was good. She ate some of the sculpted vegetables, so he ate his, recognizing them by taste. Again, she ate only part of her food, leaning back in her chair while others finished.

Conversation seemed careful. The king asked about the domains and governors of Dirklan. Jaikon's father, seated on the king's right, replied without mentioning the political positions that had caused so much trouble around the election. Lord Yaeger seemed remarkably attentive to every detail, which might be why he said so little. Telamien, blocked from Jaikon's view on the other side of Fanteal, said nothing. Was he supposed to keep silent?

Queen Trissina asked Jaikon about his home domain of Northeshur and about Governor Brakentel's family. Somehow, it seemed strange that she knew them. On second thought, the governor and his wife were older than she. Of course, she would remember people in Dirklan. At least he could easily answer her, for he'd spent as much time in the Brakentel household as his own.

Again, plates were removed, drinks were poured, and another round of plates appeared. How many times would they do this? Was this why Fanteal didn't finish her food? Jaikon ate part of his, though he didn't need it. Such appalling waste!

King Darinneth steered the conversation back toward matters of the day. "Your associates are dissimilar to those Sir Nirundale brought."

"I supposed so," Jaikon's father said. "Sir Nirundale brought his own aides, but I chose to bring a broader representation of Dirklan. I gather that the severity of the situation may have been understated in the past few years. It's time you learn the realities of life belowground."

"I find these realities rather disturbing," the queen said. "I am concerned for my daughter. I trust that someone is waiting to meet her."

"Many people will be waiting for us. She will be warmly welcomed."

"What is your wife's name, please? I'd like to write a letter for you to take to her."

Jaikon's father took a couple seconds to answer. "My wife died thirteen years ago."

The queen pressed a napkin to her lips. "I'm sorry to hear of your loss." She paused after the gently stated words. "But it causes me even more concern. Will there be no one to receive Fanteal? Not even a maid?"

Jaikon held his breath. What did a princess expect of a maid? They employed no such person in their household. What would his father say?

"Certainly, she may have a maid, though I assumed she would prefer to select her own staff. It would be impossible to designate only one person to welcome her. In spite of all the discord you heard today, the entire city of Jourendia, plus visitors from other domains, is anticipating her arrival with great excitement." He smiled. "She is more likely to be overwhelmed than neglected."

"Oh, dear."

He set his fork down. "Not literally overwhelmed. I will be at her side, and we will ride the entire trip up from Passage Lake." The queen still shook her head, and he said, "Madam, your concerns mystify me. What, exactly, is the problem?"

"You don't seem to have any idea what it is like when abovegrounders first arrive in Dirklan," the queen said. "She is used to an abundance of fresh air. Indeed, air so rich that it makes our Dirklian visitors hyperventilate. Has it even occurred to you that she needs time to acclimate? A public appearance is the last thing she should be subjected to. Do not expect her to address the crowd."

Jaikon's father nodded. "That will not be necessary. Thank you for explaining. It's true that we know little of aboveground Welcia. Not only has it been eleven years since the last ambassador died, but he was not publicly active during the later years of his life." He swept the table with his gaze. "You see, I hope, why it's critical to reestablish the bond between our peoples."

Fanteal leaned forward. "Do not be alarmed, Sir Mikkael. I am going with you."

"I am delighted to hear you say so, lady."

"I wonder why," Fanteal murmured.

Jaikon and his father raised their eyebrows at her pensive remark.

"When I think of the envoys," Fanteal said, "of how they treated the Queen of Welcia, the Ambassador of Dirklan, I cannot believe they place much value on the crown, the royal line of de Noviam, or the office of ambassador. So please tell me frankly, sir, how much of Dirklan looks favorably toward my arrival?"

During the brief pause, Sir Mikkael's eyes never wavered from hers. "Indeed, all of Dirklan desires a royal ambassador. Some may wonder whether your presence will alleviate our difficulties, but they are a small minority. Sir Nirundale always spoke highly of your gift and your knowledge. He wouldn't hear of asking for anyone else, despite the long wait." He added even more warmth to his voice. "We look forward to good years with a gifted ambassador among us again."

A servant removed Fanteal's plate and replaced it with another. She used the distraction to let the matter drop. Out of the corner of her eye, she watched Jaikon, who didn't even pick up the next fork. What was wrong now? Had her comment and question offended him?

She cut a slice of sautéed pinnpear and ate it. The tart juice flowed over her tongue, altering in flavor as she bit into the pods hidden within the fruit. "This is pinnpear," she said to Jaikon. "I understand it doesn't grow in Dirklan. You should try some, for there's nothing quite like it. Several different flavors lurk within each fruit."

He complied without enthusiasm. "Yes, I see what you mean. Unique. I don't believe I've ever seen any with the fruit shipments."

"No, it must be eaten within a couple days after it's picked. It turns bitter very quickly."

He laid his fork aside.

"You dislike it?"

When he finally answered, it was barely above a whisper. "I am not used to such excess. No one eats like this belowground."

Well, that killed her appetite. Her favorite dessert was served, but she barely noticed the taste. Would she even know how to host a dinner in Dirklan? Then, her father said something so uncharacteristic that it jerked her attention back.

"Can we truly rely on the word of a prime minister?" he asked.

He'd spoken the words casually, but Fanteal couldn't blame Sir Mikkael for the look he shot at the king or the firmness of his answer. "Yes."

"Invariably?" the king asked, a trace of skepticism in his voice.

"Yes, invariably."

"Then there should be no problem in honoring Sir Nirundale's word to Ambassador Fanteal."

"What word, specifically?" Sir Mikkael asked.

"He promised that she would have a choice in her husband."

"So you mentioned earlier. First, let me assure you that I would never force anyone to marry against their will. Still, Lady Fanteal does not know anyone belowground." He glanced to the queen and back to the king. "Am I correct in assuming that you trusted Sir Nirundale to advise her in choosing?"

"You are."

Sir Mikkael nodded. "Which is no longer possible, and a man you have known only a few hours stands in his place."

"Exactly."

Despite the king's coldness, Sir Mikkael remained calm. Perhaps there was more to him than Fanteal had yet seen. Surprisingly, he turned to her. "Lady Fanteal, I realize that you expected to have one good friend in Dirklan. Perhaps it now seems that you will have none, but that is not true. I am not the individual you expected, but I am prime minister. I'll fulfill my duty, not only to an ambassador, but to you personally. In the matter of your husband, I will advise you with all the care for your happiness that I would give if you were my daughter."

She inclined her head in respect. "Thank you."

He looked to her mother and father again. "That promise is made equally to both of you."

"Comforting *words*." The king's emphasis made it all too plain that they were only words. "Fortunately, it will be easy to convince us that you have honored them. Simply bring Fanteal with you on your visit next year."

All warmth left Sir Mikkael's features and voice. "There is no precedent for this. Have you ever sent our ambassador back to Dirklan for a visit?"

"No, and yet she saw her father every year. Since I am the streamer who lifts your vessel, I am the one person who absolutely cannot pass through the waters. If I am to see my daughter ever again, she must come to me. Is a visit of one brief day really so much to ask?"

A tense silence stretched between them.

"If it is," the king continued softly, "I have to ask myself why. And until I am comfortable with the answer to that question, I find it impossible to entrust her to your care."

"Your request is not unreasonable, yet I do not give my word unless I'm certain that I can keep it. I promise only that I will *permit* her to make the trip *if* it is possible."

"Sir Mikkael," King Darinneth said, "you have questioned our commitment. The envoys of two governors have all but accused us of outright lies and breach of covenant. The truth is, it never occurred to us that the covenant *could* be broken. Clearly, that thought occurs belowground. It is Dirklan's commitment that I now question." He let those unpalatable words sink in. "I have no way to communicate with Ambassador Fanteal. No way of knowing how she fares. Therefore, I will see her in this palace, one year from today, and hear from her lips that her wishes are respected. If not, I will know that *Dirklan* has forsaken our covenant."

CHAPTER 5

Heat tingled through Jaikon's ears. Impossible for his father to refuse the king's demand. Dirklan Province was free to choose its prime minister—but if he defied the king, he would instantly forfeit his office. Jaikon almost shuddered at the thought of the political upheaval that would wreak belowground. To think that he had worried about marrying an unknown woman!

Was there anything that had not gone wrong today? Bad enough that Fanteal might not marry him. She'd end up in some other province, rather than Northeshur where she was needed. They'd have to rely on trips, which may or may not be enough. Now, she might not even stay in Dirklan if everything wasn't to her liking. What chance of success did they actually have? This was going to be an awful year!

He thought again of Mount Estelle. The way things stood, his idea was more critical than ever. Was it even possible? He'd never know if he didn't get time to study that mountain. The chances of him ever coming aboveground again were about...zero. And the hours were slipping away.

When the queen rose from the table, the rest of them did as well. Light still glowed through the windows, but without blinding intensity now. Was this what they called sunset? Had the protracted meal consumed the remainder of the day? Oh, for an hour marker to tell him the time.

By protocol, he should direct his request to Ambassador Trissina, but her sharp rebuke still lingered in his mind. Would Ambassador Fanteal grant it? She looked so solemn. If only he could bring back the smile that had appeared when he'd returned the doll to her little sister. Would they have some time to talk in whatever room of this vast palace they were headed for?

They went no farther than the drawing room. The king and his eldest son left them immediately. Was there no custom of after dinner conversation? The queen drew her daughter aside, and they conversed in hushed voices, not bothering to sit. Were they about to leave too?

Hoping that his father and Lord Yaeger would keep talking, Jaikon positioned himself near the door. A good strategy, for Fanteal left her mother and headed straight for it with clear intent.

He opened it for her and followed her through it. She paused and raised a questioning eyebrow.

"May I have a moment?" he asked.

"Of course."

That sounded far more like obligation than pleasure. Better get to the point. "There was one sight I was hoping to see while here. Mount Estelle. Can it be viewed from the palace?"

"The peak is visible from the north windows, and you'll be able to see the axis star straight above. It's the brightest one—unmistakable."

"Sounds lovely, but is there a place within reach to see more than the peak? I realize it's some distance away, but I'd like to view as much of it as possible."

"Oh, to view it as a former? I could send for Chief Former Wuldour, and he can—"

He shook his head. That was the worst possible offer. "No, I'm not a former. It's nothing like that...not a matter for the Formers' Guild at all."

She stared at him, her lips parted. "But..."

Should he tell her why he must see it? If she knew, would she refuse to go to Dirklan after all? He couldn't take that risk. "It's difficult to explain, but I would very much like to see the mountain."

She swallowed and cleared the surprise from her face. "There is a hilltop nearby that offers a fine view. One of my favorite walks."

Promising. "Could we go there now?"

"You'd barely get a chance to see it before the sun sets, and I am going with my father to help open the passage." She shifted. "He doesn't truly need me for that, of course, but I've helped him for several years now, um, training and such."

Her voice grew tighter with every word, and he touched her arm. "I won't interfere with the parting moments you treasure."

Her smile quavered, but at least it was a smile. "If you rise at dawn, I can take you to see Mount Estelle."

"I'll be ready." Movement at the far end of the gallery caught his eye. Two servants near the wall, one with a tank and hose. "What are they doing?"

She followed his gaze. "Filling and lighting the oil lamps."

One lamp flickered then glowed, and the servants moved on to another. Unbelievable. "You still don't have magnery in the palace?"

"Some. Such lighting was installed in the ballroom—as a demonstration project, according to my father. Later, the copper pathways were extended to the kitchens and a few workshops with magnery powered tools." Irony touched her voice. "Oil is abundant aboveground. Copper is rare, and we cannot waste it on simple conveniences like lamps."

Fanteal hurried through the palace to join her father, but her thoughts stayed with Jaikon. How could he not be a former? If he had no substance gift, then the life gift statue would have been revealed, not the formers'. It just wasn't possible. But what reason could he have to lie? That made no sense either, for she would surely find out in Dirklan. Yet if he spoke true, what could the vision have meant?

A servant opened the door, and she stepped out into the fading light.

The last thing she needed was another matter to worry over. Her father, whom she was supposed to represent, had angered the prime minister. Then her mother stressed that Fanteal must show full commitment to Dirklan. So, she shouldn't take the lifeline her father provided. And frankly, circumstances could prevent her trip even if she wanted it. Her grandfather hadn't been able to come during one opening of the dome due to an injury. She knew how violently that whirlpool spun.

Fanteal shook her head hard. She had a year to make that decision. Sir Mikkael's assurances worried her more. What did he think she could deliver? As though Dirklan would instantly become a better place when a royal ambassador arrived. Not just anyone—her, specifically. No ambassador was *that* good! Had her grandfather's praise raised expectations to unattainable heights?

J aikon lengthened his stride to keep up with Fanteal, who flitted up the rugged steps of the hillside as though it were nothing. For once, he needn't curtail his breath, not with this demand on his muscles. The climb made the gem hills of Crysalan seem small. His legs complained before he crested the hill. At least the morning here was cooler than belowground. Strange after yesterday's heat.

She pointed to the top few steps in front of him. "These blocks wobble. Best to use the left side."

He angled across and followed her between coarse hulks of rock, oddly matched. "What are these?"

"Statues—or they were. Some sort of animal, I suppose."

"What happened to them?"

Once again, she quickly masked a look of surprise. "Centuries of weather. Rain and snow wear away rock."

Now she probably thought he'd never learned about erosion. Just because he hadn't predicted how it affected a carved statue.

She chose an indirect route away from the stairs, hopping over scraggly greens between flat stones.

He kept a close watch on her feet in order to follow her, unsure how deep the gaps were beneath the unfamiliar plants. He could ask or feel for the ground, but her surprised looks wore on him.

She slowed in an area where the old slabs fit close together, though their edges could still trip the unwary. "This is called the pavilion, though we really don't know its original purpose. The formers say that the hillside covers toppled stonework, so likely a quake destroyed most of the structure." She halted and extended her arms dramatically. "May I present—the star pointer."

He lifted his eyes from tilted stones underfoot and gazed past her, almost gasping aloud. No wonder Mount Estelle was said to be gorgeous. The symmetry of her cone seemed too perfect to be naturally formed. Beyond a green plain and hills that wore a darker shade, she rose majestic and harsh. The verdant cloak of the hills—those must be trees—climbed her lower slope before thinning to reveal bare rock. Finally, he understood why the mountain had been deemed solid before that long-ago collapse. The same promise called to him. Probably because of how badly he wanted it to be true. He wasn't about to let appearances fool him.

"What do you think of the view?"

That sounded like a tease. "Dare I answer? I'll sound like a belowgrounder, for sure."

Her brief laugh held a musical quality. "Everyone gapes at Mount Estelle the first time they see her. Feast your eyes."

"This feast may take a while." Hopefully that hint would give him the time he needed...and hide what he was really doing. They crossed the old pavilion to a stone railing that was kept in good repair, probably because the hill dropped sharply beyond it. Jaikon called on his rarely used forming sense. He swept it across the plain—loose matter, likely soil. Not that he could confirm that. At least, no real formers were near, so he didn't have to explain why.

He reached to the hills, comprehending the distance that vision couldn't interpret. The hills were denser than the plain, but they didn't matter either. Only Estelle did. He swept his awareness around her, reveling in the chance to use his freakish range.

"You *are* a former."

Fanteal's accusing voice jerked him back to mundane senses. Oh, by the caverns! "I'm not," he blurted out.

She looked affronted. "I can sense all three substance gifts. At least, when they are active."

Great! She *would* have high sensitivity. And that made him sound like a liar. "I mean that I'm not a former in the regular sense. Not the sort that is useful belowground. I'm not sure how the gift manifests up here." That expression on her face...why did she look so inordinately relieved?

"Hmm." She tilted her head. "We don't have nearly as many formers as Dirklan. Most of them are polishers, medic formers, architects, and the like."

"Then I'm even more out-of-place up here. Please don't call me a former when we get home. At least not in my presence. You'll just get an explanation of why my gift isn't useful, and I don't enjoy hearing it."

"Ah." Her lips lifted wryly. "I have my own version of 'no one understands' to deal with, so I won't make your situation any worse."

He studied her. These moments made him wonder who she really was. "Now I want to ask questions, but I did come here for a reason. I don't have to be a streamer to know the tides will not wait."

She half laughed. "No, they will not." She stepped away and gestured to Mount Estelle. "Send your gift to wander the mountain. We can compare our view of it tomorrow."

Had she climbed its slopes? Seen it from all sides? He watched her walk farther along the railing and sit on its wide stone top facing the harbor. Sunlight glowed through her golden locks, which stirred in the wind. Beautiful, but he was glad the wind didn't reach him. That phenomenon was far stranger than he'd guessed. Later for that. He had a mountain to deal with.

Its massive bulk awed him. Oh, how limited were eyes! Estelle's visible majesty was nothing compared to the true weight of her. Belowground, solid matter just went on and on. Yet this mountain was discrete. A single enormous entity with boundaries where it met the nothingness of air. He could actually sense where it stopped on the far side.

He paused—simply enjoyed the rare moment of grasping the entirety of a mountain. He wished he could linger in this fullness, but he had to know more.

He started exploring density at the peak. Again, his eyes had lied. *Solid* was a relative concept. Myriad fissures left gaps—no doubt filled with the air or water that he could not sense. Channels and pockets, he expected near the surface. How deep did they go? Down and down, he explored, his progress slowing as the cone widened. Denser rock offered him hope, soon proven false when it rested on pocked and creased matter. Rigid bubbles and fault lines. Some still supported the burden above, while others had already been crushed to treacherous powder. Unfused, it would act like grease in a rockslide.

What held this mountain up? Only its wide base and jagged interior, apparently. At some point, it must be heavy enough to compress the gaps. A memory taunted him. He'd once heard a streamer say that trapped water was harder than rock…would refuse to compress if it couldn't flow out. Did these pockets hold water? Surely air could not be trapped so. Or could it?

He sensed near the base now, and still he had not found the dense structure he sought. Even the symmetrical cone had given way to sheered cliffs with rubble below. Proof that mighty Estelle hid weakness within.

The last drop of his fading hope evaporated. Jaikon exhaled a long breath. Even though he'd known how unlikely it was, the disappointment was a bitter reward for his effort. No tunnel—neither the old route nor a new one—could ever stand secure within Mount Estelle. Not when both the foundation and upper reaches were this unstable. It would be a worse disaster than that ill-fated attempt to tunnel beyond Illia Domain.

There really was only one hope for Dirklan. Fanteal. As long as she was as powerful as Sir Nirundale had always said, they'd be able to keep trade moving. Provided she stayed.

What a blow the king had dealt them, demanding that she come aboveground next year. That should be fine, but what if it wasn't? Once she realized—no. He couldn't solve all of that in this moment. Today, they just needed to get her through the passage. He'd better not screw up anything else. Nor let her see his disappointment. Wait…would she know what he was doing? Heat crept up the sides of his neck.

She glanced his way and caught him looking at her. He smiled belatedly.

She stood and approached. "Are you satisfied? You were frowning so."

"I guess I frown when I get really intent on something. I basically just confirmed what has been true all these years." He angled his head. "Did you already know that through your ability to sense a forming gift? How much can you discern?"

She flicked her hand. "Only that you're using it. In fact, the very first time I have sensed a former was yesterday." She quirked her lips at his expression. "Strange, isn't it? My father can do it too. He told me I had sensed your chief former bidding the dome to shift."

"Wow!" Her father's streaming gift was greater than any in Welcia above and below. Did this mean hers was just as strong? If so, they didn't need a tunnel anyway.

She shrugged it off. "We should probably head down to the dock. The tide is flowing out."

"You can tell that from up here?"

She laughed with a tilt of her head. "Easily. The tide is *moving,* after all. None of this *stability* that formers love."

Excellent—as long as she could move water as well as she could sense it. They crossed the pavilion to the formless statues. "On this deserted hillside, may I offer you the Dirklian style of escort?" He extended the crook of his arm to her.

She slipped her hand into it. "Certainly. I am an ambassador now, not a princess." She swept a hand toward her clothing. "I even dressed the part."

He had noticed the style—leggings under a dress shorter than she'd worn yesterday. Dark, satiny green swirled over a white underlayer, reminiscent of her sash. "So I see. Did your mother have it made for you?"

"No, my grandfather brought it last year. He wanted me to go down early, but that surprised us all. So, we agreed to one year early instead of two. He left the dress for me. What could be more suitable?"

The last line stunned him more than the rest. Green and white? "For *your* gift?"

"Green for ambassador." She cocked her head. "Doesn't Dirklan still use green to represent the life gifts?"

She sounded so incredulous that he worried he was messing up again. "Ah, yes, of course."

Fanteal left Jaikon at the palace with Lord Yaeger, who was organizing their departure. He and his father exchanged formal partings with the nobles still present and with the queen ambassador. Servants opened the palace doors to a subdued roar. The sparse trees along the cliff bent hard against the wind. How would they make it to the dock?

Lord Yaeger paid no heed to it as he led them down the walkway to the shore. Experience must guide him, for the wind stayed high.

Below them, the vessel pressed into the dock's recess. A loud *thunk* resounded with each impatient wave. Dockhands stood ready near ropes looped over irons. Jaikon sensed the cliff walls that held the harbor. Extremely dense. No surprise, for the area was mostly ipenrock. A pity he didn't have time to reach through the peninsula on the far side.

King Darinneth and Lady Fanteal stared out over the water. The streamers below often motioned, but these two remained still. The king's arms were spread as though he held an invisible ball. Even Jaikon could imagine it as the harbor resting in his grasp. Fanteal also spread her arms but with her palms upward, like she lifted the water from below. Perhaps they were maintaining what they'd already commanded. The roar was louder here. Was it the sound of water swirling past the cliffs? So different from echoes belowground.

The Dirklians reached the shore, and the king glanced their way. "It is time. Board your vessel."

CHAPTER 6

Fanteal released her protection of the walkway, only shielding the dock area from the raging wind that circled the harbor. Such a delight to hold the air and all of its power as it whisked obediently over the palms of her hands.

Sir Mikkael bowed to the king, then turned to her. "Lady Fanteal, would you like to board first?"

Her father shook his head. "She is helping me open the passage. She will board last."

Deltum stared at her with an open-mouthed smile before he followed Sir Mikkael along the dock. Leaning forward to grip the open hatch, the first two men climbed through it.

Jaikon looked into the rocking vessel, then back at Fanteal. "May I help you board?" he shouted above the roar.

She glanced at her father. His hands crept nearer together. "You may help me from below. Get in." Another presence rose, barely discernable against her father's active gift. "The former has called to us. Hurry."

Jaikon climbed through the hatch sideways, still watching her. Lord Yaeger gripped her waist and one elbow, supporting her as they ran along the dock through misty wind. Up close, the dark seams between the red and white stripes on the vessel gave her pause. Could they split?

She braced a hand beside the hatch. The entire top was encased in clear crystal, smooth as glass. The work of a polisher, no doubt. As trustworthy as her grasp of the wind.

She passed from Lord Yaeger's grip to clutch Jaikon's arm. With his feet wide and one hand gripping overhead, he steadied her down the few steps inside the lurching vessel. Four full-body seats were mounted on a ring anchored to a central post. He guided her into one and fastened straps over her. Good thing he was paying attention, for the wind still occupied her.

"Why aren't they closing the hatch?" he asked with a nervous glance at the opening.

"They will soon. Hush." She stared at nothing, concentrating deeply. Wind and waves screamed past the cliffs.

Jaikon hurried to the empty couch opposite her and strapped himself in. A dockhand's weathered face appeared in the hatch, looked them over, and withdrew. The hatch slammed shut, blotting out the sun. Latches snapped into place. The vessel lurched, banged the dock, then moved freely. One of the men groaned, for pitch and yaw played havoc with a circular hull.

Fanteal's eyes adjusted to dim light, not nearly as dark as she'd expected. Ah, the seams in the top were narrow light shafts, channeling sunlight to them. The vessel began to spin, lazily at first, then picking up speed as it circled the whirlpool that she helped to stabilize. She understood the mounting ring now. Since it was anchored to a cylinder around the center post, rather than to the outer wall, it spun separately and spared the occupants from the full force of the spin. But nothing could completely isolate them, and the metal sang as it rotated.

Her body pressed into the seat, the high backrest cushioning her head and neck, and the long footrest protecting her knees. The Dirklians seemed to brace themselves. Would it be worse than she thought? Or easier for her since she understood the vortex above?

She embraced that invisible structure, reveling in the energy, for it was hers alone until it entered the water. There—it pressed a divot into the harbor. This was where she had promised to let go. A promise she could not break.

Fanteal blew out a huge breath and looked around the three faces staring at her.

"Are you finished with your part?" Jaikon asked.

"Yes." They looked so worried that she added, "All is well. My father holds us now, and the whirlpool is straight and tight." She snuggled deeper into her couch. "Time for the fun!"

"Uh...actually, it isn't," Deltum said.

"My mother didn't like it either. We'll see."

Jaikon rocked his head against the seatback, an incredulous grin stretching his mouth. "Just keep your hands tucked inside the couch and remember to breathe."

That was getting a little harder. The vessel's distorted swing must mean that they were very close to the center. Fanteal's luggage, strapped to the outer wall, darted behind Jaikon out of sync with the movement she felt. Her stomach heaved. She closed her eyes and focused on her weight in the seat. Much better, though her stomach rode high. A wobbly jerk—then her world became a pure weightless spin.

Amazing! She imagined herself as a feather in a wispy whirlwind. Her chuckle blended with the metallic song of the ring. *Oh, please let the ride down last long.*

The moments ended with a jolt that drove her stomach into her lungs, then down to her guts as the vessel bobbed to the surface. That could only mean they'd passed through the opened dome and landed in Passage Lake. Whew! Harsh but worth it. The spin soon wore itself out, no doubt stilled by a belowground streamer.

Heavy breaths ruffled the quiet. Fanteal opened her eyes to find Jaikon watching her.

"Well?" he prompted.

She let out a giggle. "The descent was great fun, but the landing...not so much."

Sir Mikkael groaned a few words. "Worse than coming out at the top." He took a slow breath through his nose. "We rest now while the streamers drain the excess water from the lake."

She hoped he wasn't going to be sick. All three of them were paler than usual, even in the dim light of the cavern. In truth, her stomach also felt tipsy. A scrape overhead drew her eyes. Air swirled through the vessel.

Jaikon explained, "That's the vent. A former opens it by command when they're sure we are stable in the water. The local streamers will bring us to the lakeshore when the level drops."

"Why wait?" Deltum turned his odd gaping smile her way. "Why don't you bring us to shore?"

Her jaw dropped. What under the skies could he mean?

Jaikon's voice ground. "Don't you think she's done more than enough already?"

"Most certainly," Sir Mikkael said, blending firmness into quiet words. He gave her a reassuring smile. "From here on, you will rest, and we will see you to your new home."

They spiraled through the lake in a gentle glide. The trip to shore ended with a rigid locking sensation. The latches snapped, and she prepared herself for the change. The hatch opened, causing the air to shift, but she sensed no difference. What had her mother thought would happen? Trust the non-gifted to predict air? Never!

Sir Mikkael helped Fanteal up, though she was steadier on her feet than he. Jaikon stepped through the hatch ahead of her, then he took both of her hands to help her climb out.

Her foot touched stone. She was standing in Dirklan.

Jaikon offered a supportive arm behind her back and a firm grip under one of her hands. His father quickly joined them, and the two men hovered on either side. She felt cocooned, which she would normally dislike, but not in this indescribable moment as her eyes sought the heights.

The sky...was closed! In its place stood the rock dome, damp and glistening. Jaikon tightened his arm around her, and she realized she had swayed. How could she be so unprepared? She'd been inside domed buildings in Regissa—even studied a model of the opening dome of Passage Lake. But never had she imagined it like this.

Immense didn't begin to describe it. Decorated, too, with alternating textures in a geometric pattern. Magnery lights faced upward to illuminate it. The design merged into a latticework pattern arching between columns that were etched around the cylindrical walls. They lent a completeness to the design, though she'd heard that the column etchings were a jest among formers.

And yes, formers were here, mingled with streamers. She sensed them more than heard them, despite their echoed voices. Opening and closing the dome required both gifts, and the work continued afterward to ensure that it was properly sealed.

Time to be done with all this awe. She straightened and glanced around to place the other things she'd been taught. Passage Lake nearly filled the entire cavern. The vessel was locked into a recess of the platform she stood upon. Across the platform, lights glowed through a window and open door. Magnery powered equipment filled that room to operate the double set of gates, which had to be closed when the dome was opened. At least these simple things were as expected, since nothing else seemed to be.

Her mother had said Jourendia was nearly as bright as aboveground. Spoken by someone who didn't like going outside. Throngs waiting to welcome her? Not here. But most important, the air was as rich as aboveground. Heavy with moisture, though. And rather still.

Sir Mikkael broke the silence. "Are you well?"

"Yes, I just needed a moment."

"Everyone needs a moment after riding the whirlpool."

She'd been misunderstood again. Excusable, though. Deltum stood off to one side, bent over with his hands braced against his knees. She looked in the other direction, where a knot of people—the formers and streamers—glanced curiously at her while they worked. She could at least give them a faint breeze. "Which of them is Dirklan's chief former?"

Sir Mikkael motioned with a finger to a man who watched them steadily. "I'll introduce you."

The former with iron-gray hair left the group and approached them. Jaikon slipped Fanteal's left hand into the crook of his arm, and they strolled to meet him.

The breeze she had started overhead lazily reached the platform, and she let it flutter her skirt as she walked.

Sir Mikkail said, "Lady Fanteal, allow me to introduce Agriben, Provincial Chief Former of Dirklan."

He stared at her, asking in a voice rough as gravel, "Are *you* the ambassador then?"

Who else? His surprise mystified her, but she recognized him, and that delight was greater than any puzzle. She offered her hand and a smile. "Yes. And you are the former who called to us."

He cradled her hand in both of his, as though it were precious. "I am. And you are surely gifted, though never as I expected. Yet there must be good reason." He seemed to recollect himself. His tone lost a little of its wonder and gained formality. "I am from Crysalan, and many friends asked me to convey their greetings. It's an honor to be the first to welcome you to Dirklan, Ambassador Fanteal." He stepped back, stiffly bowing.

Why did it always seem like people were saying the strangest things?

Sir Mikkael urged Fanteal toward an open carriage, which also seemed out of place. Ah, it was parked facing toward a tunnel. That meant the inner gate was already open, and the dark wall beyond the glowing magnery lamps was really the outer gate. Sir Mikkael climbed to the seat ahead of her, then Jaikon handed her up the ladder-like steps and followed. There would be just enough room for the three of them on the bench seat. The carriage had no driver's seat, and where horses should have been harnessed, a man sat atop a squat, wheeled device. She'd learned of such motors but never seen one.

Fanteal shifted her skirt to sit, but Sir Mikkael took her arm. "Better to stand so everyone can see you. Don't worry. The ride will be smooth, and we'll steady you." He spoke louder to reach someone standing at the far end. "Open the gate."

The woman grasped a lever and lifted it. The purr of a motor began in the equipment room. Ahead, a vertical crack of light split the cavern wall, and air rushed from the cave.

Fanteal's ears popped. The carriage rolled toward the parting gates, and Jourendia spread before her. She blinked at the flood of light and the cheer that burst from the crowd. But it was all a distant blur—for the air had fled.

CHAPTER 7

Fanteal shrank back, would have fallen, but Sir Mikkael and Jaikon supported her.

The chief former must have followed close, for his gravelly voice reached her. "Breathe deeply, lady. All will be well."

Fanteal sucked in great gulps of air and tried to gather her wits. Nearly impossible, but somehow, she had to look happy to be here. If only they would let her sit.

Jaikon whispered, "Please do something. Wave, nod, smile—anything."

Right. Royal ambassador and all that. With supreme effort, she managed to smile and raise one hand to wave. Within moments, that hand went numb.

The broad street climbed between two rows of three-story houses with barely a walkway separating each from its neighbor. More people jammed the flat roofs and leaned from open windows.

Jaikon supported her weight with an arm around her waist. "We have to let her sit," he hissed to the prime minister, none too soon.

The remainder of the trip passed in a haze. The seat back and the shoulders of her escorts propped her up. They passed under elaborate arches into an even bigger cavern. More buildings, more people. Did her smile and nodding head make her look like a broken doll?

They reached a square with a fountain shooting high at its center. So many people crowded around it, some must be getting sprinkled. Impressive buildings surrounded three sides of the square. The carriage turned left, then right, following the street. This elegant mansion they passed—*please let it be Dirklan House*. Her new home.

But they didn't stop at its broad steps. Instead, they entered a narrower, nearly deserted street, which led to another large house. At last, the carriage stopped, and voices called orders. Fanteal was lifted from the carriage and borne inside.

She blinked, trying to recover her fading vision, as Jaikon laid her flat on a couch, then piled cushions to raise her legs. Her head ached. She kept forcing her eyes open, trying to figure out where she was. All she saw was Jaikon frowning down at her.

"We're home," he said. "Rest."

Sweet relief. Her eyes fell shut.

Sir Mikkael stepped from the salon into the hall and motioned for his chief aide to draw near. He kept his voice down, for the hall reached to the ceiling of the third floor and was far from private. "Colrin, you must find a maid for the ambassador. At once."

"A maid? I'm sure we have adequate staff to clean for her."

"No, a personal maid. Lady Fanteal became quite faint within minutes of arrival. She requires a woman to assist with basic needs. Immediately."

"I will see to it, sir."

"Then find out which medic attended Ambassador Melthindi—or at the very least a medic streamer who knows something about abovegrounders. Summon them."

"Uh, yes, sir."

Why did he linger? "Well, see to it then."

"I will, but do you have orders about your guests?" Colrin angled his head toward the large reception room across the entry hall. "Would you like refreshments served?"

Sir Mikkael surveyed the members of government who had invaded his residence. The pocket doors stood wide open, and a couple governors looked in his direction. At least they'd had the courtesy not to swarm the hall when the ambassador was carried in. "Serve nothing. The orders I just gave are your highest priority."

He strolled to the reception room, taking quick stock of who was present. All the governors—except Nirundale, of course. Also, the two envoys. Deltum must have just arrived, but he'd joined Tershel. By the way they all stood, Tershel had been addressing the governors. Sir Mikkael had ordered him to say nothing of the meeting until after the full delegation had returned. Apparently, he'd interpreted that as one second after their return.

Governor Brakentel asked Sir Mikkael, "It went well then?"

"Is that what these fools tell you?" Even though he kept his voice calm, surprise opened every eye. He wasn't one to use extreme words, but he needed to silence the envoys before they did even more harm here than they had aboveground. "The meeting was disastrous. These envoys..." He directed his next words at governors Weltinfall and Zeardell. "...whom you appointed, will never accompany me again."

"But, but..." Deltum cleared his throat. "We did exactly as instructed. Remained firm in the truth that we send all the required ore and gems in payment for food."

"Were you also instructed to close your eyes and ears to their reactions? Could you not see the expressions of the nobles when you refused to consider possible flaws in our export cataracts? When you essentially called them liars?"

Both envoys began to speak at once, but Governor Yaldeeth raised her palm toward them. "What of Lady Trissina?" she asked, "Our own ambassador. Did she not help?"

"Tershel and Deltum ignored her, never permitting her help. In the palace, Lady Trissina is Queen of Welcia and Ambassador of Dirklan." He gestured to Tershel and Deltum. "To these fine envoys, she was invisible. Imagine, if you will, what I had to answer at dinner. Lady Fanteal wondered why we wanted her to come here, since we have no respect for ambassadors."

Governor Weltinfall bridled. "She said such a thing? The audacity!"

"That was the gist of it, but I will allow no criticism. She had ample grounds for the question after enduring hours of your envoys' disrespect toward her mother. Our queen and our ambassador! Be very sure of this." He swept his gaze across the governors' faces. "Next year, *I alone* will choose who accompanies me."

Governor Trezman's worried voice cut the silence. "Sir Mikkael, what of the covenant? What of the trade cataracts?"

"Trade seems to be as safe as it was before our visit. They promise to do all in their power to ensure viable food shipments."

"They have done so for years, but it only worsens."

"I am aware. As for the covenant, the king was quite clear that the royal family has always considered it unbreakable, which is indeed their promise. And ours." He let anger slow his words. "However, the accusations thrown at the king and the nobles have raised doubt of *Dirklan's* commitment." He paused. "It now falls to me to prove otherwise."

With a careful voice, Governor Yaldeeth asked, "How, exactly?"

Sir Mikkail answered softer than ever. "The king informed me that Sir Nirundale promised Lady Fanteal that she could choose her own husband. The king considers it a prime minister's promise and demands that I fulfill it. He also demands to hear from her own lips that she is well treated and the promise is kept."

Expressions fluctuated. Mouths opened and closed. Governor Armeen quickly hooded his eyes, which had opened wide for a split second.

Sir Mikkael surveyed them. "Yes," he drawled. "I'm sure that you're all realizing the ramifications of that, but I'm rather busy just now, so I'll let you return to your lodgings."

He remained still as his guests gave him respectful nods and filed past him.

When the outer door closed behind the last of the visitors, Sir Mikkail returned to the hall. A thump from above drew his attention to the second floor. Luggage was being carried along the open gallery.

This rented house...he should have moved into Dirklan House months ago. Still impossible. Ornate wrought iron railings embellished the gallery that ringed three sides of the hall. A wide staircase led to the second floor, and two smaller staircases on either side led to the third. A final narrow stairway provided access to the roof garden. The rooms were spacious and tastefully furnished. A fine house, by most standards, but less impressive than Dirklan House and far inferior to the palace Fanteal grew up in. The problem named *Governor Nirundale* irked him more than ever.

Colrin stepped through the back doorway of the hall, followed by a staff member. "Nilkie has agreed to be aide to the ambassador," he said.

Sir Mikkael considered her for a moment. A young woman he'd hired in Jourendia after taking office. On a few occasions, she had acted as a page, but speed was not one of her qualities. Probably not important in a maid, and at this moment, he would accept almost any female. "Good. You will need to take particular care of her until she has adjusted to Dirklan. Air is different here than aboveground, which is causing faintness. I'll bring her upstairs soon, so go up to her room and get things ready."

Without waiting for an answer, he returned to the salon where his son watched over Lady Fanteal. She opened her eyes as he approached.

"How are you feeling?" he asked gently.

"A little better." Fanteal gripped the couch's back to sit up.

"You needn't get up."

"I have to try sooner or later."

Jaikon moved cushions and helped her to a comfortable position. She leaned back and sighed, pressing a hand to her brow. "I had no idea it would be this difficult."

"Nor I," Sir Mikkael said. "We'd have had a medic waiting for you if we'd known. I've sent for the one who attended the former ambassador, but it may take a while."

She nodded.

Already, her breathing was growing faster, more labored. The opposite problem he'd constantly struggled against at the palace. But while Dirklians inhaled too much air aboveground, she must be getting too little. Worrisome. "In the meantime, I'd like to take you up to your room. You could rest in bed until the medic arrives."

She nodded again and extended a hand to be helped up from the couch.

"You don't need to walk," Jaikon said. "I can carry you."

"I have to get used to this. Even if I don't make it very far, I'm going to try."

"We don't want you to fall," Sir Mikkael said as they supported her on both sides.

A weak smile played at the corners of her pale lips. "I doubt you'll let that happen."

"Indeed, we won't."

Fanteal made it into the hall and paused to take it in. Nothing like her mother had described. Could it have changed so much? The Mikkaels watched her carefully. "I don't think I can manage the stairs."

In an instant, she was back in Jaikon's arms, and he carried her up the staircase.

Sir Mikkael preceded them into a room and looked around. He frowned at a woman who was arranging plants by the window. "I told you to prepare. Turn down the bed."

She hurried to do so, while Jaikon watched, untroubled by Fanteal's weight.

The room was of decent size, though smaller than she'd expected. Perhaps because her luggage crowded it. Drab hangings. Only one window. This couldn't be right. "Is this the suite my grandfather prepared for me?"

The two men exchanged a glance before Sir Mikkael answered. "No. This is not Dirklan House."

"I don't understand. All the prime ministers live in Dirklan House. Why don't you?"

"Because your uncle, Governor Nirundale, refuses to leave it."

"But why?"

"Why indeed?" Jaikon murmured, setting her down on the sheets. "He gives many reasons, though I doubt he has ever stated the real one."

"It needn't trouble you, lady," Sir Mikkael said. "Nilkie, see to the pillows."

"But it does trouble me. I need to go there."

The prime minister's voice remained level. "You need to rest. Perhaps you'd like to change into something more comfortable. This is Nilkie, who will be your maid. She'll bring you whatever you need."

Nilkie straightened her spine at the introduction. "I don't know how to find her things in all that luggage."

Couldn't she look? "My clothing is in the long leather packs."

Sir Mikkael took Nilkie aside, keeping his back to Fanteal. She couldn't make out his low-pitched words, but the maid's chin dropped, and she mumbled, "Yes, sir," multiple times.

He soon returned to Fanteal's bedside. "We'll leave you to rest now. Dinner will be brought to you, and I'll come to check on you later. Is there anything else I can do for you right now?"

She needed air and answers but couldn't think how to ask for either. "Could the window be opened, please?"

"Of course."

Jaikon cranked it open, though the air did not shift. Stifling.

"Anything else?"

She let her eyes close. "No, thank you."

CHAPTER 8

Jaikon paced in this father's study. "Her breathing is so…" He swallowed and tried again. "She sounds like Momeer did. Before…the end."

Pain flicked in his father's eyes. It had been many years. They sometimes mentioned fond memories of Jaikon's mother, but they didn't revisit her slow gasping death. His father sighed. "I noticed."

"What if she dies here?"

"Your mother died of emfiduria, which takes years to cause such labored breathing. Lady Fanteal was fine until she arrived. The cause cannot be the same."

"But now she can't breathe!"

"I suggest that you wait a few days before panicking. She may simply need time to adjust, as Lady Trissina told us."

"This is far worse than she described. Don't you realize what will happen to the covenant if the ambassador dies?"

His father waited several seconds before saying dryly, "Forgive me for being so obtuse. I thought you were concerned about Lady Fanteal's wellbeing. Obviously, I was mistaken."

Jaikon stopped pacing and stared at him. "I am."

"Your words were, 'Don't you realize what will happen to the *covenant* if the ambassador dies?' As though her life and her death are only relevant if they help us."

"Can't I care about both her *and* us?"

His father sighed his answer. "Of course, but you only mentioned us."

"You must know what I mean."

"Must I? Jaikon, you have got to start considering the impact of your words before you speak. The blunders you made in Regissa came from speaking your thoughts with no care for how they sound to anyone who doesn't live inside your head. Communication is two-sided. Partly what is said and partly what is heard."

Loud banging on the front door filled a brief silence. Both men ignored it.

"I don't have any control over what another person hears," Jaikon replied. "I speak the truth. What more can be expected of anyone than that?"

"What I expect of you is an understanding of viewpoints other than your own. And be wary of asserting that you speak *truth* when you speak your *opinions*. Those may be entirely different things."

A shrill voice in the hall penetrated the study door. "I'm a medic streamer, and that girl needs me. You show me which room she's in and don't give me any more of your insolence."

Jaikon reached the study door first and jerked it open. His father followed him into the hall. Colrin was confronting a wiry and aged stranger, whose sparse hair stuck out from his head at demented angles. Only the stiff-sided case he carried made him look anything like a medic.

"Ha!" the stranger exclaimed. "Now we'll see."

Colrin turned to Sir Mikkael. "He claims to be a medic streamer, sir, but he was not sent by—"

"Claims! Claims, you say?"

"Enough," Jaikon's father said. "I'm not interested in your offended dignity. Have you ever attended anyone from aboveground?"

"'Course I have." He pushed his chest out. "Ambassador Melthindi himself. I traveled all the way here from Alluthin just for this girl. And she's a mighty pretty one. I saw her in the carriage, right there at the beginning." He turned his gaze to Jaikon and added with a knowing grin, "You must be countin' the hours till your wedding night. Don't look down your nose at me. I know what you're thinking."

Jaikon couldn't get a word out, but his father did. "Is that how you intend to speak to Lady Fanteal?"

The old man blinked at him. "What? No. Sorry to have overstepped. I'll be respectful to the king's daughter."

Well...maybe he could be trusted. Jaikon's gut disagreed. If there was anyone else...but there wasn't.

His father must have been thinking the same, for it took him a moment to speak. "Jaikon, go upstairs and make sure that Lady Fanteal is ready to receive a visitor." He turned back to the medic. "What is your name?"

"Harbane, sir."

As Jaikon climbed the stairs, his father said, "Listen closely, Harbane. Lady Fanteal has had a tiring day. The air aboveground is richer than here. She grows faint when she stands, or even sits for too long. You are to examine her and tell us what she needs. Nothing more. Understood?"

"Yes, sir, but I'll be needing to ask her some questions."

Jaikon wished he could hear more, but he'd reached Fanteal's door. He accomplished his task, then looked over the railing to his father, who watched from below.

When Jaikon nodded, his father said to Harbane, "Come with me," and headed for the stairs.

Harbane didn't move. "This ain't Dirklan House."

Sir Mikkael stared back at him, and Colrin said, "It is, however, the prime minister's residence."

The medic blinked again. "Quite right. And I'm here for the new ambassador. If you'll just show me where, sir."

Jaikon's father turned slowly and climbed the stairs.

Jaikon went to Fanteal's bedside. "My father is bringing the medic streamer up."

She murmured assent.

"His manners are...unusual. He's elderly, but he used to care for Ambassador Melthindi. We'll stay with you." It was the most he could think of to say before Harbane entered. Jaikon took a position where he could watch him closely.

Sir Mikkael went to the opposite side of the bed. To Nilkie, he said, "There is paper in the desk. Be ready to write down instructions."

Nilkie found some in a drawer and set it atop the desk, where it drifted toward the edge. She glared at the open window, then anchored the paper with a letter opener.

Harbane set his bag on the nightstand and lifted Fanteal's wrist. "Ah, my lady, you've had a hard trip, I hear. You just keep on resting while I check you over."

Fanteal lay still.

His fingers moved up and down her wrist, as the medic streamers did to sense the nature of blood. He drew his breath in sharply. "Well, my, my! I never expected you to be such a one." A puzzled frown crossed Fanteal's brow, as Harbane blinked and looked around. "I'll just check how your blood is flowing through your heart and lungs," he said, moving his fingertips to key points around her chest. "Have you ever had difficulty breathing before?"

"No."

"How about after doing something strenuous? Has it ever been hard to catch your breath?"

"Never. I don't think the problem is in me. The air here is thin and lifeless. Like part of it is missing."

He moved his hands to a different position. "Does your head ache?"

"Yes."

Harbane straightened. "Well, it's what I expected. Abovegrounders have weak blood, but after they live with us for a bit and eat our food, it gets stronger."

"What foods?" Sir Mikkael asked.

"Oh, all the usuals we give to emfiduria patients."

"How can it be emfiduria?" Jaikon demanded. "She ran up a hillside just yesterday."

"I didn't say it was. Just that the treatment is the same. Her lungs are strong, and when her blood is, too, she'll be fine." He opened his bag, knocking over the glass of water on the nightstand, which he didn't even seem to notice. After pulling out bottles and shoving them back in, he finally chose two and rattled off instructions on dosage and frequency. He walked to the desk and peered over Nilkie's shoulder, perhaps to make sure she was getting it all down correctly.

She sidestepped, nervously. He followed her.

"Harbane," Sir Mikkael said.

The medic turned around and looked every which way. "This isn't Melthindi's bedroom."

Oh, quakes!

His gaze found Fanteal. "Ah yes, the new ambassador. Such a pretty one." He turned to Jaikon and flashed that knowing smile again.

Jaikon grabbed Harbane's arm and walked him toward the door. "Thank you for coming. That will be all." He jerked it open, grabbed the medic's bag, and continued walking him to the stairs.

"What's the hurry? What are you all worked up for? You're gonna get her soon enough. Easy on these stairs. I'm not as spry as you."

Was the man's mind as frail as the bone Jaikon felt within his skinny arm? He guided Harbane down the stairs. "You're leaving. Do not speak again."

"Oh, I see what it is," Harbane said. "You don't want me telling. You're trying to keep it a secret that she's no use with the trade cataracts."

"You don't know what you're talking about. She's a highly gifted streamer."

"Gifted streamer?" Harbane's voice squeaked and turned into a cackle. "A streamer, is she?"

The senile laughter grated on Jaikon's nerves. "You will go back to Alluthin first thing in the morning."

"You're not prime minister. You can't order me around." Harbane squirmed, trying to free himself from Jaikon's grip. "Besides, you still need me to check on your pretty lady. I'll be staying right at the Crescent Inn. You'll come asking all nice and apologetic, you will."

Colrin hurried across the hall to open the front door.

Jaikon put Harbane out into the street more gently than he wanted to, then shut the door on the tirade that spewed from him. Closing his eyes, he leaned against the door. "Colrin."

"Sir?"

"You need to find a medic—a sane one—who understands abovegrounders."

Colrin's expression offered little hope. "I will try, but I can only find people who exist."

In the end, they had to make do with their own medic, Prenard, who arrived as the cavern darkened. Jaikon wished the man was gifted as a streamer rather than a former, but all medics received the same education in medicine. At least they knew this one could be trusted.

Since Fanteal had fallen asleep, Prenard chose not to examine her. Instead, he listened carefully to every detail the Mikkaels could relate.

Jaikon's father finished with, "Ambassador Trissina told us that her daughter would need time to adjust, but she didn't describe this much difficulty. From what we've told you, does Ambassador Fanteal's reaction seem unusually severe?"

Prenard angled his head. "It's hard to say. We'll see how she fares after a few days." As he spoke, Nilkie entered the room with the medicine and instructions. He leaned forward in his chair to take them from her, then read the notes. "These are what I would have recommended. Despite his rambling, Harbane got this right." He looked at Nilkie. "You are her maid, I gather?"

"Her *aide*," Nilkie said.

He snorted. "I didn't think you'd be sweeping the floor. The title is apt enough because she will need considerable aid for a time. See that you follow these instructions exactly. Send for me if her breathing becomes more labored." He handed the items back to Nilkie. "Return to the lady. She must not be left alone."

He rose from his chair. "I'll find this Harbane in the morning and see what I can learn from him."

"Probably not much you can trust," Jaikon said. "He slips in and out of senile ramblings."

A thin smile lightened Prenard's unshakable calm. "Perhaps I can get more out of him than you could. I've had a few senile patients over the years."

A recurring dream taunted Jaikon. The trade cataracts were jammed, and when he tried to clear them—in absurd ways—everyone acted like nothing was wrong. Each time he woke, worry over Fanteal kept him tossing and turning until the next version of the nightmare swallowed him.

Sleep was making him more tired, not less! He tossed his blanket aside, felt his way to the magnery lamp on the wall, and turned it on.

One look at the slide timer, and he groaned. Only four hours through the night?

Fine. If worry about Fanteal was igniting these dreams, he'd just go make sure she was all right. Maybe then he could sleep.

He pulled on some clothes and went out to the gallery. A chain lamp with three faceted crystals hung from the hall's high ceiling. Dimmed for the night, but enough to spread a glow over each level's gallery. He reached her door and tapped his fingertips against it, then his knuckles. No response.

He turned the knob and peeked in. The lamp had been left on its lowest setting. In the faint light, Nilkie lay peacefully asleep on the couch.

Jaikon curled his lip. Pity that he couldn't shout. He pushed the door wider but still couldn't see Fanteal, for the bed was curtained. Common enough when one person needed sleep while another needed light, but it irked him. He still didn't have the answer he sought, and he didn't want to risk waking her.

Wait. That sound. Rapid gasping breaths. He strode to the bed and jerked the curtain aside. She didn't even jump. "Lady Fanteal, is it worse?"

She turned strained eyes to him and whispered, "The window."

Why was it closed? He hurried over to open it wide. The night air was usually still, but a breeze wafted past him. "Nilkie. Wake up!" he demanded on his way back to the bed. She didn't stir.

Jaikon dropped to one knee and took Fanteal's hand. "Do you feel worse? Would you like me to summon the medic? We found a better one for you."

"Give me a moment."

He was no medic, but he could count her pulse and breaths. After a few minutes, their frantic pace subsided a little. "Has Nilkie been giving you your medicine? How long has she been asleep?"

"I don't know. These curtains shut me in...couldn't call loud enough to wake her."

Jaikon gritted his teeth. "A rockfall wouldn't wake her!"

"It's not fair to...keep her awake...day and night. If you could just persuade her...to leave the window open."

"Do you know where she left the instructions?" He glanced around. "Ah, this must be them." He took the paper he found on the desk to the lamp and turned it up. After a moment, he asked, "Did she give you anything after eleven?"

"I don't know."

"Then she must be awakened."

This took some effort, but Jaikon finally got Nilkie upright and able to babble out a half-coherent apology mingled with excuses.

"Never mind that. When was her last dose of each medicine?"

She was able to give no clear answer, but after several questions, he decided they must be overdue.

"Enough apologizing, Nilkie. Go down to your own bed and sleep as long as you need to. I'm going to sit with Lady Fanteal the rest of the night."

"I can do it. I promise I won't fall asleep again."

"No. You must stay with her tomorrow. Sleep now."

He closed the door behind her and began to measure out the doses. One he recognized from his mother's illness, designed to help the body make efficient use of the little air that it received through failing lungs. Gently, he slid an arm beneath Fanteal. "I'm going to raise you a little, just for a moment. Here, drink this. And this. Good." He laid her back down. "Are you comfortable?"

"Yes, thank you," she murmured, her eyes already closed.

He watched her for a while. How wan and exhausted she looked. Her breathing grew a little calmer, and he began to draw the curtain to block the light.

The sound of the rings sliding along the rod instantly awakened her. "What are you doing?"

"Easy. Just moving the curtain so the light doesn't shine directly on your face."

"You won't close it all the way?"

"No. I promise. Go to sleep."

Her breathing steadied again, and Jaikon was left with nothing to do but stay awake in the dim room and ponder the events of the worst day of his life. No, not the worst. The day his mother died still held that distinction. But today, or rather yesterday, left him with unsolved dilemmas and additional problems.

The timer's marker glided far too slowly past the hour notches. Was the rod damaged? Or did looming troubles stretch time? Harbane's demented laughter echoed in his mind. Why had he laughed over the ambassador being a streamer? Again and again, Jaikon reminded himself that the old medic was senile, but his exhausted mind refused comfort.

Relief only came when dawn's light shot through the crystal shafts above Jourendia and his father's tread approached along the gallery.

CHAPTER 9

Fanteal ate her breakfast in bed. This had better make her stronger, for nothing else would convince her to eat such food. At least the tea was pleasant. Unlike the company.

Sir Mikkael sat in the desk chair, watching, perhaps to ensure that Nilkie was doing her job. The woman could hardly have fulfilled requests more stiffly, and she never met Fanteal's eyes.

Fanteal forced herself to swallow another bite. Even more frustrating than being so weak she required a maid, was the knowledge that Nilkie resented her duties. Could that ever be changed? Doubtful, considering how badly the relationship began. Fanteal needed a trustworthy servant. Desperately. And not just for personal matters. She should be requesting applicants and interviewing, not lying limp in bed.

Well, sitting in bed, if one used the word loosely. She set the teacup on her nightstand. "Please, take the breakfast tray, Nilkie. Also, take those dresses and press the wrinkles out."

Nilkie paused with the tray in her hands. "I can't do all that and stay with you at the same time."

Clueless. "I will be talking with Sir Mikkael, so there is nothing for you to do here."

When Nilkie left, Sir Mikkael pulled the desk chair near to the bed. "How do you feel?"

It was the third time he had asked. Maybe a smile would help. "Still better than yesterday."

"Sorry if I'm overdoing it. I'm just concerned."

"But don't you see? I can sit propped up with pillows and still manage to speak. That's better than last night." Had her lighthearted tone eased his mind?

"We'll probably receive a lot of visitors today," he said. "Governors and some potential suitors. I'm not trying to restrict your contact with them, but may I suggest that you wait to receive them until you are stronger?"

"That, you can easily persuade me to do. But there is one person I would like to see." He raised an eyebrow. "My uncle, Governor Baelan Nirundale."

Sir Mikkael's eyes lowered for a moment. "I will let you know if he comes, but thus far he's the only governor who has never visited this house."

"I gather there is a problem between you. Will you tell me what lies at its core?"

"Are you aware of the law pertaining to the death of a prime minister?"

"Certainly." She picked up her teacup. "The governor of Jourendia assumes the temporary role of prime minister, responsible only for emergency matters and organizing an election to replace the prime minister."

"Exactly. When Prime Minister Mardone Nirundale died, there were still almost four years left to his term. Instead of arranging the election, Governor Nirundale asserted that the people of Dirklan had elected a Nirundale only a year earlier and announced his willingness to complete his father's term. He did this in a speech delivered here in Jourendia, while all the other governors were elsewhere."

Sir Mikkael crossed one leg over the other. "I happened to be in Jourendia on business, so I attended the governor's speech. He stated many plausible reasons why this course of action was best for Dirklan." He angled his head in a conceding manner. "The name of Nirundale is beloved in Dirklan, particularly in Jourendia, and for good reason. Add that to Governor Nirundale's skill at omitting inconvenient facts, and he was swaying his audience very well indeed. I felt the situation needed to be dealt with before it took firm root, so I mounted the platform and challenged him with the law he was so willing to break."

"Mm. I don't suppose he liked hearing that from another candidate for the office."

"I wasn't a candidate yet. I was rather beneath his notice, but he had prepared a rebuttal." Sir Mikkael's nostrils pinched. "Insufficient, in my opinion, but he is very smooth. He managed to keep roughly half of Jourendia on his side, even to this day."

He paused, eyeing her. "I'm not sure what your grandfather told you about himself. Perhaps not much, for he was a modest man. In Dirklan he has always been held in high regard. He was extremely knowledgeable and equally wise. His son *sounds* a lot like him, so don't think I fault anyone for wanting to extend good leadership. On the other hand, there are a number of people who believe that Baelan's resemblance to Mardone lies only on the surface."

Fanteal sipped her tea. Past discussions she'd heard between her mother and grandfather took on deeper meaning. Would sharing them help her relationship with the Mikkaels? Worth a try. "When Prime Minister Nirundale told Ambassador Trissina that Jourendia had elected his son as governor, she was...concerned. Granted, I was young and only listening at the time, but I got the impression that my grandfather was equally concerned. He suggested his idea for a law that limits the number of consecutive years one family can hold the prime minister's office. The king and queen were pleased when he brought news the next year that the law had been passed."

"Interesting," Sir Mikkael murmured. "I heard those deliberations here at Government House. Some wanted to exempt the Nirundale family from it, but he consistently spoke against that. The compromise was that *he* was exempted, but not his family. The prime minister never mentioned that the crown had an interest in the matter. He always did know when to keep quiet."

Fanteal smiled. "Wise, as you say. But this is odd. Even if Baelan had gotten around the first law and finished his father's term, the law of office duration would prevent him from being re-elected. He would be better off waiting for a future election."

"He may have had a plan for that, or he may have only wanted delay. He did *start* planning the election, but the number of postponements became almost laughable. It wasn't held until a most unlikely group offered to collect and count the votes in Crysalan."

"Who?"

"The Keepers of the Writ."

Fanteal laughed. "What have they to say in politics?"

"Nothing. Their impartiality was the reason it could have worked. A great many people agreed. If it did work, Jourendia stood to lose control over this and probably future elections. Suddenly, the governor declared a firm date, and the election was held as always. That is, with each domain bringing their ballots to be counted here in the square."

She ignored the implication that she didn't know the election process. "I had no idea this sort of political controversy was going on. Neither does Dirklan's ambassador to the crown."

Sir Mikkael took a second to reply. "It has been building gradually, though it jumped to new heights when the prime minister died."

"Eleven months ago, Jaikon told me. When were you elected?"

"Four months ago."

That long without a prime minister, and no one above even knew! "Of all the years," she said, "for the half-year communication to fail, this was the worst."

"Agreed."

"I still don't understand. Why did Governor Nirundale delay so long when he cannot retain the office?"

"I am quite sure he wanted to be the one to bring his son aboveground."

Her cousin, Dalbred. Hmm. She stared out the window. "Is this related to the unspoken reason why he still resides in Dirklan House—and you do not?"

"It could be."

She turned back to Sir Mikkael and studied him for a moment. She had probably said enough. Besides, her fingers were growing numb. "Interesting." She set the cup aside and began to slide down in her bed. "I will rest for a little while before I get up. Please send a message to Governor Nirundale that the crown's ambassador wishes to meet with him today in this house."

"Are you sure you are up to that?"

If she told him why she *must* be up to it, he wouldn't believe she could do it. "Just make sure the windows are open in the salon where we meet."

When he closed the door behind him, Fanteal pulled a gust through the window. Where was the ocean breeze her mother had described flowing through Jourendia? Even her mother wouldn't claim this air was moving. Yet Nilkie said it was unusually windy, which she blamed on the recent opening of the dome. Odd conclusion. Why were they so hyper-sensitive to a breeze?

Garbed in lavender silk, Fanteal sat at her dressing table and put in amethyst earrings that matched her necklace. She winced as Nilkie fastened the sides of her hair back in a clasp. Nothing elaborate, for Fanteal didn't want to sit up any longer than necessary. She adjusted the hair that had snagged in the clasp. "Tell Jaikon I am ready."

He entered, scolded Nilkie for the luggage still piled around the room, then offered to carry Fanteal.

"I can walk," she said, "but you may help me stand."

She permitted him to keep an arm around her waist, hating that the precaution had merit. As soon as they reached the gallery, she said, "There are gentler ways to motivate people. Your approach isn't the best for someone like Nilkie."

"She is not taking proper care of you. That is unacceptable."

"I appreciate your concern, but I prefer that you let me deal with Nilkie."

When he didn't respond, she glanced up at his profile. His mouth was tight. She suppressed a sigh. His gentleness to her sometimes made her wonder if she had misjudged him. Then, in an instant and over such a trivial matter, he grew angry with her.

He guided her into the salon at the top of the staircase that led up from the hall. It was arranged like her mother's reception salon, with a couch in the center of the room facing the door. She took her place in the middle of it and spread her wide skirt.

Sir Mikkael watched with a hint of amusement. "Do you know that, even though you don't look very much like your mother, you somehow resemble her?"

Perfect. "That was my hope."

"You succeeded." He glanced over his shoulder at Colrin, who waited in the doorway. "Please bring the governor up."

The Mikkaels stood to either side of her couch, waiting. She located the draft coming from the two open windows behind her. Excellent. She drew the air to flow around her, in one window and out the other. That should provide her more of the meager air, without prompting anyone to shut the window.

Footsteps mounted the staircase, then a man entered, tall and broad-shouldered as her grandfather had been.

Sir Mikkael said, "Governor Baelan Nirundale, it is my honor to present Lady Fanteal de Noviam, Royal Ambassador of Welcia."

"My dear niece, it is pure delight to meet you at last!" He bowed, though not too deeply.

She inclined her upper body. "Likewise, such a pleasure for me to finally meet you, Uncle Baelan."

His smile was as perfectly formed as the dark hair combed straight back from his forehead. Some substance held every strand in place. "Do tell me, how did you leave my little sister?"

"My mother is well, but—little?"

He uttered a jovial laugh. "So I always called her when we were children. Oh, but I hope I haven't offended you, for I begin to think you inherited your height from her."

She gave him a playful smile. "Nonsense. I am a full two inches taller than she."

He laughed again, then turned aside. "And you must be Jaikon."

Jaikon inclined his head.

Fanteal raised a brow. "Have you never met him?"

"There's been no particular reason to. I've heard of him, of course, and of his delightful manners."

Out of the corner of her eye, she noticed Jaikon stiffen. She kept the smile on her lips. "Really? I've heard of your delightful manners too. Won't you sit down, gentlemen?"

For an instant, her uncle cocked his head, then took the chair across from her. "Oh? But perhaps we don't mean quite the same thing. I wonder who you heard it from."

"Sir Mikkael. He told me you sound like my grandfather."

Her uncle looked genuinely gratified. "Thank you, Sir Mikkael. It's a compliment I never expected from you."

"No? But then you don't know me very well."

Sir Mikkael's calm voice held just enough amusement that Governor Nirundale dropped that subject and turned once more to Jaikon.

Odd that her uncle focused on the man he'd never bothered to meet rather than the ambassador who'd summoned him.

"I've heard, also," the governor said, "of your devout faith in Ellincreo. I do trust that the chapel in the palace grounds didn't disturb you."

Jaikon dropped his voice to its driest. "Seeing a chapel is hardly disturbing."

"Ah, but I don't suppose you had to actually enter it." He turned back to his niece. "Forgive me. You must be wondering what I'm talking about. Jaikon is well known to deplore anything resembling what he would call an idol, so naturally—"

"Spare yourself the effort, sir," Jaikon said. "I have indeed entered her chapel. She knows exactly what I think of the grotesque statue in the back. So you see, all these subtle insinuations are quite pointless."

Realization bloomed on the governor's face. "You saw one of the statues? Grotesque, did you say?" He laughed deep in his throat.

"Governor Nirundale." Fanteal rivaled the quiet sternness her mother could achieve.

That stopped his laughter but didn't remove the smirk from his face. "Yes, my dear?"

She held his eyes for several seconds. "You know of the taboo concerning the statues, don't you?"

"Certainly."

"Why have you never conveyed that information to the new prime minister?"

He widened his eyes. "But my dear niece, the people elected him. Surely you don't question their ability to choose an adequately educated man."

"Perhaps they expected you to fulfill the duty of an exiting prime minister, even of a temporary one. You were to inform him of every detail of Welcian interactions. Law specifically declares it thus, because so few people can make the trip aboveground."

He opened his mouth, but she continued.

"However, that is in the past. You know of the taboo. You know its purpose is to prevent misinterpretation, for such a vision can only be understood by the recipient. Imagine what fools people would make of themselves, pretending to interpret something they couldn't possibly understand. Imagine how despicably malicious it would be to repeat a negative message. This is why no Welcian is ever tempted to break the taboo." She let the sentence leave her tongue slowly. "They would discredit themselves."

His smile remained fixed. "You have no need for concern."

"I hope not. I have good reason to believe that Jaikon has not mentioned it to anyone else. If I hear the least whisper of this, I will know it came from you. We are family, and I have no wish to hear the House of Nirundale being shamed." She leaned forward, softening her tone. "And believe me, Uncle, you are the last person in Dirklan I wish to be on bad terms with."

He finally gave her a serious answer. "I understand. You will hear nothing more of this."

"Thank you." She hid the deep breaths she was forced to draw.

Before she could start the only subject she wished to discuss, her uncle did it for her. "My dear Fanteal, you look tired. Has the transition been difficult for you?"

"It has. Worse than I expected. My grandfather told me last year that he'd made special preparations for my arrival at Dirklan House."

"Indeed, he did. I advised Sir Mikkael of this and suggested that he bring you to Dirklan House directly from the passage. The invitation still stands. In fact, I would be happy to bring you to your rightful home at once."

"My rightful home? What does that mean?"

"Surely you must know that Dirklan House has been our home for decades. Three generations of Nirundales have dwelled there. Your own grandfather built a suite just for you. Where else could you possibly belong?"

"King Darinneth and Queen Ambassador Trissina committed me to the care of Prime Minister Mikkael. Where else could I possibly belong?"

"But they could not have been aware of the circumstances."

"Quite true. They never expected a governor to be living in the prime minister's mansion. Your 'little' sister never once suggested I should live with my uncle. I will be living in Prime Minister Mikkael's household until the day that I marry. And so, uncle, if you are truly concerned for my health at all, will you please relinquish Dirklan House immediately?"

"Oh, my dear, I am so sorry, but that just isn't possible. It will take—"

She stopped him with a raised hand. "Will you explain what preparations were made for me?"

"Redecorating, of course. It's light and airy—truly a charming suite. There are abundant plants in holders along the walls, and it has a dedicated roof vent. That modification was the most puzzling, but he believed the architect and workers were successful. I daresay it is common aboveground, and it may be a comfort to you. May I escort you to see it now?"

"I need to rest. Please leave me."

He hesitated. "So soon? I had hoped—"

Sir Mikkael stood. "Her words were clear."

"Of course, if you are tired, my dear niece, I will not linger. I trust you will be stronger when we meet again."

She let her eyelids fall, rather than acknowledge his parting bow. A moment later, Sir Mikkael shut the door behind the departing governor and returned to her.

Fanteal used the interlude to refresh the room's air, drawing deep, intentional breaths. What a mess—and she'd only gotten half of that mess out of the salon. She opened her eyes and turned to Jaikon, who hovered nearby, apparently concerned.

"May I carry you back to your room?" he asked.

"Jaikon, you do not understand the damage you are doing to yourself. You must *stop* talking about the statues!"

He flung himself away from her. "Oh, the unbreakable taboo, to which we must all mindlessly submit."

"What's really mindless is to babble of things you don't understand."

"This is Dirklan, not Welcia above. No one here cares about your statues or even knows of your taboo."

"Governor Nirundale knows of their significance. That was quite clear from his laugh."

Jaikon sneered. "Wouldn't it be nice if I knew of their significance, too? Oh, but that cannot happen. They can never be spoken of. And yet, a moment ago you challenged Nirundale for *not* telling us. Well, he certainly won't, and you won't, so we'll never learn, will we?"

"The taboo is only against speaking of a revelation. Not of learning about the statues."

"Revelation? What are you talking about?"

"Don't you remember when you first saw them? They were in shadow, obscured. You even commented on it."

"Ah, yes. And you evaded my question."

"I did not. You just weren't listening. Think for a moment. Why would the back of the chapel be so dark when the rest is all light? The statues are not hard to see because they were placed in shadow. They are obscure *because* they are hard to see. Without a revelation from Ellincreo, no one ever sees a statue take on form."

"I wish I hadn't seen one."

Fanteal remembered the way fungi hung over the statue's eyes, blocking its vision. "That certainly fits."

Sir Mikkael cut off his son's response. "Enough, Jaikon." He pulled a chair forward and sat in front of Fanteal, his voice calm. "This isn't productive. I need to know whatever is necessary to maintain the best possible relations between Welcia above and below. I've never been in a chapel—never seen a statue, not even in shadow. Please explain what it would mean if I did see one."

She looked at her hands, clutched in her lap. How was she going to explain this without making everything worse?

"Is this so hard?" he asked. "You said learning about them is allowed."

She tilted her head toward Jaikon. "He'll be angrier than ever if I explain."

"I have no interest in his temper. What are the statues like? Are they carved as people?"

"No, they're just columns of gold, refined and polished until they are translucent like the vision wall belowground. They are...blank canvases through which an image is seen. There's one to represent each substance gift—forming, streaming, and wind weaving—and a fourth to represent all the life gifts."

"Blank canvases? What does that mean?"

"They take on form when Ellincreo molds them. It's only when he illuminates a statue that it can truly be seen."

"For what purpose?"

"Uh...to convey a message."

"What sort of message?"

The corners of her mouth worked. "Sometimes to give direction, to show one what to do at a difficult turning. Sometimes to show one..."

"To show one...?" he prompted when her pause lengthened.

"One's self," she replied, dreading the result.

"One's self?" Jaikon strode nearer, his skin white about the mouth. "You sanctimonious— Is that how you see me? As a—"

"Stop it." She jumped to her feet. "I have never said what I saw. It is *you* who announces that your revelation was grotesque. It is *you* who refuses to keep it private. *I* did not invite you to the chapel. *I* did not reveal that statue. *I* did not ask to see it. Stop blaming *me* for what Ellincreo revealed, for what *you* interpret, and for what *you* shout to the world." Her voice faltered, and she swayed as the room began to spin.

Sir Mikkael looped an arm around her before she could fall. He picked her up and carried her from the room and down the gallery.

Her head lolled against his arm. Desperate, she sought airflow. Finding it above, she drew a stream down to her face. For the first time, she examined the ceiling of the three-story hall. Wrought iron grillwork concealed vents. There was air up there. "Where do those stairs go?" she murmured.

Sir Mikkael stopped and looked down at her in surprise, then followed her gaze to the flight that rose from the third-floor gallery to the ceiling. "To the roof garden." He continued to her room. "Nilkie."

The maid opened the door, and he carried Fanteal to her bed. "Rest," he said, then left at once.

Nilkie looked down on her and huffed. "Would you like me to help you change?" she asked, disgust coating her voice.

Fanteal turned away. "Leave me."

"But it's time—"

"Leave."

"Fine." The door clicked shut.

Silent tears fell to the pillow Fanteal hugged. She was alone.

The only person who'd known or loved her in this whole land was dead. Her uncle saw her as a pawn to be captured from his political opponent. For all his affectionate talk, he cared not at all that she fought continuously for air.

Jaikon's concern evaporated the instant she displeased him. After today, he would probably never speak to her again. His tone echoed through her mind. All of his gentleness had been a façade. And Sened Mikkael...the way he had carried her out of the salon with barely a word spoken...he probably didn't want any more to do with her either. After all, what man wants to witness his son's humiliation?

Even her maid despised her.

Fanteal's shoulders began to shake, and her sobs quickened. The throbbing in her head beat ever faster. Her sobs turned to gasps. Desperation overwhelmed her loneliness. Air! Why couldn't she get enough? It finally dawned on her that Nilkie had closed the window while she'd been out of the room. Fanteal called out, but no one answered.

She had to get that window open. Gripping the bedpost, she dragged herself up. She clung to it while disentangling rumpled silk from her legs. The window looked so far. It couldn't be more than ten feet. She took a few steps, staggered, and ended up leaning over the back of a wingchair that hadn't been in her path. She tried again. The window tilted out of reach at the end of a tunnel. Then the floor rushed toward her.

CHAPTER 10

"I will not marry her," Jaikon declared. He paced across the study while his father leaned back in his desk chair. "To think I was angry when King Darinneth insisted that she choose her own husband. I could embrace him."

"You will never see him again," Sir Mikkael said.

Jaikon glared at him, annoyed to have his rant interrupted by an obscure statement.

"What are you thinking, Jaikon? That I will take you to Welcia above so you can insult the king's daughter while embracing him? You may consider that an entertaining spectacle, but I do not. Her husband will go with me to the palace."

"Dalbred Nirundale, no doubt."

"Unfortunately, no."

"What?" Jaikon jerked to a stop. "Do you want her to marry that scum, with his sweet, false words?"

"Not in the least, but it would keep her in Jourendia. If you paid attention, you would know that it won't happen."

"How, exactly, would I know that?"

"Her grandfather didn't want her to marry Dalbred. Add to that her disappointment in her uncle. She isn't going to like his son any better.

Instead, she will marry the son of some other governor, who will take her to some other domain—neither Northeshur nor Jourendia. She will be out of our reach. Since you have decided to alienate her to the fullest extent possible, she will probably avoid Northeshur more than any other. And that is where we need her."

Jaikon clenched his teeth, for it was true.

"So, now that we at last have an ambassador and a gifted streamer, you will throw away every hope. The grain shipments will continue to deteriorate, for if a word of truth was spoken aboveground, then the problem lies somewhere within the cataract itself. We've seen what the years have wrought. Erosion never reverses."

Jaikon cleared his throat. "Perhaps...if she lived in Weslin or Silcopton, she could at least improve the export cataracts." Pathetic suggestion.

His father gave him a deserved, flat look. "As though exports will continue if edible food does not come in."

Jaikon paced away. "I know—small help, but it would keep Welcia above, uh, willing to keep trying."

"They already are." His father leaned forward and rested his forearms on the desk. "For a while, Dirklan will continue to make do with just enough. But there will come a day when trade fails, and then history will repeat itself. Read up on the collapse of LourEstelle and the access tunnel. Some version of it will play out again. Alluthin will survive, but the other domains will dwindle away. You may consider that a price worth paying, but I do not."

He stared across the room at his father. Right as usual. And yes, Jaikon was at least half responsible for the proverbial cave-in with Fanteal. "I admit my share of the fault, but I cannot see any way of repairing things."

"Your share," his father repeated dryly. "Then I will explain the path you cannot see."

Jaikon stopped pacing and gripped a chairback, for his hands shook. "You still want me to marry her?"

"You flatter yourself. What fascinating charms do you think you possess that would induce Fanteal—an ambassador—to marry a man who cannot think beyond his own view of reality?" His father left a pause, which Jaikon was not about to fill. "Forget about courtship. I have more specific instructions."

Jaikon nodded, trying to look committed.

"First, you will never again speak of whatever you saw on that statue. It may be that Lady Fanteal's intervention will keep Governor Nirundale silent, but he cannot be trusted. Consider how you will respond if you hear talk of it. Your reply must be calmly stated, it must diffuse negative repercussions, but it must never include descriptive words about the statue. Is that clear?"

"Yes, sir."

"Second, you will discover what modifications were made to Dirklan House for the ambassador's arrival. Find the architect, the workers, the drawings, anything. Get a look at the mechanical device in the vent, if at all possible. Figure out a method to get more air into Lady Fanteal's room here."

"All right." This wasn't so bad—the mechanical aspect would even be interesting.

"And now the difficult part. You will repair the damage you have done to your relationship with Lady Fanteal."

Jaikon's breath quickened, but he kept his voice steady this time. "Damage that I have done? Did you not hear her?"

"I heard her clearly. I grant you no excuse whatsoever. You are a man, not a child. You will behave honorably, whether she treats you well or not. I hold you fully responsible for restoring the relationship."

"Isn't a relationship a shared responsibility? I cannot perform her half."

"Half! Are you really willing to give only fifty percent of your effort in order to prevent the collapse of our economy? Hunger. Threadbare clothes. Lack of countless commodities. In-fighting. Despair. And you offer to meet her *half*way? Is Dirklan worth so little to you?"

Jaikon couldn't meet his father's eyes.

"I cannot leave Jourendia during the legislative session," his father said, "which will be lengthy after skipping the year with no prime minister. Our plan that you would serve as Fanteal's escort has not changed. You will accompany her everywhere. Even if you have rocky times in private, you must show her courtesy and respect in public."

"Right, even if she doesn't show it to me."

"Think back a few minutes. When you misspoke, it was Governor Nirundale whom she reprimanded in front of us. She waited until he was gone before she said anything to you."

Great. His father defended Fanteal at his expense. And again, it was true. Just as well that his father kept talking.

"You do well in Jourendia, so I'm not worried here. A few small gatherings or outings might be good before any large public events. Then, we can make certain she will be up to it. That will be followed by invitations to the other domains. Invitations we cannot refuse. And there, you will learn the ramifications of your free tongue when we toured the domains before the election."

"Am I supposed to suddenly reverse my words now that you are prime minister?"

"You are to remember that—as prime minister—I, and therefore you, represent *all* of Dirklan. Not just Northeshur. You will be escorting an ambassador who represents the crown of Welcia to *all* of Dirklan."

"Yes, sir. But I do still believe that the import cataract in Northeshur is the most important concern to all."

"That needs no belaboring, since it is the common belief. The first domain I want her visiting is Northeshur."

"Of course. No one will object to that being the first."

"No one? They may not win that point, but they will still be clamoring for her to visit as soon as possible. You have very little time,

Jaikon. She must *enjoy* her trip to Northeshur, be willing to stay a while, make friends there, want to return. Do you understand?"

"Yes, sir."

A distant beating reached them.

His father sighed. "The knocker, yet again. No doubt another suitor or gift arriving. The competition for her is going to be intense. Whoever wins her will be prime minister next term."

Jaikon leaned his hands on his father's desk and fixed him with a gaze both subdued and determined. "My goal has never been to obtain an office. Not even for you. That is not why I joined you in this. It is because of Dirklan. It always has been, and it always will be."

Sir Mikkael stood and placed a hand on Jaikon's shoulder. "Oh, my son, I know that. You are the one who forgets your purpose when the world is not as you think it should be. Learn to listen. To consider before you speak."

Knuckles tapped the study door, and Sir Mikkael said, "Come in."

Colrin entered and closed the door behind him. "Two visitors have arrived, sir. Governor Yaldeeth is here to see you, and Prenard has come to check on Lady Fanteal."

"Jaikon, take Prenard to her room and let me know what he has to say about her condition. Colrin, bring Governor Yaldeeth to me."

"There is one other thing I believe you should know."

Jaikon stopped on his way to the door, and Sir Mikkael asked, "What now?"

"I heard it at the Tea House earlier today. Two of the pages report hearing it also when they were on errands. A rumor is spreading that Lady Fanteal is not a streamer."

Jaikon groaned. "Harbane!"

"Were you able to diffuse it?" Sir Mikkael asked.

"I didn't need to. Deltum was at the Tea House also. He claims that she was helping King Darinneth open the passage. A local woman said she heard the rumor from a senile medic streamer. It seemed that most everyone was dismissing it. I've told the pages to treat it as a joke and say they've heard that it started with a senile old man."

Sir Mikkael smiled at the change from *medic streamer* to *old man*. "You are a treasure. Let me know if you hear more of it. You may show the governor in."

"**S**he's doing a little better, I think," Jaikon replied to Prenard's question as they climbed the stairs. "She was able to receive Governor Nirundale and talked easily with him for a little while. She tired quickly, though, and fainted after she stood for a few minutes."

"Has she been taking the medicine regularly?"

"There was one delay when her maid fell asleep during the night. Whoever is sitting with her is now required to write down the times when she takes it." He knocked lightly on her door. The pause lengthened. He knocked again and called, "Nilkie?"

This couldn't be happening again. For the second time, he opened the door uninvited. The bed was empty and the room silent. He threw the door wide and rushed in. Lady Fanteal lay in a heap between the window and a chair, unmoving.

Jaikon started forward. "My lady!"

"Don't touch her," Prenard snapped.

Jaikon halted, then hurried to the window and cranked hard to open it.

Prenard knelt beside her and moved his hands down her head, neck, and spine, doubtless sensing with more than his hands. "No bones are broken. Pull that chair around so we can raise her feet."

Fanteal became aware of throbbing between her temples. A moan amplified the pain.

"Wake up, lady."

Bad idea.

A vile smell wafted into her nose. Another moan. Was that coming from her own throat?

"Lady Fanteal, wake up."

She turned her head away from the smell and tried to object. Her words sounded much like the moan.

"That's better. Open your eyes."

What was better? Two faces hung above her at odd angles. Jaikon and a stranger. Her gown was twisted around her torso, and her legs stuck out from a pile of lavender silk. Memory returned. "No." How could that pitiful whimper be her voice?

"Take a deep breath," the stranger said. "Another." He fiddled with something. "I am Prenard, a medic former. I'm going to give you something to help you feel better."

Her head was turned, and liquid dripped into her mouth.

"Swallow. Breathe deeply."

Air. There wasn't enough. Where was it? Her silent call went out, groped, found a little to pull in. Found more. She sucked in great gulps.

She opened her eyes, focused, then squeezed them shut again. Jaikon was looking down on her, his face full of worry and compassion—like before. But he despised her. Tears stung her lids. Crying—and he was going to see it.

She closed herself within, shutting out thought and feeling. Now that she was breathing deeply, they stopped trying to get her to respond. Maybe they wanted her to be still. She didn't care what they wanted. She wasn't going to let them see her cry. But she couldn't avoid the humiliation of being picked up and carried to her bed like an infant.

Nilkie arrived. If only Fanteal could close her ears as well as eyes. She tried to ignore Jaikon's stern questioning of Nilkie. Why was the window closed? Why hadn't the last dose of medicine been written down? Why hadn't she given it? And Nilkie's resentful answer that she had been told to leave when she tried to offer the medicine.

Instead of the scathing remarks Fanteal expected, all Jaikon said was, "Wait on the gallery so you are close at hand if she calls for you."

The door clicked again, and Fanteal waited for voices to reveal who remained, hoping Jaikon had left with the maid.

"Were you able to get any useful information from Harbane?" he asked.

"Some," Prenard replied. "I brought a specific list of foods that will help her blood adapt more quickly."

"Excellent."

"I suspect he's forgotten much from the days when Melthindi de Noviam first arrived, but he told me there are books he studied to learn how to care for abovegrounders."

"Books? Does he still have them?"

The eagerness in Jaikon's voice mirrored Fanteal's feelings. She opened her eyes despite her desire to hide.

"He says they're kept in the prime minister's library."

"Dirklan House!" Jaikon exclaimed.

"So I would assume. I went there but was refused admittance."

"What?"

"Governor Nirundale was away from home, but I saw his son, Dalbred. He refused—quite bluntly—to let me enter the library or to bring me the books."

Jaikon inhaled audibly and snarled the breath out as he stomped away to the window.

Prenard returned to the bed and counted her pulse. "Do not worry, lady. Sir Mikkael can get access to the books. It will only be a slight delay. Does your head feel better?"

"Yes."

"Don't let yourself be too cast down. You will grow stronger."

"Mm."

The medic soon left, after once again telling her to rest. How tired she was of hearing that. As though she had a choice. A moment later, someone tapped on the door.

Jaikon answered it, then tentatively approached her bed, a potted plant in his hands. "This just arrived from Governor Yaldeeth. She is governor of Illia."

Fanteal forced herself to turn her head in his direction and stared at the gift. "Why did she send me a plant?"

"Uh...they are a common gift."

"Is that why there are more plants in my room every time I open my eyes?"

Jaikon carried it to one of the tables and made room for it. "Yes, plus the fact that everyone knows you're having trouble adjusting to the air."

"Bizarre."

"What is?"

"What have plants to do with air?"

"They make the air richer." She only stared at him, so he tried again. "They make better air for you to breathe. It works best when light is shining on the leaves. Isn't that known in Welcia above?"

"Uh-uh." She rolled over on her side, turning away from him.

He hurried around the bed and dropped to one knee. "Please don't. I didn't mean to offend you again."

"I don't get offended over every little word."

"I...well...after today, I wouldn't blame you. I've been trying to figure out a way to apologize, but...I can't think what I can possibly say to... I suppose I'm just making a bigger mess of it, but I am sorry."

She stared into his eyes. "All right."

He started to reach toward her hand but drew back, then opened his mouth and closed it again.

"I'm tired, Jaikon. I'd like to be alone."

He hesitated. "As you wish. There's something I would have told you before if I'd realized Nilkie would leave you. See this lever on the wall? Do you have these aboveground?"

She glanced at the lever mounted beside her bed within easy reach. "No."

"Each room here has one. If you pull it down, a bell will ring and someone will come to your room. There's always someone on duty in the staff's hall where the bells sound. Please try it. I want to make sure you can call for help without getting up."

She complied, and the pressure of a spring snapped the lever back into place. A moment later, hurried footsteps and voices sounded from the gallery.

Nilkie tapped on the door and opened it. "Do you want me?" she asked.

"Not right now," Jaikon answered. "I was just showing Lady Fanteal how the bell works."

He left her then.

Finally, some privacy. Fanteal rolled onto her back. So, there'd been no need for her to get up to open the window. This whole fainting episode could have been avoided, but that knowledge didn't alleviate her helplessness. If anything, she felt worse. Limp and useless, dependent on a bell to call other people to perform even the simplest task for her. People who despised her.

And now Jaikon was back to the concerned and gentle routine. Her uncle was all sweet words and affection, too, but she was a pawn in his eyes. Probably in the Mikkaels' view as well. A trapped pawn—too weak to even stand alone.

Tears stung her eyes, and her heart cried out to Ellincreo. *Why did you send me here? I'm no use, just an object to be fought over.*

Words her father had spoken long ago whispered in her mind. "It's hard to have faith in Ellincreo when you're telling him that he's got it all wrong."

Oh, fine. I'm whining, and I ought to know better, but I don't know what to do. When things went wrong in Welcia above, there was always someone I could talk to. I know you're with me, but oh, I could use a friend. And somehow…I've just got to have more air.

Look. The word, gentle but firm, reverberated within her mind.

Look? Look at what? Jaikon's words replayed in her memory—that plants make the air richer.

The voice within grew insistent. *Look completely.*

She strained to sense with her gifting. So often she had sensed the currents of air. Warm air and cool. Air laden with moisture. Dense air. High, thin air that was barely discernible. Currents that moved and twisted, their edges rubbing, causing little eddies to swirl into existence. But those currents filled the sky, big enough to comprehend. Here was a little patch of still air hovering around a cluster of plants.

She sensed Ellincreo's voice again. *Some formers, like Jaikon, feel deep through many layers of rock. Some, like Prenard, feel the tiniest matter, even the structures I made to carry air through your body. Look closely.*

She propped herself up on an elbow and stared, not letting the faintest current disturb the air over the table. And finally, she perceived it. Almost as if a hazy layer rested on each leaf. It reminded her of the way water fused into the morning air over a still pond. But this was not water in the air. She carefully drew it toward herself—inhaled deeply—sensed it entering her lungs. This air…held life.

CHAPTER 11

Chief Former Agriben watched the street from the second-floor window of Fountain Inn, keeping out of sight behind the half-closed draperies. The narrow balcony outside his window commanded a view of the square and the length of Fountain Avenue all the way down to Passage Avenue. Not that he dared step out onto it.

He spotted Charlis, his apprentice, winding his way along the crowded street as people left their daily work. Ordinarily, most would have been heading home, but today they gathered in knots, exchanging wild stories they'd heard of the new ambassador. All manufactured within a single day.

As early as last night, the rumor that she wasn't a streamer had flown through every tearoom in the city. By morning, it made the short hop to the market. What disturbed him was not that the rumor was true, but the reaction to it. Those who believed it were shocked and horrified. The majority still scoffed at the idea. After all, House de Noviam produced the strongest streamers ever known. As though the gifts came by birth. What nonsense.

More convincing were those who quoted Prime Minister Nirundale. He had occasionally spoken of the king's streaming power, calling it 'truly remarkable' in his calm, understated way. In recent years, he had also commented on Princess Fanteal's power and range. If only Agriben could remember the actual words of that beloved leader.

Now, he dared not go into public. What could he say if anyone asked him to confirm that she was a streamer? Lying would be unthinkable. But what havoc would ensue if he stated the truth? At what point had the people forgotten that the covenant guaranteed them an ambassador, not a streamer? Their great need could never cause an ambassador to become something she wasn't. But no matter how obvious this was to him, the masses had somehow convinced themselves that the words *ambassador* and *streamer* were synonyms.

All last night, he had tried to convince himself that the uproar would die out and be forgotten. He'd sent Charlis out early, and again at noon, to glean what information he could. And now, as the young man slipped into the sitting room of their suite for the third time, the frown below his curly dark hair looked ominous.

Charlis closed the door and said, "It's worse."

Agriben sank into a chair by the round table and sighed. "Tell me."

"Well, most everywhere it's all hashed together, but I'll try to sort out the main points." He rested his hands on the opposite chair and stared at nothing. "Among those who assert that she is *not* a streamer, most say Harbane was an unusually gifted medic streamer. So even though Harbane goes off into senile ramblings, quite a few people are convinced that if she is a streamer, he would have recognized it."

"That is actually true," Agriben grumbled.

"For what it's worth, Governor Armeen has sent Harbane home to Alluthin."

"That won't help a thing."

Charlis began slow pacing. "On the other side of the rumors, both Deltum of Silcopton and Tershel of Weslin insist that they saw her opening the passage with King Darrineth. But it appears that all is not well with these two. No one knows why Deltum and Tershel seem to have so little to do on behalf of their governors. In the Tea House in

Jourendia Square, someone was needling them, trying to find out what's amiss. Deltum started to imply that Jaikon had been at fault in some way, but Tershel stared him down." Charlis shrugged. "Foolish attempt. For all that Jaikon gets himself into trouble elsewhere, he is well liked here, so that wasn't going to win them support."

Charlis gripped the chairback again. "Then there were questions of how the ungifted could physically *see* a streamer do anything. Tershel admitted it was too dark to see, but that she stood beside the king during the second opening of the dome. Deltum had daylight, but when questioned by a streamer, he didn't *see* either, for he was inside the vessel before the whirlpool formed. Jaikon watched her from the hatch, so he saw her the longest—for whatever that is worth." He shrugged again. "Then someone had the audacity to imply that the ambassador could have been pretending while the King did the actual streaming."

Agriben's jaw dropped, and his eyes widened.

Charlis nodded grimly. "Just so. Most reacted like you. Deltum shouted that the king himself said she was helping him, and asked how the fool dared slander the ambassador. The owner of the Tea House threw the idiot out, and things started to calm down."

Agriben almost had a moment to relax.

"But then..." Charlis said, wrecking it, "I overheard a group in the corner. Some woman from the prime minister's household has spread the story that the ambassador is a pathetic thing who must be coddled night and day. She's so spoiled that she can't even dress herself. One of them insisted the story came from her maid, but I can't imagine a maid spreading such tales about her mistress. I heard the same thing in the street on the way back here. Twice, in fact. I even heard speculation that Ambassador Fanteal will die, and then King Darrineth will blame us and break the covenant."

Agriben slumped in his chair and groaned. They'd waited so long for the ambassador. Hopes had been so high. How could this be going so horribly wrong? And what could he do about it? He closed his eyes and listened, hoping for guidance from Ellincreo. Nothing. When he looked back at Charlis, the young man was regarding him with a strangely anxious expression. "What is it?"

"There's one other thing I think you should know."

"Don't keep me in suspense, Charlis. Out with it."

"Some people are saying that *you* said she's a gifted streamer."

"What? I never said any such thing!"

"I know. But you did say she was gifted. I think it's been coupled with what everyone assumed would be true."

A knock made Agriben bite back his response. He stared at the door for a tense moment, then barked, "Come in."

A young lady pushed the door open and took a tentative step inside. She carried a bulging travel bag in one hand. Several strands of her brown hair had escaped from their bun.

"Bella!" Agriben exclaimed.

She gave him a wavering smile but turned her attention to Charlis, who hurried over to relieve her of the bag.

"Let me take this," he said. "How did you get here?"

"Thank you. On a train, of course," she said. "Two of them, in fact. Making the trip from Illia all in one day is less than fun. I had to run across Crysalan's station to catch the Jourendia-bound train, and I barely managed to jump into the last carriage after it started moving. Scared the children in it so bad that the little one started crying. I don't think her mother forgave me."

Charlis straightened after setting her bag out of the way. "When did you last eat?"

"Breakfast."

He shook his head and left the room.

"Bella, my dear," Agriben said, his rough voice no mask for affection. "Come and sit down."

She complied, though with an uncertain look in her eye.

"Don't think I'm not delighted to see you, child, but—why are you here?"

"You're going to think I'm terribly unstable."

"I doubt that. I've never known anyone more determined to follow Ellincreo's leading."

She stared at her hands folded on the table. "Well, I *want* to, but I don't seem to be any good at figuring out what it is. For years, I couldn't think of anything but studying the Holy Writ and all the other documents. Everyone was sure I was destined to be a Keeper of the Writ, which made perfect sense. Why else would his words have been so engrossing to me?" She drew a loud breath. "And then last year—well, you know how it was, because I talked with you about it. All of a sudden, I just knew I had to go into medic studies—which made *no* sense, because I don't have a substance gift to go along with it."

"Haven't your studies gone well?"

"Oh, it's not that. I just finished the first-year training. My instructors compliment my understanding, though remarks about my gifting are noticeably absent. One of the medics wants me to start nursing some of her emfiduria patients." Bella fell silent.

Agriben laid a hand over hers. "You know I'm expected to be back in Crysalan in a few days. You didn't come all the way to Jourendia just to tell me this. What else?"

"Last night, I went up to the roof garden to watch the light fade. I was just sitting there enjoying it when I heard him." She splayed her fingers. "I'm just sure it was Ellincreo's voice, and yet it's so inconsistent with everything he's led me to in the past. Anyway, the first part was to come to Jourendia—at once. I was struggling with it—so bad! And then he reminded me that you were here. I decided to obey at least that much of it and get your counsel before I...make a fool of myself."

"I'll never be able to give you counsel, Bella, if you can't bring yourself to tell me the rest of it."

She took another deep breath and blurted out, "He told me to become maid to the new ambassador."

Agriben had determined to show no surprise, but he could only stare at her with his mouth drooping open.

She looked away. "I knew it."

Charlis returned at that moment with a dinner tray, which he set in front of Bella. She attacked a piece of bread like she'd gone days rather than hours without food.

"You'll never believe what's happening downstairs," Charlis said. "There's a woman demanding a room for the night and spouting off how unfairly she's been treated by the Mikkaels. Dismissed for no reason, she says. Someone told me she's the maid who spread the story about the ambassador."

Understanding dawned, and Agriben chuckled.

Bella swallowed her bread. "What? I don't understand. Please tell me."

"Eat up, child," Agriben said. "There's more to this than you realize."

"Or I, apparently," Charlis murmured. "How can you laugh?"

"Because Ellincreo sent Bella to be the ambassador's maid."

Charlis's mouth rounded for an instant as he stared at her. Then he smiled. "Ah!"

Bella slapped her hand on the table. "Tell me!"

"I'm about to," Agriben patted her hand. "That looks like oyster stew, and it's quite tasty here. You can eat and listen at the same time. All is not going as expected for Lady Fanteal."

Bella took a spoonful of stew and watched him expectantly.

"To start with, she's not a streamer."

"Not a streamer? Oh no!"

"And to make matters worse, everyone's assumed that she absolutely must be one. An old medic streamer got close to her and started a rumor that she's not."

"But Agriben," Bella cried, "she has to be. Who is this old medic? He must be wrong."

"I greeted her at Passage Lake—took her hand in my own as she brought a breeze through the cavern. You know, don't you, that I'm sensitive to other gifts?" When she nodded, he continued. "I assure you, she is a wind weaver, most definitely not a streamer."

"What purpose could Ellincreo possibly have for sending a weaver here?"

He regarded her solemnly for a moment. When he answered, he softened his rumbling voice. "Why would Ellincreo have you study the Writ, when you're not to be a keeper of it? Why would he have you study medicine, when you're not to be a medic?"

"Like I said before—I have no idea."

"Well, the ambassador certainly could use a good nurse," Charlis said. "It's all over Jourendia that she can barely get enough air."

"Do you suppose," Agriben asked Bella, "that Ellincreo might want someone close to her who has studied the Writ?"

Bella stirred her stew, frowning. "There are some in Crysalan who worry that she'll bring idol worship here."

Agriben shook his head. There seemed no end to the chaos people liked to stir, but he could only deal with so much. "As for why Ellincreo sent us a wind weaver, I don't pretend to know. But as the years pass, I've seen time and again that there are reasons behind his, uh...inexplicable acts. He's just given you an example of that. The question you must ask yourself is whether you'll trust him enough to become a helper to the ambassador he sent us." He let that hang in the air until her expression softened. "And believe me, she's going to need help."

Her eyes met his. "What do you mean?"

"Eat. Charlis, tell her all the rumors."

She listened to Charlis, working her way slowly through stew, bread, and a pile of river grapes. At the end of his recital, she uttered a long, "Hmm."

"Are you still undecided?" Agriben asked.

"Undecided? Oh, about being her maid? Not at all. But one thing strikes me as really odd about all of this."

"What, child?"

"Prime Minister Nirundale—wouldn't you think he must have known she is a wind weaver?"

Agriben cupped his chin against thumb and forefinger and considered the ramifications of her statement. "That is strange. Charlis, does anyone state specific quotes of his past remarks about her?"

"Not that I've heard today. I've been trying to think back, but all I can remember are passing remarks...not the main point of whatever he was saying."

"How about our current prime minister?"

"There's no word from him at all. Not surprising, though. He must know by now, but how, in all this uproar, could he make a statement?"

"Politics!" Agriben groused. "Makes me glad I'm a former. Masses of rock are so much more manageable than masses of people." He turned to Bella. "I think we should get to the prime minister's residence before he has time to find the wrong replacement for the maid he dismissed."

"You're coming with me?" She fisted her hands. "Oh, thank you so much! All the way here, I couldn't figure out what I'd say, walking up to his door and announcing I'd come to be the ambassador's maid."

Rising, he laughed, then pulled on the cloak he'd worn at Passage Lake. No real need for a cloak on the streets, but he used its hood to shield his face as he hurried Bella out of the inn and through the square.

She stared at Dirklan House as they passed it and grumbled, "It irks me to no end that Governor Nirundale still squats where he has no right."

"You're not alone."

"Then why doesn't Sir Mikkael throw him out?"

"This is Jourendia, not Crysalan. There's loyalty to the House of Nirundale. The city's divided on it. Sir Mikkael has enough problems without turning half the city against himself."

He led Bella to the Mikkaels' rented house and knocked on the door.

Colrin greeted the chief former with a bow and stepped back to let them enter. "I didn't realize you were still in town, Agriben. Is there some issue of concern within the Formers' Guild that brings you so late?"

"No, though a matter of equal importance. I heard that the prime minister dismissed the ambassador's maid. A critical position, but not easily filled. I happen to know an ideal candidate, so I brought her."

A flicker of surprise crossed Colrin's features as he looked between Agriben and Bella. "I see. Sir Mikkael is meeting with someone at the moment, but I'll inform him of your arrival."

Out of the corner of his eye, Agriben noticed Jaikon on the gallery above. He strode to the stairs and descended, then bowed to Agriben. As he straightened, his gaze rested on Bella.

Agriben said, "Jaikon Mikkael, this is Bella Karabeth of Crysalan."

"Pleasure to meet you," Jaikon said. "What makes you an ideal candidate?"

The way she startled, he'd probably been too abrupt. But they could not afford to get this wrong twice.

Bella licked her lips. "Well, I have completed the first year of medic studies. Though I have no substance gift, I do understand the breathing ailments, which might be helpful."

Jaikon's father and Prenard stepped from the study as she spoke. Prenard launched into questions about her training, which soon turned into instructions. Apparently, he approved.

Sir Mikkael's questions drew out attitudes. The woman's answers indicated that she understood loyalty and respect.

"Are you willing," Sir Mikkael asked, "to stay within the house for a few days?" She nodded, but he kept talking. "I don't just mean to serve her, but for your breaks as well. If you haven't heard yet, there are damaging rumors circulating. She doesn't know of the rumors, and I will not have her distressed by them while she is still so weak."

Strain seemed to flit through Bella's expression as she answered. "Understandable. I will not bother her with such, nor will I ever gossip about her."

Sir Mikkael's gaze shot to Agriben. "How long have you known this young lady?"

"Since her childhood, sir, for she grew up in the house beside mine. I have always found her to be trustworthy, as is her family."

"For tonight, Bella, you are hired," Jaikon's father said. "Your continued employment depends on whether you please Lady Fanteal and take good care of her."

"I understand."

"Come. I will take you to her."

Jaikon followed them up the stairs.

Fanteal considered the young woman as Sir Mikkael introduced her and offered a simple explanation. At least she didn't stiffen with indignation at the word *maid*.

"Can you endure a breeze?" Fanteal asked.

"That will be no problem at all. Prenard told me the window must never be closed."

"Perhaps this may seem a strange question," Fanteal said, "but I need to know. Has anyone within government encouraged or ordered you to fill this position?"

Bella widened her eyes. "Nothing like that, lady."

"Who or what prompted you to come?"

She lowered her eyes and took a moment to answer. "I hope I don't sound presumptuous, but I believe Ellincreo really does speak to us. And that we all have a destiny, whether it is large or small in the eyes of others. For years, Ellincreo directed me to study his words. This past year, he directed me to study medicine. Last night…well, no one could be more shocked than I, but I felt quite certain he was telling me to come to Jourendia and become your maid." She swallowed visibly. "I didn't even know you needed one until I reached Agriben."

The tight grip of her hands at her waist revealed how much nerve that bold statement had taken. "Not many," Fanteal said, "would claim such a recommendation."

"Well, I cannot prove I heard him correctly. To be frank, I hold a very dim view of those who write their personal revelations and claim they should be added to the Holy Writ. But a maid is a quite personal position, and it's only fair that you know what sort I am."

There was certainly a great deal more to Bella than to Nilkie.

A knock on the door interrupted them. Jaikon opened it to a page carrying a dinner tray.

Bella inspected the contents. "Good. Oreduck with wesleaf salad. I hope you like it, because it's very beneficial for your condition. If I adjust your pillows, could you sit up a little?"

Behind Bella, Sir Mikkael let out a sigh bearing so much relief that Fanteal's lips twitched. "Thank you," she said to him.

"My pleasure. We'll leave you to your dinner." He paused in the doorway. "Jaikon."

His son seemed reluctant but left with him.

When Fanteal was comfortably settled and eating, Bella pulled a chair close to the bed and sat. "Do you like the oreduck?" she asked.

"It has a rather tangy taste for poultry. Is it marinated?"

Bella scrutinized it. "Probably not, but there are various ways to prepare it that diminish the tang. I'll ask the cook to try some of them for you."

"My mother mentioned eating doves when she lived belowground. Does that meat strengthen blood?"

"I've never heard that it could, but they're extinct anyway."

Fanteal paused with her fork midway to her mouth. "Really? By what cause?"

"I doubt anyone knows. There's been talk of them dying off in one cavern or another since I was little. The last was probably around five years ago."

Strange. Fanteal chewed another bite of meat. "What, exactly, is an oreduck? I don't recognize the name or the flavor."

"I've never heard of it as anything else, but a name like ore-duck was probably given to it in Dirklan. It's a large, flightless bird that is bred near the iron mines in Weslin."

"I had oysters from Passage Lake for lunch," Fanteal said. "Do you still get fish in Descent River?"

"Yes." Bella tilted her head. "How do you know about Descent River?"

"It's protected in Welcia above. No one may net from it nor empty waste into it because it provides Dirklan with fish."

"What a pleasant hearing."

Such feeling in her smile and words. Revealing. Dirklians did need to know that Welcia above still cared about them.

Bella went to look in one of the open trunks and soon busied herself hanging Fanteal's clothing. She glanced at Fanteal occasionally, but beyond giving medicine, didn't intrude on her thoughts.

While Fanteal focused on drawing air gently across the plants, Bella opened one of the rigid leather trunks, which had not yet been disturbed. It was filled with books. She pulled one out and read the title. "Rejoicings!"

"What?" Fanteal said. "Oh, my library. You needn't unpack those trunks, but please leave that book on my nightstand."

Bella rose from the trunk slowly, as though the titles of books had latched onto her eyes. She came to the bed, staring at the book in her hands. "This is part of the Holy Writ."

Fanteal gave her an ironic smile. "Yes, I know."

Bella laughed and said, "It's just that it's one of my favorites and I wasn't expecting to see it. Why did you bring them? Didn't you know that we have copies here?"

"Of course, but I'm rather sentimentally attached to them."

"Do you have a full set?"

"Uh-huh. Though not the ones that were written in Dirklan after the collapse, if that's what you mean. But even those, I've read. My mother brought a set with her to Regissa."

A knock on the door interrupted them. Bella set the book on the nightstand and went to answer it.

CHAPTER 12

Jaikon entered and swept his gaze around the room before focusing on Fanteal. "Is all well?"

Why did he seem so tentative? "All is well," Fanteal replied.

"Colrin is waiting to show Bella around the house and where her room is located—if it's all right that I sit with you for a while."

"Yes, that's fine. Go ahead, Bella, and take a little time for yourself."

She nodded. "When it's convenient, could someone come and get these empty trunks out of here?"

"Absolutely." Jaikon grabbed one and, between him and Colrin, moved the trunks onto the gallery within minutes.

Bella watched the flurry of activity with a tilt of her head. She leaned near the bed and whispered, "Is there something offensive about trunks?"

Fanteal shook with a silent laugh. "He doesn't like dodging around them. Nilkie, my previous maid, didn't consider it her responsibility to tend to my belongings."

"I see," Bella said with marked dryness. "Is that why the few dresses that had made it to your closet are wrinkled?"

"It is. Speaking of which, there is a casual dress in mint green that I will likely want tomorrow."

Jaikon waited while Bella gathered the dress and a few other items. He closed the door behind her and said, "In at least one way, she is a vast improvement."

Fanteal laughed again. "Several ways. She can even converse pleasantly."

"I know it's only been a couple hours, but do you like her?"

"Yes, I do."

His tight forehead relaxed. "At least something went right today."

"I'm a little curious. How did it happen that you found her?"

"We didn't. Agriben brought her to us, though I'm quite willing to give Ellincreo the credit."

So was Fanteal. She considered Jaikon again. Who was this man, really? Even her uncle, though intending to deride, had mentioned Jaikon's faith. If Jaikon saw her as only a pawn, would he care whether she liked her maid? And even attribute Bella's arrival to Ellincreo? Now he watched her with a puzzled half smile. She might as well make the most of his current helpfulness.

"Perhaps something else can go right today," she said.

"I'll take any and all improvements. What are you hoping for?"

"Will you take me up to the roof garden?"

His eyes flicked wide, countered by a frown. "Now? The light will be gone soon."

"Then we should go at once."

"Wouldn't it be better for you to rest?"

Fanteal narrowed her eyes. "I've been resting. And soon I will rest again...all night long. Could you stand lying around, hour after hour?"

"No, but I won't have you fainting again."

"You'll be right beside me the whole time."

He gave in with a wry smile. "Fine, but I'll carry you to the roof."

She swung her legs over the side of the bed, appreciating the belowground style of shorter dresses worn with leggings. "I will accept that on the stairs—*only* because I want to be sure I can walk around on the roof."

"Fine."

In a few minutes, they reached the base of the roof staircase, which ascended right up to the ceiling. Jaikon unhooked a chain on one side and gave it a jerk. The ceiling panel dropped onto tracks and slid away from the stairs with barely a rumble. When he'd carried her up and set her feet on the roof, he offered his arm.

Best take it. The air was nothing like in Welcia above, but a little better than in the house. She looked out over the garden level of Jourendia. Every structure was three stories tall, each one topped with greenery. It must be the flowering season of a common plant, for yellow blooms studded trellised vines. "Oh, how pretty." She turned in a slow circle, taking it all in, then pointed to one of the raised beds. "An herb garden?"

"Yes. The rest are vegetables and fruit." He escorted her along narrow paths between beds, which forced them to stroll close together. "Are you surprised? Every square foot of space is used."

"What is that for?" She pointed to bars with pulleys and chains that extended beyond the rear half-wall of the roof.

"It's for lowering food to the kitchen and lifting compost. There's a sitting area up front. Come, I'll show you."

She accompanied him toward a pair of wrought iron chairs and a little round table. Some trellises formed a partial enclosure. "Charming," she murmured, but continued to the front wall of the roof. It was a few feet tall, enough to lean against and look down.

"You're making me nervous," he said, lightly gripping her elbow and holding his other arm in position to grab her waist. "This would be a really bad place to faint."

"But I didn't get a chance to see the city, especially this end." A quiet residential street stretched below her. Houses all built from the same stone, yet each unique in ornamental carving. White stone with faint sparkles highlighted the designs, particularly around the brightly colored doors. Some so shiny they seemed metallic. No conveyances traveled the street at the moment, just a little foot traffic coming and going.

One of those people chanced to look up and waved. Fanteal smiled and returned the gesture. Soon, everyone on the street was waving to her and calling their friends to see Ambassador Fanteal.

She laughed self-consciously. "Oh dear. Was this a bad idea?"

"No—an excellent idea."

More people stepped out of their doors and waved. At least they were smiling at her. "How long do I stay, and how do I politely walk away?"

"I will end it for you. A couple more minutes, if you can. If you need to stop sooner, just tell me or lean back."

He knew these people better than she, so she kept it up. Soon enough, he raised his arm in final acknowledgement and then brought it around her in a guiding motion. "There," he said as they walked from the edge. "If they think you left too soon, it will be my fault, not yours."

A half laugh escaped her. "Is there some etiquette to waving that I wasn't taught?"

He grinned. "If so, I wasn't taught it either. More a feeling for the crowd." He settled her into one of the chairs, studying her face as she sat. "This was a happy chance—a few dozen people getting to see you. They'll spread it around that you looked well, which will calm down the concerns about your adjustment."

"Are people concerned?"

"Everyone cares, and there are always a few who love to predict disaster." He sat in the other chair. "What my father told you at the palace dinner was true. We really have wanted our new ambassador for a long time."

Interesting. She answered only with a nod, for she hadn't come up here to talk. Best to start searching. Where was that ocean breeze her mother spoke of? An inlet had to be up there somewhere.

Jaikon remained quiet for a while, perhaps thinking she needed to rest. He must have noticed her wandering gaze. "Are you curious about the light shafts?" he asked. "They're purified crystals polished to catch sunlight and angle it through the rock into our caverns. The near ends are faceted to spread the light evenly."

"My mother told me about them, though a first glimpse is worth savoring. Especially since my history book described their creation. They must be the spreaders Devron polished—defying the masses and their fears. I love his story."

"You and all of Dirklan." Jaikon spread his right arm to encompass about half of the city, reaching toward the archway into the original settlement. "He made the spreaders in this area." With his left arm, he gestured opposite. "This half was mined out in later generations."

"Mm." She kept searching, aware that Jaikon still watched her. A few narrow air currents slipped through tiny gaps in answer to her silent call. Despite the iron chairback, her muscles eased—her shoulders settling instead of aiding the constant battle to hyper-expand her lungs.

Suddenly, he blurted out, "You can breathe up here."

She startled a little but smiled. "It is a bit easier."

"Is that what you meant about something else going right today?"

"I hoped it would be so. But even if it hadn't, I so long to run on the hills that the tiniest illusion of being outside is a relief."

His forehead puckered. "When you're stronger, I'll take you to see the gem hills of Crysalan."

She nodded, still searching for the absent ocean breeze.

"I admit, they're not as high as the hillside we climbed, but they are pretty."

"I imagine so. My mother misses them."

He sat in silence. Could he be catching a hint of how much an ambassador gave up? Probably not wise to assume so.

Finally, he said, "The light is rosy. That means it'll be completely dark soon. We need to go in."

He escorted her to the stairway and pulled a lever that slid the roof door open. "Do you need me to carry you?"

"I don't think so." That kept him at her side.

He closed the roof access from the foot of the staircase and remained near her down the next flight and along the gallery. By the time they reached her bedroom, her breathing rate had increased.

She looked back along their path. "That is the farthest I have walked in Dirklan."

"You're improving."

"It's pathetic."

"Well, I can't stand it when people harp about patience, so I'll spare you that lecture. But even small improvements should be celebrated."

She stared at the roof entrance. "Wish I could sleep up there."

"I don't think you'd like it." He opened the door to her room. "Our temperature changes are less extreme than those above, but it still cools off when the light is gone." He must have noticed her quickening breaths. "Come, sit down."

She settled into the wingchair. "Will you take me to Dirklan House tomorrow?"

His brow descended in an instant, and his lips pressed together.

"Not to stay." She touched his arm. "I want to see the suite that was prepared for me. Or would it be better if your father took me?"

He sat in the chair facing hers. "He can't tomorrow. The council is in session. That's the governors plus elected representatives—oh, I suppose you know that."

"Formally called the Dirklian Legislative Council, responsible for laws and matters pertaining to the entire province, and presided over by the prime minister."

"Right. Anyway, my father will be at Government House most of the day. But maybe..." Jaikon rested his temple against two fingers. "Do you think you can make it? I can get a cair to take us, so you won't need to walk."

"What's a cair?"

"It's a little carriage with the motor built into its front. It'll take us from our door right to the door of Dirklan House."

"That sounds easy enough."

"Here's the thing. I've been trying to find out what modifications were made to your suite, but I've only found one of the workers. The architect is off in some other domain, and it'll take at least a couple days to track him down. It would be much quicker to simply go in and look things over, but it will be a lot easier for me to get through the doors of Dirklan House if you are with me."

"They won't let you in?"

Jaikon snorted. "They wouldn't even let Prenard in. He found out they have books on caring for abovegrounders, but they wouldn't admit him without a written order from the prime minister. Even with that, he had to raise his voice enough to draw a crowd before they would let him in. He's only allowed to read the specific books they give him and only inside the library. A page stays with him the whole time."

"Strange!" She drummed a couple fingers on the armrest. "I wonder what else is in the library."

"I know of one thing. Architects always keep their drawings, but the worker told me that Prime Minister Nirundale insisted that the diagrams of your suite modifications be stored in his library."

"But why?"

"I don't know. Prenard says the library is quite large. It contains a great deal besides the few items we know of."

She murmured thoughtfully, "So...the Council's in session tomorrow. Governor Nirundale will attend it, yes?"

"True. That will keep him out of the way."

"And I suspect that my cousin, Dalbred, will want to talk to me."

"No doubt."

Fanteal laughed at his tone, but said, "I should think I can keep both him and my aunt in conversation."

"She won't be there. Governor Nirundale's wife has taken their two younger children to stay with her parents."

"Hmm. That seems a little odd at this moment. Unless...but no matter. While I'm occupying Dalbred, could you find a way to leave us, perhaps under pretense of looking at the roof vent?"

"There won't be any pretense about that. I take it you want me to get into the library as well."

"Precisely."

"There is only one flaw with this scheme."

She raised her brows.

"I don't much like the idea of leaving you with your cousin."

"I'm sure he won't harm me. Do you actually know him, or do you dislike him because he's Governor Nirundale's son?"

"We've met. There are events now and then where the governors and representatives bring their spouses and grown children. Naturally, the younger generation tends to gather. He's about five years younger than I, so we didn't associate much, but I know him."

She avoided smiling, though his lowered tone was amusing. "Well? What sort is he?"

"He's as smooth as his father, but less subtle. And if I weren't so tired of being criticized for stating honest opinions, I would have said slimy instead of smooth."

The corners of her mouth twitched. "You did such an excellent job of not saying it. Tomorrow then. What time?"

"Mid-morning to avoid crowds."

"Good idea." Already she was searching for more air. "I should probably go to bed."

He rose at once. "I'll ring for your maid." As he pulled the bedside lever, the book on the nightstand caught his eye. He picked it up and asked, "Did Bella bring this for you?"

"No, it's mine."

She wondered what was in his thoughts as their eyes held across the room, but he gave no clue.

Bella must have been waiting for the summons, because she entered almost immediately.

Jaikon inclined his head. "Pleasant night."

J aikon paused on the gallery, checking the front windows. Still faint light. If he knew the speed of rumor—pertaining to the ambassador, at least—there'd be more than one person at the Tea House telling how they'd seen Lady Fanteal this evening. Might this be an opportune moment to diffuse the more negative rumors?

He descended the stairs, considering strategy, then stepped out into the dusk and made the short walk to Jourendia Square. The fountain lighting came on as he reached the square, which was nearly empty. He kept a brisk pace, following one side of it to reach his destination. Only one person took notice of him—the peace officer who was pulling levers in a recessed cabinet to power the magnery lights along the street. He nodded and continued his routine.

Ahead, Jaikon caught movement in the lit windows of the Tea House, a narrow structure compared to its imposing neighbors. He pushed the door open and stepped inside. Chatter bounced from the walls. The place was more crowded than at its busy hours of morning and lunch. Quite a few faces he didn't recognize. Visitors from other domains? Aides to the governors, here for the council?

Jaikon nodded to a few locals. One from his own street motioned him to join his table. Finding a chair to pull to the table took a little effort, but a voice behind him drawled, "There's an extra chair here you may take."

Jaikon turned. The drawl belonged to Pamitha, daughter of Governor Armeen. Nearby, sat a man who often attended Governor Zeardell.

Unwelcoming faces showed they'd forgiven nothing from the days leading up to the election. The offer to remove the chair was a pointed non-invitation to join them. Not that he wanted to, but his father's words echoed in his mind. He'd better be careful.

Jaikon squeezed the chair in between those who scooted sideways to make room for him at their table. He accepted a cup of unnamed tea from the tray of an overworked waiter who wasn't asking anyone which tea blend they preferred.

While Jaikon took his first sip, his neighbor said, "I saw you on your roof with Lady Fanteal."

"Ah. The unplanned welcome from the street cheered her."

Another said, "About these rumors—"

Jaikon stopped him with a raised palm. "I came to relax with a cup of brew. I won't get another sip if I have to swat all the rumors flying around on bat wings."

A few chuckled over that, and a woman at the next table said, "I got a wave from her too. Three floors up, but she looked fine to me."

A man winked at Jaikon. "Did you really need to hover that close to her?"

The quip sent a lower pitched laugh around the room, but Jaikon kept a calm demeanor. "I will merely say that her adjustment to Dirklian air is progressing well, but if you think I'm willing to risk her falling from a roof, you are crazier than most. She is not one to enjoy coddling, so hopefully it won't be long before we can give her normal space."

It had grown quiet enough while he spoke that another voice reached him from across the room. "That's not what her maid said."

"If," Jaikon replied dryly, "you are referring to the maid who was dismissed for valid reasons, you should consider the possibility that she wants to divert attention from her own faults." He lifted his cup. "Enough of that boring subject." He brought it to his lips and took a slow sip. He'd gotten through his plan for the rumors about Fanteal's health and nature, and said just enough to cast doubt on Nilkie's report.

He would have preferred not to mention her dismissal, but with slander already on her tongue, he couldn't leave it unanswered.

"I couldn't care less about a sour maid," a woman next to him said, "but what is there to talk about besides the ambassador?"

"The council is in session," Jaikon replied with a smile. "They must be doing *something* interesting."

"Probably talking about the ambassador." That distant quip prompted another round of laughter.

A local streamer strolled nearer, angling around chairs. Not an old man, but far from young. "It's streaming that we all care about, and you know it. Deltum and Tershel say they saw her streaming. Did you?"

Jaikon raised a brow. "You won't get me to claim that I can *see* anyone stream."

"Then you have more sense than those two. But do you think she was streaming?"

"Yes, of course."

"Why? What indicated it?"

The room went so quiet that the clinks of teacups grew distinct. Jaikon had to get this right. He set his cup on the table and wrapped his hands around it. "Both King Darrineth and Lady Fanteal spoke of her helping to open the passage. She stood at her father's side, with her hands outstretched to swirling waves. Streamer commands are invisible—true. But it is still hard *not* to say that I saw her streaming." He shrugged. "There were little hints too. They might mean more to you. I climbed to a hilltop with her that morning, out of sight of the harbor. She told me that the tide was lowering and even joked about its movement. Later, when we descended the whirlpool—which is a *vile* form of travel—she laughed all the way down." Jaikon lifted his cup again. "You're the streamer. What do you think?"

The man released his pursed lips and gave him a nod. "You are definitely more convincing than Tershel and Deltum."

"Is he more convincing than Harbane?" someone asked.

The streamer let a wry smirk pull at the corner of his mouth. "Harbane *was* able to discern other streamers back when I knew him well, but I'll have to concede he could be past the use of his gift."

CHAPTER 13

Their departure on the following morning was delayed by the cair driver, who finally arrived with a multitude of excuses about how busy the morning had been. Fanteal looked the conveyance over. Two bench seats, plus a lower straddle seat over the motor. No cover, of course, for it couldn't rain in Dirklan.

After handing Fanteal up the two steps to the front seat, Jaikon interrupted the driver and said, "I understand your point. Can we leave now?"

"Right away, sir." The driver hopped onto the straddle seat while Jaikon climbed in beside Fanteal.

As they entered Jourendia Square and drove along one side, Jaikon gestured toward the largest building. "This one on our left is Government House. Hard to get a good view from this corner, but it's quite imposing when you arrive from the old settlement and see it spread out beyond the fountain."

He must be guessing—correctly—that she hadn't grasped much on her first trip through this square.

"We are coming up on Dirklan House," he continued, "beside us on the right. Opposite are Jourendia Hall—for local government—and Market House, the one with the sculpted label. It's commonly called 'the emporium' now." He pointed. "Do you see that narrow building between them? The first floor holds our local tearoom. The proprietor, who prefers his humor on the wry side, named it the Tea House in keeping with its exalted neighbors. You can hear political talk there any day of the week. Not the stilted debates of Government House, but the common man's views. I'll take you there someday."

"I'd like that," she replied.

Only a few scattered people crossed the square during the morning's work hours. Already several were stopping to watch as Fanteal passed. One of them turned and ran toward the Tea House as the cair stopped at the imposing door of Dirklan House.

Jaikon stepped out and offered his hand to Fanteal, keeping his eyes on the square. He wasted no time in leading her across the sidewalk and pulling the bell lever beside the double doors. Their entire surface glowed with shimmering etched silver behind clear crystal. She marveled at the artistry in the seconds before the doors swung open. A servant admitted them, offering her a formal bow, and a page ran up a staircase to summon her cousin.

Fanteal surveyed Dirklan House from within. Home to every prime minister since the day the roof had been formed. Also home to her mother and uncle, once their father, Mardone Nirundale, had been elected to that office. From her mother's descriptions, Fanteal could likely find even the pantry without a guide.

In a way, the house was three connected buildings surrounding the grand hall, all joined with galleries on the second and third floors. Family on the right side. Visitor suites on the left. The longer section across the back held kitchen, dining rooms, salons, the library, offices, and everything practical. Not that any hint of the mundane appeared.

Two grand staircases climbed to the corners, with easily enough space to hold a ball between them. Pillars of dark variegated green curved out from pale beige walls. The gallery railings were carved from the same green stone, and gold leaf ornamented their intricate scrollwork. Crystal spreaders had even been embedded in the distant ceiling, bringing a hint of sunlight into the hall. Two massive chandeliers would illuminate it at night, with crystal luminaries at all three levels.

Quite lovely—and quite stifling.

A slim young man descended one of the staircases. Her cousin, no doubt, whom her grandfather had said was three years younger than she. Though not as tall as either his father or Jaikon, he carried himself confidently.

Jaikon lifted Fanteal's hand on the back of his and said, "Dalbred Nirundale, it's my pleasure to introduce Lady Fanteal de Noviam, Royal Ambassador of Welcia."

Dalbred received her hand, also on the back of his, and executed a graceful bow. "I take even more pleasure in welcoming you to your home, my dear cousin. Won't you come into the salon? Refreshments will be brought to you at once." He paused and said as if in an afterthought, "Ah, Jaikon, it's good to see you again, and thank you for escorting her. I'm sure you have much to do for Sir Mikkael, so we won't impose on your time any longer."

Skies above, that was a blatant dismissal!

Jaikon smiled faintly. "True, but I *am* doing it, so you needn't worry about imposing on my time."

Before Dalbred could try again to get rid of Jaikon, Fanteal said, "Instead of the salon, I would prefer to sit in the suite my grandfather prepared for me."

"Of course, my dear."

She stiffened. "Use my name, please."

"Whatever you wish, Fanteal." He offered his arm, and she took it, letting him draw her close to negate the coldness of her tone. He deserved it, but alienating him would be counterproductive.

He led her to the right staircase, where she paused and withdrew her hand, turning to Jaikon.

"May I?" he asked.

"Please."

Dalbred's mouth opened as Jaikon picked her up and proceeded up the stairs.

"Unconventional, I know," Fanteal said, looking past Jaikon's shoulder, "but I still grow faint on stairs."

Jaikon continued up the next flight also, since the Ambassador's suite was on the third floor. He paused at the top to set her on her feet. "Which door is it?"

By Dalbred's expression, he was less than pleased, but his voice remained bland. "Both of the corner doors. The sitting room is to the left." He led them inside.

Double pocket doors stood open, revealing the bedroom beyond, plus another door, perhaps leading to a closet or dressing room. Fanteal smiled at the suite's décor, white and shades of blue. Trelliswork covered an entire wall in each room, and ivies climbed them, floor to ceiling.

Jaikon opened the sitting room window and then followed Fanteal into the bedroom.

Dalbred was expounding on all the effort that had gone into decorating, while he opened the other windows at her request.

Fanteal paid little attention to him. When Jaikon joined her, she pointed at the louvered vents in the ceiling.

"My mother chose all the fabrics for the chairs, drapes, and bedding," Dalbred continued. "Do you like the design?"

"Very much so. Your mother has excellent taste. Could you tell me how this vent works? Is it possible to turn the louvers?"

"You've a quick eye. These knobs on the wall work the louvers. There's a second set above the ones you can see, so you can direct the air toward any part of the suite. This lever opens and closes the roof vent, and this one with three positions controls how fast the vanes spin."

"The vanes?" Jaikon asked. "Where are they located?"

At that moment, a page entered the sitting room, bearing a tray with glasses and dainty pastries, which he set on a small round table. Dalbred addressed him. "Ask Gorden to come up here at once." He turned back to Jaikon. "Gorden does our maintenance, and he's an expert on the air system. He can answer all your questions."

Dalbred urged Fanteal to try the pastries. She sat at the table and nibbled one, listening with the appearance of great interest to every word he spoke.

When Gorden came and took Jaikon to inspect the air system, Dalbred smiled and said, "Ah, now we can be private. He wasn't too hard to get rid of. I fear Jaikon is sadly lacking in subtlety."

"Nothing like your father." She lowered the pastry to her plate. "He has such abundant subtlety that it's not at all clear what some of his words mean. I do hope you don't tend in that direction."

Dalbred chuckled and said, "He does take it a little to extremes at times. But of course, with the Mikkaels there, he had to be careful."

Air moved around Fanteal, descending through the louvers above. She inhaled deeply and smiled, utterly sincere this time. "Yes, I suppose so. Since they're not here now, perhaps you could tell me the real reason why you and my uncle linger so long in Dirklan House."

He shrugged. "Oh, the nuisance of a move—and one so unnecessary."

"Isn't it inevitable?"

"Not at all, my dear." He leaned forward and laid his hand over one of hers.

She suppressed the desire to pull away and even maintained her smile. "Oh?"

"Of course, you're not in a position to know the inner workings of Dirklan's government, but my father is a master of it."

She let him expound on her uncle's finesse in keeping the loyalty of the people despite that upstart Sened Mikkael—not even a governor—winning the election. Many had thought the election was a blow to the House of Nirundale, but without uttering one word, Baelan Nirundale had turned it to an advantage.

Under cover of drinking, she was able to draw her hand from his, then slowly sipped the sparkling juice in her glass.

"And you, my dear," Dalbred continued, "are in the perfect position to take advantage of the opportunities he has created. It must irk you to know that you—a princess—are reduced to the common title of *lady* here. You deserve so much more. Royalty shows in your every move, your every word."

She cast her eyes down then brought them back to his face. "Thank you," she murmured, in a tone that indicated both appreciation of the compliment and acknowledgement of its truth. She hoped she could keep this up without growing too nauseated. "But what opportunities do you speak of? This is a democracy. All hope for a royal position died when I came here."

"I'm sure you've been told so, but broaden your view for a moment. You have no idea what upheaval arises when a new family takes over the government. It is not at all good for the people. Uncertainty. Inequity. Needless strife. Those who were once friends arguing in the streets. Families set at odds. All for no purpose."

He made an airy gesture. "In just a few years, it will happen again. How will Sened Mikkael be able to improve trade, when Mardone Nirundale could not? His warnings of impending food shortages will be recognized as falsehoods. We will have this pointless upheaval again." He leaned forward with a tantalizing smile and said, "But this time could be different. This could be the last time Dirklan is ever forced through a meaningless change."

"How so?"

"All those who said my father could not be elected because of the law of family duration will be silenced. There has been a break in the line, so conveniently provided by a man who can never succeed in the next election. My father will become the prime minister to restart the count of duration, and when the time is right, I will be prime minister. We can either get rid of that ridiculous law of duration or..." His lips curled. "...perhaps we need not elect prime ministers at all. The House of Nirundale can rule over Dirklan just as the House de Noviam rules over Welcia above. How would you like to become Queen Fanteal?"

Skies and caverns! Did her uncle know that Dalbred was spilling all this? Had he told him to? "I've never...such a title has never occurred to me."

"How could it when you lived above? But that is past. You've plenty of leisure to think on it, for the time is not right to share the idea further. My father has the steps for the transition all planned out."

"Oh? Such as?"

"For instance, he will keep the title of prime minister, but as soon as he is elected, we will begin using your title of princess again. When people are used to it, we will legally formalize it. In many such steps, we will advance toward the ultimate goal." He reached out to take her empty glass and set it on the table, thus making an opportunity to clasp one of her hands. "Ah, my lovely Fanteal, you cannot imagine how I look forward to introducing you as my bride and my princess."

"Dalbred, are you proposing marriage to me?" She didn't even need to fake the surprise.

"Indeed, fair lady, I am."

Unbelievable how fast this was moving! "But you are my cousin."

"When our grandfather was alive, it bothered no one that a cousin was likely to wed the new ambassador. Yes, I know of his decree that you could marry whomever you please. I'm sure he intended it to set your mind at rest, or possibly to prevent unforeseen disaster which could force you into marrying someone as unsuitable as Jaikon. In fact, his decree has placed you in a powerful position. Do not let his gift go to waste."

Dalbred's many words gave her enough time to prepare a way out. "Your offer is certainly enticing, and believe me, I will not forget it. Unfortunately, I am forced to delay my answer. Imagine how insulting it would be if I were to refuse to even meet all the kind young men who have brought gifts and wishes for my swift recovery." She added a conspiratorial tone to her words. "Considering our future positions—which are not yet secure—it would be wise not to create the least offense or suspicion." She stood, sensing that he would keep pressing her. "In the meantime, perhaps you could show me a little more of my future home."

"Gladly, my dear."

"I don't think you should call me that yet. It will either give the impression we wish to avoid, or worse yet, encourage other men to call me their dear."

"So careful of appearances," he teased, offering his arm. "But it will be as you wish." He led her into the corridor and gestured. "This side contains mostly private bedrooms, and this way holds the office and meeting space on the third floor. A little boring. Perhaps we should start elsewhere."

"Yes, for I cannot walk very far yet. Both my grandfather and mother sometimes spoke of the prime minister's library. I'd like to see that."

"Then we only need to descend one flight of stairs. Would you like me to carry you?"

"No, thank you. I can manage the descent. Besides, I found my suite refreshing. Which reminds me of a question I was meaning to ask. Did our grandfather ever explain why he was building such a suite for me?"

"Isn't it obvious? He held you in great affection."

"Yes, I'm well aware of that, but why the elaborate air system?"

Dalbred laughed a little. "I doubt any of us truly understand that. Late in life, he became most interested in air movement. All I can figure is that he'd exhausted the search for knowledge on every other topic." Dalbred paused to open the library door, revealing a long room that took up nearly one entire side of the second floor. "In fact, Grandfather made us remove our personal books from the library so he could create another section for what he called 'wind records.'"

When they stepped into the room, which already held four people, Dalbred stiffened. Prenard pored over a book on the table before him, a page stood near the door, Gorden was folding rigid drawing panels at another table, and Jaikon studied titles at a bookcase.

"Jaikon!" Dalbred snapped. "What are you doing here? You said you wanted to see the air system."

"Yes, I did. I found the drawings even more helpful in understanding how it functions."

Dalbred opened his mouth to speak, but Fanteal asked, "Where is the section on wind records?"

He swallowed his retort and led her past a section labeled *Waterways* and stopped at sparsely filled shelves labeled *Wind Weaving*.

"Where are all the books?" she asked, unable to keep disappointment from her voice.

"Grandfather wasn't as successful at collecting them as he'd hoped. He sent first a request and then an order to the domains. Any and all wind records were to be sent by special courier to the prime minister's library. Very few arrived. Hardly a surprise to anyone except Grandfather. Why he thought there would be wind records in Dirklan remains a mystery."

Fanteal stared at him. Dalbred's statement, so devoid of understanding, held her in shock. "Do you not breathe?"

Dalbred uttered a half laugh. "It is the streams that concern us, lady, not the wind."

Forcing her expression to relax, she replied, "Of course." She selected one of the volumes at random and opened it. The thin cover of white stone was cool in her hand. Strange since she was accustomed to leather-bound books. It contained a daily log of the forming of Alluthin's wind shafts. Brown blotchy paper suggested this was the original copy. She selected another that referred to Crysalan. Even the pages were thin quartz. "This one seems quite new."

"It is. Crysalan wouldn't send their originals, but they offered to make copies. Grandfather agreed because, if anyone can make perfect copies, it would certainly be a scribe from the keepers."

"True. They are Dirklan's custodians of the Holy Writ, after all."

"How did you know that?"

Again, she stared at Dalbred. "I was raised to the position of ambassador," she said dryly. "By Trissina Nirundale, I must add, since you seem to forget."

"Ah, yes, of course." He inclined his head, though he looked puzzled.

She glanced around for windows. Only two, and both closed. Did bookshelves cover others in that long wall? Five minutes, and already she felt the lack. She moved to the nearest chair and sat. "Jaikon, I need fresh air again. Will you be finished soon?"

"I'll call for a cair." He strode from the library.

Prenard came and felt her wrist. "How was it for you in the suite Sir Nirundale prepared?"

"Better," she replied.

"You are welcome to stay," Dalbred urged.

"Not yet. Let's go downstairs."

He offered his arm and led her along the gallery to the stairs. "There's one other thing I wanted to mention to you. Has Sir Mikkael told you of the rumors?"

"What rumors?"

"Ah! Perhaps he didn't want to trouble you, but they're getting so out of hand that I don't think it's wise to ignore them."

As they began descending the stairs, Jaikon turned from the open double doors and glared up at Dalbred.

"There are some fools," Dalbred continued, "claiming that you're not a streamer. Absurd, of course, but some people delight in creating sensations. Quite a simple matter to dispel such nonsense, so why not take advantage of it?"

What? He didn't give her a second to collect her stunned wits.

"When you arrived, I ordered that the fountain in the square be shut off. An underground stream feeds the pool. Its flow runs deep—barely noticeable at the surface. You may simply demonstrate your gift on your way through the square."

Jaikon met them at the foot of the stairs, and she reached for him almost in desperation.

He drew her hand onto his arm, though he focused on Dalbred. "We do not need your assistance in managing her affairs. To even imply that she needs to demonstrate her streaming abilities is nothing more than an insult. Come, Lady Fanteal." He hurried her to the door.

Hadn't he seen her face? Or did he think she was growing faint? He certainly had a firm grip on her waist.

Wooziness crept nearer. Could she have misunderstood? She drew quick, deep breaths to get her brain working again. How could they speak as though she were a streamer? Both of them!

CHAPTER 14

The doors closed behind them, and Jaikon regretted his impulse to get Lady Fanteal out of Dirklan House. The cair hadn't yet arrived, and they had nowhere to go. The square overflowed with people. Those nearest turned toward them the moment the ambassador arrived on the scene. He glanced down at her face. Could she walk home? Not judging by her expression—more anxious than weak. Why?

The crowd was converging. At this rate the cair might not even get through. Jaikon called to the peace officers who stood on duty at either end of Dirklan House. "You there. And you. Keep the crowd back. Don't let them block the roadway."

They tried, loudly directing people to stay back. More officers stationed near Government House hurried to their aid.

Jaikon guided Fanteal toward one of the benches that flanked the doors of Dirklan House. "All will be well. Come and sit until the cair arrives." Once she was settled, he returned to the street and raised his voice enough to be heard, yet without shouting. "This isn't a public appearance. The ambassador simply needs to rest in the fresh air until our cair arrives. I know you only want to greet her, but you must be patient a few more days." He paused for someone's question, then said, "No, there won't be a demonstration of her streaming gift today."

As Jaikon strolled before the crowd, speaking with an ease that showed his rapport with the ordinary folk of Jourendia, Fanteal listened with her gift as well as her ears. By far, the most frequent words spoken in the crowd pertained to streaming.

This was a nightmare!

She drew the freshest air she could to herself, thinking fast. Strange remarks from the last few days came to her. Sir Mikkael's words at that first dinner—as though she could fix the trade problems. Deltum suggesting that she should bring the vessel to shore in Passage Lake. Harbane's remark when he examined her. That, she could have passed off if Agriben hadn't said something similar. Even remarks about the last ambassador, Melthindi. He'd been a powerful streamer and had worked on the trade cataracts. Was that why they thought she was a streamer? The reason didn't matter. She was *not* what they expected. Not what they *needed*.

One voice, near the street, said mockingly, "The king would never lie about such a thing. We'd be bound to find out if she wasn't a streamer, and then he would be utterly discredited."

What under the skies? Her father had never said she was a streamer! And her grandfather knew she was a wind weaver. He couldn't have lied. Could he?

Off to one side, the two envoys pushed their way to the front—Deltum and Tershel. "Now you'll see," they said to those they passed.

Jaikon returned, frowning as he studied her face. "Are you feeling faint?"

She shook her head, trying to figure out how to phrase what must be said.

"All is well," he murmured. "You needn't speak, but could you smile and wave, perhaps?"

She wanted to scream, *I'm not a streamer*. Impossible before this crowd. Instead, she whispered. "I need your help. Be careful what you say."

His eyebrows twitched, but he sat down with one arm behind her, ready to support.

Deltum and Tershel had worked their way near enough to call out a greeting that she couldn't ignore. She inclined her head to them, still trying to avoid speaking to the crowd. But she could hear them. They wanted a demonstration of her streaming. Some spoke of Jaikon's assurance that she was a streamer at the Tea House yesterday. What had he said? And those foolish envoys spoke of her creating the whirlpool in the harbor. She wished she *could* faint.

That craven desire reminded her she was the Royal Ambassador of Welcia. She would face this challenge. Great. Courage but no plan.

The only thing she could demonstrate would devastate their hopes. How could it be done so that they'd understand? And without discrediting...pretty much everyone of importance.

For some strange reason, Wandermae's fate filled her mind. No, ridiculous to think they'd stone her. But would they be furious? Probably. And what would Jaikon's reaction be? Even if he'd understood her vague request, she couldn't expect open-minded calm from him.

He whispered into her ear. "Are you able to spin the pool? It would satisfy them."

Spin? Oh, could she! Wait. This might solve two dilemmas. Fanteal set air swirling around the cavern ceiling. So thin—she needed more. She summoned with a broad command, and a waft of thicker air reached her. Strange odor, but rich. She demanded more. It felt like pulling jelly through a sieve, but she wasn't letting it refuse. Some came from a wider source. That had to be the train tunnel near the arches into the settlement.

Fanteal spoke at a natural volume and bade the air carry her words across the square. "You'll see my gift in a moment, but first I must tell you that I keep hearing a strange misquote passing through the crowd." She smiled to lighten her words. "I was on the shore right next to the king, so I think I'm a reliable source. All the king—and I—ever said was that I was helping him open the passage. Please don't add your thoughts to our words. And now…" Fanteal added drama to her voice. "Would you like me to show you how I helped the king open the whirlpool passage?"

A roar of cheers echoed around the cavern.

"Please clear a pathway between me and the pool."

No one questioned that. The officers designated a pathway, and the expectant crowd shifted apart, turning toward the pool.

She stood, keeping a hand on Jaikon's shoulder so she could face him for a few seconds and block him from view. She looked down at him and mouthed the words *wind weaver* as she made a breeze blow his dark hair away from his face. His eyes rounded, and his jaw dropped.

"Careful," she whispered, then said aloud, "I'm going to stand on the bench. Steady me, please."

J aikon's breath stopped. No! This couldn't be! He felt dizzier than when he descended the whirlpool—weak enough to faint. No! *She* might do that if he didn't support her. He must answer her request. "Of course." He stood mechanically, then gripped her elbows to assist her in stepping up. His face burned, and sweat beaded on his forehead.

No wonder she had asked for his help. But he couldn't help her. This was going to be terrible! And all he could do was stand behind her with a hand on her back as she braced against his shoulder.

Tension thrummed in her body. Familiar and yet foreign. The whispery sound high above intensified, jerking a memory into his mind. Oh caverns! The roar around the harbor. It had been wind!

He'd actually seen her weave the wind! And last night at the Tea House, he'd so adroitly convinced them that she was a streamer. His stomach contorted. Many of those people stood in the crowd.

Oh, no! Several governors and representatives were approaching from Government House. Perfect timing for the lunch recess. At least his father was with the group—all distracted now by a misty funnel that rose from the pool.

How did Fanteal even do that? But it wasn't a streaming technique. And soon, everyone would realize that the hopes of Dirklan were nothing more than the dust swirling near the cavern roof.

One of the peace officers strode up to Jaikon. "Sir, Agriben is requesting to join the ambassador. It's hard to deny him, since he is Dirklan's chief former. May we let him through?"

Jaikon glanced aside and spotted the cair he'd sent for, waiting several yards away. "Yes. Send that cair to fetch him here." The steadiness of his own voice surprised him.

He'd have to get through this, one way or another, so he took a moment to look around. Masses of people stood on rooftops and leaned from windows. Dalbred had come out onto a second-floor balcony. Jaikon wished he could punch the troublemaker's self-important face.

Beside him, Lady Fanteal called out in jest. "Better stand clear of the pool. You're going to get wet."

Laughter answered her from the crowd, but no one moved any farther away. A voice shouted, "We welcome the stream, lady. Throw it over us."

She tossed her head back and laughed. "As you wish."

Her cheeks were flushed, and she spread both arms, mirroring her control. She radiated strength. Jaikon ached for her. This was her element, the state in which she was meant to live. And for that very reason, the crowd would turn on her.

Agriben clambered from the cair and took a firm stance on Lady Fanteal's right, his face set in stern lines.

Debris spun in a tight circle near the cavern roof, but the crowd focused downward.

Someone near the pool shouted, "Look! She's pushing a hole through the water...deep into the well."

Those on the rooftops began cheering.

A tight vortex of air stood straight above the pool. If not for a little mist, it would be invisible. Couldn't they feel it? A phrase echoed in his memory...*uniquely and powerfully gifted.*

Fanteal's voice rose, spreading to all. "This is how a wind weaver helps a streamer open a passage through the waters." She chuckled low in the sudden silence. "And here is the stream you asked for."

She circled her hands overhead. In an instant, the vortex sucked the pool empty. A column of water stood erect to the cavern ceiling. Was she pulling the underground stream up too? The top splayed and sent droplets flying around the entire square. For several seconds, she let the vortex spray, then closed it off. The air-encased column of water fell straight to its pool, then rebounded a few yards above it. Her wall of air let nothing spill until it settled.

All at once, wind blew around the cavern, and hair batted at faces. With open palms, Fanteal swept both arms toward the settlement arches and vocalized her command. "To the tunnel." The whoosh swept away, and brittle silence gripped the crowd.

Fanteal spoke slowly, lifting her voice to spread through the cavern as only a wind weaver could. "In this confined space, some of you may have perceived the air moving, though not at first. Only four of you were present aboveground, so I will explain to the rest. The harbor above Passage Lake is vast and open to the sky. As my father and I prepared the whirlpool, our four visitors could not possibly see the air moving, but they could see the water surging." She paused. "Only half an hour ago, I realized that it must have looked—indeed, it *had* to look—as though I, too, were streaming. But only the king was streaming. I helped him by causing the air to start the vortex. Once it touched the water, I released it, and he took full control."

Silence. So deathly quiet that footsteps were audible along the street. She'd done her best...excusing the mistake they'd made, but it wouldn't help.

Fanteal rested a hand on Jaikon's shoulder. That pulled him from his stupor, and he steadied her jump down from the bench. He looked utterly devastated. She whispered, "Chin up."

He seemed to make the attempt, firming his expression.

Fanteal seated herself as regally as possible. A few extra yards of silk would have been nice in this moment. Sir Mikkael had reached them. Several others had followed him, Governor Nirundale among them. So, the others were probably governors and representatives.

A murmur began to move through the crowd. Halfway down the path to the fountain, a man stomped toward her. He appeared to have received more than his fair share of stream water and looked none too happy about it. When he reached the edge of the crowd, two peace officers barred his access to the street, but they couldn't stop his voice.

"You're no more a streamer than I am!" he shouted.

"Please, lift my voice," Sir Mikkael said. She did so as he faced the surly fellow. "You are addressing the Ambassador of the Crown of Welcia. You will speak with respect, or you will spend the night in jail and pay your fine in the morning."

A breathy sound whispered through the crowd. The man shuffled his feet and made an awkward bow. "I meant no disrespect. But it is still true. She's not a streamer."

"Why are you wet?" Sir Mikkael asked.

"What?" the man squawked.

"Why are you wet?"

"Well, she...you saw..." He clenched his fists at his sides. "What she did with the water wasn't nothing compared to a streamer. Why, I've seen Telona pull that stream right up out of its pool and send it running like a river down Fountain Avenue. Kept it going for hours, she did, and could've done it longer if she'd wanted to. Lady Fanteal blowing a little water around ain't gonna help with the trade cataracts. We were supposed to get a streamer."

Agriben spoke up. "Who promised us a streamer?"

"Can't you read history?" The man flailed his arms. "All the de Noviams are streamers. It runs in their veins. That's how they came to be the royal family to start with."

"I can read history," Fanteal said, "and it does not say any such thing. I have many relatives with no substance gift. Ellincreo bestows the gifts as he wishes. Don't the Keepers of the Writ share that reading on Gifting Day?" Several in the crowd were nodding, so she didn't pause. "Aboveground, we believe that Ellincreo bestows the streaming gift on a king or queen, because the crown made a covenant oath to Dirklan. Ellincreo grants them the capability of opening the passage so they may fulfill it. Listen well to my next words, for I think you are in need of them." She got the hush she'd hoped for. "King Darinneth and Queen Ambassador Trissina remain steadfastly committed to the covenant. They will not forsake Dirklan."

Sir Mikkael stepped forward. "Permit me to add to your assurance, Ambassador Fanteal." He faced the crowd, which had begun to murmur. "Our recent meeting with the crown, the nobility, and the officials of Welcia above was strained because of the severity of Dirklan's situation. Afterward, the king and queen invited my son and me to share in their family time and a private dinner. Both they and the two mature heirs to the throne have personally declared that the covenant *cannot* be broken. Their commitment is as solid as that of King Tandorad and

Queen Dizelle, who sealed it and sent Prince Queltin as the first royal ambassador."

A woman spoke from the crowd, giving a slight curtsy with her first words. "It is a pleasure to hear of the king's and queen's commitment, but many of us trusted that anyway. We know they *want* to help, but the help we desperately *needed*...was a powerful streamer."

Agriben thumped his staff against the ground. "As Provincial Chief Former of Dirklan, I speak on behalf of the substance guilds. Lady Fanteal spoke true a moment ago. Ellincreo knew who our ambassador was to be. He gifted her with wind weaving. It is a fact, and no person has the right or the ability to change it. If this disturbs you, take your complaint to Ellincreo, but spread it no more through the streets."

The first man spoke again. "*Pshaw.* Words and nothing more. Words will not fix the trade cataracts." He turned back into the crowd with a loud grumble. "The least they could have done was tell us."

Fanteal didn't blame him. "It was never hidden," she said. "Prime Minister Mardone Nirundale knew." She turned to her uncle and asked, "Governor Nirundale, did you know?"

Apparently, those nearby were not his supporters, because they immediately began saying, "He's supposed to tell what he knows of Welcia. It's the law."

He ignored them and drew near her. "No, my dear niece. My father often said that you're remarkably gifted, but he never said that you are a wind weaver. Since you're at my door, would you like to come inside and rest for a while?"

"At *your* door, Governor?" She raised a brow. "This is Dirklan House. Are you still under the illusion that you should be prime minister?"

He laughed. "Ah, my dear child, a house does not make someone the prime minister."

"That was not an answer. This is the prime minister's residence, and you do not belong here. Also, Prime Minister Nirundale prepared a suite for me here. When I am awake, I can draw more air around me, but not while I sleep. This house is the *only* place where I can sleep with adequate air."

The crowd was heating up again, but he kept his back to them. "Ah yes, I see your difficulty, but I'm sure it can be overcome. Let's go inside and discuss it in private."

"We discussed it privately yesterday, and you refused. Why are you reluctant to discuss it before the people?"

"I'm not. It's just so noisy."

"We can hear one another perfectly well. Explain to all why you won't leave the prime minister's residence."

"You don't understand these things, my dear little niece. Please let me—"

"She is not little," Sir Mikkael said. "She is a woman. You will address her as Lady or Ambassador. Further, she has been studying Dirklan law since childhood and seems to understand it better than you do. If you have a case to state, then state it."

"I have no need to make a case for what is mine. This house has been home to three generations of Nirundales."

This, Fanteal could easily counter. "It became the residence of Mardone Nirundale when he was elected as prime minister. Naturally, his young children lived here with him. You and your children lived here by his permission, not by right."

The governor puffed out his chest. "My father alone spent a small fortune on this house, far more than the government allotment. Enough to pay for it outright."

"We've heard this before," Sir Mikkael said. "If I spend a small fortune on the house I rent, it will still belong to its owner."

"But it was known to the council, and they agreed to *him* funding the changes."

"Let me understand this," Fanteal said. "If you feel that Sir Nirundale bought it, in a manner of speaking, whom does it belong to at his death? He had two children."

"To the head of the family, of course," he said, throwing his shoulders back.

"Ah! That would be Ambassador Trissina. Why do you look so startled? Have you called her 'little' sister so long that you've forgotten she is your elder sister?"

From the look on his face, she had spoken a fact that he didn't want under public scrutiny.

"It makes no difference," he said. "She cannot return here to claim her inheritance."

"Do not insult her. She respects the law and would never claim Dirklan House as her property. I am both her representative and her heir. If you truly believe that Sir Mardone Nirundale bought the house, then it is mine, not yours. I give you notice to vacate at once."

"What? Will you evict the children! Your own young cousins?"

"Ha!" A rude voice called from the crowd. "Children, indeed. Barely!"

Another shouted, "Your wife took the two youngest off with her. She knows your family should have left months ago."

And still another called out, "Aren't you doing far worse to the ambassador by refusing her the only house where she can breathe through the night?"

"No, not at all," her uncle said. "I've assured her several times that she is welcome to come and live with us." He turned back to her, extending a hand. "And, my dear, the offer still stands. Please come inside."

"The king and queen consigned me to the care of Prime Minister Mikkael in accordance with tradition and their own preference. My mother *could* have designated that her brother provide for me—but she did not. I shall live with the prime minister in Dirklan House. Enough has been said."

He drew his shoulders back again. "When I have had time to make arrangements for my family—"

A man from the group in the street stomped up the steps of Dirklan House, planted himself in front of the doors, and faced Nirundale with arms folded. "I'll not tolerate this any longer. You inherited one of the original houses in the settlement, so you can go there on a moment's notice. If you try to get back into Dirklan House, you're going to have to plow me down."

Agriben joined him. "Well said, Governor Trezman." He glared at Nirundale. "Looks like you'll have to knock two of us down."

Others joined them. Someone from the group in the street hurried up to Governor Nirundale and took him by the arm. The man whispered urgently in his ear while beginning to walk him toward Fountain Avenue.

Sir Mikkael offered Fanteal a hand. "Are you ready to go inside? I'd like to see your suite." She accompanied him. "Come, Jaikon," he added quietly over his shoulder.

CHAPTER 15

Colrin's voice arrested Fanteal's progress across the hall of Dirklan House. "Sir Mikkael."

The prime minister startled, then smiled. "I might have known. Yes, Colrin?"

"I'll be organizing the move of your belongings immediately. Do you have any particular orders?"

He looked around at a couple of dumbfounded pages before replying to Colrin. "Find out which bedrooms were used by Governor Nirundale's family. Do not disturb them."

A page cleared his throat and waited for Sir Mikkael's attention. "If you please, sir, Dalbred ordered some of us to pack the gentlemen's personal belongings, which we intend to take to their house in the settlement cavern."

"You may do so."

The page bowed.

Removing things? The thought didn't sit well with Fanteal. "Sir Mikkael, the prime minister's library—I believe it would be best if nothing were removed."

"I agree. Colrin, have one of the peace officers stand watch in the library." He pointed to it on the second-floor gallery. "Nothing is to leave the room. Also, if you or any of our staff meet Dalbred here, he is to be treated respectfully. Anything else, Lady Fanteal?"

"No." Invigorated by the air she'd pulled into the cavern, she made it up the first staircase, but required support from Sir Mikkael on the next. In her sitting room, she sank into a chair and sighed. "I can't believe how quickly the rich air dissipates."

As Sir Mikkael sat across from her, Jaikon busied himself with the vent controls, then asked, "Is this better?" as the air began to move.

How could such practical words sound so despondent? "Yes, thank you."

He wandered to the window and looked out.

She tried again. "This is hardly what we expected from our morning trip, is it?"

"No, it most certainly is not." He continued to stare outside.

Sir Mikkael caught her eye as she wondered how to dispel Jaikon's funk. He gave her a tiny shake of his head, then said, "I commend you, Lady Fanteal. You revealed yourself as a true Ambassador of the Crown, both in how you dealt with Governor Nirundale and through the demonstration and explanation of your gift."

"Thank you." She shrugged. "I suspect that I alienated the half of Jourendia who supported my uncle."

"It is impossible to please everyone, but you have now earned other strong supporters."

Really? When she wasn't a streamer? "Who?"

"Some worried that you would show favoritism to the Nirundales. There has been talk that you would be certain to marry your cousin."

"I cannot. I didn't want to say this out there, but my grandfather told me a year ago that he didn't believe Dalbred is the right husband for me." She repositioned a fold of her skirt, considering how much to reveal. "By the way, he proposed marriage to me today. And more besides, which would be nothing short of treason if I went along with it."

Jaikon turned to stare at her, and Sir Mikkael said, "Explain."

"The Nirundales have ambitious plans, though they depend upon me marrying Dalbred. My uncle believes he will become prime minister in the next election, to be followed by his son. In steps, they would change my title from ambassador to princess, and in future years to queen. Dalbred did not point out that he would become king, but I'm sure that is the intent. Obviously, this includes a complete break from Welcia above."

"That *is* treason," Jaikon murmured.

"Yes," Fanteal said. "My first outraged thought was to summon the high judge from Crysalan, but I don't have proof. Only a conversation. I assume they have taken no action, unless you could say that squatting in Dirklan House was part of the plan."

"That's hardly proof of treason." Sir Mikkael raised an eyebrow. "Your current intention?"

"I will never marry Dalbred, so I thwart their plan at the outset. Also, I make you aware of the danger, sir. I don't think we should speak of it beyond us three, but you may watch for questionable actions from Governor Nirundale."

"Good, for now. How did you respond to Dalbred's proposal?"

"That it would be rude to accept any offer of marriage until I had at least *met* other suitors." She huffed a laugh. "That is actually true."

Jaikon stepped nearer. "Do you suppose that Mardone Nirundale knew what his son and grandson planned?"

She exhaled aloud. "I so much wish I knew what secrets my grandfather took to his grave!"

"Meaning?" Sir Mikkael prompted.

"After he left last year, I wondered *why* he didn't want me to marry Dalbred. Perhaps I know now, or perhaps he thought our personalities incompatible." She shrugged. "It matters little compared to the rest. Why was he collecting wind records?" She lifted a hand toward the louvered vent. "Why did he build this when no one else from aboveground required such a device? And above all, *why* did he let everyone think I am a streamer?"

Sir Mikkael leaned back in his chair. "Are you certain that he knew?"

"Absolutely. He asked me to demonstrate my wind weaving skills for him every time he came to the palace. He only spoke of streaming to my father—and to my brother after his gift manifested."

"Why didn't *you* tell us?" Jaikon asked.

How could he ask her that? She let astonishment flow into her voice. "I thought you knew!" He looked so skeptical, she wanted to drum her fists.

"You just told all of Jourendia," he said, "plus a host of visitors from other domains, why we couldn't have known."

She glanced to his father and back to him. "I didn't want you blamed. I truly only realized that you didn't know from what you and Dalbred said on the stairs. And I was dumbfounded, because every time we were outside, I was wind weaving on your behalf."

"What?"

"When I spin the air over the harbor, it drives wind through the entire city. All the more disturbing to Dirklians, so I shielded you."

He drew his head back. "We don't know how wind behaves."

"Then remember this. When you left the dock and searched for me, how did the colonnade feel before you found me?"

He narrowed his eyes. "So windy I had to cover my nose and mouth."

"Once you were with me—in an open-air chapel, walking to the palace, on the hillside—through all of it, I bade the wind bypass you. The wind roared at our departure, beating the cliffs and bending the trees. But did it bother your walk from the palace to the dock?"

He shook his head, eyes closed. "I noticed trees a few times, but only thought wind was a strange phenomenon. That roaring...I've never heard such a sound." His voice fell again. "I thought it was the waves."

"I thought much the same," Sir Mikkael said. "I'm sure Tershel and Deltum did as well."

"For all it shocked me that you didn't know…" She flipped her hand. "I don't blame you. I understand why misconceptions happen. Perception was a common theme when I studied negotiation with Lord Yaeger. A person's beliefs and expectations always color how they perceive events and words."

"True," Sir Mikkael said. "Also, what we do *not* know impedes understanding."

Silence held them for a moment, and Jaikon returned to the window. Yet another vacillation. She wasn't putting up with this forever. "In what way have I displeased you this time, Jaikon?"

He pivoted quickly. Surprised? "You haven't. I would even say that your demonstration was masterful. That scene in the square could have gone very differently, but you pulled it off."

"Mm. For the record, you got it under control first, so *we* pulled it off." He shrugged.

"I thank you for the compliment," she said, "but you haven't told me what is wrong."

"You are still not a streamer. I don't blame you for that. But it is still what we desperately need."

She slapped the arm of her chair. "Why, in all the caverns below, don't your own streamers take care of the trade cataracts? Surely Melthindi didn't stand there every day and pull shipments through. What of the Streamers' Guild and their chiefs? Speaking of that, why haven't I met the Provincial Chief Streamer yet? I heard the name Telona in the square. Isn't she still Provincial Chief? She must be quite gifted if she kept a stream flowing straight up for hours."

"She was," Jaikon said.

"Was?"

"Emfiduria is taking her. Last I heard, she can barely lift her head."

Fanteal looked between the two men's somber faces. "I don't understand."

"Emfiduria is a disease of the lungs," Sir Mikkael explained. "It progresses slowly, but always kills in the end. When people die in midlife, that's usually the reason."

She was about to question further when she recalled that his wife had died in midlife. "How sad," she murmured, unsure what to say next.

"Did you know that it also killed Ambassador Melthindi's wife," Sir Mikkael asked, "and indirectly his son?"

She could only shake her head. Her grandfather may not have seen any reason to mention Telona's illness, but the death of the ambassador's wife and son...hadn't they warranted comment?

Sir Mikkael said, "She already had emfiduria when she became pregnant. Therefore, the child was born weak, and such children rarely live to adulthood. He died about a month after his mother. Ambassador Melthindi, unfortunately, never ceased grieving."

A distant memory stirred from childhood...her father concerned over receiving no letters from his uncle belowground. "I suppose that impacted his effectiveness."

Sir Mikkael angled his head. "He stopped attending government meetings, but he still visited Northeshur a few times a year. We also had Telona, who was a rare gift, but of a different sort. The cataracts are violent, and water erodes channels. Water-borne containers, which are harder than ordinary rock, erode them even faster. Obstructions occur, and only a streamer can remove them with brute force—provided they can find them. Telona could move huge volumes of free-flowing water, but she was never good at discerning obstructions. Ambassador Melthindi was highly skilled at just that."

"Ah. The supposed de Noviam streaming skill."

Irony tinged Sir Mikkael's words. "The ambassadors have always been crucial to maintaining trade. Your mother's role may be political, but it has a practical side here."

She could think of nothing to say—could only stare at her hands tightening in her lap. She was a complete disappointment. The victories of the past hour faded like mist on a breeze. Political victory? Public opinion? It would all be forgotten when trade failed.

CHAPTER 16

Bella arrived with Fanteal's belongings and unpacked for the second time. Fanteal leaned back in her wingchair with eyes closed, so Bella wouldn't chatter.

Her churning thoughts refused rest. Hard to say which were the worst. Everyone's blatant disappointment over the gift she didn't have, or her grandfather's omission of critical facts.

Had she known him as well as she thought? Did he care for her as much as she'd believed? She glanced around the sitting room. Fresh and pretty with every convenience she could want. He'd hidden the poor air, but he'd spared no expense to alleviate the lack.

She reached up through the louvers, sensing the draft produced by gently spinning vanes. Voices vibrated the distant, thin air. People must be in the roof garden, though they weren't loud enough to disturb.

Until one of them let frustration edge his voice. "Well, now that we know, couldn't we explain it to the king next year and ask him for a streamer instead of her?"

Fanteal clamped her teeth hard and squelched her awareness of distant air. How many reminders did she need! She'd given up the sky for *this*!

She couldn't sit here anymore. Bella was putting things away in the dressing room, and only one trunk remained near to hand. Her treasured books. Even those, she couldn't bear to open. Instead, she placed them on the bookshelf her grandfather had provided.

Bella tried to draw Fanteal into conversation at times. When that didn't work, she filled the gaps with her excitement over the column of water that had spanned the full height of the city cavern. "I ran up to the roof of the rented house in time to see it," she said. "Oh, how glad I am that everyone knows now of your gift! Agriben had told me you're a wind weaver, but then Sir Mikkael ordered me not to leave the house or speak of your gift. Such a relief that I no longer need to watch out for some slip."

At least someone was pleased—sort of.

Bella came and went many times, bringing meal trays and reporting on the rapid movement of the household. Everyone was busy except Fanteal. Bella paused in her description of the house's layout for a few seconds to measure Fanteal's bedtime dose. "And the maid's room is only a few steps away from this one. Your bell rings in my room as well as the staff's hall, and there's a way for me to show them that I am answering it. I'll be here in a moment if you need me. All very well thought-out."

"Mm-hmm."

"It's clear that your grandfather valued you greatly."

Did he? "I saw him so rarely," Fanteal said. "What was he like? What did people here really think of him?"

"He was highly respected. Very intelligent. I know the chief medic of Crysalan. She told me he was a most attentive listener, always asking questions and wanting to know the root of a matter. She said once that she thought his great listening was the source of his great wisdom."

Bella handed her a dose of medicine, and Fanteal drank it. From the concerned look in Bella's eyes, she must be hoping for a response. There was just nothing in Fanteal to say. Did wise people hide facts?

Bella adjusted pillows as Fanteal moved to lie down. "If a man like Mardone Nirundale valued you, then there is no cause for anyone to doubt you. Not even *you* have cause to doubt your own value."

Her attempts at encouragement fell short, but she meant well. "Thank you," Fanteal murmured. "Pleasant night."

"Pleasant night." Bella pulled the bed curtain to block direct light from the magnery lamp on the wall. From beyond it, paper rustled. She must have picked up the book that lay on the nightstand, just as it had in the other house. More pages flipped, then she read an ancient poem aloud.

> *When the tempests blow, I will rejoice,*
> *For you quiet them.*
> *When floods pass their bounds, I will praise you,*
> *For you recall them.*
> *When the earth trembles, I cling to you,*
> *For you reform it.*
> *Though storms rage, or the waves beat, or the earth spews*
> *boiling rock,*
> *Still I will worship the One, for your strength maintains my*
> *peace.*

Fanteal let the words flow over her…imagined them supporting her as the wind did when she leapt into it…let the verse carry her into sleep.

As Fanteal finished breakfast in her sitting room, Jaikon visited. He came with a polite inquiry over her night's rest and the effectiveness of the ventilation.

"I did sleep a little easier." She decided against mentioning the ever-present ache between her temples. "The air is still thin, but it refreshes quickly." She topped off her cup from the pot on the table. "Would you like some tea?"

"No, thank you." His gaze wandered around the sitting room. "My father and I," he said, "must go out this morning, but we'll return by noon. He asked me to tell you that several governors are inquiring when you will be available to receive them."

"Shall we say one this afternoon..." She hid the dread an ambassador shouldn't feel. "...from Crysalan perhaps, and two tomorrow from Northeshur and Weslin?"

"Is there any particular reason why Crysalan is first?"

She may as well admit it. "I suppose my choice is selfish. Perhaps I am less disappointing to Crysalan than to the others, and I would like the easier meeting first."

Since the import cataract flowed into Northeshur, and Weslin fed ores into an export cataract, her meaning would be obvious. His uncomfortable pause proved that he'd understood. Did he agree?

He paced, then must have realized he shouldn't. He picked up the nearest object as though that had been his goal. It happened to be the book *Rejoicings*, which Bella had left open on a side table. "It's illustrated." He frowned at it. "Are all your ancient texts mixed with drawings?"

"No, it's unusual. That particular scribe must have been an artist."

He angled the book toward her. "What exactly is it?"

The picture faced the poem Bella had read last night. Its imagery was obvious to Fanteal—yet meaningless here. Disturbing. "The slope on the left is a mountainside with a flow of lava pouring into the sea. The sky is heavily clouded as in a storm, and the waves are driven by it. Where the lava meets the sea, the water is boiling away into steam, rejoining the air. An artist's rendering of the elements coming together in their violent forms as described in the text."

He drew a slow breath. "Please do not misunderstand me or take this as a criticism, but I think it would be unwise to show this to a Keeper of the Writ, especially in Crysalan."

What now? "I will heed your advice, but why?"

"It is heresy to add to the ancient texts."

"That is so in Welcia above, too, but the text is not changed."

He tilted his head with a faint shrug. "Some might say that the drawing alters the meaning."

Not to her. What did he see? "Alters it how?"

"It emphasizes the power of the elements but shows nothing of the power of Ellincreo."

"Read it, please."

He scanned down the words. "The text is the same as in our copies."

"Aloud, please."

He met her gaze for a moment, and she caught a glimmer of understanding. He read it well, his cadence showing familiarity. The calm strength of his voice warmed her.

Peace coaxed her smile to form. "Thank you."

Their eyes held, and his tone gave double meaning to his reply. "My pleasure."

Irritating her one moment, then connecting with her heart the next. That was Jaikon.

After he left, she stared into her teacup for several minutes. So many contradictions.

Bella soon returned, and Fanteal finished preparing herself for the day. Just as she was about to go down to the library, someone knocked on the door, and Bella opened it to one of the staff.

He licked his lips. "Lady Fanteal, a caller has come for you. An older man named Malca Barran. I told him the prime minister is out and suggested he come back, but he said he really came to see you. He claims he was acquainted with Mardone Nirundale. I can send him away, but I thought I should ask first. Would you like to receive him?"

It seemed odd, but her curiosity stirred. "I will. Bring him here, please." When the door shut, she asked Bella, "Have you ever heard of him?"

"No." She stretched the word, a slight frown between her straight brows. "I believe I should stay with you."

Fanteal's lips twitched. "You look so suspicious and intimidating that I fear you'll scare him away."

Bella chuckled. "Well then, I shall tidy the bedroom and stay discreetly in the background. But he will know I am there."

"You may run in and rescue me if need be."

When Malca Barran was shown into her sitting room, he offered a courteous bow. "It is a great pleasure to meet you, Lady Fanteal. Perhaps it may seem odd that a stranger has come uninvited, but I trust you will understand and forgive my presumption. I was Prime Minister Mardone Nirundale's medic for many years and was with him when he passed from this life."

"Ah!" She motioned to a chair. "Won't you sit down?"

He did so, then leaned toward her. "Please let me begin by offering you my condolences on the loss of one dear to you."

She averted her gaze, taken off guard since no one seemed to grasp that the loss was a recent one to her. "Thank you. I appreciate your thoughtfulness."

He gave her a moment, then said, "It occurred to me that you may have questions, which I would be happy to answer. But mostly I came because Sir Nirundale mentioned you in his last words. I thought you might wish to know."

"He did? What did he say?"

"'Fanteal must come below.'"

For a moment she savored the thought that she had been on his mind at the end, but then puzzled over the meaning. "'Fanteal must come below?' Just that?"

He nodded. "You must understand that he had great difficulty speaking at all. There were gaps between the words. Perhaps there would have been more if he'd been able to get the words out easier."

She stared out the window. "How did he die?"

"It was very sudden. He was here in the house, walking along a corridor. One of the staff saw him clutch his head, then stagger and fall. They sent for me, and I came at once. He died a few minutes after I arrived. A blood vessel in his brain ballooned until it burst. An uncommon, but not unknown, cause of death. The end can come in seconds or minutes."

"Who else was present?"

"No one. The staff were running to alert the family, for they were away from home. But there was not enough time for them to arrive."

"It sounds painful."

"It is, my lady, but he did not suffer long. He was robust and active right up until the last few minutes of this life."

She let the pause lengthen, many thoughts jostling through her mind. "I wish I could have known him better than was possible in only one day each year. Could you tell me what he was like?"

"A very learned man, but modest. Quite approachable. One felt that he was attending to every word spoken."

"What sorts of things did you and he discuss?"

"He had an interest in the workings or failings of the body." He laughed a little. "Frankly, I think we spoke far more of the health of *Dirklan* than of *his* health. An excellent leader, committed to his people."

This sounded like the man she'd known. "Was there any illness that particularly interested him?"

"Oh, emfiduria I suppose, but naturally that is a concern for everyone."

"Oddly enough, I had never heard of it before I arrived. Is it widespread?"

He heaved a deep sigh. "It is, unfortunately. The number of new cases per year continues to rise, as does the number of deaths."

"What exactly is it?"

"Lung tissue deteriorates bit by bit until there is simply not enough left to absorb adequate air. The first symptom is a loss of energy, but it starts so slowly that most people are unaware. Later symptoms include numbness, lightheadedness, difficulty focusing, and memory loss. Respiration becomes very rapid, but victims can never get quite enough air."

"In effect, they suffocate?"

He took on the sad look medics used when delivering bad news. "Yes, you could say that."

"Can nothing be done?"

"We have learned to slow the progression, but we have yet to find the cause or the cure. Sir Nirundale often inquired after the progress of our research, and he ensured that we had every possible resource."

"My mother never mentioned it even once. How long has it been going on?"

"The very first cases occurred around thirty years ago, we think, although they were so rare that there wasn't even a name for it. Lady Trissina may not yet have heard of it when she left Dirklan. By…oh, I suppose about twenty years ago, it was causing considerable concern, at least to the medics and the prime minister. Naturally, we didn't alarm the people any sooner than necessary, but it has probably touched every family by now."

He gripped his knees. "Do not look so concerned, lady. Perhaps I err in telling you so much. The case is not desperate. Sir Nirundale studied medical texts and our research extensively, and he always remained optimistic. Just a few weeks before he died, he assured me that we would have a breakthrough soon."

"*He* assured *you*? Did he say why he thought so?"

"No." He chuckled. "In fact, I asked him that myself. He put his hand on my shoulder and said, 'Mark my words—in a year, there will be no new cases of emfiduria.'"

In a year? That would be...now.

CHAPTER 17

Governor Trezman of Crysalan brought his son, Fieldan. Nothing wrong with that, Fanteal reminded herself, even if the intent was obvious. She recognized the governor as the first to block the door of Dirklan House and dare Governor Nirundale to enter.

Both Sir Mikkael and Jaikon were present, and the conversation followed the general theme that Fanteal had requested. But though she asked Governor Trezman to tell her the concerns of Crysalan, he touched on them only lightly.

Did anyone expect her to be an ambassador? She switched her approach, asking about her grandfather's visits to Crysalan.

"Ah, yes," Governor Trezman said. "He came twice a year and spent a week with us."

Apparently, they expected her to be ignorant too. "Yes, I know of his regular tours and that he spent a week in each domain." She tried prompting. "I understand that he met with guilds during his travels."

"Yes, he always made a point of that. It was one of the things that made him so particularly well liked."

"What did each of them discuss with him most recently?"

"The Formers' Guild holds a joint meeting in Crysalan to present their structure reports. There are no significant shifts, but formers are unceasingly vigilant and report on even the smallest unplanned change, along with their planned excavation and mining."

"Of course. And who else did he meet with?"

Governor Trezman seemed to search for something to say. "You may be aware that the Keepers of the Writ are based in Crysalan. He always met with them also, even though there is never really any change in their affairs. Then, there is the School of Health, which is located in Illia, but they meet biannually in Crysalan."

"What did they discuss?"

"They gave their reports. I rarely stay for the entire meeting. Sir Nirundale had a great interest in their research. They would sometimes discuss various details for hours."

Clearly the governor saw the health of Dirklan as less interesting than the unchanged structure reports. Had her morning visitor overstated the problem?

Refreshments were served, and Fanteal strolled with her teacup to the salon's open window. Fieldan followed her, and his father immediately drew both of the Mikkaels into conversation. Oh, how blatant. Still, she must accept this gracefully. Fieldan wasn't the first and wouldn't be the last.

His looks were more what she was accustomed to aboveground. Hair more brown than black and, compared to most of the belowgrounders, he almost looked tan. His voice had a pleasant tone. Could he sing well? Now, if he just had a brain to go with his outer qualities.

He smiled down into her eyes. "I am so happy to see you recovering your health so quickly. We were rather worried at first."

"Thank you." She sipped her tea instead of explaining how she really felt.

He set his cup next to the leafy plant on a nearby table, then reached for the casement. "Let me close the window for you."

"Leave it, please."

She had spoken softly, but he looked shocked. "But...it's so breezy."

"I like it."

"Ah, yes, I suppose. I hear that opening the passage has stirred up the air more than usual this year—maybe because you were helping to open it. No doubt it will settle soon."

What? His lack of comprehension left her speechless.

He slipped a hand into his pocket and pulled out a small, decorative box. "I brought something for you. A welcome gift from our family. From the gem mines of Crysalan. I selected the stones for you. I hope you like them."

He opened the box as he spoke, and her lips formed an *O*. A pair of earrings were hooked against shimmering quartz. Enormous dark rubies set in thick gold. They were the sort of jewelry her mother liked, though stones this size were more suitable for a necklace. Just looking at them made her earlobes hurt. Whatever would she do with them?

"Thank you so much! Please convey my gratitude to your family." She felt that he expected more, but she couldn't call them pretty. She held one up to the light. "The rubies look to be very fine quality."

His tentative smile stretched wider. "We chose the very best for you. We could give nothing less when the king and queen sent us their cherished daughter. You will always be most precious in our eyes."

The warmth of his words and tone touched her. Perhaps she needn't be so cynical. "Thank you."

"Particularly in my eyes," he added.

Oh, dear! Couldn't he have kept it at the family level for at least one day? She acknowledged with a nod and took refuge in sipping her tea.

Fieldan turned his teacup on the saucer. His tone grew more serious. "There is something that I'm afraid might trouble you, and I would like to set your mind at rest. You may hear, may have already heard, that the devout of Crysalan tend to be, well...particularly devout. In fact, some are in dire need of moderation. But let me assure you that their opinions are in the minority. My family and I certainly don't share their extreme views."

Puzzling. "Extreme views on what, exactly?"

"The worship practices in Welcia above. I know you have had no time to meet many Dirklians, but you will soon. You may hear misguided suggestions. Um, this is awkward because we've barely met...I would never dream of proposing on such short acquaintance. But should you *eventually* honor me with marriage, I will not interfere in how you choose to worship. If you have, uh, objects of worship, you are free to bring them into the home I would offer you."

Objects? Prickles crawled toward her face. "Idols, do you mean? You would allow idols in your home?"

He rolled his lips. "Perhaps here it would be wise to choose a different word."

Her cheeks burned. "Be assured that I will bring no idols into any home. Indeed, I would violently object to anyone bringing them into mine. I have never worshipped wind, nor water, nor earth, nor any object made of such. I worship Ellincreo and no one else."

Her voice was not loud, but her vehemence abruptly ended the conversation of the other men.

Fieldan's mouth hung open. "I...I didn't mean..."

His father hastened to his side and spoke with calm courtesy. "Lady Fanteal, I fear there has been some misunderstanding. Perhaps I should explain that long before I was governor, there was a most unfortunate event. On one of Ambassador Melthindi's early visits to Crysalan, he was met by an overzealous Keeper of the Writ, brimming with accusations. Ambassador Melthindi never again spent a night in our domain. It was a grief and mortification to us, and we do not want it to ever happen again. You are entirely, unreservedly welcome in Crysalan."

There was no doubting the earnestness of his tone. As ambassador, she shouldn't take offense anyway, so she put it aside. "I plan to visit Crysalan as soon as I am able. It would please me far more to be welcomed as a follower of Ellincreo than to be welcomed despite assumed idolatry."

"I have no doubt at all that is so. Expect such a welcome. Would you like to come and sit down again?" He guided her back to the central group, made general conversation, and soon ended their visit.

Fanteal parted from her guests on friendly terms, not letting her concern show. What had kept the previous ambassador away from Crysalan for decades?

Jaikon's father escorted their guests out, leaving him with Fanteal. A slight frown creased her brow. Was she pensive or searching for air? "Feel free," he said, "to pull a good stiff breeze through the room."

That won him a smile. She must have followed his suggestion, for her hair swayed, though the breeze did not touch him.

Jaikon strolled to the table where she had set the jewel box. "May I?" At her nod, he opened it. He held the earrings up, letting them dangle to judge the weight, when his father returned with a flat case in his hand.

Sir Mikkael paused to inspect the gems. "Hmm." His voice dipped. "Impressive."

Fanteal chuckled.

Jaikon shook his head and adopted a solemn tone. "I cannot approve! If she wears these, her ears will be brushing her shoulders in a week."

Laughter warbled in Fanteal's voice. "At least someone understands."

"Our own gift for you has just arrived from the jeweler." Jaikon's father looked at him. "Shall we admit our mistake and tell her what we had made for her?"

"Only with the understanding that it was ordered before we met her."

"What are you talking about?" Fanteal asked.

"We had a gift made for you," Sir Mikkael said. "A necklace we intended to present on your arrival. Granted, your shoulders could support the weight, but it just didn't seem right for you."

"Once we met you," Jaikon added, "we couldn't bring ourselves to give you anything so overdone."

His father opened the case and turned it to show her the contents. Dainty emeralds set within an array of diamonds formed an arc that merged into a chain of woven gold. Enough gems for the honor due an ambassador, yet fashioned into a delicate, airy spread.

She gasped and pressed a hand to her chest. "That is *perfect* for a wind weaver!"

Jaikon savored the look on her face. He'd been right about this.

"Thank you so *very* much. It's just *lovely*."

A smile lurked in his father's voice. "I did catch a hint that you rather like it. You are most welcome, my dear." He put the case into her hands. "Do you still feel you can manage two such meetings tomorrow?"

"I should think so." She gazed at the necklace for a moment, before transferring her attention to his father. "I just wish they wouldn't come suggesting marriage and accusing me of idolatry in the same sentence."

"Mm. Charming. Your first visitor will spare you that. Governor Brakentel of Northeshur will bring only his wife. Governor Weltinfall of Weslin has no son to offer you either, but he has summoned a nephew to Jourendia." He regarded her for a moment. "My only reference to the Holy Writ will be a reminder that we are not to fear tomorrow." He left them with those words.

Was this the time Jaikon had been searching for? The difficult words refused to form. "You've been in the house all day. Would you perhaps like to go up to the roof garden?"

"Always."

They left the jewels in her suite, then he helped her up the stairs, trying not to overdo it. On the roof, they followed paths toward an enclosed arbor. Iron trellises wrought in the form of twining flowers were graced with live trumpet-shaped scarlet blooms. Despite greenery on every roof, flowers for the sake of beauty alone were rare. She paused to admire them.

"Lady Fanteal..." He took her hand, which had been resting on the crook of his arm.

"Yes?"

Now she looked worried. Great start. Jaikon cleared his throat. "That day in Welcia above, I made so many bold statements. All based on false assumptions. The limited apology I gave you was hopelessly inadequate." A huff escaped his nose. "I thought I had erred so little. I'm embarrassed to remember how I misjudged and insulted you." He swallowed. "So now, I offer you a real apology. I am so very sorry that I made an already difficult day utterly miserable for you."

Her wide eyes and parted lips—what did they mean? Nerves forced him to speak before she could. "Will you forgive me?"

She tilted her head as her expression relaxed. "I will."

Hopefully, her little smile wasn't in mockery. "Thank you."

"Jaikon, I have a feeling that you do not much enjoy giving apologies."

His lips twisted. "No, not my greatest pleasure. Does that ruin it?"

"No, it makes it all the more valuable."

He inclined his head. "Nicely said, Lady Fanteal." He gestured to the wrought iron furniture. "Looks like they spared no feathers in the cushions. Would you care to see if the lounge is comfortable?"

She settled into it. "I wouldn't mind if you used my name rather than my title when we are not in formal company." She gazed high. "This vantage point is perfect to study the cavern ceiling."

The crystals glittered with captured sunlight, obscuring details of the gray stone surrounding them. Jaikon sat in one of the chairs. "What do you search for, Fanteal?" Strangely pleasant to use only her name.

"Air channels."

"Can you still not find enough air?"

"I can draw enough for myself. It's the flow that puzzles me. So uneven." When he didn't answer, she asked, "Doesn't that seem odd?"

"Not to me, but I grew up with miners and formers." He grinned. "We like things very still down here, you know."

She laughed. "How do you use your gifting?"

"It has no use. My reach is hopelessly broad."

She swung her legs off the lounge and sat facing him. "I don't understand."

Different viewpoints...like his father spoke of. "I suppose for a wind weaver, having broad range is primary. To a former, it's more of a nice addition. Finders, for instance, must discern which minerals or ores lie within the rock, but for the most part, they are looking for what is near enough to mine. Splitters need to break it apart so the miners can start hauling it out. They needn't reach far. Polishers alter matter at finer scales. Medic formers can't reach more than a few yards but can discern and repair tiny details. I possess none of these abilities."

"What *do* you discern?"

"Well, you could say that I comprehend all of the rock at once. The pressure of it. The differences in weight, stress, and density." Did that convey anything to her? "It's rather hard to explain."

"How far can you sense?"

He shrugged. "I can feel to the surface throughout Dirklan. Not all the way up through Mount Estelle, though. That's why I wanted to examine it aboveground. That vantage point explained the pressure I can feel below it."

"You studied it quite a while. What did you learn?"

"Just confirmed that what we guessed was true. Its monumental form isn't nearly as impressive as it looks. The iron-rich rock of the foundation supports fizrock above."

"Fizrock?"

"Any type of rock that is riddled with air pockets or fissures. Mount Estelle is enormously heavy because of its bulk, but it's weak."

"Could you feel to the far side?"

"Yes, the entire thing." That stirred a rare sense of pleasure. The only joy he could take in his gift...and one he could never share with other formers.

Fanteal tilted her head in an adorable thoughtful look. "When you feel to the surface, what do you feel beyond it?"

He blinked. "Nothing!"

"Hmm."

Jaikon leaned forward, resting his arms on his knees. "What do *you* feel at the boundary of air and earth?"

"Resistance. I don't truly feel the earth, of course. I feel the air compress and scatter when land rejects its passage. But it's not all so stubborn. If the earth is sand or pebbles, they tumble in the wind. Clumsy little things."

She swayed and motioned as she described air, which made it seem visible to him. "Or if the earth and water have grown up together into a tree, then it will bend and let me pass gracefully. Especially the willows. They are my favorite. The grass, too, is pleasant. Though it cannot leave the earth, it pretends it is the air. With these, I must be careful, lest I strip away such tender forms of earth."

Jaikon savored the beauty of her movement, not wanting her to stop. "What do you feel where wind meets water?"

"Water has a mind of its own, but it's persuadable. Streamers talk of it seeking the deepest crevices. Yet it flings itself into the air—or rejoins it slowly in the rising heat. The streams may run counter to the wind, refusing to turn, but when air and water join forces, they are formidable! Stronger than rigid earth." A smile crept into her rapt face. "'Rock dissolves away, only to be rejoined and separated anew, sculpted by Ellincreo into his prize creation. The union of earth, water, and air.'"

How eloquently she had come around to quote from the Holy Writ. He finished it. "'Crowned with a will, and gifted with qualities of Ellincreo, to use as each one chooses.'"

"Just so!"

It happened again. Like when he read the poem to her. Something he couldn't fathom.

CHAPTER 18

Steam rose from the roasted oreduck as Sir Mikkael's knife pierced the crispy skin. Fanteal summoned a whiff to her nostrils. It smelled as delicious as it looked, glazed with a honey-colored sauce and speckled with chopped herbs. He carved a slice and placed it alongside the fried rice she'd spooned onto her plate.

Finally, she was able to eat in the dining room instead of hovering a few steps from her bed. Dinner was a small affair, with only the Mikkaels. The staff had placed covered dishes on the round table in a single course and left them in privacy. The golden-tinted crystals of the magnery lamps cast a cozy glow over porcelain, glass, and silverware.

Fanteal held her knife for a moment, admiring the ornate handle. "We have nothing like this above the waters. How are the colors embedded in the silver?"

"They are alloys—blended metals," Jaikon explained. "Metalwork in Dirklan is as much art as it is function."

She ate a piece of oreduck, thankful that its odd tang was well-masked.

"I gather oreduck is not served in Regissa," Sir Mikkael said. "What do you think of it?"

"Rather surprising at first." Fanteal took the bowl of peas Jaikon passed to her. "There do seem to be a lot of ways to prepare it, which is good since it's rather common here."

"More common for you than for us. We also enjoy oysters and several types of fish. Bella is quite adamant about the foods that are prepared for you. I'm sure she'll relax her vigilance once you are stronger."

"She told me ducks are the only bird species still living belowground. Do you know what caused the others to go extinct?"

"No specific cause. It was a gradual decline."

"Gradual doesn't mean without cause—only that it is hard to recognize. Did the trade cataracts also change slowly, or did they worsen a great deal in the past year?"

Sir Mikkael paused his eating to study her. "More of a steady decline over the past couple decades. Why do you ask?"

"My grandfather spoke of difficulties, but never to the degree that you described. The more I think of it, the more I wonder why."

The two men exchanged a glance, then Jaikon said, "There are some—many—who felt that he did not give adequate attention to trade. Despite the high regard in which he was held, he did not win his last election by a very large margin."

She sipped her minted water. "This is so puzzling. Am I missing some political nuance? I've heard nothing of rationing, and the people I've seen appear adequately fed." Jaikon was stiffening, so she directed her next question to his father. "If the situation is so severe, why didn't my grandfather tell the king?"

"There is enough food, but just barely. We still require imports from Welcia above. Rationing creates problems of its own. To avoid it, we are extremely careful with apportioning resources to each domain. As always, Dirklians do everything possible to increase food production, but we have limited space. Nothing is wasted."

He spread his hand toward the serving dishes. "Speaking of which, I must warn you about local customs. In Dirklan, we typically serve ourselves. We never take more than we can eat. No one will be offended if you decline food, but they will be appalled if you leave uneaten food on your plate."

No wonder. "I see now why you were uncomfortable at my mother's table, but my grandfather wasn't. He ate as we did." Was he matching custom out of good manners or hiding the lack plaguing Dirklan? She shook her head. "It makes no sense. He is reputed to be wise, but any time since Melthindi died—eleven years—he could have asked that a streamer be sent in my place. There are a few in the royal family. I realize that a direct descendant is preferred as ambassador, but my father could have sent one of my older cousins. Yet my highly educated and wise grandfather insisted that Dirklan would wait for me. A long wait, since an ambassador is expected to be at least twenty-five. Since he requested that I come early, he didn't *want* to wait. Yet he did." She angled a look at Sir Mikkael. "Don't you find that strange?"

"I do." Sir Mikkael nodded gravely. "I never had a reason to consider it before yesterday, but now I wonder. Is it possible that he didn't know you are a wind weaver?" He held up a hand as she began to shake her head. "I know it seems obvious to you, but four of us watched you weave and thought you were streaming."

"This is what worries me. I still doubt that any of you grasp it. Like Fieldan saying that it's not always so breezy here, and that people think it's from me opening the passage days ago. Everyone is going off of what they expect, regardless of what is. Like when I first approached you. Jaikon thought I was running."

Sir Mikkael lowered his fork, giving his head a tiny shake. He grew thoughtful, as though calling on a memory. "You *were* running."

"No, I intentionally walked." She quirked a brow. "My mother's influence, so I am quite sure of it. The wind was blowing—sweeping my hair and gown back. You perceived the motion as though I were running rather than that the air was moving. No abovegrounder would have seen it that way. I have finally figured out the obvious. You all expect air to be still. And since you clearly don't know, I must tell you—stagnant air is dead air. It is *not normal*."

Fanteal chewed a spoonful of peas in the ensuing silence.

Jaikon toyed with a piece of meat on his plate and exchanged a frown with his father. "I'm sure it seems odd to you, but the air here never does move. Nothing like it does under an open sky. Greehan and Wandermae created air channels after the collapse, and they bring air to Dirklan."

"They certainly *should*. My mother told me that the ocean breeze blows through Jourendia. The smell of the ocean in Regissa reminded her of home. I have yet to notice its scent. Do you ever smell it?"

Sir Mikkael shook his head.

"My mother left Dirklan twenty-six years ago. What has changed since then? Rock moves gradually. The birds died gradually. Emfiduria increased gradually. Sir Nirundale studied health and sent for wind records, which don't seem to exist. He insisted that a wind weaver come instead of a streamer. He ordered a special room to be prepared with forced ventilation, as though he doubted whether I would survive."

Jaikon leaned an elbow on the table and rested his forehead against his fingertips. "Are you saying that Dirklan is slowly suffocating?"

"Mm-hmm." She let silence emphasize her understated answer. "Now that I've gotten your attention, I acknowledge that I've only been in one place thus far. Jourendia's air is rather stagnant and thin, but you won't die tonight."

"If it is a problem here, it is a problem everywhere else!" Jaikon thrust his chair back, stood, and began pacing. "Didn't we have enough trouble as it was? Didn't—"

"Jaikon." Sir Mikkael's firm voice brought his son to a sudden halt. "You will not rant of this. It is not to be overheard through these walls. Not to be declared in the city, nor rumored in the Tea House." He pointed to Jaikon's empty chair. "Sit."

"You will keep it quiet, then? As Sir Nirundale did?" Jaikon turned to Fanteal. "And do you agree—that no one should know?"

"Why bother telling?" she asked. "I could barely persuade *you*. I'd rather spend my time determining what can be done."

Jaikon plopped into his chair.

She exhaled through pursed lips. "You thought I came to stream. I thought I came to represent the crown. It seems we were all wrong. I shall have to find some wind to weave."

"For now," Sir Mikkael conceded with an ironic smile. "But ambassador you will remain. In the meantime, how can we help you?"

Fanteal considered. "Wind records would be a good place to start, though I'm guessing they'll be inadequate. Were maps or drawings made when Wandermae and Greehan opened the air channels? Or any updates since then?"

"If so, those would be kept among the Formers' Guild records," Jaikon said, "not wind records. The rail tunnels are well documented. They must carry most of the air. I'm not sure about any smaller channels." He fiddled with his knife. "I suppose we should look at the paper drawings in the prime minister's library. Rigid drawings weren't used until paper became scarce. If we cannot find them here, Crysalan may have them."

She took another bite of duck, mindful that she couldn't waste it. "I must travel to each domain anyway. Crysalan has to be the first stop from Jourendia to Northeshur, so we can check then."

Jaikon paused with a fork halfway to his mouth. "How did you know that?"

She suppressed a huff. "We have maps. Imagine that. I even learned how to read them. The above- and belowground maps are correlated. I know where the domains, the rails, and the rivers are. I also know where the air vents open aboveground."

He held up a hand. "Right. Sorry. Since I was not trained my entire life to be an ambassador, can I get an explanation of the aboveground vents you speak of?"

She rolled her lips. "Sorry to have snapped at you. The vents are walled at least three feet high and have column-supported roofs. Locals must ensure they are maintained, and it's unlawful to block them."

"If you already know where they are aboveground, can't you find them below?"

"Not easily. They aren't vertical—nor straight. The natural ones may wend their way through miles of rock." She scooped up the last of her rice and peas. "I wonder if the streamers may have useful information. If a river has cut a deep channel, there is air above. Where does the Streamers' Guild meet?"

"They cycle between Northeshur, Weslin, and Silcopton," Sir Mikkael replied.

Fanteal's shoulders crept higher. "I'm kind of dreading this answer, but where does the Wind Weavers' Guild meet?"

His rueful look came as no surprise. "There aren't enough of them belowground to meet as a guild, nor is there anything for them to discuss or decide."

"How many are there?"

"I don't know. Perhaps one or two in most domains." He seemed to search for more words. "When plants flower, they will send a breeze across the rooftops. In public meetings, they lift voices, as you did in the square."

"Sounds like a lonely profession."

"It's not a profession. They work like everyone else who doesn't have a substance gift. Alluthin may be the exception, since they actually have open fields and varied crops. They may have enough work to pay wages to wind weavers."

Fanteal's spine stiffened. "Do you mean that wind weavers in the other domains aren't paid? Even when they do perform a service?"

He left a pause long enough to imply the answer. "Not that I have heard, and yes, I probably would have heard if they were being paid."

Brittleness crept into her voice. "I wonder how many wind weavers you would have belowground if you—that is, all of Dirklan—recognized their gift as valuable. And I wonder if your air wouldn't be a great deal richer because of it."

Neither man responded to her rhetorical comments. They couldn't, of course.

How had this deplorable situation come about? Her history book heaped praise upon the martyred Wandermae, who had persuaded a former to help her create air channels after the collapse of LourEstelle. They had saved Dirklan—and died for it at the behest of an ignorant tyrant. The king and first ambassador had decreed that wind weavers and their guild were valued and protected. What had gone wrong? And how would it affect her?

CHAPTER 19

The meeting with Governor Brakentel had as much depth as the hair on his balding head. Though Fanteal tried to get him to speak of Northeshur's concerns, she failed. Apparently, the trade cataracts were not to be mentioned since she could do nothing about them. His avoidance of the subject only convinced her how deeply disappointed he was with her gifting.

His wife, Lellia, relieved the gloomy tone. She made Fanteal laugh aloud with her freely expressed opinion of all the governors scurrying about to find bachelors.

Lellia's eyes scrunched shut as she smiled. "Well, I'm glad you can laugh over it, my dear. It must be dreadfully awkward for you. If you find them clinging, tell them you have no intention of deciding for months. Maybe then they'll give you some space. I can't see why you should decide in a hurry anyway." She included the men in her glance. "Don't we all tell our children not to be hasty with such an important decision? If anything, an ambassador should be even more careful than the rest of us."

Jaikon regarded her with an impish smile. "I wonder," he murmured, "what you would be saying if you had an unwed son."

"Enough of your sass. Don't think I'm telling her to marry *you*, for you were the most troublesome boy. I swear you asked more questions than all my children put together. Always taking apart anything that moved and leaving the pieces scattered about."

"Unfair. Now I can put them back together again."

"Humph." She turned back to Fanteal. "Would you believe, my dear, he took apart the timepiece I inherited from my grandmother? The sort created aboveground. Passed down through generations since before the collapse. It hadn't been in my house a week when I found the works scattered across the hall table. And all he said when I called him to account was, 'But it didn't work.'" The lady stood to take her leave, giving her skirt an indignant shake and smiling down on Fanteal as she laughed.

"I will never hear the end of this," Jaikon complained.

"Nor will any of us," said Governor Brakentel, "for you must always tease her."

After they left, Fanteal asked Jaikon, "Are you related to the Brakentels?"

"No, but I spent many a day in their house, for my father was Governor Brakentel's aide and then chief of staff."

She remembered his mother's failing health and early death. She wanted to ask more but couldn't bear to destroy the lighthearted look that the visit had brought to Jaikon's face.

Governor Weltinfall of Weslin brought Fanteal a plant stand crafted from his domain's metalwork. Enamel in shades of jade and ivory covered the aged bronze, except where it was tastefully allowed to show. Gilded vines climbed the legs. A beautiful work of a master artisan that she could accept with heartfelt pleasure. Unfortunately, the only pleasure in their meeting.

Governor Weltinfall responded to her questions about Weslin with a sourly stated, "There is no point in talking about that." He then launched into a list of his nephew's accomplishments, while that quiet young man looked increasing uncomfortable. Was he even twenty yet? Poor kid.

The following days offered little variation as she met with each governor. Regarding her role as ambassador, they presented two attitudes: condescension or disregard. More young—or not so young—men were presented, often revealing their misconceptions about Welcia above in general and wind weavers in particular. Some betrayed their unease, and others hid it under assumed confidence. She did her best to forgive them all, since they had no opportunity to gain either knowledge or experience.

Only Governor Yaldeeth of Illia provided a truly pleasant visit. Her white curls framed keen eyes amid myriad fine lines. Though the eldest of all the governors, she didn't bother with attendants.

Having no need to draw attention away from Jaikon to some descendant of her own, she included him in the conversation. They spoke of a project the School of Invention had undertaken. Passion animated him and sparked a smile in Sir Mikkael's eyes as they rested on his son.

"How do you know so much about this?" Fanteal asked Jaikon.

"Oh, it was the latest big idea during my final year at the School of Invention." He gave her a boyish grin. "Sorry for derailing your meeting."

Interesting. Fanteal had assumed he'd completed his upper education with the Formers' Guild. When did his unusual gift bring that to an end?

Though her attempts with other governors had met with no success, Fanteal asked her guest, "Are there any particular concerns in Illia?"

Governor Yaldeeth treated her interest as normal. A delightful change. They had a lengthy discussion of the manufacturing and technology projects underway in Illia. Granted, no trade cataracts were located there. Did that explain the governor's willingness to talk of other matters? Fanteal couldn't believe that anyone in Dirklan was indifferent to food shipments. When the governor finally broached the subject of marriage, she seemed to do so under duress.

"I understand..." Governor Yaldeeth lifted her upper lip. "...that my fellow governors are parading a succession of eligible bachelors before you. I do have an unmarried grandson, but nothing will induce me to throw him at you. He told me some years ago that he intends to marry *someday*—just hasn't gotten around to it yet. He's in his thirties now. You can draw what conclusions you like from that. You're welcome to meet him if you desire. However, I will be in no way offended if you do not desire it."

Fanteal laughed. "Already, I like him better than all the rest."

Governor Yaldeeth smirked. "It must be intolerable for you to be hunted like this. Sir Mikkael, why don't you tell them to stop making fools of themselves?"

"I did not ask them to bring their young men, and I will not tell them to stop. Lady Fanteal may see them all as they *are*, rather than as they are *told* to be."

"Hmm. Some value in that, I suppose." Governor Yaldeeth turned back to Fanteal. "You do realize, I hope, that there is no hurry for you to decide. Melthindi de Noviam waited three years before wedding the prime minister's daughter."

Fanteal arched a brow. "Three years?"

The governor nodded. "I looked up the dates to be sure. The situation was a little different, for she was only sixteen when he arrived. I honor him for not arranging an immediate marriage, even though the delay caused some angst at the time. To hear people talk, our traditions are more inviolable than the law of gravity!"

She uttered such a dainty snort with the words that Fanteal nearly laughed.

"But it is not so," the governor continued. "I've been wondering what Prime Minister Nirundale intended. Had *he* brought you to us, I am quite sure you wouldn't have faced this mad rush. He was always very careful with timing."

"What do you mean?" Fanteal asked. Could she get more insight into her grandfather's thoughts?

"He would introduce an idea in a very casual way, let a few days pass, then bring more details to light. But I have always believed he had a certain end in mind when he made his first casual statement."

Governor Yaldeeth set her empty teacup aside. "A few months before your arrival, he would have spoken of how inadvisable it is for cousins to marry. In another week or so, he would have chatted about how most of us choose our spouses. If he had certain people in mind, he would have spoken to their parents. There would have been dinners and entertainments in certain households." She flicked a glance to the current prime minister. "Unfortunately, Sir Mikkael had no knowledge of the promise he'd been committed to. We all had to find out immediately, or the delayed wedding would have made it seem that something was very wrong indeed."

"Everyone thinks that anyway," Fanteal muttered, "though for a different reason."

"I have been wondering about that a great deal." The governor eyed Fanteal. "Don't take this amiss. I suppose the answer is obvious, but I want to be sure. Are you certain Sir Nirundale knew what your gifting is?"

Ah, the endless question. "Positive. There can be no doubt."

"Then be very sure that he would have made it known before you arrived. *So* unfortunate that he died suddenly. I wish I knew what was in his mind."

"Yes, we all do," Sir Mikkael said. "I have no doubt that he very much wanted a wind weaver."

"I must ask what is probably a silly question," Governor Yaldeeth said. "Please understand that I have no gifting whatsoever and excuse my ignorance."

Sir Mikkael's eyes creased. "I will not let that pass. You have an amazing ability to see the practical applications of knowledge that so many others miss. It is a gift most rare and precious. Now, lady, you may ask your *supposedly* silly question."

Governor Yaldeeth chuckled, inclining her head. "Thank you, sir." She turned to Fanteal. "Is it possible for you to make use of the wind in some fashion within the trade cataracts?"

Fanteal blinked. "I...don't know. My father took me to all three cataracts, but I never even tried to reach within them. Streamers were present. They would have been the ones to..."

"What?" Jaikon asked.

"It has dawned on me that I don't really know how far the streamers reach into Northeshur's cataract. A little way, at least, for they hold the water back until enough pressure builds to force the canisters through. It's an interesting question though. I will see what is possible. I plan to tour all the domains soon." She paused and grinned at her guest. "And when I come to Illia, I would like to meet your grandson."

"As you wish, Ambassador, but without obligation."

Jaikon laughed. "In fairness to Renauld, I have to point out that Lady Fanteal might like him better than most." He turned to Fanteal. "He's quite intelligent. He has several inventions in production that have significantly improved irrigation. He is good-natured and courteous...as long as he remembers you are there. Just a little apt to start puzzling out some obscure problem in the middle of a social event. On the other hand, it would never occur to him to be condescending, or to devise political schemes for his personal advantage."

"Ah, yes. It would be a relief to meet such a man."

"In time," Governor Yaldeeth said, "you will meet many such men. I will be glad when all of this nonsense calms down. Before I take my leave, Ambassador, may I have a moment with you in private?"

"Certainly."

Governor Yaldeeth waited for the Mikkaels to exit and close the door, then asked, "Do you realize that your choice of husband will have a substantial impact on the next election?"

"The way I am being pursued has suggested that."

"I believe you have met most of the governors now. I understand that Governor Armeen of Alluthin has arranged to be the last to meet you. The Armeen family is extensive. I do not know the man he has chosen to present to you. However, I know the governor and his ambitions."

Governor Yaldeeth stroked her wrinkled hand along the arm of her chair. "He is determined to be the next prime minister. The election is three years away, but he has already approached me, suggesting an alliance of sorts with Illia. Alluthin is the only domain that produces enough food to supply others. He plans to use food shortages to win the election. Not that he phrased it that way."

"Ah." Interesting that Governor Yaldeeth was telling her this.

"In some ways, I am loathe to influence you," the governor said. "Sir Mikkael is no fool and can advise you. However, I don't know what your relationship is with him. Governor Armeen will never reveal his intentions to Sir Mikkael, so I set my scruples aside. Be cautious in regard to Alluthin."

"Thank you for the information. I am willing to listen to Sir Mikkael's advice, but he will also have a bias in favor of his own son. I can ask his opinion about anyone except Jaikon." Hopefully that was enough of a prompt.

"Ah, Jaikon." Governor Yaldeeth considered for a moment. "He has a certain way about him that attracts, which is a useful quality in a leader. While it cannot be said that *everyone* likes him, it can be said that *no one* is indifferent to him. He sometimes alienates people, being rather adamant in his opinions. A common fault in the young, which is usually tempered by experience, so it doesn't worry me."

She swayed her head side-to-side. "But let us set politics aside. It seems likely that you will marry. The man will always be your husband, but he may not always—or ever—be prime minister. Times are chaotic. Chose a man, not a position. Did your mother tell you how to discern the qualities of a husband?"

Fanteal sighed. "She told me to trust Sir Nirundale to choose. That worked well for her. You can imagine how well it's working for me!"

Understanding glimmered in the governor's eyes. "Here is what I told my daughter. Most men will treat a woman well during courtship, but you need to know how he will treat you afterwards. Consider how he treats his mother or other women. That is your future. Is he interested only in his own affairs, or does he show genuine concern for others? Do you respect him? Can you work with him toward a common goal? Can you laugh with him? Can you argue without coming to hate one another? These are things to consider. They are a foundation on which respect and love can thrive."

That sounded like good advice. But could a man fake such things?

Governor Armeen's pale grey eyes locked with Fanteal's. A direct and appraising gaze. "A pleasure to meet you, Ambassador. Let me add my welcome to the many you have no doubt received."

Why did he look familiar? Ah, the day she'd challenged her uncle in the square—Armeen had led Nirundale away. "Thank you, Governor. I, too, am pleased to meet you and look forward to hearing more of Alluthin."

"Yes, of course. It so happens, we've brought a little bit of Alluthin *to you*. But first, allow me to present Grellin Armeen."

Fanteal exchanged a formal greeting with him. He must be the bearer of their gift, for he set a covered basket on the table.

He unbuckled the closures, saying, "In keeping with tradition, we wanted to bring you a gift that is uniquely from Alluthin. Ours is the only domain with space enough to grow full-sized trees. We also have an art of growing very small trees." He removed the cover and lifted out the specimen in a shallow, ornate pot. "This one is over a hundred years old."

Fanteal bent to inspect it more closely. "A hundred years? How can it be so small at that age?"

"The growth is controlled by pruning, not only the branches but also the roots. Some skill is required. We would be happy to prune it for you, or to teach you how if you have the inclination. This one was planted by my great grandfather and passed down through the generations."

"A living gift! And one that is no doubt precious to your family. I do not know how to thank you enough."

A smile warmed his cold eyes. "You already have, lady, for you perceive its value."

Sir Mikkael invited the guests to sit. This was the moment when such meetings started their decline, but she forged ahead. "Governor Armeen, what concerns do you have for Alluthin?"

"None, at the moment. We are well supplied with the type of streamers we need for water management. We are also upgrading the mechanical forms of irrigation, which is ongoing work for us. Naturally, food shortages elsewhere in Dirklan could become a future problem. For that reason, excavating new caverns and preparing them for crops is also an ongoing effort in Alluthin."

Wow. He neither condescended nor avoided the subject of streamers. Could he keep this up?

As the conversation progressed, both he and Grellin responded to her questions about crops, rotation, irrigation, and techniques for increasing yield. She felt like an ambassador for a change.

"Consistent control of water is essential to us," the governor explained. "Alluthin is fed by many natural flows. The issue is getting it to the right place at the right time—and back out again. Rice, for instance, grows best in flooded paddies, but they must be drained before harvest. Several types of berries are harvested by flooding their bogs, but if they stayed flooded, it would kill the plants. We used to rely on streamers, but in recent years several inventions have relieved us of that need."

Odd. "Why do you want to be relieved of the need to use streamers?"

"It overtaxes them, for one thing. Streamers are a diligent sort, but no one should be expected to work such long hours so frequently. There is no sense in placing all dependence on a single method. We have developed cisterns, pumps, piping, and the like. Such water handling systems are crucial to the survival of Dirklan. Yet I daresay, you have not even heard of them."

"I have. Jaikon explained some of the recent inventions to me."

The governor widened his eyes, and Grellin stepped into the pause. "I didn't know you had an interest in such matters, Jaikon. Are you acquainted with Renauld Yaldeeth?"

"I've known him for several years. His inventions are most intriguing."

"True. A brilliant man, though not always easy to converse with." Grellin turned back to Fanteal. "I look forward to showing you what we have accomplished when your upcoming tour brings you to Alluthin."

Refreshments were served, and this time, it was Fanteal who arranged to step aside with the young man presented by the governor. Not that Grellin looked all that young. Thirtyish, perhaps. He had the same gray eyes as the governor, but no other resemblance. "You must tell me how to care for this little tree," she said, moving to the window where they had placed it on a table. She began slowly increasing the air flow to gauge his reaction.

He followed and glanced at the tree. "For watering and feeding, it's not so different from other potted plants. But the pot must be small to inhibit growth, which leaves little room for soil. I brought you a book..."

He pulled it from the basket under the table. "…that explains how to care for it. You won't need to prune or repot it until the half-year. Please let us help you with that the first time."

She took the book. It was bound in the typical quartz cover, with its title engraved. "*Tiancient Trees?*"

He inclined his head. "It's a merging of the words *tiny* and *ancient.*" He glanced at the window. "It really is breezy here. I overheard talk of that in the restaurant this morning."

"More so than Alluthin?"

"Yes, at the moment, at least."

"Don't the trees need air movement?"

He smiled a little, as though she had said something silly. "A little during pollination season, but primarily just light. There are broad crystal shafts running all across our cavern roofs. Alluthin is brighter than any other domain." By the straightening of his broad shoulders, this granted bragging rights. "As for your tiancient tree, it will want plenty of light too. Perhaps you should show me where you intend to keep it, so we can make sure it will be able to survive."

Thus, he arranged to carry his gift from the salon to her private sitting room. She removed a pot from the plantstand the Weltinfalls had presented to her. "Please set the tiancient tree here."

"That's a handsome piece," Grellin said. "A fitting throne for this monarch among trees."

"It was a gift from Weslin."

"I'm not surprised. Many fine artisans live near the mines, I'm told."

"You haven't been there?"

"No reason to."

"How about Northeshur?"

"What would I go all that way for? There's plenty in Alluthin to meet our needs. You'll see when you come. Prime Minister Nirundale would always tour to the north first and then he came around westward and south, saving Alluthin for last. Is that the route you plan to take?"

"I believe so."

He nodded. "Alluthin is a good place to end your journey. You'll like it. People always used to spend holidays in the gem hills, but more and more come to us now. It is so bright and green. The air is richer because of all the growth. And maybe best of all, you don't have to try to avoid those sanctimonious Keepers of the Writ that clutter Crysalan."

"Are there so many?"

"One is too many! But why bother with even one? The gem hills are pretty in their own way, but Alluthin is like an enormous living gem—emerald or peridot—sparkling with light. Even the patients in the emfiduria sanatorium live longer than anywhere else in Dirklan. Ambassador Melthindi made his home with us, too, but perhaps you already know that."

"Yes. Do you happen to know why?"

"I didn't know him well. I daresay it was the rich air, since he was Welcian. By the way, Governor Armeen owns the house that the Ambassador used. The lease has expired, and the latest tenants are moving out even now. You can use the house as much as you like."

"How convenient. Thank you."

"It's not as big as Dirklan House," he said, looking around the sitting room, "but very pleasant, nonetheless. Is this the suite that Sir Nirundale had prepared for you?"

"Yes, it is."

"I heard about some device for moving air."

She showed him what he was clearly looking for. "Is there any such arrangement in the ambassador's house in Alluthin?"

"No. It does have a great many windows, though, so I don't see why it would be needed. Whatever his reason, Ambassador Melthindi preferred it to living in Jourendia. Who knows? Perhaps he had a foresight that so many others lack."

"What do you mean?"

"Our world is changing. We may as well face the facts. The worst thing we can do is fixate on the way it has always been. We need to look to the future. And the future is in Alluthin. After all, what does Jourendia, the smallest of all the domains, have to offer? I suppose the gem mines still yield, but gems lose value when food is scarce. Government is the major business now, but that can be done anywhere. Jourendia has little to offer the future."

His value for the domain was clear! She let her voice dip pointedly. "There is a certain passage."

"True, but..." He adopted a serious expression. "May I speak candidly?"

Wasn't he already? How bad would this get? "Please do."

"Has Welcia found other sources of ores and gems?"

"No. Nor does Welcia *above* seek other sources. The crown honors its covenant with Welcia *below*."

He inclined his head. "Then, the passage retains its value. But change must still occur, for the old trade system is failing. The Mikkaels hope to restore it, which would be well if it were possible. Unfortunately, there isn't the least indication that it is."

She maintained an interested look, wanting him to continue.

"Welcia must grow and harvest all the food they send us, regardless of whether we receive it wet or dry. We understand that better than anyone in Dirklan. At some point, the cost will become too great, and they will give up. Conditions only worsen. They do not improve. No amount of complaining or begging will change the cataracts. They are out of our control. Food growth in Alluthin is within our control, and that is where the focus needs to be."

This was clearly Grellin's passion, for he did not pause. "In Alluthin, you will hear no complaint about your gifting. There will be no demand for public displays. An ambassador may actually be an ambassador instead of a cataract worker. Negotiations will be needed to revise our covenant. Your position will become very significant. It will be far easier for you if you are allied with the most powerful domain."

They did indeed aspire to much. Were they also correct?

CHAPTER 20

Jaikon unfolded a map of Jourendia and snapped the panels into place. Fanteal held one edge, for the map was bigger than the rooftop table. He positioned it to align with the actual caverns, then pushed chair backs against its sides. "That should keep it steady."

She swept her fingertips over the clear crystal surface. "My mother told me about these level maps, but it's still amazing how they look thicker than they are. We have relief maps in the Substance Guild Hall in Regissa, but this...wow! Like a relief map compressed into glass."

"Quartz, actually, but clarified. Or did you know that?"

She twitched a shoulder. "They both look the same, but I know clarified quartz is used for glass in Dirklan. No point in a manual process to make glass when you have so much quartz to get rid of and plenty of formers to polish it." She traced a river line in the map with her finger. "Etched to show depth features too. This is beautiful."

Endearing that she saw beauty in something as practical as a map. He unfolded an unmarked clear layer over the top, then pulled a wax pencil from the case in his pocket. "Now, oh wind weaver, about those air channels..."

She chuckled and looked up, turning in a slow circle to take in the entire cavern. Like a streamer—they also moved while they worked.

He stood still to sense the caverns. Rather, the rock surrounding them, for the caverns were the absence of rock. The city cavern, biggest by far. The settlement cavern, lower and to the right. The lake cavern beyond it with its dome closed against the harbor. Where were the cliffs he'd seen hemming in the sea? Ah yes, there. He returned to the familiar and discerned the long, narrow emptiness of the rail tunnel stretching toward Crysalan. Others branched from it toward Jourendia's lesser caverns. Downward, he searched out the river channels, one powering the magnery turbines, another providing fresh water to the citizens, and the deepest one carrying away waste. Their purposes he knew from normal experience, for gaps in the rock felt no different to him whether they held air or water.

Fanteal pointed almost straight up. "Do you sense that one?"

"What do you mean?"

"I can feel you working. I thought maybe you were looking for the air channels."

He blinked at the assumption. "Uh, no."

She laughed. "Well, I meant the *gaps* that air travels through. I can pull a little through there," she said, eyeing a spot, "but it's hard to get continuous motion. What does it feel like to you?"

"Hmm. Which way?" After Fanteal's pointing and describing, he finally realized what he was looking for. "Oh...maybe...that gap gets thin and flat through a long shallow dip. The matter is less dense beneath the dip. What do you know about the area above it?"

She knitted her brow and then gestured. "Off that way somewhere is a vent on a hillside covered in massive old trees with exposed roots. There's dirt on the riding trails. I've no idea how deep."

"Exposed roots? Was that caused by a shift?"

"No, erosion by rain." She pressed a finger to the side of her chin. "There was a mudslide when I was, oh, five or something. It could have been in that area."

"I know about erosion and sediment in rivers, but not how it works in air channels. Can they fill in? What's obvious to you, is mystery to me."

"Mystery for me too," she said. "I'm used to the vast open sky. Can you move any of that…uh…less dense matter?"

"Caverns, no! Even if I could, we don't excavate without a dual assessment."

"I didn't mean excavate. Just turn over what might already be loose. Now that I'm working the air back and forth, the shape of the current is changing. Something must be moving. It sounds different too."

"I don't hear a thing."

"Not with ears. Sound is carried in the air, and I can *hear*, so to speak, with my wind weaver sense." She pulled a sudden breeze down to them and sniffed. "Yes, something organic is in the channel."

He smelled it, too, and wrinkled his nose. Oddly familiar.

She looked at the map, though her face remained intent like she still sensed upward. She traced a twisting and turning path along the map.

He used his forming sense to find it overhead. "Yes, I can follow the entire channel now." He drew it onto the top layer of the map. A polisher would have simply etched it. One of his many failures during former training. He'd learned how to map, yet he drew with wax pencils like a child.

Movement along the channel made him gasp and snap the tip off the pencil. His panic lasted only a second. The ipenrock stood impervious while loose matter skittered inward. The wind picked up again. "What are you doing?" he demanded.

"Cleaning the channel."

He followed her gaze. A narrow twist of debris spun downward. Like a vortex that a streamer would create to suck filth from the duck pond and send it down the waste stream. But this one was a dark smudge casting a shadow amid light shafts as it snaked down past the rear edge of the roof. He ran to the back of the house and looked over the half wall. A mess dropped to the street. She reached his side as dust and leaves swirled down around the growing heap.

"That," he groaned, "is going to get some comments."

She giggled. "It's probably good compost. Consider it a gift from Welcia above."

He narrowed his eyes at her. "When you're not being dignified, you're a bit of an imp."

By the look on her face, she took that as a compliment. Strands of hair crossed her forehead, the wind pulling them from their clip. She inhaled deeply and kept the air flowing across the rooftops. He turned so the irritating wind struck his back. He had to admit, it did smell fresh. Probably didn't in the street beside that pile of muck.

He walked to the roof access and pulled the bell lever. When a page arrived in response to his summons, Jaikon said, "Some—compost—has fallen from one of the vents in the cavern roof." He pointed. "It's in the street over there. Have it cleaned up."

The page looked upward, wide-eyed. "Uh, yes, I'll see to it, sir. I've never heard of compost falling. Should I send for a former to have the opening sealed?"

"No!" Fanteal and Jaikon said in unison. "Whyever would you do such a thing?" she demanded.

"Someone could get hurt if debris hit them."

She calmed her voice. "It was a controlled fall. I was cleaning the vent. No one will get hurt." She waited for him to go down into the house before exclaiming, "Ellincreo preserve us! Will others react the same way? Do you suppose formers have purposely closed some of the vents?"

Jaikon sighed. "I wouldn't have thought so, but—well, I suppose if one person reacted so, others could have. Agriben is still in town. I think it's time we invite him for a visit."

"Yes, please do." After a dramatic shudder, she returned to the map and her work. In a moment, she said, "There's a narrow channel over that way."

At least she didn't seem interested in clearing it. He focused his gift again, located the entire length, then began sketching it.

"Can you smell that?" Fanteal snapped.

He startled out of intense absorption. "What?"

"The ocean air. I found the harbor-side opening. There."

He moved to stand behind her, following the length of her arm as she pointed, searching the cavern wall with both his eyes and gift. Unconsciously, the two of them gravitated toward it, stopping at the corner of the roof that faced the square and Government House. The strengthening breeze stirred Fanteal's hair. He sucked his breath in. "Oh! Yes, I most definitely smell it!" He coughed. "Do you like that?"

She laughed at his pained expression. "Well, maybe the guano scent is a bit thick. But don't worry. It makes great fertilizer."

"Don't you dare pull that into Jourendia!"

She laughed again. "If you insist. Actually, I don't think I can. Drawing the air in is like pulling mud through a sieve. Much easier to push." Her voice grew vague when she concentrated like this.

The breeze she had pulled down from above their roof changed course. It intensified to a throaty roar as it sucked relentlessly through the air channel overhead and beat against a crevice high on the far wall.

Jaikon studied it. The gap began as a sort of shelf, tucked away near the ceiling. It narrowed gradually but remained wide enough to crawl through. Something within resisted the onslaught. Dense, yet pierced. And beyond that, a porous structure. A piece tumbled. Clumsy. She had described it well. Smaller pieces shifted, slid, or rolled in the wind's path.

She laughed. "Ocean eagles. I knew it."

She drew in air from above, twisted it, and drove it spinning through the cliffside channel. She frowned. "There's some kind of structure in there. It's messing with my vortex."

"I can sense it. Symmetrical. Bits are breaking off, but the rest of it may be iron." He almost told her not to tear it out, but he recognized its stability.

"I thought you couldn't detect what type of matter something is."

"I know natural properties as well as anyone. If a grid that dense was placed there on purpose, it is likely iron." A clump of matter slid away from the grid. "You're moving something."

"That's the plan. I want their nests out. And the guano, too, or there'll be no end to complaints. I sense you there. Can you feel the loose stuff?"

"Yes." His voice lightened. "And there it goes."

"All of it?"

"Most. The smaller bits are moving." He waited, sensing the changes. "Pebbles are falling now. I think you got it all out." The pressure against the grid ceased. No, worked back and forth, in and out. "Are you cleaning that grid?"

"Trying to. Air is not the best scouring tool."

He laughed. "I'm sure we can come up with something better. Send a person up there if we must." At some point, he had wrapped an arm around her back, and her body relaxed against it.

She whispered, "Peace now, fair wind. Return."

He looked down into her rapt face. Her eyes swept around as she directed the air. The ocean scent filled the cavern, moist and salty.

She looked up into his eyes. "Now do you smell it?"

"Indeed, I do." He smiled. "Much sweeter than before."

She leaned sideways against his chest, joy in her eyes. If they weren't in view of the square, he would have embraced her. Instead, he said, "We're getting an audience."

She straightened. The moment ended.

"Come." He drew her back toward the arbor, where the forgotten map showed signs of the recent tempest. He swept bits of dirt from it, until she cleared it with a breeze. He grinned, then drew the angles of the channel and the cliff-side cavity. He met her eyes again. Was that a realization lurking in them?

It stirred within him as well. What might come of this? Too many unknowns. He pointed at the cavity he'd drawn. "What was here?"

"An aerie. Do you know what ocean eagles are?"

"Never heard of them."

"They're enormous birds that hunt out at sea and nest on cliffs. They pick up dead branches and even rocks and carry them to their nests." She wrinkled her nose. "Tidiness doesn't appear to be one of their values. Over the years, they must have blocked the opening. Two adults took flight when I flushed air though, and some smaller ones as well. They've nested in that spot for years. Even as a child I used to watch them lift fish to their chicks. But I never dreamed that their aerie was the opening to one of Dirklan's air channels."

"Will they be back?"

"Probably. I think I should flush that channel frequently for a while, or they'll be stinking it up again."

"We're planning a tour soon. What happens when you're gone?"

"Not to worry." She flipped her hand. "Abovegrounders will have noticed and will realize I caused the unusual airflow. Besides, the birds took flight shrieking. If they persist in returning, my father will order them hunted. Telamien will be delighted. He's getting quite good with a bow and will be thrilled with an excuse to use it."

A bow? Jaikon had seen a bow and tethered arrow used for sport fishing, but a flying bird? How little he knew of life aboveground. How little any of them knew. He watched her for a moment. She looked both vibrant and relaxed. From the rich air? The joy of using her gift? A joy denied him, but he did get a little pleasure out of searching. Now that he understood what she needed, he sought channels with less density and even found a couple to sketch.

The breeze hit him first, then a putrid odor. "Yuck! What is it this time? And can you direct that interesting bouquet out to the ocean?"

She didn't answer.

He craned his neck to look at Fanteal. Her stricken expression made him drop his pencil.

She covered her mouth. "Oh, Jaikon, I am so sorry!" Her voice squeaked.

What in the caverns? He crossed the roof to her. "It's all right if you can't. I'm sure it won't last long."

"Don't you recognize the smell?"

"It's not—Oh!" An image of the statue in the chapel forced itself into his mind. "I try to avoid that memory."

"I am so very sorry! That I, of all people…" Her lips trembled. "It's just that I was so upset and angry, and I thought it was you, but I should have known better. And then I said…" Tears filled her eyes, and she drew a trembling breath. "But it couldn't have been you. It was Dirklan."

He stared above her head, the image almost as clear in his mind as it had been that day in the chapel. The thing's mouth and nose—so encrusted that it could barely breathe. Yet it remained oblivious to its condition. Deep within, her words registered as truth.

"I am so terribly sorry," she repeated. "Please, will you…can you ever…"

Her voice failed again, but he understood what she was asking. Anger and the pain of humiliation demanded their due. Refused to let go. He knew what the Holy Writ said about forgiveness. But it spoke of just penalties too. Pathetic excuse. That was the trouble of spending time with Ellincreo and the Writ—Jaikon also heard *him*. Even when he didn't want to.

The quiet nudging within reminded him that some of his humiliation resulted from his own haste. Then reminded him of the day she forgave him on this very rooftop. He still didn't want to forgive *this*. Well, sort of, but not entirely.

Ellincreo spoke more clearly yet. *Didn't I forgive you when you falsely accused me of killing your mother?*

He had to bring that up. Caverns, there'd be no peace until Jaikon did this. And did it completely. He blew a long breath out over the top of her bowed head.

Jaikon slipped his fingers beneath her chin and lifted until she met his eyes. "I forgive you."

A shaky sigh escaped her, and she rested her head against his chest.

Awareness of her permeated him. When had he wrapped his arm around her? He had to comfort her, but he also had to stop this intense—he wasn't even sure what this feeling was. Or how to stop it.

Bits of leaves in her hair caught his attention, and he started to laugh. She drew back as he pulled one out and showed it to her. "Who would have thought that wind weaving was almost as dirty as mining?"

She uttered a little chuckle and pulled something from his hair. "I didn't realize that the men of Dirklan adorned themselves with pine needles."

"It's a new fashion I'm starting. Or maybe I should say that *you* are starting." Irate voices reached them from the street. "I don't think it's going to be an instant success." He grew serious. "I still don't know that I understand. If that was a vision from Ellincreo, why did he show it to us?"

"It must have been to prepare us in some way. Perhaps to give us a glimpse of what needs to be done." She looked disgusted with herself. "I should have realized. It's not in Ellincreo's nature to show us the faults of others. Since he showed *both* of us that vision, it must be because of what we need to accomplish. *Together*." She tilted her head with a hint of dawning comprehension. "I'm the most gifted wind weaver in generations, but if an air channel is fully blocked, I won't be able to find it without your help."

So much in what she said sparked both answers and more questions. For once, he felt like he could safely say anything to her. Ask her anything.

The roof's access panel slid back. No! Not an interruption now!

Bella came up onto the roof, accompanied by Charlis. Agriben's apprentice hung back, looking unsure of his welcome.

Much as he wanted to send them away, Jaikon said, "Lady Fanteal, may I introduce Charlis Torgan. He is an apprentice to Chief Former Agriben." Hopefully, she understood that only the highly gifted could apprentice to a provincial chief.

Charlis bowed. "It is a pleasure to meet you, Ambassador. Forgive me for intruding without an invitation."

Fanteal offered a friendly smile. "I would say it is good timing rather than intrusion. Jaikon and I were just speaking of our desire to meet with Agriben."

"You may carry our invitation to him to dine with us," Jaikon added. "Do you know if he is available this evening?"

"I believe so. Is it, by any chance, related to the, uh, strange winds we've been having?"

"No," Fanteal replied. "I am far more interested in the winds you do *not* have."

Charlis's brows shot up, but it was Bella who responded. "Everyone else sees the opposite. I happened to meet Charlis in the Tea House. We've known one another for years, so we were *trying* to talk. But the place is swarming with, well, speculation, to put it mildly. If they weren't asking me what you were doing, lady, they were asking Charlis whether we were about to suffer a collapse."

"You set their minds at rest, I hope," Jaikon said to Charlis.

"Certainly, but there was no way to answer their questions."

"Lady Fanteal was simply clearing a couple of the channels that provide us fresh air. Nothing very remarkable. You are welcome to join us for dinner along with Agriben."

A smile crept through Charlis's formal demeanor. "I'll inform him of your invitation, and we'll see you at dinner."

He left, and Jaikon turned to Bella with a wry smirk. "I feel like I owe you an apology. I had no idea that sending you out for a break would drop you into a swarm of conjecture."

"I'll have to get used to that."

"Maybe," Fanteal said, "it wouldn't be so bad if they could talk *to* me instead of asking *about* me. You did say, Jaikon, that you would take me to the Tea House someday. Is this the moment?"

Didn't she know what she was asking for? Or was she that courageous? He remembered the day in the square. Courageous. "If you're ready."

"As ready now as I will ever be."

"May I come with you?" Bella asked.

Jaikon grinned at her. "Not fed up enough?"

"Oh, I am. But I can't bear it if they all end up knowing more than I do."

CHAPTER 21

Fanteal stepped through the Tea House door, which Jaikon held open for her. A sudden hush spread from the front of the long room to the back.

A man behind the counter on one side turned, his brow lifted in question. Then his smile stretched, and he hurried forward.

"Lady Fanteal," Jaikon said, "this is Dillent, the proprietor of the Tea House."

Dillent bowed. "Ambassador, I cannot tell you what a delight it is to welcome you. Please let me find you a seat."

Behind him, a waiter swiftly wiped a circular table in the center of the room, and another rearranged chairs. Dillent led them to the table and held a chair for Fanteal. He nodded to Jaikon and Bella, but addressed Fanteal first. "What may I serve you, lady?"

"I would like pyret," she said, careful to use her mother's accent on a word that was utterly foreign aboveground.

"Ah, so you know of it, do you?" he replied. "Sir Nirundale always ordered a supply of it the week before the passage was opened."

"Yes, he brought it to my mother, for it is not grown in Welcia above. Did you know Trissina Nirundale?"

Background chatter had been building, and a couple voices asserted that they knew Trissina. This entire event would be a group discussion, of that Fanteal was sure.

"Only a little," Dillent said. "I was working my first job in one of the Fountain Avenue tea shops when she left. I served her occasionally, but I lack the effrontery to claim that I knew her." The background assertions ended as a waiter slipped a loaded tray onto the table in front of him. He poured for his three guests, then sat in the empty chair. "However, I am honored to be her tea supplier," he added with a wink, "and to give her a taste of her first home. What kind of tea will your father send to you?"

"None, I think." She stirred sugar into her pyret. "I'm rather fond of mint tea, but he knows it grows here. There is another reminder of my first home that my mother also told me to expect belowground."

"What is that?"

"The smell of the sea. She told me that the ocean breeze blows through Jourendia."

His brows rose, as did comments in the room. Everything from "nonsense" to "indeed, it used to" circled between the tables.

"Do you remember it?" Fanteal asked her host.

"Now that you mention it, vaguely. It sort of faded away. I haven't even thought of it in years."

"I finally found it this afternoon, though it took a great deal of searching."

Someone at the next table asked, "You don't mean that dreadful stench, do you?"

"No." She laughed. "That was rather awful, wasn't it? Some birds had blocked the inlet. I pushed their guano and nests into the sea."

"Well, I hope you don't intend to do that anymore," someone said. "There's a coating of dust over every inch of Jourendia. What was that collapse above Dirklan House all about?"

A sing-song voice complained, "Why is everything so dramatic with you? Collapse, indeed. It was just a little dirt."

"True enough, but what's so great about having dirt fall on us?"

"Oh, hush and let her answer," a woman said.

Fanteal hurried to squeeze a word in. "It didn't fall on anyone. I drew it down into an empty backstreet. There are air channels in the roof of the cavern. Some have gotten blocked, so the air has stagnated. That allowed even more dirt to collect. Once I get them reopened, the wind will keep the air clean and fresh."

"Wind! We don't have wind in Dirklan, except when the passage is opened. And mighty unpleasant that is!"

"That's only once or twice a year," another replied. "Stay inside if you don't like it. I, for one, remember the breezes we used to have, and I'd love to feel them again."

"She could at least have asked first. Has the council approved this?"

Fanteal's eyes rounded. Didn't these people know history or law?

Jaikon cleared his throat. "Remember that law forbids the council from controlling the substance gifts. Ambassador Fanteal did, however, discuss the state of the air channels with Sir Mikkael. Like any sane person, he agrees that our air should be clean. Regardless, the prime minister would never prevent those gifted by Ellincreo from using their gift."

An irate voice started speaking near the back, but Dillent spoke over it. "The prime minister. Now there, you bring something to mind. Lady Fanteal, there is one thing that everyone has been wondering about more than all else. I do hope you don't mind my asking, but I just can't stand hearing any more speculation."

She gave him a wry smile. "Then ask, for I doubt your question will surprise me."

"Did Prime Minister Nirundale really know you're a wind weaver?"

"Absolutely. He would ask me to demonstrate it for him every year and took pleasure in my developing skills. He used words like *air*, *wind*, and *weaving*. He never spoke to me of streaming, never asked me to move water."

"I told you so," someone nearby said in an under-voice. "Sir Nirundale wouldn't have sent for wind records if he thought a streamer was coming."

Murmured conversations spread around the room. Dillent ignored them. "What did he have in mind?"

She shook her head. "I very much wish I knew. Expectations were never even hinted. He always asked my brother, Telamien, to demonstrate his streaming gift, too, so I simply thought he was interested in the things we cared about. No different from my grandmother aboveground while she still lived. When Sir Nirundale talked of my future, he spoke of the domains and the matters of life in Dirklan."

Fanteal sipped her tea amid the resuming conversations. Too many revolved around the annoyance of wind.

"Has your tea cooled?" Dillent asked, "or is the taste not to your liking? I can bring you mint tea if you prefer?"

Oh, she was frowning. She cleared her expression. "It's not that. But this idea people have—that air should be still. It's so very unnatural."

"It must be hard to get used to Dirklan," he replied with a sympathetic smile. "Especially when you are used to the gales that Deltum and Tershel described."

"Wind isn't usually so harsh. That was just because of the forces needed to open the passage. But still, it is normal for air to move."

"And it's so thick there, too," he said. "But you'll soon grow used to it here. Perhaps you'll even wonder why you used to prefer it so dense and restless."

She only regarded him.

"Did I offend you?"

"No. I like to hear what people think. Yet your ancestors once breathed dense, moving air."

"True, but we got used to it this way."

"Used to it, yes. People can get used to a great many things. But that doesn't prove they are desirable."

Before he could answer, someone else approached the table. "If you'll permit me, Ambassador, I'd like to ask you something."

From the corner of her eye, she caught Jaikon's expression hardening. "What do you wish to know?"

"What do you have against the Nirundales?"

Fanteal let her voice carry surprise. "Nothing."

"Then, why don't you wish to bear their name?"

Jaikon's chair scraped backwards, but Fanteal answered before he could. "Odd questions. My full name is Fanteal Nirundale de Noviam, so you see, I already do bear that name."

The speaker scowled. The room's silence felt brittle. "I meant by marriage."

"That's another oddity," Fanteal said. "Neither my parents nor grandfather ever suggested that I marry my cousin. How it came to be expected here, has me quite puzzled."

A man at the back of the room stood and left money on the table. "Well, it's nice to know there's common sense aboveground. Why anyone here thinks it's their business whom she marries is yet another puzzle." He made his way toward the door as he spoke, pausing by Fanteal's table to give her a bow. "It's a pleasure to see your health improving, Ambassador."

He continued on his way, and the first speaker bowed despite looking disgruntled. "Thanks for your answer." He stepped back, and conversation again swirled through the room.

Dillent leaned forward and folded his hands on the table. "I do hope," he said quietly, "that none of this has given you a distaste for my humble establishment."

She flicked a smile. "Humble?" He chuckled, and she joined him. "Jaikon told me days ago that I would find plenty of debate within these walls."

"This is true. Unless some fool gets slanderous, every opinion is fair here. And you, lady, will always be welcome."

Even with guests, dinner was served in a single course. Tonight, they followed it with dessert drinks in the salon. Something else for Fanteal to learn, for she had no idea what this concoction was. Thick, with a touch of sweetness and a spice like cinnamon, yet different. She would ask Bella later. The young woman was a treasure, ready to answer any question and able to explain nuances that Fanteal didn't know to ask about. Maid, aide, and friend.

This salon was arranged in a more informal, family style, allowing all six of them to relax without any hint of status. Though the chairs were made of stone, they were so intricately carved and polished that Fanteal could imagine their beige and brown frames to be wood. The ample linen cushions, dyed in varied shades of blue, aqua, and green, hinted at an outdoorsy look that she missed.

Agriben plumped the back cushion of his chair and leaned into it as he returned to their earlier conversation. "Now that you've explained the condition of the air channels and your ability to clean them, I am certain that Sir Nirundale knew our air supply is compromised. Also that he expected you to resolve the problem."

"I believe so," Fanteal replied. "It's really the only explanation that fits his actions."

Sir Mikkael set his drink aside. "I'm planning to give a speech on this soon. I've discussed the air situation with medics Prenard and Malca, who are willing to emphasize the benefits of fresh, moving air. I'll explain Sir Nirundale's preparations and my appreciation for the wind weaver gift. Two consecutive prime ministers agreeing to the work should help silence those who object to the gift they have forgotten."

"It seems so strange to me," Fanteal said. "Wandermae's story is still read aboveground. I would have thought it would be even more important down here."

Agriben shrugged. "Perhaps because formers are so much more common belowground. Although Wandermae found the air channels, Greehan opened them. I assume you need a former also. Charlis told me that he sensed a former, whom he didn't recognize, at the same time that you were clearing Jourendia's channels."

Fanteal looked to Charlis. "Can you sense all the gifts too?"

"No, but I can sense other formers particularly well. Did you notice one active, and...by any chance, could you tell if he was active because of what you were doing?" He dipped his head. "I know it's unlikely, so please pardon my odd question."

How much should she say, since Jaikon didn't want his forming gift mentioned? Could she avoid it? "Most certainly, I felt the former—and needed his aid, for I cannot directly sense the debris clogging the channels."

Charlis widened his eyes. "You mean...you were working with a former...intentionally?"

"It was I," Jaikon said, reluctance oozing from the short sentence. Both Agriben and Charlis stared at him open-mouthed. "Don't worry. I wasn't forming, only sensing and mapping."

"You're a former?" Agriben couldn't have sounded more astonished. "I've never once seen you at a Formers' Guild meeting."

"Rather pointless. I cannot manipulate matter. Just sense so far that my range couldn't even be confirmed. Northeshur's chief former gave up on training me."

Agriben snorted. "Nedford! As opinionated as he is skilled at polishing. Which is saying a lot on both counts."

Jaikon angled his head in a noncommittal motion.

"Reach up through the cavern roof," Agriben ordered.

Fanteal could sense all three formers active, though they didn't even look up.

"Reach on toward Crysalan." Agriben angled an irritated look toward Charlis and Fanteal. "If the two of you don't mind!"

Fanteal jerked her awareness back. At least Charlis looked as sheepish as she felt.

"The primary cavern is here," Jaikon said, "and the market cavern here. Do you want me to name the rail spurs?"

"No, it's obvious you're there. Reach toward buried LourEstelle."

A few seconds passed before Jaikon spoke again. "I cannot get to the far side of LourEstelle from Jourendia, but the access arches and the scree that buried them is in this area." He looked at Agriben. "But I can no longer feel you there with me, so I can say anything I want to about it and never be proven."

Agriben's lips were tight. "Charlis, reach with us."

The three of them were silent for a moment, then Charlis said, "I can sense where you fade out, Chief Former, but just barely. I might reach a hundred yards beyond, if that."

Jaikon squinted. "Maybe eighty, but you are both quite nebulous after the Crysalan caverns."

Agriben leaned forward, gripping the arms of his chair. He appeared more excited than bothered to find a former who could best his range. "You're coming with me to the sealed tunnels."

"If you want me to reach through Mount Estelle, there's no need. I assessed it from aboveground."

Agriben's pitch rose as high as his gravelly voice allowed. "And?"

"More fizrock than anything. It's riddled with fissures, tiny voids, and crushed rock. That volcano produced nothing like ipenrock. Believe me, I wanted to find a tunnel route, but I couldn't. And I *did* sense through the entire mountain."

"So..." Agriben sniffed. "You are not among those who claim that over a hundred years of stability means we can safely tunnel now."

Jaikon shook his head emphatically. "There are stress points in the mountain." He shifted in his chair. "I don't mean to speak out of turn. I never did an apprenticeship, but I did study with the Formers' Guild in my teen years. When I was aboveground, I found the debris field that was associated with the collapse of LourEstelle. It was huge. Enormous. There is no way we could tunnel below without requesting approval from the formers above. Even though I have no credentials, I would have to tell them that I believe it is unsafe."

Agriben's lips twisted downward. "That is your obligation, since you are gifted." He huffed. "I have to admit I'm somewhat annoyed that you didn't apprentice, Nedford's biases notwithstanding."

"No one else would have taken me on either. I cannot identify types of ore, nor can I cut or drop stone. I can neither alter nor etch matter."

"And yet you can sense structural stress and density at incredible distances. Even in Devron's day, when long range was a primary requirement of chief formers, I don't think anyone could reach from Jourendia to the access arches."

"I know, but they *could* manipulate matter within a portion of their range. I cannot."

Agriben grunted. "I won't pretend to understand why your gift is so odd, but Lady Fanteal says she needs your aid. I expect you to provide it to her." He looked to Fanteal. "What do you plan? Simply clear channels that Greehan formed, or do you need new channels created?"

"I won't know until I have checked each domain. Any caverns hewn after Wandermae designed the airflow might need new channels. Also, I cannot find fully blocked channels, because the air will not move. This would all be so much easier if records of the channels could be found."

"If Greehan was mapping them," Agriben said, "those records were likely lost when he was murdered. We may have little to go on, but I am leaving for Crysalan tomorrow. If I can find anything useful, I'll have it ready when you arrive."

"Thank you."

Agriben turned to Charlis. "Change of plans for you. Stay in Jourendia and assist Lady Fanteal in whatever she needs. Also learn about Jaikon's gift."

Charlis uttered a faint sound in his throat, quickly silenced. He wiped surprise from his face. "Yes, Chief Former."

Jaikon rolled his eyes and said dryly, "Don't worry, Charlis. It won't take you more than an hour to learn about my gift."

Agriben glowered at Jaikon. "Apparently, you can assess a mountain, so I imagine you can assess an air channel. If Charlis needs to carve any in the future, he will need someone on hand to assess them." He darted a glance to Charlis. "Make sure he knows how, then prove the skill here. I'll confirm it when he comes to Crysalan. Also, figure out a way to map what he can sense and you cannot."

CHAPTER 22

Jaikon looked over Fanteal's shoulder as she pointed out an entry in one of the books on the library table.

"This winter reference to a western inflow confirms that we haven't found all the air channels yet. We'll need to search that way."

West. She said it as though she'd told him exactly where to look.

In the doorway, a page cleared his throat. "Charlis has arrived and asked to see you, sir."

"You may bring him up here." Jaikon's inner defenses rose, and the former wasn't even in the room yet.

Charlis soon entered. "Pleasant morning."

They returned his formal greeting.

He stood rather stiff. "I admit, lady, to not having any idea what I should be doing to help you. Or when, so I thought I should check in first."

"First, before what?" Fanteal asked.

"Well, Agriben just left. Which means I have to leave the Fountain Inn too, and I'll need to find another spot to stay. It would be useful if I knew how long until you leave for your tour."

"Oh. I don't know." Fanteal rolled her lips and looked to Jaikon. "Perhaps it would be easier if he just stayed here."

Little though Jaikon wanted a former residing in the house, he couldn't ignore a hint that strong. He turned to Charlis. "You are welcome to stay in Dirklan House if it suits you."

His lips parted. "I...I didn't mean to sound like I was begging for a room."

"You didn't." Jaikon waved toward several bookcases. "These contain what records Sir Nirundale was able to gather in preparation for our wind weaver's arrival. You are welcome to study them, though I'll warn you right now, wind records are *nothing* like former records."

Fanteal chuckled. "Ask me if they are too obscure. I realized yesterday that the more we understand each other's gifts, the better. But for now, I've discovered a reference to a winter inflow to the west. I want to find those channels before we set out from Jourendia."

Charlis cocked his head. "Wouldn't that negate the inflow from the ocean inlet?"

Jaikon caught the quick lift of Fanteal's brows. At least he wasn't the one asking the silly question this time.

"Wind is not a river," Fanteal said. "Not forced to seek the lowest point. A channel can carry air in either direction."

"Oh. But...we don't need it to switch, do we?"

Fanteal skipped the surprised look this time. "Our primary wind is out of the southeast, but in winter it shifts around, coming from the southwest or even from direct west. The ocean inlet—ah, no—the ocean *channel* is in a cliff face, which will block it during part of the winter. So yes, the airflow direction will switch at times, and the channels must accommodate that."

"Ah."

Oh, the look on Charlis's face. Jaikon had felt that sort of ignorance enough times to sympathize. Not much, for this former would doubtless make Jaikon feel ignorant in other ways. "If we are going to look for west-facing channels, let's get up to the roof."

On the way, Jaikon sent someone to tell Colrin about their houseguest. Soon, they gathered around the rooftop table that held the map of Jourendia and its surroundings. Fanteal didn't even look at it, and Jaikon recognized the distant expression that meant she was weaving her beloved wind. He bent over the map with Charlis and pointed out what he had marked. "The ocean channel is here. I suspect an iron grate within, if you'd like to confirm that."

Though Charlis's gaze fixed on the map, Jaikon sensed him reaching across the cavern to the ocean channel. "Well marked," Charlis said. An etching of it began to appear in the upper layer of the map. "Yes, iron and quite rusty. I'll let the local formers know they need to add it to their maintenance routine."

Not five minutes, and Charlis was demonstrating all the things Jaikon couldn't do. Laughter from Fanteal interrupted his internal grumping. He stepped to her side. "What is it?"

"The ocean eagles are back. And oh, are they mad at me!"

"Serves them right."

"Regissa's chief wind weaver is active there too. I'm guessing she's right atop the cliff. I told you they would notice."

"That, you did. Is there any chance you can be more specific than simply *west* for these channels you'd like to find?"

She strolled with a swaying movement. Was her grace born of her gift? Lovely either way. He caught the subtle sounds that indicated air testing the surface of the cavern face. How would Charlis react?

He still bent over the map. Oblivious.

Good. At least there was something he didn't know. Jaikon began his own search, just to get the overall feel of the westward mass of ipenrock encasing Jourendia's caverns.

Charlis suddenly exclaimed, "Do you sense that?"

What did he look so excited over? He was still sensing through the ocean channel, so Jaikon followed. "What do you notice?"

"Chains!" He grinned, still intent. "Oh, yes. A mesh of iron chains. Broad spaces, but the formers above must know the bird size well enough to keep them out. They've dropped them from above, and I believe...yes, they are anchored atop the cliff." His grin stretched wider. "I've contacted the aboveground former. If he can sense emotion like most of us, he absolutely knows how happy I am about their barrier."

Like most of us. Jaikon sensed upward through the cliff until rock met the void, but encountered no former's touch. Perhaps they focused on the chain barrier rather than the mass beneath their feet. No consolation.

Charlis jerked his head back. "Wow! One of those birds must be attacking the chains."

"Yes, I can hear them screaming," Fanteal said. "Is the chain structure withstanding them?"

He nodded. "It's far too heavy for them to lift. Whoever made it knew what creature he was dealing with."

Fanteal turned her back on the ocean channel. "That problem was solved quicker than I expected. Let's see about the western channels." The joy in her face dimmed as she glanced at Jaikon.

She probably expected him to feel the same excitement they did, so he forced a smile. "Were you able to find any likely places to search?"

"Perhaps. Give me a few more minutes."

Jaikon waited, delving the rock again while she looked. He became aware of a faint presence flickering about. Charlis was no longer fixated on the map. Was that him trying for...what?

After a few minutes, Charlis stepped to Jaikon's side. "I can feel you there. Your range is quite broad."

He wasn't even feeling it all if those scattered touches were any indication. Jaikon didn't answer—even when peripheral vision told him Charlis was looking at him.

Charlis murmured, "I know what it's like to have an unusual gift. One that is not appreciated."

"Do you?"

"Some hate it that I can identify what specific formers are doing while a group is working together. I only talk about it if there is some need to do so. Otherwise, formers don't want me around…like they feel watched or something."

"Mm."

"Well, anyway, I just wanted you to know that I get how uncomfortable it is to be different."

Jaikon turned his head to look Charlis in the eye. "You just likened your enhanced gift to my woefully lacking gift. No, you don't get it."

Charlis opened and closed his mouth.

Fanteal pointed. "If you could use the enhanced part of your woefully lacking gift to look for a channel over that way, I'd appreciate it."

He suppressed an urge to growl. He was almost angry that he found the channel, blockage and all, within minutes.

They proceeded much like they had yesterday. During the morning, they cleared three channels, and Charlis etched their locations into the map's top layer. Charlis's ability to ensure that debris fell safely also eased a worry. Not that Jaikon wanted to admit it.

Bella accompanied a delivery of lunch trays, which prompted Fanteal's odd habit of looking at her bracelet. Jaikon's stomach applauded, and a glance at the hour markers confirmed they had lost track of the time. After he and Charlis got the map out of the way, the four of them sat around the rooftop table to share the meal. A welcome break. Less welcome, Fanteal expressed her appreciation to Charlis.

Jaikon hid a sigh. Sometimes he thought he'd gotten past the blemish of his freakish gift. The mere presence of a skilled polisher proved him wrong. Though Fanteal also thanked him, it didn't mean much. She didn't know what was expected of a former. Besides, Jaikon found channels best when she pointed out an opening within Jourendia's cavern.

Barely thinking about it, he spread his forming sense wide. *Could* he find channels on his own? What if a new cavern needed a channel where none existed? He took note of the lay of ipenrock near the channels they knew of...searched out the overall structure, reached deep through the vast mass...found the curve of the harbor walls, then the extension of the peninsula.

Jaikon pointed. "Fanteal, is there any sign of an air channel to the southeast? Along the peninsula rather than through the cliffs over the harbor?"

She wiped her fingers on a napkin, though he was sure she focused distantly. "Not that I can tell...although I'm not quite sure where to look. Any air I push that way just wants to head out the ocean channel. Why do you ask?"

"Just noticed some density variations. Nothing important." Once again, no value to what his gift revealed. Odd about the peninsula though.

Within days, Charlis declared Jaikon's assessments proven. He hardly knew if he should be elated or furious with Nedford.

"Really," he told his father during their daily meeting, "I'm amazed at how easy an assessment is. It's all about structural stability. I detect that at the first glance."

"How did Chief Former Nedford fail to notice you could do it?"

Jaikon huffed. "He never let me try. Assessing is important. I couldn't do the simple, ordinary tasks, so he didn't let me advance."

His father leaned back in his chair, sliding a pen through his fingers. "I now entertain serious doubts about Nedford's judgment. Are you interested in apprenticing under a different former—one who isn't obsessed with polishing?"

Jaikon shuddered. Join the half-grown at his age? Most of whom could probably polish a chair to his shape while he lowered himself into it? Never! "Don't even think about it. If I had to assess the quality of detailed workmanship, I'd be lost. Nedford was right about that. Nor does Charlis nudge me in that direction."

"Does he criticize your gift?"

"No. He's too determined not to talk about my limitations."

"You think too much of them as it is." His father handed him scribed notes. "Today's session."

Jaikon took them, a rough copy of the council's debate and decisions. Hard to focus, for it always irked him when a non-former spoke as though he viewed his gift wrong. He forced himself to attend while his father told him of the nuances that were not in the notes—mostly the underlying challenges of initiatives and those who obstructed or championed proposals.

"Governor Nirundale," his father said, "actually agreed with Governor Armeen today. A minor point, but watch Nirundale's alliances now that his support is eroding in Jourendia."

Uhf. All these details that a prime minister's son must be aware of. So much more to his role than he had envisioned before the election.

As they headed to the dining room, they joined Fanteal and Bella near the stairs. Jaikon's father offered Fanteal his arm as they descended. "I must tell you of my walk through the square today. I chanced upon Malca Barran, who was watching the children play. By the delighted look on his face, I thought he must have some young relative among them. Not so. He told me there has been a distinct change in the children's energy level since you cleared the air channels. They play longer and more vigorously."

She uttered a joyful squeak and added little hops to her next few steps.

Sir Mikkael chuckled before continuing. "Malca said every medic in Jourendia is now your firm supporter. He's traveling with us to Crysalan, and then on to the School of Health to report on the benefits of clearing air channels."

"Excellent! One less battle to fight during my tour."

"Indeed. I plan to talk with the Chief Keeper of the Writ when we arrive in Crysalan tomorrow. This news is certainly worthy to be shared during the Savoring Day service."

"I cannot wait to see the sacred chamber." Fanteal danced into the dining room, ending with a spin. She stopped, facing Jaikon's father. "Why do you stare? Am I breaking some etiquette?"

"Not at all, my dear. Such a short time ago, you could barely walk. Now you dance."

His father was right. Jaikon would keep *this* relief in mind no matter what was said at the Savoring Day service.

They gathered around the table. Colrin joined them this evening as well as Bella and Charlis. The talk centered around their upcoming trip. A new experience for Fanteal. Common for Jaikon, but he'd enjoy seeing her reactions.

His wandering attention returned to the conversation when Charlis surprised him with a comment about the high number of air channels. Fanteal would never agree.

She shook her head in broad sweeps. "I just don't understand Dirklians' barely-enough attitude. *One* passage to aboveground, with travel once, maybe twice, a year. As though that is enough despite the blatant lack of communication. *One* river brings you fish, *one* import tunnel. I'm actually surprised that you bother with two export tunnels. Only *one* domain grows enough food to sell it in other domains. If any of these fail, you expect dire consequences. Yet in all these years, you have never created another access tunnel."

"It's not that easy," Charlis said.

"I know." Impatience edged her tone. "And Mount Estelle is unstable. But most of Dirklan is not under the mountain."

"True, but that alone doesn't make it suitable. The old access tunnel ran horizontally out of LourEstelle. In a manner of speaking, it was within the mountain rather than under it. We don't have that landform anywhere else. There have been other failed attempts."

She rolled her lips. "I have seen the depression aboveground from one of those attempts. Doubtless there are aspects that I, a non-former, cannot understand. But the idea of continuing to rely on a barely adequate supply system still mystifies me. And I am being generous in calling it barely adequate."

She was right, of course. Everyone agreed that their food supplies were stretched to the snapping point, though lately it seemed a taboo subject. Surprising that she brought it up, for air was her sole passion. Something he tried hard to accept. Odd that she proposed a tunnel. Jaikon knew all the reasons it couldn't be done. Not from his own gift, but from the true formers. Only they possessed the knowledge. They had to be right.

Even as he thought it, the obvious assumptions writhed into knots. Were they right? What if a tunnel really was the only option left to Dirklan? What if the only reason it wasn't worth the risk, had been the fact that they didn't need it? A swiftly faltering fact. The image of what he'd sensed within the peninsula made him completely unaware of the food he ate.

Only when his plate was bare did he notice how Fanteal and Charlis leaned near one another in conversation. Heat overtook him. He needed to get out of this room. The moment he could excuse himself, he headed up to the roof.

The door panel slid shut at his feet. He glanced around, relieved that none of the staff had come up to relax at day's end. He took a moment to stroll and shake off the irritation he couldn't name. A breeze flowed. Odd that he found it welcome.

He reached the northeast corner of the roof, stopping just out of sight from the streets. Formers would not be working now. Fewer to notice him reaching deep within the ipenrock beyond the eastern wall. Analyzing...searching out the density variations...following them. A dead end...then another. Turning inland was no good. Farther and farther, he searched. Well beyond the harbor cliffs, extending through the peninsula. Ever rising. Reaching the surface.

Tingles prickled along his shoulders and neck with every hint that this was possible. And died with every doubt. Why was he bothering? If he told another former he'd found a potential tunnel route through ipenrock...no, he wasn't dealing with another load of scorn.

CHAPTER 23

Fanteal accepted Jaikon's hand and stepped from the train carriage at the Crysalan station. She glanced down, looking for the live magnery rod. There it was, barely visible between carriages. She was still a little nervous of it, for one touch could kill a person. Strange that such a danger was tolerated, though according to her mother, horses killed more people aboveground than magnery did below. Her mother had been right about the comfort too. The train ride had been incredibly smooth. The motion created a steady breeze, for all carriages were open in Dirklan.

"How is the air?" Bella asked.

"Not great, but not too bad. I even detect a hint of the ocean. Can you smell it?"

Bella shook her head.

"I suppose not," Fanteal said. "Let me know if you hear any comments that the air has improved. It flows, in part, from Jourendia, so it ought to be better than it was." She glanced over the plaza. "Is it always this crowded?"

"Only on the holidays," Jaikon replied, stopping beside his father near the steps that led down from the platform. He whispered a tease. "Or when ambassadors arrive. Time for a little waving."

Fanteal's smile needed no urging, for the welcome was quite touching. She addressed the crowd, using her gift to spread her voice so she could keep her tone conversational. She shared a greeting from King Darinneth and another from Queen Ambassador Trissina, confirmed her own commitment to Dirklan, and ended it with thanks for their warm welcome.

Sir Mikkael also addressed them briefly, then the crowd began to disperse.

Fanteal waited between the Mikkaels, surveying the broad plaza and imagining the scenes from her history book. Atrocities had played out here after the collapse of LourEstelle. Including the mob murder of Provincial Chief Wind Weaver Wandermae and of Former Greehan who had helped her. Where were the bronze statues of them? Her mother had said they stood in the plaza. As the people went on their way, she spotted one near Crysalan Hall. "I'd like to see the statues, please."

"I'll escort you." Jaikon guided her down the steps as his father headed elsewhere with others of their travel party. Bella followed Fanteal, for she was now formally known as the ambassador's aide, and Charlis fell into step beside her.

They approached the life-size statue of a man. Greehan, obviously, rather than Wandermae. A flowering bush overflowed from an ornate stone tub beside it. Unusual to find a purely ornamental plant belowground, but the fragrance seemed a fitting tribute. Fanteal took a moment to remember Greehan's sacrifice and honor him in her heart.

Jaikon held silence too, but Charlis came to her side, gesturing to the statue. "This is Greehan, the former who opened air channels after the collapse, thereby saving all of Dirklan from slow suffocation."

Fanteal nodded and waited, but he made no reference to Wandermae. She looked at him and found no intent on his face to continue. "I know the story," she said, "but understand the value of speaking it. Are you going to tell the rest?"

His eyes shifted beneath puckered brows. "Uh, he had to do it in secret, because all forming had been forbidden. When they discovered who did it, the mayor stirred up the mob and they killed him. Especially tragic since he saved their lives."

Worse than his first brief statement. Fanteal couldn't think what to say—other than an alienating rebuke.

Jaikon filled the breach. "She meant the part about Wandermae."

"Oh!" Charlis's perplexed look faded. "Yes. She, um…I guess she helped him find the air channels. They—"

Fanteal held up a hand. "Please don't explain anything else." She looked all around as she spoke. "Jaikon, where is the statue of Wandermae?"

"I…don't recall ever seeing it."

"They moved it," a woman's voice said, "back when I was just a girl."

The others looked around, for no one stood near enough to speak so softly and still be heard.

Fanteal didn't need to search. The woman, a dozen yards away, had lifted her voice as only a wind weaver could. "At last…" Fanteal whispered, sending her voice in reply, "…I have found another weaver."

The woman approached. The look on her face, Fanteal could understand in part. Relief to find a fellow wind weaver, and yet she looked…worn down. Creases near the drooping trend of her mouth hinted that she might be nearing her forties. She curtsied and said, "I am honored to meet you, Ambassador Fanteal."

"I am equally delighted to meet you. Your name, please?"

"Audrea. If you'd like to see the statue of Wandermae, it's in the loft dwelling that used to be her home. I can show you the way."

"That would be lovely."

"Uh…" She twined her fingers. "Would it be all right if only you came?"

That would never ride on the breeze, but what could Fanteal say? And why did it matter?

Jaikon cleared his throat. "I must accompany her. I am Jaikon Mikkael, son of the prime minister."

"Mm, well, at least you know that Wandermae existed."

Bella picked up on the hint. "Please excuse us, Lady Fanteal. I must see to arrangements." She turned away, saying, "Will you come with me, Charlis?"

Audrea led Fanteal and Jaikon across the plaza, then down streets between four-story buildings, always angling toward one side of the cavern. A few times, she whistled softly, giving the notes flight with her gift. As they neared the cavern wall, Fanteal noticed a long diagonal slash running up it. Reaching the base, she realized it was a staircase carved into the wall itself. Four feet of stone shielded the steps on the open side, but enough light shone over the half-wall to glint off reflective quartz wearing thin on the steps' edges.

Audrea ascended the first few stairs and looked over her shoulder. "A long climb, I'm afraid. I hope that's all right."

"How is the air?" Jaikon asked.

"Been growing richer lately," Audrea said, apparently thinking he was asking her. She smiled at Fanteal. "Was that your doing?"

"Yes." Fanteal looked to Jaikon. "I have found a clear channel to draw from. I should be fine."

He offered his arm anyway, and she slipped her hand into the crook. The ceiling of the staircase barely allowed Jaikon to stand upright as they followed Audrea. At the top, the half wall leveled, forming one side of a large room. Fanteal rested her forearms on the wall and looked down on the rooftop gardens below. "What a perfect home for a wind weaver."

"I suppose so." Jaikon studied the high ceiling, an amber shade of quartz which glowed softly. "A polisher did a masterful job of diverting a light shaft."

Fanteal turned inward to discover what he meant, though another sight grabbed her attention. Against the back wall stood the statue she had sought. Assuming it was life-sized, Wandermae had been a slight woman, but her face was strong. She stood with her hands spread, one reaching higher in a wind weaver's gesture. The artist had rendered her long, curving locks as though a breeze were sweeping them aside, and a dove sat perched on her bare shoulder. Though the statue was bronze, somehow the dove was white, Wandermae's hair was black, and the irises of her eyes were a penetrating blue. "Stunning!"

Audrea gazed upon it reverently. "It is said that Devron himself formed and polished the statue."

"Easy to believe," Jaikon murmured. "Some of his art remains on display in Jourendia. He could alter metal to reflect colors beyond their natural hues. Even the door to his old home is a rich teal that I have never seen duplicated."

"Why is the statue up here?" Fanteal asked.

"On account of that so-called Keeper of the Writ, Scourtau." Audrea snarled his name. "It used to stand beside Greehan's where they put that bush. As though flowers can fill the gaping absence of the true hero."

That still made no sense. Maybe Fanteal could get a better explanation from Bella later. She took in the rest of the room. Bare except for two benches that seemed out of place against etched walls. Built-in soil pots stood empty at each end of the balcony. Trellises rising from them arched over the half wall within easy range for picking the fruit that must have grown here long ago. Closed doors in the back corners of the airy room seemed to hide secrets. "You say Wandermae lived here?"

"Yes. This was her welcome room..." Audrea gestured vaguely to the doors. "...with her private rooms back there. Nothing left in them but an ancient oil stove in the kitchen wall. Magnery was never brought this high."

Footsteps ran up the stairs and reached the top. The newcomer panted as she stared, awestruck. Fanteal sent the freshest air toward the young woman, who inhaled it rapturously. "Ah, lady, your gift is true."

"Ambassador Fanteal," Audrea said, "this is Lezzilie, who is also a weaver."

She curtsied. "It gives me great pleasure to meet you, lady."

"And to me as well." Fanteal glanced to Audrea. "Was your whistle a call to weavers? Are others coming?"

"Yes—at least I hope so."

Lezzilie shook her head. "I saw a couple heading this way, but they noticed..." She cast a nervous glance at Jaikon. "Well, they don't want their gift known. Not beyond the weavers, that is."

"Whyever not?" Fanteal demanded.

"They wouldn't be allowed to travel. One is from a market family. If she cannot travel through the domains, she'll lose her livelihood."

Cannot travel? "And the other?"

"Well, she's not twenty yet and still finding her way. Why risk her options by being tied down with a weaver's gift?"

Tied down? "I don't understand this at all. A wind weaver *must* travel."

"Not an option since Scourtau found that stupid book," Audrea said. "We cannot leave our domains, and if we say one word crosswise, there's no hearing the end of it."

"Who is this Scourtau, and what book are you talking about?"

Audrea sniffed. "He was the Chief Keeper of the Writ for a couple years before he died. Emfiduria caught him, I think. The book is *Wind Weaver Admonitions*. He found it in some archive and claimed it's part of the Holy Writ. Lots of arguing over it when I was too young to understand how much it would hurt me in the end." She slid her entwined fingers in and out while she spoke. "Ever since I heard you were a wind weaver..." Her furtive smile peeked out. "When everyone else was ranting that you were supposed to be a streamer, I was jumping for joy inside. I've been wondering what you might do."

"Clearing the air channels is my first priority, and I will reestablish the Wind Weavers' Guild, for something has clearly gone wrong. Perhaps this book is the cause, at least in part. I've got to get a look at that, for it is *not* among the Holy Writ books aboveground." She pivoted. "Jaikon, have you read it?"

"No, but with that title, it's probably only read to new weavers."

Audrea huffed. "Bits and pieces of it are sometimes read on Savoring Day. Especially if a weaver said something the keepers didn't like."

Lezzilie watched Jaikon with narrowed eyes. "I've heard you're devout."

Why did she pronounce *devout* like it meant *enemy*. What was going on here? "I also follow the words of Ellincreo," Fanteal said. "But not false words. And if this book is keeping wind weavers from using the gift Ellincreo granted them, I must question it. How many weavers are there in Crysalan, and how many share their gift?"

"Five that I know of," Audrea said. "Only us two are publicly known."

Fanteal shook her head. "Do you know how many are in the other domains?"

"How could I? I cannot leave Crysalan, and they cannot come here."

"Not even for the Gifting Day ceremony? Or for weddings?"

Audrea rocked her shoulders. "I wouldn't think so. If they dared come, they'd be hiding their gift, for sure. It's not easy. If we get denounced as a troublemaker in the sacred chamber one day, we're mocked or shunned for weeks and months."

"No wonder the air channels are compromised," Fanteal said. "The wind weavers cannot act."

"Well, we do pull fresh air through when it gets stale," Lezzilie explained. "Between us, we can usually check each cavern of Crysalan every week or two. I'm not sure what you mean, though, about clearing the channels."

"If they were clean, there would be a continuous flow. Does anyone pay you for your service?"

Lezzilie snorted. "Caverns, no!"

The champion spirit within Fanteal surged ever stronger. "Have you had enough? Are you ready to seize the freedom of your gift?"

Their eyes rounded, and they leaned back. Audrea gasped. "I cannot. I lift the voice of the Chief Keeper of the Writ and serve among the keepers. But I haven't studied the full Holy Writ, so I am forbidden to speak."

"What? Why?"

"Lest anyone mistakenly believes I speak for Ellincreo."

Jaikon frowned like he was as appalled as Fanteal. "What service is it that you do, beyond lifting his voice?"

"I work in the kitchen to prepare the common meals for the students."

Fanteal would hate that, but the palace cooks loved it. Did Audrea? "Is that enjoyable work to you?"

"I thought it would be, but it's nothing like preparing a delicious meal or trying new combinations. Just assembling the same things in the quickest way possible to fill bellies, then cleaning up and starting it all again." Audrea shrugged. "But I must earn a living, after all."

It seemed Audrea's life gift was as trammeled as her substance gift and her tongue. And Fanteal thought *she* had it bad. "Well, I have nothing to say about cooking, but plenty to say about wind weaving."

CHAPTER 24

Almost there. Footsteps echoed as they entered the tunnel. Fanteal had waited so long for this. Savoring Day in the sacred chamber. The cavern with the golden vision wall. The inspiration for the golden statues aboveground. There was nothing like it in all the kingdom.

Sir Mikkael escorted her, his retinue following. They stepped from the tunnel into the cavern, about two thirds of the way up the sloped floor, then traversed a wide aisle. All around, chairs clustered on irregular terraces edged with wrought iron railings. Formers of old had leveled them within the natural shape of the cavern floor. They turned to descend the center aisle.

Where was the vision wall? Fanteal had expected it to draw her eyes instantly. Shouldn't she see it by now?

There was the pool her mother had described, with the platform in front of it. Keepers of the Writ would speak from there, and musicians already gathered at one end, plucking strings to tune instruments. But behind the pool stood a twenty-foot wall draped in lush greenery. Vines perhaps, for they spilled from a garden atop the wall. Beyond the garden, she glimpsed the rounded peaks of the gem hills sparkling beneath light shafts. Pretty. But no vision wall.

How could this be? Surely, they hadn't mined out that pristine gold! Not when it had been dedicated forever to Ellincreo.

The disappointment ran so deep that her cheeks heated. They'd nearly reached the lowest terrace. Seats of honor—front and center. People stared at them. She mustn't let her distress show.

Sir Mikkael guided her to a chair, and she sat between him and Jaikon. The others filed past to take seats on their left. As soon as she could do so, she whispered into Jaikon's ear, "What has become of the golden vision wall?"

He inclined his head toward the pool. "It is there—behind the ivy. Don't you see the gold between the leaves?"

Barely! She made out glimmers here and there. More, the longer she studied it. At least it still existed, but *oh,* what a letdown! Her chest ached. "But how can one see?" she murmured.

Jaikon answered under his breath. "Visions are...a thing of the past." His final word twisted like he was choking. He swallowed hard, staring at the wall.

No wonder! The gaps sparked with golden light. Every leaf was etched in radiance. Then as quickly as it began—it was gone.

Jaikon exhaled, his face white.

Fanteal faked a casual look around, checking people's expressions. Not a one showed surprise or interest in the wall. She settled back in her chair and whispered, "I don't think anyone else saw it."

Jaikon moved his lips, but no sound reached her.

This was no time to discuss it, anyway. The Chief Keeper of the Writ, Thilleon, clad in a deep green robe and a bejeweled sash, strode onto the platform and began the Savoring Day service. It proceeded much like it would aboveground. A greeting, including acknowledgement of the ambassador and prime minister. Music. Then the offering of gratitude for recent events and accomplishments. The list grew long, and Fanteal began to wonder if he would even mention the improvements in air.

As time passed, she sensed with her gift. A wind weaver—Audrea, no doubt—was lifting the keeper's voice to the farthest reaches of the cavern. She was skillful enough to maintain even volume throughout and to dampen echoes from the distant ceiling. No other weaver was active. Fanteal stirred the vines with a subtle breeze, hoping weavers would notice and reach into the wind with her. None did.

The chief keeper cleared his throat and left a dramatic pause. "And now, I must share an unusual development. It seems that the air of Jourendia had grown stagnant over the years." Finally! "Lady Fanteal, being a wind weaver, has refreshed it for them. We offer gratitude on behalf of Jourendia. Doubtless they are savoring the freshened air in their gatherings today. Now, let us move on to savor a reading from the Holy Writ."

Fanteal's jaw drooped. That was it? All he had to say about the most important event in over two decades? She glanced at Sir Mikkael. His lips formed a thin line. It wasn't just her, then, thinking too much of herself. What to do?

The chief keeper announced the title of the reading, jerking her attention back. "Wind Weaver Admonitions."

Far down the terrace to her right, a man's voice growled, "Take care what you are about."

Fanteal recognized the voice. Governor Trezman of Crysalan. Audrea instantly dampened his words. Few would have heard. She must have orders.

The Chief Keeper made a palm-down gesture, and his words were barely audible. "You needn't worry. I've heard no hint of idolatry for me to rebuke."

The hand motion must be his cue to Audrea. Fanteal probably wouldn't even have heard the exchange if not for her own gift. At a stir to Fanteal's left, she glanced around. Bella had risen from her seat and hurried toward a narrow tunnel beyond the end of the platform. Where did that lead?

"Not that I believe," the Chief Keeper said with a humorous lilt, "that Lady Fanteal needs admonition." A few chuckles answered the mild jest. "However, I'm sure she'll want to hear the text for belowground wind weavers."

He began his reading with an introductory paragraph. The book looked thin. Still, was he going to read the whole thing? The text described how wind weavers would gather four times a year and wander through all the domains. Ah, the Guild had once thrived, but *wander*? Strange word choice, for they must have been working their gift. Then the reading grew much stranger.

It made no further reference to their gift or to air. Instead, it spewed accusations of gossip and igniting trouble, of deserting their families, and of extorting wages when they had performed no work.

Fanteal's nails bit into her palms. Her chest heaved until it was all she could do to keep her breath silent. Sir Mikkael gripped her knee. He wanted restraint, did he? Fine. She was a trained ambassador. She would consider her words before uttering them.

The Chief Keeper was a polished orator. Expressive intonations. Moving around the platform. Looking at his audience more than the book. But he never made eye contact with the front row. He flipped a stiff page. "Many of you know that the next section addresses individuals of days past, so I will skip to the closing directive." He flipped more pages, then resumed. "Wind weavers are to heed these rules or surrender their gift. They shall tend the work of their own homes and own domain. They shall not infringe upon any other domain, nor travel to them. They shall spread no tales between other wind weavers. If they discover a matter of importance, they shall take it to the lead Keeper of the Writ in their domain. The keepers shall judge the significance and deal with it by their wisdom."

The reading closed with a summation, but Fanteal was too furious to hear it.

Sir Mikkael dug his fingertips into her flesh. "Choose your moment and words wisely." Barely audible. He narrowed his eyes. "Is my voice being suppressed?"

"He has a wind weaver controlling what is heard. I can lift your voice if you speak." She looked to the side where she sensed the weaver. Bella had returned to the tunnel opening, but Fanteal still couldn't see Audrea. "He must keep her hidden."

The chief keeper closed the book and finally looked at them. "Lady Fanteal, I have already been assured that you are an earnest follower of Ellincreo. Therefore, as a wind weaver, no doubt we can trust you to follow this portion of the Holy Writ. Your position is unique, so if you would rather discuss important matters with me instead of Jourendia's lead keeper, please send me a message and I would be happy to come to you."

Her answer—that all of Dirklan was her home—was on the tip of her tongue. But something felt off. Like she was being led into a trap.

Sir Mikkael gave her a subtle tap, and she lifted his voice. "That will not be necessary," he said, "for the Royal Ambassador of the Crown may travel wherever she pleases, throughout her life."

"Even the crown," the keeper said, "is subject to Ellincreo's words."

Bella strode onto the platform. "Were they Ellincreo's words?" The hidden wind weaver tried to dampen her voice, but Fanteal lifted. "You read a copy," Bella declared, "and I hold the original, just now pulled from its shelf in the archive below this chamber." She held it open before the chief keeper's face.

The keeper swayed his hand, palm-down, perhaps trying to make it look like a natural calming gesture. "You left the keepers, Bella, and have no right on the platform."

"I know that copies of this book omit the date, thus pretending that the writing is ancient. A lie that should shame the scribe who copied it. Read the date of the original and attest that no vetting date was added."

He stared at it, his lips tight.

Bella didn't allow him even silence as an out. "Will you not state, sir, that it is long past its vetting period and was never confirmed as a book of the Holy Writ?"

He maintained his erect stature. "Thank you, Bella, for bringing this to my attention. I will address the scribes for their omission, and the copies will be updated."

"Better to shatter the pages to dust," Bella said, "for this book contradicts the Holy Writ of Gifting."

"Give me that book. You are not a Keeper of the Writ and cannot judge its writings."

Bella slapped it into his hand. "It was under you that I studied." She stomped off the platform and dropped into her seat.

The chief keeper resumed his benign tone and addressed the crowd. "It grieves me that the peace of your Savoring Day has been disturbed like this. Yet the disruption is providential, for it gives proof once again that this book is true. Wind weavers bring turmoil. Ponder this as you return to—"

"The audacity!" Governor Trezman shouted. "*You* chose the reading, and a foolish choice it was. Lady Fanteal hasn't even defended herself, though she knows better than all of us that these nonsense dictates have robbed Dirklan of a critical substance gift."

"Robbed?" The chief keeper smirked. "In truth, Lady Fanteal is robbing me at this moment, for she prevents my own wind weaver from using her gift. We would not be enduring this outrage otherwise."

"I am lifting all voices equally," Fanteal said with utmost calm. "The only outrage is that you claim ownership of a wind weaver. How long have you forced her to silence any voice you do not want heard?"

"This is not a public forum."

Sir Mikkael stood and drew Fanteal up as well. "Then you shouldn't have used it to publicly assert authority over wind weavers." He led Fanteal up the few steps onto the platform and faced the audience. "This is not the place I would have chosen to address you, for I honor the purpose of this gathering. However, the Keeper of the Writ omitted most of the good news I related to him. Thus, I will share it."

Whispers grew silent as gazes fixed on him.

"I was puzzled when I first realized that Ellincreo had sent us a wind weaver. Now that she has shown me the state of our air channels, I am beyond grateful. Jourendia is only the first beneficiary of her amazing gift. Already, the medics report health improvements. She travels as ambassador, yes, but as a wind weaver, she will open the air channels wherever they are needed. She will also reestablish the Wind Weavers' Guild."

The chief keeper pointedly faced Fanteal. "You have not been duly chosen to lead any guild."

Someone shouted from the terraces. "Only a former has the knowledge and authority to move matter, even if it is in an air channel."

Fanteal did her best to level his shout and still let it be heard, but this meeting was about to explode all around the compass. "Please don't shout," she said softly. "I will lift the voice of any who are recognized by Sir Mikkael."

Agriben stood as she spoke. What a relief that he was present.

Sir Mikkael held up his hand, palm forward. "This is still not a public forum, but I recognize Chief Former Agriben."

The rough cadence of his voice soothed Fanteal. "As Provincial Chief Former, I am aware of Lady Fanteal's wind weaving plans. I have assigned a former specifically to documenting and clearing the existing air channels. Two formers are with her whenever she works, so if a new channel does need to be formed, an assessment can be made immediately."

Oh, did that delight Jaikon, as it did her? He looked more bemused than anything. Wait...was he staring *past* her? But she must pay attention, for Agriben had more to say.

"The contention raised—in this, of all places—has proven the need to formalize the Royal Ambassador's restoration of the Wind Weavers'

Guild. Prime Minister, if enough wind weavers are present here, I suggest an immediate vote to—"

The woman next to him jumped to her feet. "I, Lezzilie, nominate Lady Fanteal as Chief Wind Weaver."

Fanteal gasped. This could go wrong. The legalities teetered on the edge. She jumped at the chief keeper's voice.

"You are not allowed to speak in this chamber." But it was not Lezzilie he silenced. He pointed a shaking finger toward the tunnel.

Audrea stood, trembling, just within view. She opened and closed her mouth.

Sir Mikkael said calmly, "A keeper may not forbid a citizen to speak. Are you a wind weaver?"

She nodded, twining her hands. "I...Audrea...nominate Lady Fanteal as Chief Wind Weaver."

She looked so pale that Fanteal wafted fresh air in her direction.

"It makes no difference," the chief keeper said. "There are only two confirmed wind weavers in Crysalan, and that is not enough for a vote."

"There are more," Sir Mikkael said. "Wind weavers, I ask you to ignore false words you've been taught. Instead, call to mind the Holy Writ of Gifting, for Dirklan *needs* you. Please stand if you are willing to vote."

One stood. Then another. Then two more.

"That will be enough," Agriben said, "although, it has just occurred to me that I don't know how weavers prove their gift."

Fanteal held in a laugh, though it probably showed on her face. "They can each send me a draft. Audrea, come stand here with me, so we have dual proof." With that done, Fanteal was just about to declare it finished. Then the air shifted again, though unfocused. She looked to the source, but no one was standing there. Had someone been recently gifted? She smiled. "Yes, young wind weaver, I can feel your breeze. You are welcome to stand."

A stir began, and a young man—a teen, really—stood to his feet amid a few gasps.

"Excellent," Fanteal said. "You may always feel outnumbered, but I have attended many guild meetings, and I assure you they are better with both women and men."

"Are all confirmed, then?" Sir Mikkael made a point of getting Audrea's agreement too. "I've never run a guild meeting, Lady Fanteal. What's next?"

"Are there any other nominations?" she asked. After a silent moment, she said, "I call for a vote of assent or dissent. Those in favor of me as Provincial Chief Wind Weaver, raise your hand." She looked around. "I would ask for dissenters, but all hands are up. Thank you for your trust. I commit to leading our guild until Dirklan's airflow is restored and all wind weavers are found and trained. We will vote again when the guild is fully restored."

"Lady Fanteal, as prime minister, I hereby recognize you as Chief Wind Weaver of Dirklan." He offered the partial bow accorded to provincial guild chiefs. "We will announce this in the plaza shortly. Chief Keeper Thilleon, thank you for allowing this unorthodox meeting of the Wind Weavers' Guild. We will depart now and return the service to you."

The prime minister's retinue began rising, and Fanteal quickly added, "Wind weavers, please accompany us." Tempting though it was to ignore the chief keeper, Fanteal inclined her head to him.

He returned it. "I congratulate you, Chief Wind Weaver Fanteal."

What was most surprising, her new title or his gracious response? Saving face? She'd see how things played out before she trusted his revised stance.

Fanteal stepped from the platform. Though Jaikon congratulated her and bowed formally, his eyes darted to the ivy-covered wall and away again. She longed to ask why but settled for taking his arm instead of the prime minister's. Maybe she could whisper something. They climbed the steps as the chief keeper pronounced the traditional benediction, stretching it out long enough for them to traverse the upper aisle. Through that short walk, Jaikon stared over her head toward the wall.

She found no free second to whisper a question during the swirl of activity that followed. First, a quick word to the weavers about where they would meet with her after lunch. Then, she stood upon the same platform as yesterday, between Sir Mikkael and Chief Former Agriben. The attendees at the service must have run to spread news. A throng flowed into the plaza and choked the streets that flanked surrounding buildings.

So little time for her to take everything in. The three conferred on what should be said, then each took a turn at formal remarks and very brief plans for the future. Through all of it, she lifted voices, while trying to get a feel for the crowd. Faces showed neither pleasure nor displeasure. *Stunned* might be the best description. Some held tablets and jotted swift notes. Ah, Crysalan's fascination with record-keeping. At least the wind weavers—clustered on the steps below her—hung rapturously on every syllable. Bella and Charlis looked thrilled, and Jaikon...what was going on with him?

Again, she remembered the long-ago murder of the wind weaver who had saved Dirklan from suffocation. A very different story was playing out for Fanteal. Not that the crowd was shouting joy or anything. Oh. Of course not.

They still needed a streamer. And she still wasn't one.

CHAPTER 25

Jaikon escorted Fanteal to the inn's lounge. Empty, but he knew that wouldn't last. Though the masses had remained on the plaza, a dozen people accompanied the prime minister.

Fanteal dragged Jaikon to a corner. "What are you thinking?"

Way beyond vague! "A hundred things, give or take. Are you asking about anything in particular?"

"A hundred is a fair estimate." She pressed a hand to her brow. One of her own hundred thoughts triggered a smile. "Two formers always with me. I loved it when Agriben said that—calling you a former in front of everyone."

"He'll regret it if anyone asks who the second former is."

"He can handle a dispute quite well." She stepped closer, whispering, "But, Jaikon—the vision wall—it *glowed*! I know you saw it. And later, when my back was to it, did it glow again?"

He closed his eyes. Did she have to bring this up? As though he could avoid it. "A little. More like an amber haze. From what you could see, did the audience notice?"

"I don't think so. They didn't stare at it, anyway. What do you suppose it meant?"

He shrugged. "That part was all about wind weavers. It may have been Ellincreo's approval. Or a message to you weavers. Or something entirely different. I'm not exactly fond of interpreting glowing gold, you know."

"Mm. The first one...I'm sure that was for you and me. But impossible to interpret under all that ivy. Why is it allowed to cover the gold?"

"Because it could. Plants enrich the air. Maybe they dampen echoes behind the musicians. The wall hasn't granted a vision in my lifetime, so who would care?"

"You knew it was there. How?"

"More of it showed when I was a boy."

"How can you be sure that it doesn't grant visions? Only those a vision is meant for can see it. But right now, no one can, because it's covered up."

Why must everything be so contradictory? Better to trust the truth he knew. "Be careful, Fanteal. This isn't a time to irritate the chief keeper any further. We are to know the voice of Ellincreo within, not to rely on external visions."

She seemed to contemplate the buttons of his shirt for a long moment. "There have been times I have known within my heart what to do, but even with the best intentions, we can make mistakes. Sometimes we can recover from a poor choice, but not always. In the midst of a critical decision, a vision helped me move forward. So maybe both ways of seeing are good."

He didn't want to go there. "As you say—*maybe*."

He couldn't hide from the scrutiny of her beautiful eyes. "What vision," she asked, "has he placed in your heart that you doubt?"

To think he used to hate being around medic streamers because they could sense pulse rates. Could a wind weaver sense his soul? Silly. Yet it seemed *she* could.

Someone approached, ending the uncomfortable moment. Then he recognized the person, and the next moment became that much worse. What was *he* doing here?

Jaikon had no choice but to introduce him. "Ambassador Fanteal, this is Nedford, Chief Former of Northeshur."

The instant Nedford finished his bow to her, he focused on Jaikon. "Do I understand correctly that *you* are one of the two formers who accompany Lady Fanteal?"

Jaikon inclined his head. "If it bothers you, take it up with Agriben."

"I shall."

Sooner than he expected, perhaps, for Agriben approached behind him. "I understand," the provincial chief said in his gravelly voice, "that you have overlooked Jaikon's primary expertise in years past."

"Long range is only as good as what it can shift."

"Ah, my friend, your impressive polishing skills blind you. Jaikon assesses faster and farther than any former alive."

"Alive. That is rather the point, isn't it? The collapse of LourEstelle killed all the longest-range formers of their day, so I must hold to the opinion that it isn't useful."

"It also," Fanteal said, "killed many who had no forming gift at all. Those who died ignored the vision wall's clear warning. That alone caused their deaths."

Crysalan complete, Northeshur next. Jaikon buttoned his shirt, torn between relief and worry. Well, he'd survived his first week as prime minister's proxy and formal escort for the royal ambassador. That was something.

He crossed the inn's hallway to Fanteal's sitting room, where they gathered for breakfast. Just the four of them, now that his father had returned to Jourendia. Nice to be free of the aides and visitors who surrounded a prime minister. They spoke little, for Bella was making a list and Fanteal seemed pensive. Charlis passed a dish of eggs to Jaikon as he sat down.

Jaikon enjoyed a mouthful of the well-seasoned eggs. At least he'd known those who had gravitated toward Fanteal as he'd guided her through the many caverns of Crysalan domain. Air channels here were well documented—typical—which left him with less practical work.

While Charlis dealt with debris in the channels, Jaikon had navigated politics. Keeping Fanteal's suitors from infringing on her wind weaving duties. Smoothing jagged feelings that he had scraped before the election. Even fending off snide remarks directed at the wind weavers who studied every twist of Fanteal's gift. This had better not become his life!

Charlis reached for the teapot and refilled Fanteal's cup. Catering to her as always. He filled Bella's cup too. So preoccupied was she with the notebooks beside her breakfast plate, she didn't seem to notice—until she smiled her thanks. Jaikon waved Charlis's offer of tea away and turned to Fanteal.

The hint of a smile hid behind her teacup, and amusement lurked in her eyes, which rested on Charlis squeezing lia juice into Bella's tea.

How was tea service funny? Any subject was better than Charlis's overdone courtesies. "Did you enjoy the dance last night?" Jaikon asked Fanteal.

She looked surprised. He'd been there, so this was hardly a creative topic. "Lady Trezman is a fine hostess," Fanteal said. "I enjoy dancing, although displaying the exact level of favor to each political suitor does tarnish the pleasure." She leaned back. "A nice change of pace, though, after days of convincing wind weavers that they're allowed to practice their gift."

"How do you think the weavers here will do when you're gone?"

"Well enough. Audrea and Lezzilie have been subtly training the others even before I came. Now that they can practice unhindered, and understand the overall air flow, they may sharpen their skills through use." Fanteal turned her wrist and looked at her bracelet, then set her cup down. "Almost time. Excuse me."

She left the table, and Charlis stared after her. "Why does she do that?"

"Look at her watch, you mean?" A tease hid in Bella's eyes.

Charlis had an odd way of wrinkling his nose when he was puzzled. "Look...watch...? What is she watching?"

Bella laughed aloud, gathering up her notebooks. "Oh, that was priceless. A *watch* is what they call their circular timepieces."

"No," Jaikon said, "they are called *clocks*."

Bella stood. "The tiny ones are called *watches*. Don't ask me why." She followed Fanteal, still chuckling.

"I wonder what she needs that for," Charlis mused. "It's not as though we don't have hour markers."

Jaikon laid his napkin aside. For once, he possessed an understanding that Charlis didn't. "We know the time from the sun angling through a light shaft onto a marker. She knew the time from the sun itself. Our method cannot be intuitive to her." He stood. "I have little doubt that she is correctly predicting when we should be on the platform for the train to Northeshur."

Charlis left with him. "Doesn't really matter. Bella reserved carriages. They'd wait for us."

That was true, but Fanteal wasn't the sort to make people wait for her. How could he have thought her a spoiled princess?

The train ride to Northeshur took far longer than Fanteal expected. Governor Brakentel's wife, Lellia, knew better and had a late supper ready in her dining room when they arrived.

Lellia studied her when Fanteal finished eating. "You look tired, Lady Fanteal. Is the train ride to blame, or the air?"

"Both, perhaps. The air is quite stale."

Lellia clicked her tongue. "Then I imagine you will like the gift that Governor Yaldeeth had delivered here. Her grandson, Renauld, designed a portable, motorized fan for your travels. It's already connected to the magnery copper in the bedroom I prepared for you. Come along, and I'll show you."

What a relief. Though the fan's steady whir was annoying, it made the night bearable.

Breakfast was an informal event, prepared by her hostess and served at the kitchen table. Quite homey in a way that Fanteal had never experienced.

Jaikon relaxed in this setting, doubtless because he'd spent much time here as a boy. As they lingered over their tea, the Brakentels' daughter, Vrendi, arrived with her youngest child, Jules. All formality dropped after the introduction. Vrendi grabbed a cup, helped herself to tea, and joined them at the table, chattering about the dance her mother planned in order to welcome Fanteal.

Jules squeezed into a space next to Jaikon, setting a box on the table.

"What do you have there?" Jaikon asked.

"It's a model cair." Jules opened the cover. "See, I've put the chassis and wheels together, but the instruction plate is lost, and I can't figure out how the gears fit in." He pulled out little parts and handed them to Jaikon as he spoke. "Berta says Drahon must have lost a part, but he says he didn't. Can you make it work, Uncle Jaikon?"

Uncle?

Fanteal's surprise must have shown, for Vrendi said, "Not really an uncle, of course, but the little ones just started calling him that at family gatherings. Do you need to do any shopping before the dance? I know all the best shops for everything."

"Thank you, but I need nothing. Today is already full."

"Official events," Vrendi asked, "or that air channel stuff we've been hearing about?"

"We're going to visit the import cataract."

In the stunned silence, Jaikon's soft instructions to Jules continued. "This shaft goes vertically into the motor. Do you see how that lets these grooves align with the gears?"

Vrendi found her tongue. "*That* is the worst idea I have ever heard."

Before Fanteal could think of a response, Jaikon said, "Worst? I seem to remember an idea you had about a certain duck."

Lellia shuddered dramatically, and Vrendi rolled her eyes. "Oh, very funny." She clinked her cup into its saucer and leaned toward Fanteal. "But why, in all the caverns, would you go *there*?"

"Because it's important to Northeshur and Dirklan."

"Well...not to be rude, but...it is the one place where you were most wanted and, well...are the least capable."

"Definitely rude," Jaikon murmured, holding a portion of the model while Jules worked a piece into it.

"I am not going as a streamer," Fanteal said. "I am going as an ambassador and a wind weaver."

"But—"

"Not your concern, dear," Lellia said to her daughter as she stood. "Help me clean up."

Jules squealed and pumped his fist. "I knew it!"

Jaikon chuckled. "I see the Mechanics' Guild in your future."

Jules ran to his mother, cradling the half-finished model and shouting, "Look!"

Jaikon grinned at the boy, then said to Fanteal, "The workers will be at the cataract by now. We should be going soon. I would have thought Bella would be down by now."

"Charlis took her to breakfast at the inn."

"Oh." He blinked but didn't add words to his blatant surprise.

Her laugh bubbled out.

"What?"

"You haven't noticed how Charlis treats Bella?"

"He caters to *you*," Jaikon grumped. "Is there anything he hasn't served you at a meal? He can't even wait for your cup to be half empty before he hurries in to fill it."

"Protocol, Jaikon. Bella drinks tea like she lives in a desert. He cannot fill her empty cup unless he tops mine off first."

"Oh."

That syllable sounded so inordinately pleased, that Fanteal's laughter almost escaped again.

The couple in question returned at that moment so they could set out. A double-seated cair took the four of them from the residential area, past several larger buildings, and through an open market. Unlike Jourendia's featureless gray, Northeshur's caverns were reddish-brown, sometimes ribboned with creamy shades.

Fanteal pointed to a fine example as they neared a tunnel. "That's lovely."

"Indeed," Jaikon said, his voice tight.

"Is there anything I should know about the people I'm about to meet?"

"Hmm. Well, the gifted will all be streamers, except that one former is always on duty. The chief streamer and chief former rub one another all wrong, so we probably won't see Nedford."

Their cair entered a broad tunnel. Linked carts rattled past along another rail. She hoped they held food. Would any improvements have been implemented yet? Were any possible?

In a quarter of an hour, the groan of gears and rush of water echoed beyond the tunnel's far end. The cair stopped at the platform, and Jaikon offered Fanteal his hand, while Charlis did the same for Bella.

"How's the air?" Jaikon asked as usual.

"Moist and richer than in the main cavern."

A woman came to greet them, and Jaikon introduced Fanteal and Bella to Northeshur's chief streamer, Zendel. Charlis joined them, carrying the map case and resting a folded tripod against his shoulder.

Zendel gave him an odd look. "Haven't seen you in a while, Charlis. Is Agriben visiting?"

"No, he assigned me to accompany Ambassador Fanteal."

She eyed his gear. "What do you need all that for?"

"To confirm the level maps and update if needed."

She turned away, grumbling, "We know where the cataract is."

They followed her, and Fanteal finally got a look at the import cataract—the prime contention that refused to cease haunting her. Not what she'd expected. The underground river descended in a steep torrent. Thick rods angled from it toward a narrower chute, which leveled amid mechanical works, then rejoined the river's course on its way to unfathomed depths. Raging water and clanking metal grated the air, but at least it didn't echo. Odd.

She swept a gentle wind through the chamber, partly irregular and partly formed to accommodate equipment and tiered seating up one wall. Her sweep explained the absence of echoes. "Have the walls been roughened on purpose?"

She felt a touch of surprise from Charlis as he extended his gift. "It seems so. I wonder why."

"The echoes would have been intolerable," Fanteal said.

More than a dozen people lounged around. Some were clearly streamers, perhaps others handled freight.

Fanteal turned to Zendel. "Have there been any shipments yet today?"

"One, so far. Six canisters came through. We'll know when the next one's coming because the flow diminishes while they prepare for the next push."

Fanteal nodded, for that matched what she'd seen above. To Jaikon, she said, "The air is turbulent above the river, causing a diffuse spread." She pointed. "There are open air channels there and there."

Charlis set up his tripod and opened the map, while Jaikon began inspecting the channels for loose matter.

Zendel huffed. "There's nothing wrong with our air, as Sir Nirundale and his medic friends could have told you. Always here asking questions."

That caught Fanteal's attention. "Were they? Why?"

"The cataract streamers don't get emfiduria."

"Did they determine what protects you here?"

"Some thought it was moisture in the air, but many streamers get moist air. They took plenty of samples from the river to test, but I never heard that they discovered anything."

Another hint and dead end. Fanteal returned to wind weaving, but these channels proved clean, and the lower portions were already on the map. Jaikon showed Charlis where to etch the far end, which she confirmed by sending a gust through.

"Ah! There's a wind weaver above." She loved that touch and couldn't keep a smile from her face.

"Meeting an old friend?" Jaikon asked with a grin.

She laughed. "I don't recognize her, but it's awfully fun to spin a helix with her." Fanteal noticed a change in the cataract—more space for air—and began reaching through it.

A man's whisper behind snapped her concentration. "Instead of a streamer, we get a lame former pretending to be useful and a wandering weaver playing games aboveground."

A woman answered him, scoffing. "No more help from the king than the prime minister."

Fanteal went rigid. Likely none but she had heard. She turned slowly and found the twosome sitting on the top tier of benches. "Did you whisper that to purposely reach only the sensitive hearing of a wind weaver?" That wiped the smirks from their faces, but she didn't want an answer. "Or are you unaware that sound travels upon air..." She altered to breathy words and lifted them to resound from the wall behind the two. "...and your whispers are loud and clear to me?"

They both shuddered from the unnatural sound. The man bumbled through an apology, and the woman muttered something similar.

Jaikon hovered protectively over Fanteal, a hand on her back. "What did they say?"

"I shall not repeat it."

Jaikon's muscles stiffened. "You will leave this chamber immediately after reporting your names to Ambassador Fanteal's aide."

The culprits had edged along the bench and now scrambled down the steps, where Bella met them, her notebook open.

"Forgive my interruption," someone said, "but the cataract flow has begun to lessen."

"Actually, that started before those two interrupted my work." Fanteal turned again to the water. How many more shared the same attitudes, though unspoken? "When the water is held back aboveground," she said, "more air enters the waterway. Wouldn't it be nice if streamers recognized that an ambassador knows the procedure, and a wind weaver perceives the cataract's changes before you do?"

Zendel looked disturbed, though she kept her shoulders erect. "Yes. Quite. Uh, only the woman was a streamer, by the way."

An annoyed voice spoke from the chamber entrance. "The other was a former, I regret to say." Chief Former Nedford advanced a few paces and bowed. "Allow me to assure you, Ambassador Fanteal, that disrespect is not condoned by the Formers' Guild."

She swiftly turned back to the cataract. "Thank you, but I must focus." The torrent was half its strength. "Follow me up it, Jaikon."

She felt Charlis, Zendel, and other intent streamers. Workers moved into positions near the chute.

Fanteal wrapped awareness around the column of air that ascended the widening gap in the cataract. Not halfway up, she lost track of the chief streamer. Fanteal had expected better range from her. Odd. Charlis fell away too, but Jaikon was still with her. His presence hovered above the air's path—also beneath, where water must be charging along the rock he sensed.

Her column met resistance. "There," she snapped. Air hissed through a tiny gap. She raced along the thread, then surfaced. Only in the open air, did she lose awareness of Jaikon. He'd made it all the way! Joy pulsed for him—then was swallowed by even greater joy.

She touched her father's awareness and slid a breeze to caress the flow where his presence lingered.

Great force plummeted against her column, nearly ripping it away from her. She squeezed it high in the channel as the mass surged by, then sucked more air down from above and followed it, sensing the shape that it filled. An odd faltering, then the mass surged past, picking up speed, then faltering again before surmounting the obstacle. Finally, she sensed the streamers below again. Fanteal withdrew all but slight awareness, lest she disrupt their work.

A great splash erupted from the cataract. Streamers forced water up and arched it over to the outbound flow. "Dirty," one of them grumbled. Canisters squealed along the rods.

Fanteal let go of the air, for she must see with her eyes. Skies above, she was swaying, and Bella had a grip on her arm. Jaikon stood rigid—fixated within his forming gift.

"Look at this mess. This is what we deal with every day."

Fanteal wasn't even sure who said it, but clearly it was directed at her. Crumpled metal filled the chute with four intact canisters compressing it. Sort of intact. White muck bubbled from a crack in one of them.

"Spare her a minute," Zendel said. "Can't you tell when the gifted have been working?"

Jaikon snapped out of it and gazed down on her in concern. "You needn't cry." He wiped a thumb across her cheek. "This is nothing new. We'll use the part we can."

"They are not sad tears." Bella said. "You should have seen her face, just after she said, 'there.'"

Zendel leaned in. "What did you sense, lady? What was the good part?"

Fanteal sniffed and tried to still her trembling lips. "My father." Oh no, that probably sounded stupid. "Other streamers too, of course, but it just felt so good because I miss him." That wasn't any help to belowgrounders, either.

Murmurs circulated around Fanteal.

"Her father—she means the *king*."

"The *king* is streaming our import cataract?"

"You see? He *does* care!"

Several more of the same carried a note of hope until someone said, "No disrespect intended, but it didn't help."

Zendel cleared her throat. "Don't jump to conclusions. We'll figure this out sanely. Lady Fanteal, how high up did you reach, and do you have any way of knowing how much farther it was that he was reaching down to you?"

She'd better get her wits together...remember the ambassador part. "I reached all the way to the open air aboveground, but the distance through rock isn't really something that a wind weaver can judge in terms of miles."

"What, exactly, did you sense when you said 'there'?"

"The column of air met the restrained water." Several streamers murmured, but Fanteal turned to Jaikon. "I thought you might want to know where that was, so you can map it."

He nodded, but Nedford said, "That's just below ground level. No one can judge well enough to map that far away."

"Maps aren't the point." Zendel kept her focus on Fanteal. "Could you tell whether the canisters were intact when the held water was released?"

"I can only sense pressure against the air, not discern the canisters within the water."

"They were intact," Jaikon said, "when they first surged ahead."

"You cannot tell that," Nedford said, dropping the words like rocks. "I grant your ability to perform an assessment, since Agriben vouches for it. But I will not allow guesses—even educated guesses—to spawn false information. The import cataract is too vital."

Steady voice, she warned herself. "I felt him reach the surface."

"You are an impressive wind weaver, Lady Fanteal, and sensitive enough to recognize other gifts. But by your own words, you know nothing of the canisters until they arrived here."

"Then prove my words yourself," Jaikon said. "I wouldn't know if they were leaking, but I felt seven identical objects." He flipped a hand toward the mangled metal the workers had pulled from the receiving chute and dropped on the floor. "Straighten that mess and see whether it's three canisters."

Nedford focused on the scrap. It shifted slightly, and part fell away. He angled his head, then conceded. "Not worth separating, but it was three, so yes, seven in total. Which could also have been a guess. Not that it matters, for we already believe they are loading solid cargo."

"Exactly!" Zendel splayed her hands. "Enough formers' ego. We should be talking about water. Figuring out exactly what is happening when damage occurs."

"True," Fanteal said. "But the cataract is not just water. It is water and air within a sheath of rock. While streamers, weavers, and formers talk about what they think others cannot do, we make no progress."

She dropped her gaze squarely on Nedford. "As liquid and solid mass press against the air, I can sense obstruction if it exists. Please take note of my hand." She turned her back to him and swung her hand behind to rest against her spine, with two fingers extended. "Jaikon, are there solid obstructions, and if so, how many?"

"Yes, in two distinct places."

She brought her hand forward and held her two fingers overhead. "Two is the number I revealed to those behind me. Charlis, please map what Jaikon shows you. I can give an approximate confirmation." She spun to the workers. "In the meantime, open these canisters."

"Pardon me, lady," Nedford said, "but you don't have the right to interfere in food handling."

Oh, for patience! "I am inspecting imports from aboveground. I suggest you find a copy of Welcian law and familiarize yourself with the rights and responsibilities of a royal ambassador. While it makes no mention of smiling, waving, or marrying politicians, it says quite a lot about matters of trade."

She turned to Zendel but paused, for the chief streamer had shifted away and pressed a hand against her lips. A problem? No, for her eyes danced. On with what mattered. "Before they attempt another shipment," Fanteal said, "I want to send wind up the cataract, and I request help from the Streamers' Guild."

Jaikon sketched on the map layer with his wax pencil, rattling off former terms to Charlis, while Fanteal explained her plan to the chief streamer. As Fanteal sent the hair-whipping gust upward, she felt him already encasing the cataract from base to top. "Lower...upper," she said, as she reached the snags impeding her wind.

Afterward, Jaikon pointed them out on the map. "Her word comes shortly after the obstructions."

Nedford had finally deigned to look at the map Charlis was etching. "Then, she does not actually confirm anything."

"Understand that she moves very quickly. It may just be the delay for speech. Or it may be that she notices the effect after the wind catches." He looked to Fanteal. "I've noticed when you blow through a dirty air channel that the dust is most chaotic *after* the first disturbance. Am I interpreting this correctly?"

Wow. A former who noticed her. More thrilling than being seen by other wind weavers. "You are. What do you find there?"

CHAPTER 26

Jaikon's hunched shoulder muscles released. That smile Fanteal gave him...so different from the one she used for introductions, or toward crowds, or in a greeting over breakfast. It replaced the energy Nedford's blatant disregard had sapped. "I sense the obstacles," he replied to her, "though I will study this longer before I state conclusions."

He caught Nedford's look of disdain but focused on Fanteal, for she glowed with approval. A good thing, because he needed all the encouragement he could get. Sensing so much land at once, analyzing obstructions, trying to follow moving objects—it wasn't easy. He even had to avoid the former he'd begun to sense aboveground. Why others enjoyed such encounters, he couldn't imagine.

Jaikon watched through several transits. It soon became clear that abovegrounders were experimenting. Zendel assigned a streamer to record every possible detail. Too bad it would be months before they could compare notes with those aboveground.

Different lengths of canister chains came through, and then different weights. Shorter and lighter did seem to fare a little better. Less waste, but no more food received. Disappointing. Then another cycle commenced and ended with nothing at all.

The chamber seemed to chill. Streamers speculated on the purpose of the empty surge. But he knew they were wrong, even while he hoped *he* was wrong. He waited for another cycle. Small canisters clustered at the top, they bounced around the highest obstruction, then plummeted down a narrow side channel.

Jaikon placed a single dot on the map but said nothing to Charlis.

Two more empty cycles. Fanteal sent up a gust after each one, frowning as she wove it. Was she trying to communicate disappointment?

She rubbed her forehead, and Zendel said, "Enough, Lady Fanteal. I don't know about moving air, but if I streamed that much water all by myself, I'd be ready to drop. Besides, you hardly ate any of the lunch we had brought in."

Jaikon felt much the same—for an entirely different reason. Charlis folded the map and tripod, and Bella closed her notebook. Jaikon returned to Fanteal. "You do look tired, but at least it doesn't seem to be from poor air this time."

"No, indeed. This chamber gets a complete refresh of aboveground air with every cycle."

Interesting.

The cair trip back to the Brakentel home was silent. Were the others tired, or had they noticed? If so, they would never speak of it in the cair driver's hearing.

When they stepped from the vehicle, Charlis asked, "May I come in and talk with you for a moment?"

"Of course." Jaikon led the way into a salon off the welcome room.

Charlis spread the map on the table and pointed to the dot. "What is this?"

Jaikon grimaced. "Opening of a side channel."

Charlis gave him a grim look. "Which you found when the transits were empty."

"What does it mean?" Fanteal asked.

"They started sending smaller canisters. The big ones don't fit down the side channel, but the small ones do."

"They send, and we get nothing?" Fanteal asked. At his nod, she said, "Well, I hope my father got the hint that I wasn't happy with those cycles." She paced—unlike her. "I just loathe the communication issues." She looked back and forth between the two formers. "Can someone close off that side channel?"

"No." A bald answer, but Jaikon was too discouraged to smooth it. "I can feel where other formers reach—and do not reach. None but I was near the obstructions and side channel."

"No surprise," Charlis said. "Obstructions have been cleared before, but all were lower down. How bad are they?"

"Fragmented rock without much room to get around. On that highest one..." He fiddled with his pencil. "A split rock is wiggling."

"Caverns, no." Charlis exhaled the words as ominously as they deserved.

"But it is. Someday it will break. And depending on how it breaks, it might block the cataract."

Fanteal paled. She plopped into a chair. "How much longer till that happens?"

"A day, a decade, a century. We won't know until it occurs."

"It felt so good," she murmured. "Like we were learning something useful. And now it's all a disaster again."

Hard to avoid agreeing with her, but her hope needed support, not collapse. "It isn't a disaster yet. What of the air? You liked that, didn't you?"

"Yes." She put on a positive expression. "It reinforces my suspicion that stagnant air causes emfiduria. Unfortunately, the prevailing flow in Northeshur is going *out* the cataract chamber, so the other caverns get no benefit. We'll have as much work to do here as we did in Jourendia."

As Fanteal spoke, their hostess entered, carrying a tray of tall glasses and a pitcher. "Save time for the dance, my dear," Lellia said. "I've already had to turn away three of your suitors, who hoped to visit you today."

Fanteal tsked. "The dance, yes, but I don't have time for pointless visits. I need to find Northeshur's wind weavers and clear the channels, so I can continue to the other domains."

Lellia poured a glass of amber juice and handed it to Fanteal. "I understand, and I don't blame you. I can send them all away if you like. *Or* I could invite one to dinner each night that you are with me."

Fanteal took a mint sprig from the tray and swirled it through her drink. "Not a bad idea. That would avoid giving offense, and I must eat dinner anyway."

Jaikon stiffened as her gaze settled on him. Was that a question lurking within it? "Am I supposed to discreetly eat elsewhere?"

"Don't you dare abandon me," she said. "You represent the prime minister."

That didn't make him a suitor, but at least she wanted him nearby. That alone would defeat the sting of any sneers they threw his way.

As the dinners played out, the sneers diminished. Jaikon noticed it more every day. Fanteal's suitors couldn't avoid conversing with him, and a truce of sorts became necessary.

Even the dance was more enjoyable than he'd expected. Being Fanteal's escort meant he got more time with her than any suitor did. The grand event brought in swarms of hopefuls from beyond Northeshur. Most showed him a subtle deference. Why?

It didn't hurt that Fanteal stared incredulously at anyone who mocked him. Maybe part of her ambassador role, for he was the prime minister's proxy, and she tolerated no disrespect of the prime minister, king, or queen.

Respect for position was one thing. Respect for a person was another. Did she...was it possible that she...respected him? It seemed so. But what if he was wrong?

Fanteal wandered through the first-floor rooms of the house Governor Yaldeeth had loaned them. Bedroom and kitchen in the back, dining and welcome rooms in the front. Two floors above held more bedrooms and such.

Jaikon came down the stairs. "This has to be one of the original houses of Illia domain." He gave her a wry look. "I'm guessing it's smaller than you expected."

"We'll call the rooms cozy. I'm just so relieved not to be at a public inn like we were in Weslin and Silcopton." She shook her head. "Always on display—careful about everything we said."

He stepped into the kitchen and began opening cupboard doors. "Stocked with all the usual. How are you at cooking?"

"My mother insisted I learn the basics. Breakfast and lunch may not impress anyone." She added a lilt. "But dinner should be good." The governor's son would host their dinners while his mother was in Jourendia at the council sessions.

Jaikon chuckled. "Not to worry. I can cook." He bent to inspect the shelves of cool storage. "We won't starve."

Bella came downstairs and opened the mail pouch waiting for them on the welcome room's table. She pulled out two stacks and held one out to Jaikon. "Here's yours." He took it and went to the couch, while she sorted Fanteal's stack, pausing to read a few unsealed cards. "The Schools of Invention and of Health invite you to visit, and the four wind weavers of Illia invite you to meet with them at a location and time of your choosing."

Fanteal savored the result of her public letters to the domains. So much easier than drawing wind weavers out of hiding in Crysalan. "We'll meet here after breakfast tomorrow. Get a note out to them right away."

Standing beside the table, Fanteal read the weekly letter from the prime minister, then moved on to the others, ending with a letter from Grellin Armeen. He didn't follow her from one domain to the next like her other suitors, but he sent her news of Alluthin and asked her opinion about some point or other. Not bothering to be present, yet discussing more of interest than those who dined and danced with her. Hmm.

Fanteal sat down and started her letter to Sir Mikkael, while Jaikon continued reading the council session briefs his father always sent. "Interesting," he murmured.

"What?"

"Nirundale supports another of Armeen's proposals. Getting quite friendly, these days."

Charlis accompanied Bella when she returned from sending a response to the wind weavers. "The local chief former was easy to find this time," he said.

Jaikon looked up from reading. "And?"

"I didn't even need to persuade him. He just listened to my report, then I asked if he had any concerns about us working in Illia. He waved it off with, 'I approve of whatever Dirklan's Chief Former and Chief Wind Weaver have agreed to.' He wants a copy of the updated level maps, but I do that anyway."

"Perfect," Fanteal said.

"I love this about Illia." Bella flipped through her notebook as she sat down at the table. "They skip the drama and just *do* things."

"That," Jaikon said, "and Governor Yaldeeth understands preparation."

So it seemed. "How? She never misses any council session in Jourendia."

"Her son handles everything while she's gone. Has for years. Two dedicated couriers travel back and forth between them."

"Imagine," Fanteal murmured, "if the ambassadors could do that."

The entrance chimes rang, and Charlis opened the door. A pleasant voice said, "Jaikon asked me to visit."

Jaikon jumped to his feet. "Renauld! Come in and let me introduce you. Ambassador Fanteal, this is Renauld Yaldeeth, the governor's grandson and, arguably, the most prolific inventor in Dirklan."

He bowed to Fanteal. "A pleasure."

Succinct. So, this was the suitor who wasn't interested. She matched his brevity in her response. By the time they'd completed introductions, Bella had cleared the mail from the welcome room's table.

Renauld narrowed his eyes at Jaikon. "That friendly little note you sent...why do I feel like there is more to it?"

Jaikon drew out his answer. "We have a problem."

"I don't do politics."

Laughter shook Jaikon's voice. "As though I'd ask *that* of you. This is about the export cataracts. We've just arrived from Silcopton—and Weslin before that."

Renauld kept his eyes on Jaikon, ignoring all the movement of Charlis spreading a map on his tripod while Bella unfolded another on the table. "Interesting subject, at least. Particularly since you know that I am less a former than I am a politician."

"You see?" Jaikon said to Fanteal. "I told you he would get to the main point quickly."

"You did." If Fanteal had any other choice, she wouldn't trust someone she'd just met. Still, Jaikon had no qualms. "What we're about to discuss is mostly common knowledge, but not entirely. We'd like to keep that portion out of the rumor stream."

"That won't be hard for me. May I ask about your air channel work, or is that also hushed?"

Fanteal smiled. "That, we announce at every opportunity. All the domains I have visited now have natural airflow. The wind weavers I find in each domain are now paid to monitor the flow and to check on the small caverns associated with their domains. Those still concern me, for

I've not had time to get through every tunnel and mine. I'm training the weavers so they can continue the improvements I have begun."

"Impressive start, Lady Fanteal. I happened to talk with a medic who knew Sir Nirundale." Renauld furrowed his brow. "Can't remember his name—started with *M*, I think."

"Malca?" she prompted.

"That's it. He's been visiting domains after you depart, then brings reports to the School of Health. Medics tend to gush about health improvements."

Gush didn't begin to describe what Fanteal's heart was doing, but Renauld turned to the map on the table—Weslin domain. "What's the issue?"

Jaikon leaned over it and pointed out aspects of the export cataract. "Weslin's cataract transports only slurry, predominately iron. This point here is the farthest that the local formers can reach." He moved his finger much farther along the course to the panels that Charlis had recently added. "I can sense this far."

Renauld held up both hands. "Wait a minute. Have you found a niche for your gift?"

"Apparently." Jaikon's shoulder movement still revealed how little he enjoyed speaking of his gift.

"After all these years, they're acknowledging it?"

"Not with awestruck wonder," Jaikon snarled.

Charlis chimed in. "Agriben has confirmed his ability to perform largescale assessments. I also vouch for his skills."

Renauld rested his eyes on Charlis. "Which will matter only if you become Dirklan's chief former...someday."

Fanteal caught the drift. Agriben was aging, and Charlis was still in his twenties. Not likely to be the next chief former for the entire province. "That sounds like Formers' Guild politics," she said.

Renauld flashed a smile at her. "Good point." He turned to the map of Silcopton domain. "Where is the cataract here?"

Jaikon pointed again. "This one is used for both slurry and raw gem pods. Local formers can reach this far, and I can sense almost to the end."

"Almost? Then how do you know it's the end?"

"Partly because of Ambassador Fanteal's knowledge of the cataracts, and partly because of...what I sense of the surrounding land." Again Jaikon sounded uncomfortable. Strange. Immersing himself in his gift always delighted him. Almost always.

Renauld stared at the map in silence, then raised his brows in mute question.

"Here's the issue," Jaikon explained. "Ore slurry is abrasive. The pod surfaces are fused smooth, but they are harder than the surrounding rock. Formers belowground monitor the cataracts and repair damage. Formers above do the same, but their reach is even shorter than our formers'. All that space between gets no attention. The walls are cracked in more places than I can count."

"I suppose every crack is full of ore?"

"Yes, and I suspect they are widening. Payment for food is lining the cataract instead of pockets aboveground."

Renauld watched Charlis spread out the map of Northeshur domain. "Same problem with food imports?"

"Similar." Jaikon explained about the side opening that swallowed their food.

Renauld rubbed the divot in his chin. "Why wasn't any of this a problem early on?"

Charlis answered. "The cataracts were formed into useful conduits in Devron's time. Back then, the formers had greater range than they do now." He angled his head. "We aren't sure if they could sense as far as Jaikon, but some could effectively command stone alteration at least halfway down the cataracts."

"I thought all the long-range formers were killed in the collapse of LourEstelle."

"People only think that because range was the high-priority skill in those days. All the chief formers had it, and *they* were killed. But that doesn't mean everyone with long range died."

"If so, why don't formers have long range now?"

Fanteal flipped her palms up in disbelief, gesturing to Jaikon while directing her stare at Renauld.

"Oh. Well, yes. But I mean, other than him."

Even Bella was shaking her head now.

Renauld braced his knuckles on the table and looked under his brows at Jaikon. "This, my friend, is why I hate it when people introduce me like I'm brilliant. It always comes right before someone is shocked by my stupidity."

Unrepentant, Jaikon said, "Well, at least you're making the same assumption as everyone else."

Renauld came close to shouting. "Are you accusing me of thinking like the masses? That's worse!"

Jaikon laughed. "Oh, calm down. If you really want to know why the gifts have changed, try asking the chief keeper or any of the substance guild chiefs. You'll get opinions ranging from, 'Ellincreo provides exactly what we need,' to 'He is still providing all the gifts, but we don't recognize them.' Bella favors the first explanation, Lady Fanteal the second, but I only care about fixing the cataracts. No former can reach the central portions, but they are in desperate need of repair."

"Mm." Renauld rubbed his chin again. "You're looking for a mechanical solution then?"

"Any type of solution you can think of. Dream on it."

Renauld straightened. "I will, then. One little point you politicians should be aware of."

"I'm not a politician," Jaikon retorted, "but what is it?"

"Governor Armeen asked the School of Invention for help with water issues in Alluthin. When I developed powered irrigation, the streamers were furious."

"Oh, yes. I remember, now that you mention it."

"Probably not as well as I do," Renald half-growled. "If I step into the formers' realm of rock, you better have a defense ready. My inventive gift is only valued if it doesn't touch what others consider to be their own."

CHAPTER 27

All through the days of clearing air channels in Illia, Fanteal's hope rode high. Touring the School of Health delighted her heart, for they lauded the benefits of fresh air. The School of Invention provided an interesting tour, but Renauld put in no appearance.

Afterward, Jaikon led Fanteal to Renauld's *office*, using the word loosely. So cluttered that, at first, Fanteal didn't see him bent over a table with a strange contraption on it.

It wasn't until Jaikon called his name that Renauld straightened and blinked at them. "Oh. Is the tour today?" He looked side to side as though he had misplaced something.

Jaikon grinned. "Yes, but don't bother trying to remember. It's over. Your grandmother is back, and she's hosting a dance in honor of Ambassador Fanteal. Remember that instead."

Renauld put on an air of superiority. "I know all about that. And that your father arrived in Illia today. My formal attire is already pressed, and I will be present for the first dance." He bowed to Fanteal. "You and I, fair lady, are to open the dance along with our esteemed elders, so I humbly request the honor of leading you out."

He spoke with such excessive pomp, Fanteal almost giggled.

Jaikon apparently missed the humor. "I always have the first dance with Lady Fanteal."

Renauld shook his head in mock reproof. "Shockingly selfish. My grandmother has decreed otherwise. But fear not, I shall concede the floor to you thereafter."

Jaikon looked ready to argue, even though he couldn't claim the proxy role when his father was present. Interesting, but Fanteal replied to Renauld. "I grant your most humble request, sir." She dropped the bantering tone and included Jaikon. "Really, it makes no difference, for I dance precisely once with each potential suitor."

"You'll probably be forced into dancing with some governors too," Renauld said. "You have my deepest sympathies, lady." She laughed aloud this time, though Renauld asked Jaikon, "Has the council session finally ended?"

"No, just a recess to add a few days to the weekend. Enough to let the representatives travel home and back."

"Or allow the governors to chase the ambassador's favor."

"Ah..." Fanteal teased, "so you do politics after all?"

"Never, but that doesn't mean I cannot recognize it." He sent a questioning look to Fanteal. "But I am guessing that you didn't come to hear my opinion of certain politicians."

"No. Any interesting ideas about the cataracts?"

"Don't give me that hopeful look. I haven't earned it. A few *ideas*, yes. An auger, of sorts, within an adjustable cage that could follow the cataract's contour. A spinning device that could coat the cataract walls while following it. But my ideas all have the same flaw as the formers' gift." When they only waited in silence, he said, "Deployment. I cannot figure how to place automated tools so far into the cataracts. And worse, if some failure prevented movement, they would block the flow far more than it is now."

Fanteal's hope plummeted. No matter the success of her wind weaving, they could not find a trade solution. She looked to Jaikon, dreading the disappointment on his face. Not there.

Instead, he stared at nothing. "Imports are most important. The biggest obstacle is relatively high in a steep cataract. Consider lowering a device from above. Gravity will help instead of hinder."

"True...on the way down," Renauld mused.

"Getting stuck..." Jaikon drummed his fingers on the table. Suddenly, his frown cleared. "Would there be a way to make it shatter into small pieces so the current can flush them out?"

"Ah! I never have designed anything to destroy itself. Intriguing."

Why that made Renauld so happy, she couldn't imagine, but she propped up hope. "So, you're not giving up?"

Renauld jumped. "Giving up? Caverns, no!" Her face must have shown far too much relief. "Lady Fanteal, I won't give up because my nature defies the word *impossible*. But I must be honest with you. My chances of *success* are still quite low." He spread his hands and smiled. "I have until the half-year, right? The tides allow for at least one trip of the small vessel, so we could send the plans up, maybe even a prototype of the device. Assuming I can figure something out by then."

Usually true, though the last half-year had failed them. She pasted her smile on. "Of course. I look forward to our dance."

Tonight, Prime Minister Mikkael escorted Fanteal through the doors of a governor's house. Fitting protocol, though she missed the simpler escort Jaikon provided. The spacious hall glittered. Polished silver and brass helixes dangled from the galleries, scattering light as they spun. The wide-open pocket doors of the side rooms made the hall feel even larger.

Fanteal's gown suited the occasion. Full-length in weaver's white, trimmed with dainty green stitching and embellished with her ambassador sash. But that wasn't her favorite part. Only the emerald and diamond necklace the Mikkaels had given her could hold that place.

Governor Yaldeeth stepped forward to greet her guests, sprightly enough to give the lie to her white hair. Fewer introductions were needed these days, and Fanteal felt less like an outsider. Might she someday feel like a Dirklian? Soft music flowed from the band in one of the side rooms. And, oh, look at that. A young wind weaver stood by the doorway, ensuring that echoes didn't spoil the melodies. Fanteal smiled at her, and the girl grinned back like she was bursting with pride.

Renauld, quite impressive in his formal attire, came to claim Fanteal's hand for the first dance.

"Ah, so you remembered," she teased.

"How could I forget a lady as beautiful as you." Renauld quirked an eyebrow at Governor Yaldeeth, whose hand rested in Sir Mikkael's. "Is that the kind of thing I'm supposed to say?"

His grandmother cast her eyes to the distant ceiling. "I told you it didn't matter one way or another."

The gentle strains gave way to the first measure of dance music, and Renauld swept Fanteal into a spin. He was a surprisingly good dancer.

"Tell me," Fanteal said. "Were you teasing me or your grandmother?"

"Her. She's annoyed by your other suitors and strictly forbade me to behave like them."

Fantail laughed. "I do believe she is my favorite of all the governors."

"Mine too. No one is even a close second. A pity, isn't it, that her only bachelor descendant is in love with his workshop?"

"Are you trying to get out of marrying me?"

He looked shocked. "No one is pushing that on me, so there is nothing to get out of. It's quite impossible anyway. An ambassador must travel, but an inventor must stay in his workshop."

Governor Yaldeeth invited other dancers to the floor, and Renauld guided Fanteal between couples. "So...many...people," he murmured. It was no surprise that he ended the dance near Jaikon. "As promised," he said with a wink, and vanished into a side room.

Never was Fanteal allowed to sit out a dance, for every suitor was present. Even Grellin, whom she hadn't seen since her visit to Crysalan. He arranged to have the dance right before the musicians took a break. Thus, he escorted her to the buffet in a long dining room at the rear of the hall.

Fanteal selected a few delicacies, and Grellin poured her a glass of chilled pyret tea.

He guided her to a small table and pulled a chair out for her. "I would have thought Governor Yaldeeth could provide a better repast for such an honored guest as yourself."

Wow. She took a bite, gaining time to formulate her answer. "I had dinner before the dance, but it was kind of her to provide refreshments."

He sat down to his own rather full plate. "When we host you in Alluthin, we'll provide kindness *and* plentiful food."

"At the moment, I would rather hear courtesy to my current hostess."

That gave him pause, but Grellin recovered quickly. "Forgive me if I made you uncomfortable. When do you expect to visit Alluthin?"

"I have two more domains to visit first. Since I don't know what may be needed there, I cannot give you an exact date."

"Small domains. I've heard that you're training wind weavers. Perhaps you should send your students to the remaining domains. An opportunity to try their skills alongside Jaikon and the apprentice former who does the work. The men could join you afterward in Alluthin and let you know how it went."

"I journey as ambassador as well as chief wind weaver. I will not slight any domain."

"Your dedication is commendable. No doubt you are right, especially so soon after your arrival. Don't worry that you will have to maintain such an arduous schedule. Ambassador Melthindi didn't find it necessary." Grellin washed down a bite with a draught of tea. "I'm excited to show you around our domain. Restfully, of course. Our wind weavers are already organized and skilled, so we won't put you to work."

"I enjoy weaving the wind."

"Then Alluthin will be perfect for you. Spacious and vibrant. I'm sure you will love it."

She swiped her last river grape through a delicious sauce. "You certainly do—understandable, since it is your home. This first visit will not be long, though. I have engagements in both Jourendia and Crysalan."

His gaze dipped, but he said, "Then, I will hope to persuade you to return quickly. By the way, I want to introduce you to Alluthin's chief former, Creflon Lawfertee. He was an apprentice to Agriben in his earlier days, and thus is able to tend the dome of Passage Lake."

She swallowed her grape. Where had that subject change come from? "Oh?"

A hint of surprise entered his eyes. "I assumed you had heard about Agriben—that he collapsed or had some kind of fainting spell."

Her stomach tensed. "No."

"Well, in any case, I believe he recovered, so a change isn't imminent. Of course, it will happen someday. You are such a diligent ambassador, I thought you'd want to meet the domain chief who will likely be selected as the next provincial chief former."

Disturbing. She couldn't shake his words. Not even while talking with other dance partners—until the last dance was announced.

Renauld abruptly stepped between her and the man who was approaching. "May I have this dance, Lady Fanteal?"

She wanted to accept, but a few suitors stood near enough to hear her answer. "I'd enjoy it, but I cannot show favoritism among those who court me."

"Then you *may* enjoy it, for I am not courting." He took her hand and drew her toward the dance floor before she could respond. "Besides, those who follow you around Dirklan have already had more dances than I."

She wouldn't let anyone else get away with this, but she was intrigued. The dance floor was less crowded than before, and she was certain some motive hid behind his surprising request. She moved to his side in the opening promenade steps. Could he have news about an invention? Something he couldn't say when the floor was crowded. The time came to join hands, and she faced him, speaking softly. "Do you have news for me?"

"Nothing that deserves such a smile, but it is a good cover." He twirled her away and back again.

"Then what?"

"You spent more time with Grellin Armeen than anyone else. And no, I am not jealous."

Now she must promenade with another dancer. Returning to Renauld, she grumbled, "This is a terrible dance for conversation."

"True, but I only have one thing to say." Another spin interrupted.

"Say it at once."

"Listen with your gift," he whispered, barely audible. "I spent too much time in Alluthin. The Armeens are bats in dove plumage. Grellin, especially. I just wanted to warn you."

They started weaving between couples, then promenaded toward the band to offer a bow and curtsy of thanks for the evening's music. Through all of this, she must keep up a gracious smile. How long before she could have a private talk with the Mikkaels?

She managed that a few minutes after the crowds left. "Sir Mikkael, Grellin told me that Agriben collapsed or fainted or something. Do you know what happened?"

"I heard of it after the fact. It seemed a minor event, and he quickly recovered. What had Grellin to say about it?"

"He spoke of Alluthin's domain chief former and said he is likely to be the next provincial chief."

"Rude to speak of Agriben's replacement so prematurely."

"But is it likely true? Grellin said Creflon apprenticed under Agriben and is able to tend the dome over Passage Lake. Is anyone else equally qualified?"

"I don't know." Sir Mikkael considered for a moment. "Agriben undoubtedly knows and, when he is ready to relinquish his duties, he will only recommend those who can open the dome."

"What if..." She fidgeted with her sash. "What if he didn't relinquish his duties before...what if he passed suddenly?"

"That would be an unfortunate disruption, but the result would be the same. The guild will vote, in either case, to choose a new provincial chief former. They will choose someone who can open the dome." When she only frowned, he added, "You know as well as I do that the choice lies *only* within the purview of the Formers' Guild. There is no point in worrying over things you cannot control, especially something that is not imminent."

He glanced to Jaikon, including him in his next words. "Current matters are more important. You will soon be visiting Alluthin. Governor Armeen holds considerable sway in the council. Remember that his family is large and owns most of the cropland of Alluthin. Both of you need to be careful with your words. Avoid giving offense."

Jaikon rolled his eyes. "Do I get any credit for improvement? Whom have I offended lately?"

His father laughed softly. "I have heard no shock waves, so I gather you deserve a great deal of credit." He took Fanteal's hand. "You, my dear, are the one at greatest risk of offending. Grellin Armeen will likely propose marriage. My advice is that you wait several more months before choosing. Also, I made a promise to you and your parents. Please discuss your choice with me before committing yourself."

"I will not accept any marriage proposal before the air channels are cleared and my entire guild has completed a tour of Dirklan. They must learn about the province-wide air flow."

Sir Mikkael nodded. "That may be enough of an answer, but Grellin may press hard. If he is not your choice, you will eventually have to say *no* outright. Avoid that until you are ready to announce the proposal you *do* accept. Nonetheless, it is crucial that we maintain a good relationship with Alluthin."

Jaikon escorted Fanteal out of the governor's house. The guests had departed, and the city square lay in shadow beyond the street's magnery lights.

A cair waited for them, and the driver bowed to Lady Fanteal before offering his hand to help her climb in. This fellow treated her with distinct honor, even ensuring that her gown didn't hang out of the cair. Was someone he loved suffering from emfiduria and now inhaling the first hint of relief?

Such courtesies were growing more common, offsetting the disgruntled looks from those who thought of Fanteal as not-a-streamer. Jaikon took his place beside her, and they set out for their borrowed house. If only he had some offsetting attribute to counter the not-a-real-former grumbles.

They soon arrived at their temporary home—their last night here. A magnery light glowed at its lowest setting in the welcome room. Bella and Charlis must have gone up to their rooms already.

Fanteal looked worn down. "Are you tired, my dear," he asked, "or not looking forward to another train ride?" She blinked and stepped back to lean against a chair. Yi! How had he called her *dear*?

"Both," she said, "but that's of little matter. It's just..."

"What?"

"It seems that when I hope things will get better, they get worse. We've learned plenty about the cataracts, but that only proves they are in terrible shape. Not enough time has passed for an invention yet, but one doesn't seem likely. By what I've heard about Alluthin, I should love the place, but I have such a bad feeling about it. Then hearing of Agriben's poor health is disturbing. Obviously worse for him than for me, but he has been such a reliable and necessary supporter—for both of us."

"That is true." Jaikon had to do better than this. She didn't need agreement that things were bad. "Sometimes hope seems as dim as a cavern when the light shafts wink out. But light returns every morning, no matter how dark the night."

Vague. Would practical encouragement help? "The invention—it definitely needs more time, and we have that." He hoped. "Agriben— that worry may be nothing at all. We'll see him in Crysalan in a couple weeks, and he will probably set your mind at rest. Alluthin—it is beautiful. I'm not looking forward to the Armeens either, but we don't need to think about them for at least a week."

A brilliant idea flashed into his mind. "Let's plan something to look forward to. In Crysalan, there is this wonderful inn tucked away in its own private cavern. You'll love the history of the place, and love the hot springs even more. We'll take a few days, climb the gem hills, stroll the gardens, then soak in the mineral waters." Her expression lightened as he described the plan. "Does that make tomorrow look a little better?"

"It does."

He wished for a bigger smile. "Who knows, maybe you'll find another wind weaver aboveground at the next domain."

She inhaled like she did whenever she thought about her gift. "That's always fun." She tilted her head. "Do you ever sense a former near the surface when you follow me along a channel?"

Ugh. Why did she have to ask that when he was trying to cheer her up? "I guess, maybe. It's not the same for me." She looked like she was going to ask for details, so he kept talking. "I suppose every wind weaver up there knows you and enjoys a friendly touch." He winked. "I'm rather short on *old friends* in Welcia above."

Even her grin looked tired.

"Get some sleep—" Just in time, he stopped himself from ending with *my dear*.

CHAPTER 28

Fanteal sensed Alluthin before they reached it. Airy in a vast sense. Several light shafts beside the rails revealed tan stone, paler than anywhere else. Even the echoes changed, for the tunnel roof angled steeply into a shadowy realm. She wafted a breeze through it to discern its shape. "Does any portion of this get near the surface?"

Jaikon followed her gaze, and she felt his gift sweep past hers. "Not really."

They approached a split in the tunnel, and Jaikon shoved the steering lever to the left. He nodded right. "That leads to food storage in a dedicated cavern." He leaned back and stretched as they passed it. "Almost there."

The carriage emerged from the rail tunnel into the cavern. Brilliant and immense. Actual trees reached for the distant ceiling. These were not the little fruit varieties she'd seen in other domains. She stretched her awareness, merely for the joy of reaching farther than anywhere else—then squelched disappointment. The pale stone and plentiful light must make it look bigger than it was. Still, this was by far the biggest cavern in Dirklan. Others just as big adjoined it.

The carriages stopped, and Jaikon's words reached her. "Give her a moment. She is sensing."

She blinked. Everyone else had climbed out, and Grellin awaited her. As always, a demand for public appearance. She accepted Grellin's hand and stepped from the carriage. The station was long but not as broad as some. No room for a crowd, but a cluster of people waited to greet her.

As Grellin introduced each, she realized this was a select group, nearly all with the same family name—Armeen—and a few bearing the name of Lawfertee. Many offered curtsies, bows, and murmurs of "Such a delight, Ambassador Fanteal." No cheering. No reference to her wind weaving gift, even though the chief streamer and chief former were among those introduced. A very dignified welcome, entirely focused on her role as ambassador. They would already know Jaikon, of course, though it seemed odd that they didn't acknowledge him. Apparently, Bella and Charlis were invisible. If Grellin had his way, all three of them would have been left on the platform.

Fanteal turned to her companions, allowing time to unload the luggage piled on the extra seat in each carriage.

"Come, Lady Fanteal," Grellin said, "the station workers will assist your attendants and show them the way. I have refreshments ready for you at a reception."

Reception? The little crowd was shifting aside, allowing space for them to pass. He touched her hand again, light but clearly intending to lead her away.

"*We*," she said, "will appreciate the refreshments."

"Naturally, I assumed Jaikon would also join us."

Irritating, but they still had an audience, so she kept her voice soft. "Bella and Charlis, also. As for the reception, that is less convenient. In the future, please do not make engagements without consulting me."

"Don't worry. I have allowed time for the meetings that you requested and plenty of time for you to simply enjoy a rest."

Short of making a scene, she could think of no way to get her message through. Bella seemed satisfied with the luggage arrangements, so Fanteal began walking along the platform at Grellin's side. No surprise that he reached for her hand again, but instead of drawing it to the crook of his arm in the Dirklian style, he formally supported her hand on his open palm.

Never had she expected this mistake here. "What are you doing?"

"Acknowledging your station."

She wanted nothing more than to pull her hand away. Again, that would create a scene in front of the entourage that now followed them.

Jaikon, immediately behind her, said, "Palm down," in an under-voice.

Grellin flicked a glance back at him. "I know exactly what I'm doing. Alluthians were familiar with Ambassador Melthindi's formal manners."

"Doubtless he escorted his *wife* this way," Fanteal said. "At least have the courtesy to turn your palm down."

This time, Grellin complied. "Is there some nuance I have overlooked?"

"Either you have missed the entire meaning, or your presumption is in the skies above. If you escort me in the future, please offer your arm as the prime minister and his proxy do."

They reached a turning point with a few steps down, and Grellin smoothly altered as if to assist her, then drew her hand to the crook of his arm. "Please forgive my misconception, lady."

"Of course." She kept her expression and voice neutral, difficult though it was. The hand position wasn't the issue—no one here could interpret that, for the gesture was rare belowground. Regardless of that fine point, she was still sure he'd intended to portray himself as husband to the ambassador. And he had done it before an audience that made it difficult for her to decline his gesture. Or so she assumed. She could be wrong, so she'd better get past this. "Am I correct in guessing that you invited specific people to meet me at the station?"

"Yes. I didn't want you mobbed as you are elsewhere."

"Why these particular people?"

"They are the most...shall we say, significant...citizens of Alluthin, for they own the controlling interest in the croplands. There are other crop owners too, but with so many people to meet, I want to spread out introductions. You'll meet them at the reception."

Significant? This almost sounded like a class structure. How far did it reach?

Fanteal strolled with Grellin toward a cluster of people at the edge of a grove of trees.

"Does our little forest remind you of home?" he asked.

Forest? Evenly spaced trees without undergrowth? "Not really, but the grove is pretty." Spindly too, but she omitted that. It wouldn't go over any better than when she'd said Alluthin's air was no longer the best in Dirklan. A slip at yesterday's reception, while she spoke of opening their air channels. Her words had prompted stony glares.

Hopefully the wind weavers she was about to meet wouldn't resent the truth. By their expressions, at least, they seemed pleased.

Grellin stopped before the group. "It gives me great pleasure to introduce the Royal Ambassador of Welcia, Fanteal de Noviam."

They all curtsied—ah, no—one man among them bowed.

Fanteal received their courtesy with a smile, giving Grellin a second to add her title of Chief Wind Weaver. He didn't, so she spoke. "It is a pleasure to me as well to meet the wind weavers of Alluthin. In a moment, we'll sit down to talk so I can meet you individually, but first I will introduce my companions." She turned enough to draw them forward. "Perhaps you already know Jaikon Mikkael, who is the prime minister's proxy while I travel. He is also a former."

He nodded to the group, and Fanteal introduced Bella and Charlis.

Grellin seemed to want her introductions even shorter than she'd made them, for he promptly moved on. "This is Percuff, the lead wind weaver. Not a guild chief, since there is no true weavers' guild in Alluthin, but he reports to the cropland owners. This way to the circle." Grellin began to lead her toward a ring of benches within the grove.

Nerve-wracking. She hung back, eyeing the tall, skinny trees.

"What's wrong?"

"The branches seem...rather thin."

Grellin looked vaguely surprised. "These trees are young."

Young? At this height? Strange, but the locals had already entered the grove, so it must be safe. Fanteal let Grellin escort her toward the benches.

The eldest woman drew near her. "We heard rumors that you were elected Chief Wind Weaver of Dirklan in Crysalan's sacred chamber. Some say that the weavers of other domains have added their votes in confirmation. Is it so?"

"Indeed, it—"

"You may sit here, Ambassador." Grellin guided her to a bench before addressing Percuff. "Apparently, there has been some problem bringing in enough fresh air yesterday. That should be the first order of business."

That quick, defensive looks clouded their faces. She wished he would keep quiet. Now she would have to start with damage control. "Oh, I doubt there has been any problem with that. I would far rather start by simply meeting all of you." Her smile cleared the clouds, and they began sitting down. "Grellin, thank you for escorting us here. I'll likely take quite a while for our meeting, and I don't want to detain you."

"It is my pleasure to attend you."

Figured. She started around the circle, learning names and what they enjoyed most in their weaving gift. That usually revealed any specialties as well as a demonstration. The scratching of Bella's pen assured her she would have help with remembering all of the details. There were only ten wind weavers, but this was the most that dwelled in any domain.

When each one had answered her, the eldest, Oganzie, asked, "What is *your* favorite way to use your gift?"

Fanteal opened her mouth to answer, but Grellin spoke first. "Do not be presumptuous."

Fanteal was facing Oganzie, so Grellin missed her gritted teeth. Oganzie didn't, judging by her sneaky smile. Fanteal said, "My favorite part is to reach through the vast spaces. I didn't realize it at first, but I'm now sure that is why Ellincreo gifted me as he did. Soon, we will walk together through Alluthin's caverns, and I'll show you what I mean."

Grellin jumped in again. "I told Percuff to delay the morning refresh until you joined them. That needs to be done first."

So aggravating! Nonetheless, she smiled at Percuff. "Do you refresh it every morning?"

"Yes. Not me, though. Oganzie and Ettora do it."

"You may go ahead, if you like." Fanteal watched with her gift, sensing where they drew a current inward, coiled it through the largest caverns like a lazy snake, then sent it out again.

"That's most of it," Oganzie said. "We go to the fringe caverns next and refresh each one. They don't have channels of their own."

Grellin couldn't stay out of it. "Is the air now fresh like aboveground, Ambassador?"

She gave him a long look. "It is fresh at the moment, but already the breeze has stopped. I noticed it thinning last evening. Air needs continuous movement, so—"

"Percuff," Grellin interrupted *again*, "arrange for two refreshes a day."

"Grellin, that is not the solution. I know how to direct wind weaving."

"I'm sure you do." He reverted to the respectfully affectionate tone he used with her. "Indeed, you've proven that elsewhere, beyond question. But, my dear lady, I invited you here to relax, not to work."

"Kind of you. Yet, I wish you would believe me when I say that I enjoy wind weaving. Even with no invitation, I would have come anyway. I am both ambassador and chief wind weaver, and I need to finish opening channels."

"What you've done for the neglected wind weavers in the other domains is admirable, though not needed here. Alluthin has always honored the weaving gift, and we use it regularly. In fact, we are the only domain that has paid them a wage through all generations."

"Speaking of that," one of the wind weavers said, "I hear that they get paid in other domains now, too, and the rate is even higher than ours."

Fanteal didn't know what Alluthin paid, but she confirmed the hourly rate elsewhere.

Grellin addressed the local weavers. "They still make less than you, for they rarely get a day's work as you do. Naturally, you'll earn less if you no longer refresh the air on a daily basis."

Was he suggesting that she should *not* clear their air channels? Fortunately, the weavers looked to her in question. "There is plenty of work for weavers in Dirklan, and you are now free to travel. For instance, you may earn more by training other weavers on your pollination techniques. I've read—"

"No other domain," Grellin said, "has space for such crops. I hear that it is a pleasant duty for our wind weavers, though. Would you like to see a demonstration of their techniques?"

"Yes, in due time, though I doubt that needs my attention. The air channels do. There should be no need to refresh daily. The breeze should flow through on its own. Alluthin should participate in the fresh airflow that the rest of Dirklan Province now enjoys."

"How?" a young weaver asked.

Good—a question that Grellin couldn't answer for her. "I will show you." Fanteal stood, and they followed suit. "We'll tour Alluthin's caverns." She flipped a hand toward Jaikon and Charlis. "The formers will map the air channels, and we'll search for new ones in the fringe caverns. As we go, I will draw air back and forth to find obstructions in the channels." She strolled between trees. "Spread out a little and observe my technique, for this task will become yours. It must be done four times a year through all of Dirklan.”

The trees creaked. A sound as unnatural as their stiff movement. Shouldn’t thin branches be more flexible?

A few extra lines creased Oganzie’s face. “We usually keep the main flow higher during a refresh.”

“So I noticed, but searching and cleaning techniques require stronger flow and reversal.” Fanteal stopped, and with a glance over her shoulder to Jaikon, she pointed to what she sensed. “Up there.” He nodded, and she asked, “Is matter moving in the channel?” She felt his sense following hers, so she worked the wind back and forth through a narrowed portion. Overhead, entire limbs creaked their opinion of foreign winds.

“Yes,” Jaikon said. “The narrowing is—”

A creak morphed into an ominous groan. Branches ripped through a neighboring tree, caught directly above her, then both limbs snapped.

Fanteal barely had time to cover her head. Jaikon grabbed her around the waist and dropped, forcing her to the ground beneath him. He twitched and grunted. What had happened?

She blinked hard. Black hair on Jaikon’s arm came into focus. Her cheek rested on the back of his splayed fingers. She twisted and peered through a maze of twigs and stripped leaves. Shattered limbs lay several feet away. Charlis released Bella from a protective embrace, but they stood just beyond the mess. Wind weavers stared with mouths agape. Thank Ellincreo they had spread out. Grellin darted toward her from the circle of benches. Hadn’t he been at her side?

Jaikon demanded, “Are you hurt?”

“No.” Uncomfortable, but not in pain. Because of him. He was on hands and knees, his torso above hers. “Are you hurt?”

“I’m fine,” he said.

Charlis reached them, lifted a branch, and flung it away. Jaikon shifted and straightened upright on his knees, giving Fanteal space to turn and sit up.

She caught his grimace just as he tried to clear it. He *was* hurt. Before she could say anything, Grellin reached her, all solicitude, and helped her up. Couldn't he be quiet?

At least Charlis offered a hand to pull Jaikon up. Without even asking, Bella lifted the back of his shirt.

"See to Lady Fanteal," Jaikon said.

"Medics tend the most serious injuries first." Bella dropped her pitch. "Those welts must sting. Do the bones hurt when I press here?"

"No. More drama than injury. I'm fine."

With a smirk, she shook her head and eased his shirt down. "This got all snagged up when those branches whipped across you."

If they were talking about shirts, he couldn't be badly hurt.

Bella looked Fanteal up and down. "You're all right, I take it?"

"Yes. Nothing hurts."

A few wind weavers clustered around her, brushing leaves from her dress and leggings. Fanteal smoothed her hair back and refastened a clip. A couple men arrived in the grove, out of breath from running.

Grellin leaned near her ear. "Don't worry. I'll protect you."

What in the caverns?

He strolled over to join the men as they stared up at injured trees and dangling limbs. At every mention of wind, he steered the conversation back to some kind of experimental enhanced growth and weak limbs. Apparently, it was from blame that he protected her.

Fanteal stepped close to Jaikon and looked up into his face. "Thank you!"

His expression lightened, and he answered softly. "You're welcome, my dear." He cocked his head. "Shall we find a better place for wind weaving?"

They did so and managed to confirm the air channel locations and clear a few without destroying any more trees. That done, they headed for the fringe caverns, which required cairs. Fanteal deftly drew a few people with her into a cair so Grellin would be forced to take another.

Thus she, Bella, Percuff, and Oganzie gained a few minutes of privacy, enhanced with her gift.

Fanteal asked Percuff, who looked younger than she, "How did you get chosen as the lead wind weaver?"

He exchanged a look with Oganzie, and they both uttered a humorous snort. "I married into the Armeen family last year," he replied. "The change came a month to the day after my wedding. Don't worry, though. I know I'm a rookie. In reality, Oganzie still leads us."

"Oh, dear," Fanteal turned to Oganzie. "Do you mind? Does it affect your pay?"

She laughed. "Not a bit. I hated going to those stupid cropland meetings. The only difference is that we meet in his house instead of mine. The crop owners probably feel they have more control that way. If we need to do something they don't understand, we talk about it later and just get it done."

"Oh, I see." Fanteal hoped it was that simple, but she wondered if she had...not a *spy*, exactly. Possibly an *ear* in the background, who might report to the crop owners. Still, she didn't work in secret.

That couldn't have been more obvious once she stepped from the cair at the first stop. Jaikon and Charlis began their routine, and Fanteal explained her techniques to the wind weavers. Local growers stopped their labor in the fields and gathered to watch. Everyone would know.

Grellin wandered off at one point to talk with a cair driver. The fellow jumped onto the motor and headed away. Odd, but his purpose became clear when the driver rejoined them at the next fringe cavern, bringing Chief Former Creflon.

Not what she wanted, considering his glib remark at yesterday's reception. *There will be no need for forming in Alluthin.* Uttered like she was an idiot.

CHAPTER 29

Creflon greeted Fanteal, then asked, "Wind weaving here?"

She matched his pleasant tone. "Alluthin lacks natural flow. Perhaps you already know that the caverns excavated after the collapse do not have air channels."

"Of course. That is why the access tunnels are so wide."

"Spoken like a former." Fanteal said it with a lilt and smile, but Creflon stared at her.

"That is what I am."

No sense of humor. "Quite so. Speaking as a wind weaver, I'll elaborate. The wide tunnels allow space for air movement, but without a source, they cannot provide fresh air."

His gaze had wandered to Jaikon, who was searching through rock. Creflon narrowed his eyes, and his forming gift reached out to follow Jaikon's.

Perhaps she should explain. "Jaikon is searching for possible routes for air channels. He can sense all the way to the surface."

"So I have heard. Regardless of what he can sense, we cannot excavate to the surface."

"How far can the longest-range former of Alluthin reach?"

"That is not the point, lady. Even if we were willing to risk opening a hole that someone could fall into—which we are not—holes on the surface would allow water to enter, causing all manner of harm."

"The air channels are protected aboveground to guard against either problem."

"Abovegrounders would have no idea that new channels were being opened."

What kind of idiot did he think she was? Fanteal pointed to where Charlis bent over his map, following Jaikon's references to document the route. "Level maps have a purpose, you know. Communication may be painfully slow, but it does occur."

He regarded her for too long. "I respect your role as ambassador, Lady Fanteal, but the decisions to form are the purview of the Formers' Guild."

"Naturally," Fanteal replied. "Jaikon's and Charlis's work is approved by Provincial Chief Former Agriben."

"True, at the moment, but Agriben has never ordered a domain's chief former to—"

"Creflon," Grellin said, "please come and review the updated map. Confirmation of everything within your range would be advisable."

Creflon's nostrils twitched, but he walked toward Charlis.

Grellin touched Fanteal's arm, detaining her. "It's one thing to protect you from a couple of foresters, but quite another when you challenge any of the Armeens."

"Isn't his family name Lawfertee?"

"Yes—descended through the daughter of the original cropland owners. They are still considered Armeens. A different approach will be needed, but that is for the future."

Future? Was he referring to marriage? "I don't see why this is a family matter at all. We are speaking of the Formers' and Wind Weavers' Guilds."

"Quite, but this is Alluthin, where food production is paramount. The locals who are blessed with substance gifts would never forget our highest priority." His brow twitched as he watched her reaction, and he altered his tone. "All of Dirklan depends on us for food."

She tilted her head. "So this is why you like the wind weavers managed by someone with the Armeen name, rather than by Dirklan's chief wind weaver."

He smiled winningly. "Ah, but I very much hope we will soon have both."

She understood him, but better to let him state his intent fully. "Pardon?"

"Couple your titles with my name. That will grant you all the cooperation you could ever want in Alluthin. And in Dirklan, after the next election."

"What a charming proposal," she remarked drily.

"Don't think that I value only practicality. My admiration of you grows with every moment I spend in your company. Nothing would delight me more than to exchange marriage vows with you."

She had to admit his tone and expression were utterly sincere. Not that they ignited any spark within her. Still, she wouldn't risk offending him. "Unfortunately, personal preference isn't a luxury allowed to an ambassador, so the practicalities must be considered."

"I know. That is why I speak of them more than my affections."

"With that clear," she said, "I do not understand why a royal ambassador and a provincial chief wind weaver would need a local family name in order to fulfill her duties."

"Nothing happens in Alluthin without the approval of the Armeens."

"I must consider *all* of Dirklan."

"Exactly. Alluthin is the only long-term food source of the province. We *will* win the next election. Wed to me, you will have all the authority you could possibly need. Without my name, you will be fighting an endless battle for anything you may want to do. Please forgive me if I am too blunt, but I must be honest. Your chances of winning those battles will be slim, indeed, if you do not bear the name of Armeen."

Grellin's proposal haunted Fanteal through every unoccupied moment. Once she'd gotten her anger under control, she couldn't help but wonder if he were correct. Ominous thought. She sipped the last of her morning tea, staring out the inn's window at a field, while Bella sorted through invitations at the sitting room table.

She'd heard nothing else from Renauld, who had promised to send word of any breakthroughs. If the import cataract couldn't be repaired, then Alluthin was crucial to the survival of Dirklan. Even if it was repaired, Alluthin was still an important food source. There simply was no other domain that approached the criticality of this one. Every time she reached that conclusion, she hid a sigh.

She strolled back to the table and set her cup down. If only Grellin stirred emotion within her. It wasn't for lack of effort on his part. After his *honest* declaration, he spared no pains to win her affection. To find her preferences and cater to them. He was good at it, too, though it left her cold. Was there any way to build a friendship, at least? Something that could make marriage...what...mildly pleasant? Maybe someday grow into...companionable love?

Ugh. Was this the most she could hope for? Even this felt uncertain. Why, though? He was courteous. Mostly. Awfully prone to interrupting her. At one point, he'd apologized afterward, assuring her he'd only done it to protect her from making a mistake. That reason made her like it no better. Maybe less.

Perhaps such annoyances would resolve once he knew her better. He certainly tried to accommodate her, so communication might be all they needed in order to reach an understanding.

Marriage wasn't about her preferences anyway. She was here to represent the crown. Unfortunately, the crown was a distant glimmer beyond the view of most Dirklians. That made her sad in a deep, inexplicable way. She slid into a chair by the table. They had lost something precious here and didn't even seem to know it had once existed. Could she resurrect the awareness that they were part of something far grander than they could see? Could she hope to succeed without the influence that Alluthin wielded? Or more accurately, that the Armeens wielded? Doubtful.

Every consideration pointed in one direction—to marry Grellin. She failed to hide the sigh this time. Unfortunately, Jaikon walked into her sitting room in that moment.

"Is something wrong?" he asked.

Fanteal produced a calm smile, for Bella had turned to look at her too. "Just that the last couple days have been so tedious."

Bella may not have been convinced by that excuse, but Charlis, following Jaikon into the room, distracted her.

Jaikon looked over the invitations on the table and lifted his lip. "We're never going to get done at this rate. Not with Grellin and company arranging breakfast, lunch, and dinner in one exalted house after another."

Fanteal couldn't blame him for griping. The Armeens and Lawfertees pandered to her. Jaikon, they treated as an afterthought. In company, he took it with outward patience, though it must be galling.

Charlis, who had just repeated one of Creflon's reminders that their work was unnecessary, said, "I don't understand him—any of them, really. It's like they don't want Alluthin to have good airflow. Why, I cannot figure out."

Fanteal had puzzled over that as well. "It could have something to do with maintaining control over Alluthin's wind weavers. A reason perhaps to insist that they must all stay here for the daily refreshing. At the moment, crops requiring wind pollination are only grown in

Alluthin. The Armeens may not want those skills available to other domains."

"Doesn't seem like an adequate reason." Jaikon rubbed his jaw. "Nowhere else has the necessary space for grains."

"No, but one thing is certain. They don't want me in control of the wind weavers." Unless she was an Armeen, but she wouldn't say that. Jaikon was irritated enough by the need to squelch what looked suspiciously like jealousy. Something else she wouldn't speak of. "You're right about the delays, though. Grellin will monopolize my time, no matter what. I think you and Charlis should analyze and map the fringe caverns without me. I cannot help you, anyway, for there are no gaps for me to flush air through."

"I don't want to leave you alone with him."

"Bella will accompany me." Fanteal gave her an apologetic smile. "Sorry, for they lack courtesy."

"I'll just sit in the background and pretend I'm not listening." Bella added a sly wink. "A good way to learn."

"True enough." Doubtful that she'd learn much, but Fanteal was sure something was hidden here. Removing Jaikon from social events might loosen tongues. "You could get more work done," she said to the men, "if Grellin wasn't constantly interrupting. I'm not sure if I can rid you of Creflon, though. Will he be able to stop you?"

"Let him try," Charlis growled. "I have orders from Agriben to map the levels, and I'm doing it."

"If you anger Creflon," Jaikon warned, "it could affect your future career. He is likely to be the next provincial chief."

Creases deepened between Charlis's eyebrows, and Bella murmured, "Oh, no."

"Let me deal with him." Jaikon clapped Charlis's shoulder. "I'll stress your need to obey the current provincial chief former, whomever that may be."

How it must aggravate them to tread carefully before the Armeens. Could she fix that for everyone if she brought her titles to bear from within the family? The tension in her chest began to hurt. She hid her eyes from Jaikon and tried a cheerful tone. "We'll divide and conquer, then."

They implemented their plan and got the work done before the grand ball the Armeens held in her honor. Governor Armeen even returned for the event.

Despite Fanteal's enjoyment of dancing, she couldn't look forward to it. Not with all the meticulous planning. They even had meetings about it! At least, this was the only one of them Fanteal had to endure. She almost lost her temper when the governor's wife handed her yet another list. "Here are the dances and your partners."

"What? Do the men here not know how to ask for a dance?"

"They did ask," Lady Armeen said.

"Oh. *I* am the one who doesn't have a choice."

Lady Armeen gave her a deadpan look. "Is there a man on the list with whom you do not wish to dance?"

Oh, to say, *every one of them*! Ambassador training dictated that she accommodate local custom. She kept her lips closed and scanned the list. She had met so many people in the last few days that she recognized the names. "I do not see Jaikon Mikkael on the list. He will undoubtedly ask me to dance, according to the more usual custom, so a dance must remain open."

"I see. The men have already been informed of their dances. Which one do you want to offend by removing him?"

"It is not I who offend. I suggest that the person who prematurely accepted on my behalf inform the gentleman that he or she made a mistake."

The lady's expression made it clear that she was the one who would be forced to admit a mistake.

Grellin stepped into the breach. "Or you may add a dance."

Thus, the long night was made even longer. Every dance seemed identical. Only a few of Fanteal's partners came up with original conversation. Still, her feet didn't consider them worth the effort.

Jaikon's dance came late in the evening, without the pomp of each partner being formally presented to her.

He took her hand but looked into her eyes before leading her out. "How are you holding up?"

"My feet hurt, and I am fed up with this charade. Can we slip away somewhere?"

He drew her hand onto his arm. "There are balconies behind these curtains. You may enjoy a breeze."

A casual stroll took them from the room. The curtain dropped shut behind them, muting the music and the ballroom's overdone lighting. She rested her arms on the cool stone railing. Jaikon was perceptive enough to give her silence. A faint breeze already wafted in the darkened cavern, and she savored it. Until a voice caught her attention.

"Did you hear that Shenelle Lawfertee is requesting compensation for lost income?"

The next few words were too faint to make out, but was that Grellin's voice? Fanteal held a finger to her lips, making sure Jaikon saw. She sensed with her gift as well as her ears.

The first voice said, "Her emfiduria sanatorium will fail since Alluthin no longer has the best air. If it's true that poor air caused the disease, she soon won't have patients, anyway."

"Shenelle will have to pivot to a new business." Definitely Grellin. "She cannot complain about falling on hard times because others are healthy."

"Be careful." That one sounded like Governor Armeen. "Wind weavers can hear too well, and the ballroom is above us."

"She is dancing with Jaikon," Grellin assured him.

The first voice spoke again. "I'm not at all sure it's a good plan to marry her, Grellin. She's done nothing but cause harm. The foresters are going to have to take down the experimental trees that were growing so well—until her wind snapped them off."

"More height does not equal more fruit," Grellin said. "Shorter trees that grow with wind in the early years are sturdier and produce better."

"Starting over is still a loss of ten years. The owner isn't happy. But that's not the worst of it. Our wind weavers have asked for the same wage the weavers in other domains are getting. One has even announced her intention of leaving. What if the others leave?"

"She's from a different domain." Grellin sounded dismissive. "She only came here because her husband had the early signs of emfiduria. The rest of them were born here."

"Well, if we're forced to increase their pay, we've already decided to increase the food prices to cover it."

"Then what are you complaining about?"

"We'll be criticized, and you better believe we're stating the real reason for the increase. She is trouble, Grellin. Better to get her out of Alluthin. Marry her, and we'll be stuck with her for life."

"All these matters will soon be trivial."

A new voice whispered, "New air channels are not trivial. They'll spark hope of a tunnel."

"Delay until Agriben dies, then stop it permanently." Who was Grellin speaking to? Creflon?

The whisper continued. "If she gets to Welcia, she could convince the aboveground formers to begin work."

"Nine months away," Grellin said. "Plenty of time. Once we are wed, I'll stop her meddling. She is our means to control all the wind weavers of Dirklan, and more importantly, to put an Armeen in the office of prime minister. As for the trouble she stirs, far better to keep her here where I can control her."

Heat swelled up the sides of Fanteal's face. How dare he?

"If you can," Governor Armeen said. "I was there when she jerked Nirundale down from his pedestal. Her mother's brother. Family who bears her name, mind you. She didn't hesitate to destroy his influence."

"Indeed? Is he not still governor—and powerful enough for our purposes?" Some silent gesture must have been used, then Grellin continued. "Nirundale grew overconfident and didn't bother to understand whom he dealt with. I won't make his mistakes. Enough of this. The music is ending, and I must return to the ballroom."

Fanteal stepped back from the railing. She breathed her words. "Did you hear?"

Jaikon shook his head and whispered, "Important?"

She nodded. "We have to get back into the ballroom." He pulled the curtain aside, and they stepped through. A quick glance told her that Grellin hadn't yet returned, but Lady Armeen's stern gaze rested on her. Would Grellin learn that she had been on the balcony? Would he suspect that she'd heard? Whether he did or didn't, what was she going to do about it?

CHAPTER 30

The so-called Growers' Guild came to see Fanteal off. The same people who had greeted her. Only in Alluthin was that guild made up of cropland owners, rather than the people who did the work. The wind weavers also came—uninvited—with a common question. Could they come to Crysalan for the feast day?

"Of course!" Fanteal spread her smile over the group. "You may travel as freely as anyone."

"Unless," a woman's arrogant voice asserted, "they have orders to fulfill, which is true every day."

"*Requests*," Fanteal said, "for their services may be presented to the Wind Weavers' Guild in advance. This will enable them to determine an equitable division of who stays and who travels for the various holidays."

"The growers do not request. They order."

Governor Armeen rounded on the woman. "A great many of us have the manners to request."

Grellin leaned near Fanteal. "Don't let this worry you. It's just splitting hairs over terms, for the weavers always meet our needs."

"I hope it is nothing more than splitting hairs, for the substance guilds are autonomous by law."

"Quite true." He patronized her as usual.

The woman who'd spoken earlier started ranting something about the Growers' Guild, but Governor Armeen advanced on her and interrupted. Fanteal didn't catch what he'd said to shut down the overbearing creature.

As though nothing unpleasant was happening, Grellin guided Fanteal toward a rail carriage. "I look forward to seeing you again in a few days."

Fanteal and her companions stepped into carriages without further challenges. She leaned back with her lips closed. The tunnel darkened as they left the area's abundant natural light shafts behind. Finally, she murmured, "That was horrible."

"The departure scene," Jaikon asked, "or all of it?"

"The entire visit."

He waited, but when she didn't elaborate, he said, "The mapping went well for Charlis and me. But I never got a chance to hear about your days with Grellin. Or what you overheard on that balcony."

How much should she tell him? "Well...Grellin plans to marry me. Nothing new in that. To my face, he makes it sound like the marriage will benefit me greatly. What I overheard was quite the opposite."

"Are you disappointed?"

Startled, she met his gaze. "No! Not even surprised, really, although I was trying to give him fair benefit of the doubt."

"Then why do you look so depressed?"

"He makes a fine case that the marriage will benefit Dirklan."

Jaikon took a moment to answer. "Why believe that if he is lying about your personal benefit?"

"The problem is that Dirklan is very close to being wholly dependent on Alluthin—or I should say on the Armeens." She opened her eyes wide and shook her head. "And I thought the Nirundales were bad."

He chuckled. "Ah, but now you know what game Grellin and the Armeens are playing. Forewarned is forearmed."

The carriage tilted to accommodate a curve in the rail. "Forearmed implies that I have a weapon, but I don't. At least, not a weapon that can overpower Dirklan's food problem."

"You are the daughter of the king. Royal Ambassador of the Crown of Welcia."

"Will that matter if the import cataract cannot be repaired?" She had her answer in his silent frown. "I'm not even sure if repairing the cataract will solve the underlying problem."

The carriage leveled again, and he asked, "What underlying problem?"

"It seems like everyone belowground has forgotten they are part of the kingdom of Welcia. The laws of Dirklan are founded in the kingdom. Thus, law will fail if the kingdom is deemed irrelevant. You heard it a moment ago. Substance guild autonomy is guaranteed by law, yet the Armeens control the guilds in Alluthin. They want to control them throughout Dirklan."

"I suppose they will have the Formers' Guild if Creflon becomes provincial chief." He rubbed his jaw. "The Streamers' Guild isn't at risk, though, and I cannot imagine that you will let them take over the Wind Weavers' Guild."

"That's partly why he wants to marry me—to control all of Dirklan's wind weavers."

Jaikon stiffened. "He said that?"

She nodded. "While we were on the balcony. Governor Armeen was with him and two others."

"Any idea who?"

"Only that they were part of the Armeen clan. One considers me trouble and doesn't want Grellin to marry me. The other..." She flipped her hand. "He was whispering, and I couldn't be sure who he was. I thought he might be Creflon, for he spoke of not wanting air channels to be formed." She slowed her words. "Because they would raise hopes of a tunnel. Hmm...a tunnel would feed Dirklan and restore trade. Only

Alluthin would gain nothing from it. As for the Armeens, their excess food would lose value, both in money and in power."

"A tunnel," Jaikon mused, "would also give Dirklan access to the king and queen."

"Yes...trouble for the Armeens. Their so-called Growers' Guild is also teetering on the edge of law."

"You mean about usurping authority over the substance guilds?"

"Somewhat, but they aren't a guild as much as a family cartel, wielding an undue amount of power. Or they will be. If they were actually doing it right now, I would challenge them myself in court. But they will wait for food shortages, and then no one will dare defy them."

He chuckled.

"What?"

"You doubted your own authority a moment ago, but you speak of taking on the Armeens in court."

She huffed a laugh, unconvinced. "I didn't say I thought I would win."

"Grellin's pursuit of you proves one thing very clearly. He isn't confident that his strategy will succeed unless you marry him. *He* knows that you possess authority."

She looked at Jaikon for a long moment. "Interesting point. He told me I won't be able to accomplish anything unless I am his wife." She tilted her head. "Phrasing it a little nicer than that, of course."

"He must have phrased it nicely, indeed, to convince you of such a lie."

"He could make it hard for me."

"So could you...make it hard for him. What does he need you for?"

"Primarily to win the election. Secondarily, to control the wind weavers. At least, that's all he said."

Jaikon pursed his lips. "Governor Armeen knows they are at risk of being charged with illegal control of the wind weavers. That's why he shut what's-her-name up. If you reveal the Armeens' intent before we run low on food, they won't have a chance in the election."

"I have no proof. In fact, the governor stood against an illegal demand just moments ago."

"That, he did, in front of witnesses." Magnery light shifted over Jaikon's frown as they passed a lamp. "One thing is certain. They need the food supply to remain tight."

"I suppose that's why they don't want anyone thinking about a tunnel. But there isn't a tunnel route available, is there?"

He stared at her—far too long. "What else did they actually say?"

"Um…" What had come first? "Grellin said to delay air channels until Agriben dies, then stop them permanently. The whisperer said that if I get aboveground, I might convince the formers to start on the air channels."

"*If*…you get aboveground?"

"Well, yes, but that is certain. Everyone knows that the king insisted I visit him at the next new year."

"Exactly. The word *if* implies that someone doesn't want it to happen. Who? The one who whispered or Grellin?"

"Both!" She couldn't help growling the word. Nor speaking the rest of his vile words. "Grellin said it's nine months away—plenty of time. That he would stop my *meddling* once we are married. Best to keep me here where he can *control* me." No matter how tightly she clenched her fists into her skirt, she couldn't stop their shaking. A night's quiet had done nothing to soothe her fury.

Jaikon laid a hand over her fists. "His plans are easily flouted. Simply decline to marry him."

She drew a deep breath and blew it out slowly. "I know. And I won't marry him! But he tried to get a *yes* from me before escorting me to the station."

"What did you say?"

The concern in his voice proved that her own was not unfounded. "Delay tactic. I told him that, for weighty matters, I always allow time to pass between the persuasion and the decision."

"Good response. How did he take it?"

"Well enough." She smoothed the wrinkles she'd wadded into her skirt. "Eventually, he will try harder. I'm worried how he will react to a definitive *no*."

Another lamp highlighted the lines in Jaikon's forehead. "Whatever you do, don't say that you want to consult with your parents."

That *if* seemed to have taken strong possession of his thoughts. Had she misrepresented it? To her, the conversation had been about the channels...or a possible tunnel. "Really, a tunnel would change the entire situation."

He grumbled, "Why do you keep going back to that?"

She widened her eyes at his vehemence. "Why does it bother you?"

"Sorry." He rubbed his fingers through the hair at the nape of his neck. "It's...possible but not possible." He rubbed some more, then dropped his hand to his lap. "As frustrating as a figure-eight rail."

"You have funny expressions down here."

"A conundrum. Infinite travel with no arrival."

Apt enough. "How about if we focus on the possible side?"

"I do, but it always loops me back around to *im*possible." He forced a smile. Unconvincing. "Renauld will probably come to the feast in Crysalan. It's deemed a time of breakthroughs. What could be more fitting than to announce a solution for the import cataract during a feast that commemorates Dirklan's escape from starvation?"

True. If he had a solution.

Renauld did indeed arrive in Crysalan the day before the feast. Without a solution.

Fanteal went down to the ration breakfast, needing no effort to maintain a somber demeanor. This feast was not celebrated aboveground, but her mother had explained it. Breakfast was a reminder of the meager rations Dirklians had endured after the collapse. Lunch would commemorate the first feast held in Dirklan after the import cataract delivered adequate food.

The inn's dining room filled, though the portions needed no such gathering. Each plate held one slice of a hard-boiled duck egg and a bite-sized morsel of a vegetable. A formal prayer of gratitude for the food was uttered in unison, then the ration was eaten in silence, and everyone left.

Adults hushed the whines and whimpers of the young, and one mother whispered to her child, "This is all our ancestors could eat for each meal, so it is all we will eat for this breakfast."

How could Fanteal enjoy the feast later, knowing that they were all facing lack again? Maybe the service in the Sacred Chamber would calm her. Not if it erupted into contention again.

Sir Mikkael studied her as he prepared to escort her into the chamber. "Let your worries go, my dear. They do not need your attention. This is a day to celebrate provision at the hand of Ellincreo."

He was a rock. Unshaken by the disquieting revelations she and Jaikon had shared with him. She knew he was right—that worry solved nothing, no matter how vigorously one wallowed in it. Yet knowing that made smiling no easier.

They traversed the aisles as they had a couple months ago, and she took her seat in the front row between Sir Mikkael and Jaikon. She knew which reading to expect. The story of Dirklan's near starvation after the collapse and the solution Ellincreo had shown Devron in the vision wall. Did anyone but her find it odd that they all sat before the same vision wall—entirely obscured by ivy?

The service moved on, and the Chief Keeper of the Writ began speaking of the year's most significant accomplishments. Not many before he extolled the benefits of fresh air. He commended the revived

Wind Weavers' Guild and shared encouraging health reports. Some of them were even news to her.

Warmth flowed through Fanteal. There was no denying that she had succeeded in ways Dirklan had never expected. Lives were being saved with a gift both simple and precious. Air.

The songs began. The first celebrated the long-ago gift of food after the collapse. Fanteal felt like a streamer had doused her inner fire with a chilly current. All these words of joy and provision, and Dirklan was still on the verge of hunger. Neither her substance gift nor her life gift could help them.

The songs went on, but she didn't know them. Couldn't participate except for a few with repeating lines, like *The mercies of old rebound in our need.* It echoed from the audience after scattered singers around the chamber offered stanzas from the Writ's Book of Remembrances. This song had a theatrical feel, as though witnesses had stepped forward in time to share the stories of their day. Even the act of turning to listen to each singer created a sensation of participating in a reenactment. Fanteal had to admit—this one was fun. Encouraging. Each singer walked down to the platform after their part, and it grew crowded as they joined in a rousing conclusion.

Fanteal sang, "The mercies of old rebound in our need," almost laughing through the final repeat. She turned to share the moment with Jaikon.

He stood rigid, staring at the singers. No, staring above them—at the vision wall.

She darted her gaze to it. The faint glow through the leaves—was that a brighter gold than usual? What did it mean?

She subtly glanced around. Sir Mikkail seemed oblivious, but Charlis and Bella on the far side of Jaikon had noticed something. Maybe only his intensity. Or something more?

She almost stamped her foot, for once again, she couldn't ask what he saw.

CHAPTER 31

Only the vision wall mattered in this moment, but the mundane business of leaving the sacred chamber took over. Fanteal must walk the aisles in front of everyone with a smile pinned to her lips, then make her way to Crysalan's wide courtyard, amid suitors who vied to be near her. The feast was being spread over buffet tables. A band began playing, and acquaintances converged in groups, their voices in party pitch. A good thing she'd been trained as ambassador, because all she wanted was to drag Jaikon to some private space and demand an answer. How long would this last?

The word *feast* must be relative, for she was served quite ordinary portions. Games followed, then more food, dancing, food, visiting among friends, and more food. All right, a feast it was, and a long one too.

Fanteal joined the families of her suitors, going from one to the next. Not a bad way to compare the relaxed version of each. If only her mind wouldn't hark back to Jaikon staring at the obscured vision wall. As usual, Grellin arranged to be the last to escort her among his family and through another round of dancing. Would he try to press for an answer again?

She sensed that moment drawing near and looked around for a graceful escape. More trays of food arrived, and servers set out sweet cakes. "Ah, is this the last course?" she asked Grellin.

"No doubt. May I get you something?"

She had already begun moving toward a buffet table near where Sir Mikkael sat. "Thank you, but you needn't. I have not yet had even a moment to share with the Mikkaels."

"You see them every day."

If his tone was any indication, he wasn't going to give in. She'd drawn nearer now and replied a little louder, "I would still like to join Sir Mikkael during the feast."

That brought the prime minister's gaze to them. Understanding lurked in his eyes. He rose and approached. "Thank you for escorting Lady Fanteal to me." He took the hand she extended, leaving nothing for Grellin to do but depart.

Sighing, she sat beside Sir Mikkael, who resumed the conversation she'd interrupted. A few minutes later, Jaikon brought her a little dome-shaped cake with nine swirling lines traced in the crisp frosting. She chuckled at the representation of the dome over Passage Lake. "That is so cute."

"Tasty too." He consumed his in three bites.

She nibbled more slowly, then wiped her fingers as another dance tune began.

Jaikon took the hint and stood, extending a hand. "Shall we?"

She accepted, but a few steps from her chair, she whispered, "Do you remember offering to show me the gem hills someday?"

He lifted an eyebrow. "I do."

"How about now?"

"They are best viewed at midday with a few hours to stroll. The light shafts are dimming."

"Then I will start with the nuanced light of sunset," she whispered. "You may show me more tomorrow."

They wove between couples who were trying to find space to dance in the crowded courtyard. Easy enough to obscure the fact that they were slipping away. She hoped no eyes followed them, particularly when she caught Jaikon's scrutiny.

"You look like a child bent on mischief," he said.

She uttered a dainty snort. "So do you."

He laughed. "Can you tell me what mischief we are bent on?"

"None, really. Hate to disappoint you, but I want to get out of the crowd." They reached a deserted street. Noisy good cheer lay behind them. "Can we at least see the part where the gem hills are near the back of the vision wall?"

"That's probably all we can see before dark, but it's not far. What's your real reason for this stroll, Lady Mischief?"

"I'm not telling you until we are truly alone."

"Ah. Trying to make me hurry with curiosity."

True enough that her quick steps were just short of a run. "You're the one who claimed it will get dark soon. Hush, though. Someone else is on the street."

He guided her through a couple turns and along another street. She sensed the change before they rounded the last building. The air ahead lazed between vast mounds that reached toward the distant ceiling. Footsteps still echoed behind them, hurrying as they had.

Jaikon looked back. "Ah, you couldn't escape Bella's eye, and she brought Charlis."

"Well, our reputations may be spared then. Keep moving. If we don't wait for them, she might give us a little space." They were passing through the broad cavern opening now, and the reddish glow that pierced the light shafts flickered over crystals below. "Oh, wow!"

"They get this pink and gold look," Jaikon said, "in the morning and evening. The cooler tones shine best during full day."

She couldn't help slowing. "They truly are like gem-studded hills." She gasped. "They're moving!"

"No, we are moving, and the light shifts as well, so you constantly see reflections from different crystals."

"Oh," she groaned. "I want to forget everything and just stare."

"We can."

"No. There is a garden atop the vision wall, right? Take me there."

"This way."

They skirted a hill until the path split, one fork ascending to the right. This led them to a natural platform where narrow paths wound between raised garden beds. Practical beauty. Most contained food, but a few that traced the long edge held flowers. Beyond them, Fanteal sensed the air space of the sacred chamber. She turned her back to it and sat on the rock wall surrounding the nearest garden bed.

Jaikon sat beside her. "What's wrong?"

"Nothing," she whispered. "I just want to stay out of sight—at least until I'm sure that the sacred chamber is empty."

He eyed her but waited while she analyzed the air's movement for subtleties that would indicate that a living body stirred it. Finally, she reported, "I believe it is empty."

"Mm. Are we alone enough for you to tell me why we are here?"

She kept her voice hushed. "Did you see the vision wall glow today?"

It took him several long seconds to answer—as hushed as she. "I think you know I did."

"And you saw it when we came to Crysalan before."

"That, too, you know. Did *you* see it today?"

"A subtle glow for me. What was yours like?"

"Brilliant." He sounded far from pleased. "Not that I can learn anything from that."

"It has a message for you."

He didn't answer.

"Maybe for both of us," she said, "but definitely for you." A gentle breeze wafted between them. "I know you believe we are supposed to learn from Ellincreo within our hearts, and there is truth in that. But why would it be bad to learn through a vision as well?"

His breath grew audible. "It's not that it would be bad."

"What, then?"

Jaikon stared at the hill before him. Pink crystals darkened to ruby. How could he put this into words? "It's...complicated and...must not be overheard."

"We have time." She angled her head toward the long ramp they'd climbed. "Bella and Charlis wait down there. They would surely let us know if anyone drew near. I will shudder the air surrounding us so our words cannot be discerned."

Slight though it was, the silence grew deeper. Was there no end to the uses of her gift? Unlike his.

"So, tell me this complicated thing," she prompted.

How to say this? "I do know something. But I cannot do anything with it."

"That sounds like Devron's vision."

"Nothing like that. He thought his vision was unsafe—even crazy. But he was *capable* of doing it. I am *not* able to do what has occurred to me. It's not even a vision in my heart. It's something I sensed in the ipenrock beyond Jourendia. The part that extends into the peninsula."

Shadows fell over one side of the hill as the top of a light shaft lost sunlight. Fanteal spoke slowly. "If it's not a vision in your heart, then why did you tell me of it when I asked about the vision wall?"

The last thing he'd expected her to say. Stunning how on-point she was. "Well...the idea won't leave me. No matter what I do to get rid of it."

She angled her body to look more directly at him. "Were you trying to? How?"

"Oh, like brainstorming with Renauld. I understand that we cannot fix what we cannot reach, but I hoped he'd find some solution to, um, at least make my idea unnecessary." She would ask what his idea was now. Oh, he didn't want to tell her. There was no saying what she'd do if she knew.

She stared at him in the half-light. "Jaikon," she whispered, "are you afraid that the vision wall will confirm your idea?"

What? "No. I don't expect to see anything. I'm worried that wall is going to stir up trouble for *you*."

She shrugged. "I don't care about *that*."

A smothered laugh tried to force through his throat, and his chest shook.

She smirked but didn't give up. "If Ellincreo has a message for us, we need to see it."

"There are a few vines out there. A few hundred, that it is."

"Ivy is nothing." She stood.

He followed her to a raised bed that edged the top of the vision wall. She braced herself against one end and tugged on one of the vines. "What in the caverns are you thinking?" he demanded.

"They aren't that thick. They must break now and then. What happens if they fall into the pool?"

"No idea. If the ends get long, they float. I suppose growers trim them out of the pool when necessary."

Her tugging snapped a vine, and the end stuck out. Nothing shifted. She leaned out and looked down into the pool. Yi! He grabbed her around the waist with one arm and clutched the bed's stone wall with his other hand. "Be careful!"

"This works." She leaned farther out and jerked handfuls of vines. "They're all twisted together. Pull me back."

He pulled her several steps as Bella and Charlis dashed up the slope to them.

"What in the caverns are you doing?" Bella demanded.

"Checking the vines."

"Never do that again!"

"Calm down. Jaikon held me firm."

Dim though it was, the demand in Bella's eyes shone, and Jaikon blurted out, "That doesn't mean I approved."

Fanteal flicked her hands wide. "Enough. Jaikon said growers trim the vines, so there must be tools. You lived here, Bella. Where did they keep them?"

"Uh...there's a recessed cabinet in the slope wall, but—"

"Good. Close at hand. Get them, please."

"But why?"

"We are cutting the vines off at the top, so they drop into the pool."

Bella's and Charlis's mouths hung open like tiny caverns.

Jaikon figured he looked the same until Fanteal's chuckle loosened his tongue. "You haven't made the Keepers of the Writ angry enough with you yet?"

"I am doing nothing wrong. By ancient decree, the vision wall was never to be interfered with."

"What was actually written," Bella corrected, "is that it was never to be mined."

"Permanently covering it is only a tiny step from destroying it. But us arguing the decree's intent will not stop their anger. One thing is certain. A vision appears behind the ivy when Jaikon is in the Sacred Chamber. So, he and I must choose what is most important—the keepers' anger or Ellincreo's message."

Well, that made it non-negotiable. But the way Charlis was staring at him made Jaikon's skin crawl.

"This morning…" Charlis murmured. "I could have sworn the edges of the leaves were glowing—over on the left half of it. Is that what you mean?"

So, Jaikon wasn't the only one. Tangible relief rushed through him. "It was the entire wall for me. Why didn't you say anything?"

Charlis huffed. "Why didn't you?"

Fanteal shook her head. "We really need to do something about this stigma over seeing a vision! Later. It's getting dark, and I don't see any tools yet."

Bella hurried down the ramp, and Charlis followed her. Fanteal stared into the chamber as they waited. "It's lit," she said.

"Yes, small magnery lights near the steps between terraces."

"Makes perfect sense. There are still so many things I would never think of, and you Dirklians solved the problems long ago."

He rested a hand against her back. "Light is kind of a big deal down here."

Charlis and Bella returned, and he carried two pairs of long-handled clippers. He handed one to Jaikon. "Maybe we should start from opposite ends and work toward the center."

It wasn't long before ivy sagged like thick, stiff fabric. Pressure tightened the vines, making them easier to cut. Before the two men met, the center ripped away and a whooshing splash sent an echoing whisper through the sacred chamber.

On his knees, Jaikon gripped the wall of a raised bed and leaned out. No one could make a vision come. Were they being presumptuous?

A gentle glow began to emanate from the wall. His heart thrummed. "It's starting!" Surely this meant Ellincreo approved of their action. He leapt up and raced for the ramp.

Bella grabbed the clippers he and Charlis dropped, while Fanteal joined their run down the slope and through the chamber's lower side entrance.

The entire wall glowed with an image so broad, Jaikon had to run up a few terrace levels to take in the whole thing. Amazing! He grew lightheaded.

Fanteal gripped his arm. "Calm down. You're going to hyperventilate like you did aboveground."

He let out a shaky laugh. Trust her to notice that.

Charlis stood a level below them on the left. He extended both hands toward whatever he saw. They trembled. He turned to look up at Jaikon, gasping. "This side—just like before."

Bella approached him, using a terrace railing for guidance. She looked to the wall and their faces, seeming disappointed. "What is it you see?"

"It's a level map!" Charlis's voice dipped. "Oh, you cannot see it?" When she shook her head, he said, "I'm so sorry."

"Don't be silly. I don't need to."

Only now did Jaikon realize that, even though the vision wall shone brilliantly, the chamber terraces remained as shadowed as before. "If anyone else wanders the gem hills or looks into the chamber's tunnels, they won't know anything is happening here."

"Huh." Fanteal sounded amused. "That's convenient."

He looked down at her and had to suppress an almost overwhelming desire to hug her. "What do you see, my dear?"

"It glows softly and is covered with lines that don't make any sense to me. Perhaps my part is just to give confirmation."

"That won't hurt." He began studying it in earnest.

Bella asked Charlis, "What is it a level map *of*?"

"I, uh, don't know." He gripped his head with both hands and groaned. "I just *have* to draw it, and I don't have any mapping plates."

"Oh!" Bella chuckled. "I happen to know where the supply room is. Would blank notebooks work?"

"They're small, but I could double the pages for depth."

She hustled away, then returned with an armload. The two of them opened bindings and spread panels over the platform.

Jaikon sensed Charlis working, etching the panels with what he saw. Interesting that he saw only half. Jaikon focused on the right side. He had a good guess of what it was, but he must be sure. Fanteal's hand was still tucked around his upper arm, but she didn't make a sound. Just stood with him, through time that he couldn't measure.

He confirmed the overall shape, then went back to the details. Yes, they were what he remembered, but more. A distinct pathway laced through it.

Charlis walked up the steps and into his peripheral vision. Not wanting to interrupt, apparently.

"Are you finished drawing what you can see?" Jaikon asked.

"Yes. I saved some panels if you want me to etch what you see."

Surreal. Jaikon went down to the platform and looked over the etched map, comparing it to what he saw on the left side.

Charlis asked, "Do you see the same thing I do?"

"Yes." Jaikon studied it for a while. "Accurately etched."

"Thank you, sir."

That was surreal too. Charlis, gifted enough to be apprentice to Agriben, accepted Jaikon's word as a superior's confirmation. Of a vision, no less. Jaikon held out his hand. "May I have your pencil, Bella." He closed his fingers around it and moved to the blank panels. Looking up and down, time and again, he drew the two-dimensional overlay, then instructed Charlis on the third dimension. Just like they had done in the caverns where Jaikon could sense farther than Charlis.

Finally, Jaikon looked it over and confirmed that their copy matched the vision. He let out a long breath. "That will do it."

Charlis began stacking the plates—small for maps, but sequence numbered.

"We'll need proper-sized maps if we ever want to see this approved." Jaikon considered. "Make two copies—no, three. One for the Formers' Guild below, one for above, and the third to store in the prime minister's library."

"Yes, sir."

Jaikon lifted his eyes as the glow faded. "Ah, there it goes." Odd that he didn't feel disappointment at the loss of its beauty. Just peaceful. It had appeared when he needed it, and that was enough. A shadowy mass obscured the pool at the foot of the wall. If not for the faint light from the stairway magnery lamps, they would have stood in deep blackness.

"I wonder," Bella said, "why Charlis couldn't see the whole thing, since he needed to document all of it."

"The part he could see," Jaikon replied, "was consistent with his former's range."

"Wait." Charlis turned to Jaikon. "I never saw a scale indication, and I don't know how to title the map copies."

Jaikon realized he still held the wax pencil. On the bottom of the cover plate, he wrote the scale references—one for the two broad dimensions, and another for the recessed third dimension.

"Really?" Charlis murmured. "But where in Dirklan could *that* fit?"

Jaikon was already writing the title. *Jourendia City Cavern—eastern wall through aboveground peninsula.*

CHAPTER 32

S ir Mikkael finished writing a note as the inn staff cleared breakfast dishes from their private sitting room. Jaikon tried to guess at the thoughts hidden behind his father's impassive expression. Always harder to discern when others were present.

Colrin closed the door behind the server and returned to the prime minister, who handed him two squares of quartz. "Give the note for the Chief Former of Dirklan to Charlis and Bella. Have them go in a cair so they can escort Agriben here. You deliver the note to the Chief Keeper of the Writ."

Colrin departed, and silence fell. Jaikon glanced at Fanteal. What was she thinking? After all, his father had said nothing more than *hmm* when they'd told him that they had cut down the ivy, seen a vision in the golden wall, and Charlis had documented it.

He had simply written notes after that. Enough to make any person nervous, but not Fanteal, apparently. She relaxed in a stuffed chair. Having donned one of her longer dresses this morning, she looked regal. And beautiful.

Jaikon couldn't match her calm, but at least he didn't feel driven to pace.

Sir Mikkael eyed the stack of map plates, which now had an extra blank cover to hide its shocking title. "Skip all former terms, Jaikon, and tell me what that map means."

"It shows the ipenrock structure from the eastern side of Jourendia out through the peninsula. Since ipenrock is not *entirely* as impenetrable as its name suggests, this map shows the places where it can be excavated." He met his father's eyes. "In other words, it reveals a tunnel route."

"An unconfirmable tunnel route," his father said. "Known only through a vision."

"Not exactly. I have sensed the area before, so I knew what I was looking at in the vision wall. As for the lower part, Charlis, Agriben, and many other formers will be able to confirm it. When the maps reach aboveground formers, some should be able to confirm the upper portion."

At a knock on the door, a shade of annoyance crossed Sir Mikkael's features. "Enter."

Colrin opened the door. "Sir, I met the Chief Keeper of the Writ approaching the inn, so he has already arrived."

"Send him in."

Within a moment, Chief Keeper Thilleon stomped through the door, the prime minister's note clutched in his hand. "I don't know why you sent for me, sir, but—" He glanced at the other two and gave them a quick nod as he continued. "Perhaps you have already heard the awful news, but if not, I must report vandalism in the sacred chamber."

"Shocking, though perhaps my joyful news will alleviate your distress. But news of any sort does not prevent you from properly greeting the ambassador."

Though they spasmed, Thilleon compressed his lips and bowed slightly. "Pleasant morning, Lady Fanteal."

She inclined her head. "Pleasant morning, Chief Keeper."

"And now for good tidings," Jaikon's father said. "The debris that used to cover the vision wall—as though the treasure were insignificant—has been removed." He paused as Thilleon's nostrils flared. "Are we speaking of the same event, in quite different terms?"

It took him a moment to get an answer out. "None but the Keepers of the Writ have the right to alter the sacred chamber."

"Yet you have allowed dumb plants to alter it. To obscure the only thing in the chamber that is, in fact, sacred. An entire wall of gold so pure that no natural process could create it, nor any person refine it to such a degree. The vision wall, which Ellincreo used in times past to save Dirklan. I find it quite fitting that it has been restored to us on the feast day which celebrates our ancestors' rescue from starvation."

"Who did it?"

"You may offer your *thanks* to the royal ambassador and my son."

"*Thanks,* indeed! She is bringing her heathen idolatry here!"

"Not one such word has ever passed her lips. Slander her, and you will answer charges in court."

"If I hear of a vision, that will be proof."

"If Ellincreo chooses to reveal visions, that is his prerogative, and you have nothing to say. If he does not reveal them, then your complaint is equally without merit. No, do not interrupt me." Sir Mikkael held his gaze steady, his calm at odds with Thilleon's quivering. "I asked you to come here so I could share the simple facts of what happened. That was a courtesy to you, not an invitation to debate theology. I have matters of government to attend to. You may depart."

When the door clapped shut behind him, Sir Mikkael murmured, "Such an unpleasant individual." He turned to Jaikon. "I imagine you could have argued him into contortions on several points. Thank you for refraining."

Oddly enough, Jaikon had felt no desire to do so. "Easier to hack through ipenrock with a fork than persuade an expert that he is viewing his vast knowledge from the wrong angle. The vision is more important."

His father's lips twitched. "Speaking of that, have either of you considered how you will handle the inevitable question of whether you saw a vision?"

"The four of us decided last night," Fanteal said. "We will use the aboveground custom that visions should not be spoken of lightly, lest they be misinterpreted. They are for the eyes that have seen them. We will give only that answer, instead of *yes* or *no*."

"Then what cause would you have had to cut down the ivy?"

She cast her eyes to the ceiling for a second, then smiled. "The vision wall belongs to all of Dirklan and should not be hidden. Though the ivy may have enriched stagnant air in the past, it is now just overgrown weeds."

"Well enough. Much as I want to leap at this hope, it must be handled with care." He drummed his fingers. "We were discussing the tunnel. What is the likelihood of a cave-in if we excavate?"

Jaikon figured he'd be asked this a hundred times. "No more than the likelihood that the dome of Passage Lake will collapse." If that response worked with his father, it would work with others.

Sir Mikkael considered. "Decent answer, but most consider that a possibility, slight though it is. Lady Fanteal, what damage would be done to the capital city of Regissa if the tunnel collapsed?"

Her expression turned pensive. "The eastern wall of Jourendia's city cavern is not under the city of Regissa. It's behind and below the cliffs that constrain the harbor. More wind than soil up there, so the land isn't used. The peninsula itself is bare rock."

He turned back to Jaikon. "How viable is the tunnel route?"

"It will be steep in places. One section will involve a dip. I'm not sure how walkable it will be, but our current rail and mechanical technology should be able to lift and lower freight through it."

"Carriages for people?"

"Given time, I believe so."

"Given time—what does that mean?"

"I think we should start with a small tunnel first. A single rail to move food in and ore out. That much could be done in a year. Then widen it for more rails and determine how to keep a carriage upright enough for people to ride through the tunnel."

"That all sounds wonderful. So, why hasn't anyone thought of it before?"

"Because no one could sense far enough. Frankly, there are false leads. They turn inland, which seems like the most favorable route, but they lead to unstable areas. If we tunnel the wrong direction, we will never come out aboveground."

Sir Mikkael rubbed a finger over his lips and didn't seem to notice when another knock sounded. Jaikon went to open the door, admitting Agriben, who leaned heavily on his staff. Concerning how slowly the chief former moved. Charlis followed his master, and—somewhere nearby—Bella's voice requested a tea tray. She brought it in by the time greetings had been exchanged.

Amid the movement, Fanteal stood and motioned Charlis to bring her armchair to the table for Agriben. He lowered himself into it, then seemed to be catching his breath as Charlis assembled the map plates before him and Bella poured him a cup of tea.

What had happened since the last time Jaikon had seen Agriben? His skin was too pale. At least his eyes remained sharp enough for the fine detail of the map, and his gruff voice steady in his questions. These were all technical matters, and Jaikon's father patiently waited them out. Fanteal, too, though she leaned over the table like a question was ready to burst from her.

Agriben pointed to the far left of the map. "I take it this is beyond the cliffside air channel."

"Yes," Jaikon replied, "along that back street by the rental flats for visitors."

"Conveniently inconvenient."

"Sir?"

"I assume the swarms have left Jourendia. There should be vacancies and no permanent residents to notice an unusual newcomer. Charlis may take a flat there without attracting attention."

Tight muscles loosened in Jaikon's shoulders. Agriben took this seriously.

"Do you want me to start confirming it, sir," Charlis asked Agriben.

"You'll have to. I'm not up to traipsing around back streets, and people would notice me even if I was. Do more than confirm it, Charlis. Thoroughly map from the interior as far east as you can reach. Three copies of the current structure with proposed tunnel route. We will use the naturally known structure to prove the accuracy of the vision map. We'll send one to the aboveground formers, so they can see that we have considered the matter with all diligence. They won't start if they aren't confident."

Sir Mikkael put his finger on the map. "You say that Charlis can confirm to here, which is less than halfway. How certain is it that aboveground formers will be able to confirm all the way to this point?"

Agriben drew the corners of his lips down. "Reasonable chance but not certain. That is why I want the vision map proven against reality where we can."

"Assuming this is confirmed with a double assessment," Sir Mikkael asked, "when should we expect to make connection between the tunnel descending from above and our tunnel reaching up?"

"Depends on when work starts. One of the Northeshur formers brought me word yesterday about another slippage in the import cataract." He glanced around them. "Get your jaws off the table. It didn't impede anything, but it's not in a good spot."

"Where is a good spot for slippage?" Jaikon grumbled.

Agriben gave him a dour smile. "Exactly. So, the tunnel should be started at the *earliest* possible moment. I will open the dome at the half-year, so we can send the plans up." He turned to Charlis. "I'll come a week ahead to assess your maps."

"I'll have them ready, sir."

"I know you will."

"What if the tides aren't favorable for communication?" Sir Mikkael asked.

Agriben shrugged that off. "A streamer researched the unusual high currents that troubled the harbor during the last half-year. They have always been followed by unusually low currents the following year. I expect all three low tides will allow me to open the dome for the small vessel to pass through.

"In the meantime…" His gravelly voice dipped. "I do not want a single whisper of the word *tunnel* to grind through the rumor mill. Not a soul is to hear about this."

"Agreed," Sir Mikkael said.

Agriben looked around them. "Six people in this room. Does anyone else know?"

Sir Mikkael shook his head, then added, "Colrin must know."

"Why?"

"Funds and logistics," he replied. "Charlis is not as notable as you, Agriben, but he is known. I don't want his name associated with the flat by the eastern wall. Colrin will see to it with utter discretion."

Agriben grunted. "Suppose I can't say *no*."

Fanteal still waited with tiny fidgets. "I gather this is obvious to you three formers, but no one says it." She focused on Agriben. "Is this tunnel going to become a reality?"

Jaikon was glad she'd asked. Former or not, he needed to hear it too.

Agriben used a gentler tone with her. "We formers are like that, you know. We want our double assessments before we commit." He tilted his head toward the plates on the table. "I will say that, if this vision map is proven, then the tunnel route is viable."

Her inhalation shuddered. Jaikon felt as giddy as she looked.

His father allowed himself a smile, but warned, "All of you get your excitement out before you leave this room, or you will give it away to the first person who sees you."

"That's actually my next question." Fanteal licked her lips. "Why, exactly, must we hide it? I mean, if it's only that we don't want to raise false hopes, couldn't we just describe it appropriately? For it would relieve another issue if we could tell."

Agriben narrowed his eyes. "Anything to do with Alluthin?"

"Is it that obvious?"

"Rumors fly on a feast day. I hear that Grellin Armeen is the front-runner for the coveted position of ambassador's husband."

Jaikon's every muscle tensed. Pity he couldn't punch a rumor in the face.

Fanteal lifted her chin. "As I say to one and all, I will not rush the choice of my husband."

"Marriage to you is not the only prize the Armeens seek." Agriben spread his gaze to all of them. "Creflon's kind respect toward me grows nauseating. I know full well he is hinting that I'm no longer up to the duties of Provincial Chief Former. Perhaps mentally as well as physically."

"But you are!" Fanteal's voice squawked. "Your full grasp of matters has been perfectly clear here today."

He grinned. "Thank you, Lady Fanteal. But if I chase after visions that I cannot possibly confirm, no one will believe you. Be wary of the Armeens. The governor and Grellin could use the vision against you—and against Jaikon—should that ever suit their purposes."

"I don't quite understand this," Bella said. "Won't every other domain be wildly in favor of a tunnel?"

"Definitely." Sir Mikkael tapped his fingers on the table. "To protect their interests, I can see two options for the Armeens. Kill the tunnel project before any abovegrounder hears of it, or obtain control of the tunnel site."

"Jourendia." Fanteal glowered. "Win the election and make sure the ambassador's children carry the name of Armeen. Embed their clannish talons in the capital city of Dirklan."

Sir Mikkael leaned toward her. "I understand your anger, but don't give Grellin any clues. You'll have time enough to turn him down after the aboveground formers have confirmed the upper portion of the tunnel and started work."

She blew out a breath. "I won't let him guess. He cannot force me into marriage, after all. I'm far more worried about the tunnel. Could Creflon stop it?"

Agriben snorted. "I am still the provincial chief former. *He* answers to *me*."

Jaikon wondered about the spots of color that mottled Agriben's cheeks. He worried even more when Bella, who also watched Agriben, cheerfully turned the subject.

"It's only three months to the half-year," she said. "Not very long to wait, and I have no doubt that the king and queen will give full support for the aboveground work. Charlis, are you coming with me to escort Agriben home again?"

He agreed, and during their slow departure, Jaikon began stacking the map plates. The swish and clicks seemed oddly loud when only Fanteal and his father remained.

Fanteal gripped and released the table's edge several times. "I had hoped that Agriben's ailment had been overstated, but it doesn't seem so. Do either of you know what it is?"

"An issue," Jaikon's father replied, "with the amount of blood his heart is able to pump. I spoke with his medic streamer, who told me he has seen people in a similar condition live anywhere from one to five years more. In fact, he said the recent enriching of our air will aid Agriben."

A smile tried for a place on her face but slipped away.

"What's wrong?" Jaikon asked.

"I feel guilty. Wanting him to live so our plans are not ruined, instead of for his own benefit."

"Our plans are his plans too. It's the sort of grand quest that a man such as Agriben will defy death to achieve."

"I wish I could do more," she murmured.

"Better to do what you are gifted for." Sir Mikkael turned the discussion. "Is everything set for the meeting of your guild?"

"Yes. I have selected the wind weavers who will travel with me on the first maintenance tour of Dirklan. Bella has arranged lodging. We'll convene in Jourendia at the beginning of the next work week, then travel to each domain in turn."

"How long will it take?"

"Probably at least a couple months for this first one. I must train them on so much. The overall airflow of Dirklan, the local flows within each domain and its caverns, and how to clear debris before it builds up." She spread her hands. "They all need time to try it for themselves too."

Jaikon's father nodded. "Bella and Jaikon will accompany you, but I assume you do not need a former. Uh, such as Charlis, that is."

Awkward. From his father, no less. Jaikon couldn't blame him, though. Recognitions aside, he still couldn't form.

"No," Fanteal said. "Jaikon's skills are more suitable for this tour."

Nice of her. This time around, his *skill* would be escorting her. Hardly a former's task. Would he never escape the dissonance? A former who was not a former.

CHAPTER 33

Fanteal wrestled annoyance yet again. Avoiding questions about a vision was harder than avoiding suitors.

After Grellin invaded their sitting room at the inn, he urged her toward the dim corner windows, and though he approached the question in a sideways fashion, it was still the same. The Mikkaels were present, as well as Bella, but that didn't stop him.

Fanteal let irritation bleed into her voice. "How many times must I say that visions are private? I'm done with this."

"Irritating, I'm sure." he murmured in his kind voice, which she was growing to loathe. "May I have a moment alone with you?"

"No," Sir Mikkael said flatly.

Grellin's posture stiffened. He relaxed in an instant and opened his mouth, but Sir Mikkael spoke first.

"Lady Fanteal has been pursued for three months, despite a schedule packed with the duties of both an ambassador and chief wind weaver. In the morning, I am taking her back to Jourendia, so she may rest for the remainder of the week. I will not be issuing any invitations to Dirklan House."

"Ah, I couldn't agree more, sir, that she deserves some time away." Grellin turned his smile to Fanteal. "Perhaps now I can persuade you to enjoy a truly restful visit to Alluthin."

"The king and queen," Sir Mikkael said, "entrusted their daughter to my care, not to yours. Have a pleasant evening." He turned to Bella. "Would you see if Colrin is back?"

When the door had closed on their unwanted guest, Sir Mikkael turned to Fanteal. "Forgive me for answering on your behalf."

She laughed. "Certainly not. I appreciated it too much to forgive."

"I'm glad." He strolled to the windows. "You are capable, but feel free to make use of my guardian role whenever you need it."

She lifted her brows. "Does that have some particular significance at the moment?"

He favored her with his rare smile. "I'm inclined to suggest restraint to *all* of your suitors. That should relieve Grellin's unreasonably urgent demand for an answer." Bella and Colrin came in as the prime minister spoke. "Colrin, draft a letter for me, addressed to all the governors. Include Lady Fanteal's plan for touring the domains and emphasize the purpose—maintenance of the air channels and training wind weavers on their new—no, *restored*—responsibilities. There will be little time for social engagements, and following the lady from one domain to the next is discouraged. Politely phrased but clear enough that Jaikon can demand their departure on my authority."

Unflappable as ever, Colrin nodded. "I understand. I will have the draft to you by breakfast."

Jaikon stared out the window of the flat toward the eastern wall. One of the few chances he would get to study the future tunnel route.

Fanteal's voice lilted. "Don't you just love all this rest we are having here in Jourendia?"

Jaikon glanced down at her. Banter aside, rest had never been their intent. Still, he couldn't resist. "Hmm. Bella is organizing months of supplies in this three-room flat designed for short stays. Charlis is prepping so many map boards we barely have space to keep the couch in the welcome room. I'm scrutinizing miles of ipenrock. And you are... Wait, what is it you're doing again?"

She lifted her chin. "Providing encouragement and moral support. And sneaking. It takes a great deal more effort than you might imagine."

He grinned. "If it's that hard, you could always stay in Dirklan House."

"For what? To chat with the staff? Much more exciting to come here undetected."

He grew serious. "Every visit to the flat is a risk if we are to maintain secrecy."

"It worked. Bella and I took a cair to a different street, where she bought something. Then we crossed a couple alleys on foot, and I doubt anyone saw us on this street. Besides, there isn't time to repeat the trip before we leave for the tour."

The tour. Neither of them would be coming here again for a couple months. He'd gotten mere days of scant participation in the tunnel project—for which only he could find the route. The tunnel he couldn't form. Instead, he must trail after those who *could* use their gift. Eligible to escort Fanteal because he was the suitor who wasn't a suitor. A lot like being the former who wasn't a former. That described his life.

"What's bothering you?" she asked.

That obvious? "Nothing important."

She leaned nearer. "In case you didn't notice, I have spent the last three months with you."

"Oh, *you* were that lady who was always hanging around."

"Nice try. Out with it."

He might as well say something so she would let it go. "Just wishing I could have more to do with...my own idea...my own vision."

Her expression turned pensive. "I suppose it seems like Charlis, and ultimately others, will enjoy the *doing* of it. Still, you alone are the designer—the architect. You alone are capable of assessing it." She studied his eyes. "Does that help at all?"

"Sort of. It's hard to explain."

"I think I get that part—at least some. In ways, our gifts are alike."

His mouth dropped open. If that was what she thought, she did not get it at all. "Alike *how*?"

"In what we are not."

"Are you wandering above the caverns somewhere?"

She smirked. "I'm not what anyone expected, or wants, or appreciates. I have the wrong gift." When he started to shake his head, she touched his arm. "Even though I've convinced people that fresh air is good, no one can eat it. The cataracts are still in terrible condition, and I can*not* do anything about them. As for being ambassador, I don't think anyone really wanted more than...a live body with a title. They don't like it when I make decisions or take action."

She rolled her lips. "Many days, what I am *not* seems far more important than what I *am*." Her shoulders made tiny motions. "I tell myself that, since Ellincreo gifted me and sent me here, I am what Dirklan needs—even if they don't agree. But it can be very hard to believe."

"You are what we needed!" he assured her. Why did her eyes squeeze like she was in pain? "What is it?"

For a moment, it seemed she wouldn't answer. "Need*ed*. You said it past tense."

"I didn't mean *that*."

"I know, but you see how easily it comes out?" Her faint smile returned. "I *do* understand about not being what people expect. There are formers aplenty here, and everyone thinks they know what a former ought to be. And you are not that. You cannot fix trade cataracts any better than I. But you *can* see a tunnel. All of it. Dirklians don't recognize your gift. Maybe they never will. But your gift is exactly what Dirklan *needs*."

He couldn't find words. At least, his fingers found her hand. He held it long enough that he had to come up with something. "You've got that *encouragement and moral support* thing covered pretty well."

She smiled but somehow looked apologetic too. "I'm dragging you away from your tunnel."

"Don't worry about it. This part is best done *without* me here. We won't prove anything if I hang around and tell Charlis how to map existing structure."

"That's not the point. We are more than our gifts. Just as I am more than a wind weaver, you are more than a former."

Was she going to equate being ambassador with being the son of a prime minister? He was a shadow carrying around someone else's authority. Best to keep his lips closed, for he wasn't buying this part.

"I know you're going to be bored," she said. "Watching me train wind weavers, day after day. I have suitors aplenty, but they only care about me if it gets them what they want. I truly need someone who will...care about...letting me accomplish what *I* need to do. Someone to fend off all the distractors and the people who think I shouldn't be doing it. Maybe that doesn't seem important to you, but it's really important to me."

That quick, he was so...very...glad...that he was not a suitor. "I will be there for you. Willingly."

*W*illingly. A word Jaikon reminded himself of often as the weeks stretched. Though the tour wasn't as boring as Fanteal had assumed, it was harder than *he* had assumed. Not for her. He'd made sure of that.

He glanced sideways at her, asleep against his shoulder. Unlike her to fall asleep, even though train movement could have a lulling effect. Dim tunnels, a steady swoosh, faint vibration.

Two-and-a-half months surrounded by wind weavers. A year ago, he never would have believed this could have happened. Not that the weavers were any difficulty. They adored Fanteal, and developed such camaraderie within their revived guild that he couldn't imagine infighting among them.

Naysayers had been more of a problem. It wasn't that anyone wanted stagnant air these days, but some still believed wind weavers must not travel. Until that day in Northeshur. Someone told Fanteal of the prophecy before Wandermae's birth and how she'd gotten her unusual name through a vision from Ellincreo. He smiled, remembering Fanteal's awestruck words. "Wander—may. Don't you see?" Jaikon had stared at her along with the rest. "That wasn't just a name!" she had declared. "Wind weavers...may...wander."

A musician who was present had shouted, "May wander! Those are the words I was searching for." Her song had spread faster than one of Fanteal's vortexes and even greeted them a few times as they arrived on train platforms. Nice change.

As for suitors pursuing the ambassador, they hadn't been as much trouble as on her first tour of the domains. His father's letter had ensured that he never had to deal with more than one at a time. Manageable.

In a way, the worst problem had nothing to do with wind weaving or Fanteal. Just the result of his own tongue while campaigning for his father. Long ago, in his mind. Not so long for those he'd offended. The proverbial stinging bats. All he could do was endure it, for even though he now knew of a better solution than he'd proposed months ago, the tunnel could not be mentioned. At least the offended parties kept their stinging words for moments when Fanteal wasn't nearby, so it didn't affect her.

He'd finally gotten some salve for their stings in Illia. Governor Yaldeeth had driven off one of the bats, then looked Jaikon straight in the eye and spoke with hushed weight. "You have matured." He had probably gaped, while wondering if he should be embarrassed or gratified. "You used to rant," she'd said. "Don't know how you shed the anger, but well done."

He still didn't know—neither when nor how the anger had lost its grip. A relief, though. He'd better keep an eye on that trap, for he was certain of one thing. He didn't want it back!

Crowing laughter erupted from a carriage behind them and woke Fanteal. "What? What's funny?" She blinked at the dim tunnel. "Oh." She wiped her thumb against the corner of her mouth. "Sorry, I can't imagine how I fell asleep."

"Delayed reaction."

"To what?"

"Could be all the goodbyes when we sent the wind weavers home from Crysalan. More likely the visit to Alluthin. That domain would exhaust anyone." Just remembering the unspoken resistance made Jaikon's guts feel like ipenrock.

She huffed. "Tense, wasn't it?"

"That's an understatement if I ever heard one."

"Reminded me of the thick air and green haze before a thunderstorm."

"What?"

"Oh, you've never seen it. A harbinger of lightning. No one can miss it. The sort of thing that makes parents hustle their children inside."

"Sounds like an apt comparison. It did feel like an impending rockslide. Especially when you asked the Alluthin wind weaver to teach pollination techniques."

She rounded her eyes and twitched her head. "Whew. Not that anyone got to practice it, but at least they got a demonstration." She lowered her brow. "I'm worried about the two Alluthin weavers who dared to travel with our guild. I hope they won't bear an extra burden because of it."

Nothing he could say to that.

"Did you ever hear why Creflon wasn't there?" she asked.

"No." Being spared the chief former's disdain had been a short-lived relief. Until Jaikon remembered Creflon's blatant mistrust and how he had followed them through every cavern during their first visit. What was so important that he would leave his domain now? A worry that Jaikon could do nothing about.

"Ah," Fanteal murmured, "there's the bend to the left. The long curve is next, then the last straight section into Jourendia's station." She smiled at him. "Maybe it's funny to you, but I like it when Dirklan feels familiar. We're almost home."

"Mm." What he liked was hearing her call Dirklan House home.

Fanteal changed out of travel clothes and freed her hair from the sensible roll that secured it for the train ride, then she joined the men in Sir Mikkael's study. He would want a report.

"Beginning to end, please," Sir Mikkael requested.

She and Jaikon took turns relating their perspectives of the events in each domain. Good overall, except for the tension in Alluthin.

"It sounds like you dealt with the cropland owners as best as anyone could," Sir Mikkael said. "Did Grellin press you for an answer, Fanteal?"

"He seems to have figured out how much I hate that. Let's just say that he gave me an opportunity to answer, and I didn't. He is coming to Jourendia's half-year celebration, so I'll soon get another opportunity to not answer."

He leaned forward, resting his elbows on his desk. "Only one more week to avoid offending him. The three dome openings commence the morning after the dance. I sincerely hope we can announce the proposed tunnel a few days later. That will greatly reduce the inordinate sway the Armeens hold." He turned to his son. "Did Creflon cause difficulties this time?"

"He wasn't there."

Sir Mikkael straightened. "Really? Not at all?" He didn't pause, for Jaikon shook his head. "That seems rather strange, but perhaps we can find out why this evening. Agriben arrived in Jourendia yesterday, and I invited him and Charlis to dinner."

Fanteal edged forward in her chair. "Speaking of Charlis, how is his work going?"

"He has finished the tasks Agriben assigned him. Though I cannot get him to state a definitive conclusion, I managed to drag the words 'I think you will be pleased' from him."

Fanteal silently clapped her palms in quick succession, letting a huge smile squeeze her eyes shut.

Jaikon warned, "Don't get ahead of the final determination." He must have realized that his own smile robbed his words of caution. "Agriben really will be looking for flaws. It's his duty, you know."

"Yes, I understand." She passed a hand downward before her face and presented her most serious expression and somber voice. "Even if the conclusion is favorable, it is not mine to announce." She flicked her hand up again and flopped back in the chair, letting her smile rebloom. "But my spirit shall savor this joy no less. Even when I mask it."

Jaikon chuckled, and Sir Mikkael looked as unburdened as she had ever seen him. He pushed a stack of papers toward his son. "Your last session reports. In brief, the council has finally adjourned."

Jaikon heaved a sigh in his own version of drama. "What shall I do for reading material?" He stood and picked up the top sheet to scan the subjects. "I cannot believe it lasted seven months."

Sir Mikkael smiled at Fanteal. "Our new ambassador gave us plenty of fodder for discussion and debate."

"Did they end up passing any of those proposed laws?" she asked.

"No, on either side of the questions. I managed to convince representatives that the Wind Weavers' Guild is already covered under any laws pertaining to the substance guilds. More importantly, I persuaded the majority that new laws affecting only one of the three guilds would, in fact, violate our constitution, which requires that all three substance guilds are autonomous."

"That should be obvious," she said. That Dirklan's governing body needed convincing, proved to her just how much this province had strayed from their own guiding principles. "Who is in the unpersuaded minority?"

"All of the Alluthin representatives and Governor Armeen, of course. Governor Nirundale, also, and some of Jourendia's representatives agree with him. No other governors and only scattered representatives from other domains. Not enough to matter, at least for now. I did notice that those who sided with Alluthin on this matter also tend to be rather loud about food concerns."

He stood when the sound of an arrival reached their ears. "As for those who brought up your clearing of the vision wall, there is little support for infringing on the keepers' purview. We will wait for next year's session, and only discuss the matter if an actual issue has arisen."

Colrin came in to announce that Agriben and Charlis had arrived, and the group walked down to the hall to greet them.

Fanteal watched Agriben while the party continued into the dining room. He seemed much more himself, walking at a normal pace and leaning less on his long walking stick. A relief.

The meal was served in the informal fashion, with kitchen staff departing as soon as they had placed the dishes on the table. Less food than they were ever offered in Alluthin and far less than in the palace, but enough. Though Fanteal never commented on it, she couldn't stop noticing the careful portion sizes.

Agriben's good cheer sparked her hope again, but she held her question, wanting him to bring it up.

He finished his oysters, then with a sly smile, darted a look around their faces. "You are all being *so* patient."

"Ah," Jaikon said, "so you are taunting us, after all."

Agriben chuckled. "I will tell you, then. I spent the day in that little flat, reviewing Charlis's maps. They are all accurate."

Not even close to what she wanted to hear!

"Still taunting us," Sir Mikkael murmured.

The chief former laughed again. "Fine. What he copied from the vision wall matches reality east of Jourendia. As for the tunnel route, I have assessed it and deem it viable."

Fanteal pressed her hands to the table. "So, it will be excavated and formed?"

"What I will do…" Agriben grew serious. "…is send the appropriate maps to the aboveground formers with my approval as Provincial Chief Former of Dirklan. They still need to do their own assessments. If they deem it safe and viable, they will already have my permission to begin." He scooped up a spoonful of rice pilaf. "They will have the most work to do, anyway."

"When will we start?" she asked. "Or at least announce it?"

"They'll need a little time to make their determination, more than a day. I'll send a letter with the maps, and I'll ask them—if they agree to excavate the tunnel—to make a significant alteration at the site of the aboveground opening. Something that Jaikon can sense. That way, we will know their answer."

She leaned back, unable to eat for the joy that choked her. This would solve everything! The food shortage. The communication problem. Dirklan's isolation from their own kingdom. The Armeens' impending stranglehold on the domains. Even remove the pressure for a marriage she didn't want. Her relief over that last worry…it revealed what little use it was to claim that Grellin couldn't force her into marriage. But with a tunnel, she really would be free to choose.

"Lady Fanteal…" She startled as Sir Mikkael said her name. "…you look like you're about to run out into the street and shout the news."

"Well, let's just say, I imagine enjoying the day that news is shouted abroad."

"It must not be done prematurely."

"I understand, sir."

Agriben tapped his knuckles against the table. "The timing is only one issue." He fixed his gaze on Jaikon. "The information must be handled *appropriately*."

Jaikon lowered the fork he had lifted toward his mouth. "What?"

Agriben looked back and forth between the two Mikkaels. "The Formers' Guild needs to know before everyone else."

"I suppose," Sir Mikkael conceded, "but I don't see how it will be kept quiet for many minutes after that."

"They need to learn of it in a manner they will accept." He again pinned Jaikon with his gaze. "Much of the tunnel route is based on only one former's knowledge. You need to start attending Formers' Guild meetings, Jaikon."

He dropped his fork and groaned.

"I know you don't like the way they have treated you, and I don't blame you. But if you want the tunnel excavated, then your gift must be acknowledged. That will not happen unless you take your place in the guild."

"That won't make them accept me."

"*I* accept you." Agriben's gravelly voice made his words all the firmer.

When Jaikon didn't respond, Charlis added, "I have much experience of your gift, and I am confident in vouching for you."

"Two of you," Jaikon said, "against more than a hundred."

"Two is enough, by the Guild's own rules." Agriben ground his voice again. "And one of us is the provincial chief former."

"If Nedford is present, he will say I am not trainable."

"If he has that gall, I will point out that *he* was not capable of training you. I plan to announce that I am taking you on as an apprentice."

Jaikon slapped the table. "I didn't even—"

"Don't argue with me. I don't need a list of what you cannot do. It's what you *can* do that we need." He continued over Jaikon's glower. "I cannot force an apprenticeship on you. But if you want a tunnel, you must have standing within the Formers' Guild."

Jaikon lowered his gaze to his plate.

"Do you accept apprenticeship under me or not?"

"Yes," Jaikon snarled.

"That is the worst-tempered acceptance I have ever received."

Jaikon drew a breath and inclined his torso. "I am honored to study under you, sir."

Agriben laughed. "You sound as if you think I'm going to treat you like a schoolboy. Nothing could be farther from my plans. Only by showing others that I respect your gift *as it is*, can I start swaying *them* to accept it."

"I appreciate that, sir. I really do. But to be honest, I don't think it will work."

"Immediately, no. But my faith in your gift is necessary to *start* the tunnel. Once it's finished, no one in Dirklan will dishonor your gift. Publicly, that is. Not that I advise you to rely on public accolades. They can flip in a day." Agriben curled his lip. "Even after decades of approval."

That sounded so crosswise to everything he'd just said that Fanteal straightened.

By the narrowing of Sir Mikkael's eyes, he'd caught the change too. "Does that have some particular meaning?" he asked.

"Creflon has been very attentive to me lately. In Crysalan and now here. From my friends, I hear he is quite subtle. He speaks of how sad he is to see my health declining. Little frowns in my direction. Supposedly, he's noticed me being forgetful, and it grieves him. Or so he says."

Sir Mikkael's expression relaxed. "Then, we will refute him with equal subtlety. I will have Colrin tell the pages to keep their ears open. Such rumors are not exciting enough to spread quickly, and Creflon has far less time than he realizes. Only a week until we can send our messages aboveground."

"True." Agriben gave him a definitive nod. "And I can't see it taking even another week until they give us an indication of their answer."

That firm response drew hardly a smile to Fanteal's heart. She chided herself. The news was still amazingly good, and the troubles tiny. So, what had squelched her urge to shout success?

CHAPTER 34

The Guild Hall was more than half full when Jaikon entered with Agriben and Charlis. He wanted to stand against the back wall but stayed at Charlis's side as Agriben stepped onto the small platform.

Agriben didn't even get a chance to start the meeting before a former asked, "Why did the prime minister send his son to observe our meeting?" No wonder Agriben had delayed their entry until it was time to begin.

The chief former thumped his staff on the platform. "Do you mind if *I* lead the meeting?"

The man inclined his head. "Sorry, sir."

Those who were still standing found places in the circular arrangement of chairs. Though they sat several rows deep, most attendees could see one another. Charlis took a seat immediately next to the platform, and Jaikon sat beside him. That got him a few strange looks from the chief formers of other domains.

Agriben cleared his throat. "Welcome, formers of Jourendia and those visiting from the rest of Dirklan. I'm especially glad for broad attendance today, for I must start by addressing a problem. I've noticed it several times over the years. We have become too comfortable with the familiar. This may seem trivial, but I've come to realize that it induces blindness to certain gifts, because we think that all formers must fit into predefined specialties."

He drew his staff near his body, gripping it high. "Since polishers are best suited to opening the dome, we think our skill is the most important. Strange. Trade cataracts stretch for miles, yet we disregard long-range gifts.

"If you've read the documents of old, you know that specialties were *never* used to disqualify someone whom Ellincreo had gifted. Now..." Agriben uttered a low huff. "We think we have the gifts all figured out. If a young former is not strong in certain specialties, their other abilities are ignored. The more unique a gift is, the more we dismiss it."

His voice ground deeper. "Backwards! *Think* about it. Unique gifts are the ones we *lack*. These are the gifts we ought to emphasize and develop with greater diligence than any other." He raked a stern gaze over his audience.

"We have erred greatly. It is time to acknowledge that and correct our mistake." He widened his stance. "It is only fitting that the provincial chief former begin the correction, so I am taking on another apprentice. He is a highly gifted former whose training was actually *abandoned...*" Agriben shook his head. "...only because no one else could match his astonishing range."

Jaikon steeled himself for whatever the reaction would be. Only one expression shocked him—Creflon's. The hint of a smile. Eager eyes. Why? Jaikon took a quick glance elsewhere. Other expressions ran the gamut of annoyance, confusion, and agreement.

"Some of you," Agriben said, "already know whom I mean. For those who don't, I am referring to Jaikon Mikkael. He possesses the longest range of any former in Dirklan. Possibly, in all of Welcia."

As a murmur swept through the crowd, a great many eyes turned Jaikon's way. Not Creflon's. He looked over the crowd. Was he waiting for something?

"If there are concerns," Agriben prompted, "I want to hear them now."

After a moment, someone cleared his throat. "Not a concern, exactly, but his dual role is also unique. A son is often the proxy for the prime minister, and our constitution prohibits the civil government from controlling any of the substance guilds."

"True," Agriben conceded, "although an apprentice is not in a controlling role within the Formers' Guild. Jaikon's dual role could even be an advantage, improving communication between our guild and the prime minister."

Creflon looked even more pleased, but again he waited with his lips slightly parted.

Agriben scanned the crowd. "If there is nothing more…"

"One issue does occur to me," Creflon said. "I daresay you are correct that Jaikon's range exceeds every former's. It certainly exceeds mine. A few peers have told me the same. I understand that Lady Fanteal has sensed his presence at a considerable distance, but that tells us nothing about his accuracy beyond what we ourselves can sense. Again, it may be perfect. But I don't understand how even one of us, much less two, can ever confirm his skills."

Agriben smiled. "Interesting conundrum, isn't it? We must give it more thought, since it would be a shame to limit ourselves to those with the second-best and third-best range. Particularly since we've all focused on near range skills. I cannot help but wonder. Are others gifted in the same manner as Jaikon, yet with that skill neglected?"

"Perhaps," Creflon allowed, "but we can know nothing of them. How could such an impossible constraint be overcome? Or are you dismissing the need for a former to prove his gift?"

"Not at all, but that is for another day. We have ordinary business to attend to now. The half-year approaches, and Sir Mikkael has submitted a formal request. He needs the dome opened at all three low tides for communication with King Darinneth and Ambassador Trissina."

Creflon raised no further objection, nor did he seem bothered by having it deferred. Jaikon got an example of his attentiveness to Agriben, for a few minutes later, Creflon carried his own chair onto the platform for Agriben to use. He then pulled another chair for himself to the side of the platform opposite Jaikon. From there, he silently watched the other formers throughout the proceedings. What was in his mind?

Half-year celebrations were as old as Welcia. During childhood, Fanteal had wondered why. Only twice a year did the small moon rise full in the wake of its big sister, but what was there to celebrate in that? When she grew old enough to join the citywide moonlight dance, she'd thought she understood.

Belowground, it was an entirely different matter.

Moonlight here was a set of markers on the cavern wall. Each aligned with a moon shaft so as to reflect the light of one moon on the night that it rose full. She had seen it for the big moon's full phase. Tomorrow night, the small moon's marker would glow. A crowd would wait in Jourendia Square to see it. A moment after, they'd start the celebration that had little to do with moonlight. For belowground, they really celebrated low tides. Only then could the dome above Passage Lake be opened. Now *that* was worth celebrating!

The crowds would be small compared to those of the day she'd arrived, but trains brought revelers, and a party spirit rode laughter in the square. The Tea House overflowed with thirsty patrons, causing Dillent to set up makeshift tables along the edge of the square.

Fanteal had her own reason to dance. The tunnel plans would rise on the harbor's vortex. No one need know the true cause of her smiles.

Lighthearted, she went down to breakfast and entered the small dining room as Sir Mikkael asked, "More than usual?"

Jaikon shrugged. "I don't know how much is usual."

Fanteal pulled a chair out to sit. "What are we talking about?"

"A lot of formers have come to Jourendia," Jaikon said.

"At the guild meeting yesterday, you mean? You never told me how it went."

"The hall was full this time, and I noticed even more formers around the settlement cavern in the evening. I suppose it could be because the dome will be opened, but that doesn't require more than a few." He tilted his head. "Actually, it only requires one who is skilled enough. Last time, Agriben had Charlis on hand and a few other young formers. That's the only opening I've ever witnessed."

Why did he look disturbed? "Is there some problem with a lot of formers coming here?"

He sighed. "Rumor has it that Creflon speaks mournfully of Agriben supporting me, and worse, making me his apprentice."

Unbelievable. "Mournfully?"

"I am now added to the so-called evidence that he is no longer fit for his position. At yesterday's meeting, Creflon asked who was capable of opening the dome." Fanteal let her eyes ask her question, and he added, "Since that is a primary requirement of a provincial chief former, it sounded like hinting at the need for a vote."

"Who *can* open it?" she asked.

"Of those present, only Agriben, Charlis, and Creflon are capable of all three tasks—opening, protecting, and resealing the dome."

"Could there be others?"

Jaikon pushed a half-eaten fried egg around on his plate. "Possible, though likely unproven. Agriben should know of any, and he mentioned no one." Jaikon let his fork handle fall against the plate. "One thing is certain. There are enough formers in Jourendia to elect a new provincial chief. All of the domain chief formers are either here or on their way. Charlis admitted that is unusual."

"Do you think Creflon summoned them?"

Sir Mikkael pushed a plate of skillet bread nearer to Fanteal. "Some, perhaps, but I believe that as many or more are here because of the rumors he has sparked. They may wish to see and hear Agriben for themselves. They may even intend to refute Creflon's insinuations."

Fanteal forced herself to ask the question she didn't want answered. "But they could also support Creflon—true?"

"They could, but Agriben smirks over the situation. I'm sure he knows where the formers stand better than any of us. Eat, my dear."

"I've lost my appetite. If we cannot send our letters and plans aboveground…" She spread her hands. They knew how awful that would be without her saying it.

"Jaikon failed to mention one decision made in yesterday's meeting. The Formers' Guild will not convene again until after the three openings of the dome." Sir Mikkael set the jar of riverfruit sauce beside the skilletbread. "Agriben will start *that* meeting by announcing the proposed tunnel route. And the tunnel will change everything."

She let the words sink in, her muscles relaxing.

"That is true," Jaikon said. "Don't mind my sour mood. Just hate being used as a tool against a man I admire."

That would rankle with anyone. Worse for him, considering how his gift was disdained here. She forced herself to search for flaws in their strategy. "Are all the documents ready? I know the maps are, and my letter to my parents. What about the other letters and Agriben's detailed plan?"

Sir Mikkael finished his tea. "All are bound in portfolios and waiting in our library. Additional copies are stored there, as well, and Agriben has the map and plan copies destined for the Formers' Guild archive."

Fanteal finally helped herself to a wedge of skilletbread and spooned the thick riverfruit sauce over it. "I cannot tell you how happy I will be when—"

"Where?" a muffled voice shouted.

She turned her head toward the door as running footsteps pounded across the hall.

The door burst open. Charlis gripped the handle and doorframe. Tears etched his cheeks as he panted.

Sir Mikkael stood in an instant. "What is it?"

"Agriben." Charlis's voice rasped. "He's dead."

No, no, no! Fanteal couldn't think. The clatter of her falling spoon made her jump.

Charlis let go of the door handle to cover his face. His strangled gasp split the air wide enough to receive his heartbroken sob. He choked it back. "I'm sorry...I had to hold it in until I got here."

Jaikon crossed the room and clutched him. Half support, half embrace. "Your tears honor him." By the sound of his voice, Jaikon shed tearful honor too.

Sir Mikkael grasped Charlis's shoulder for a moment. To a page hovering just beyond the door, he said, "Get me Colrin."

"Already summoned, sir."

Fanteal forced out squeaky words. "Send Bella to me."

"Yes, lady."

Fanteal pushed herself up from the table, though she had no means to help. Jaikon guided Charlis into one of the extra chairs along the wall. When Bella hurried in, her tragic expression revealed that she already knew. She twisted one way and another, seeming unsure whose side to rush to. Fanteal motioned her toward Charlis.

Turning away, Fanteal pressed the corners of her eyes. The dear man who had welcomed her. Who took her side when others looked askance. Who encouraged her...and Jaikon. The one who believed in him and practically demanded he take up his gift. Beside her sorrow, guilt wormed into her heart, for part of her shouted a silent demand. What would become of their tunnel plans?

Were the others thinking the same? She took hesitant steps nearer to them.

Poor Charlis. He bent low over his knees, sobs spiking through his attempts to catch his breath. She'd seen the affection between master and apprentice. Bella sat with one hand on his back and the other wiping her cheek. She'd known Agriben since childhood.

Colrin poured liquid from a flask into a small glass and pressed it into Charlis's hand. "Drink."

He got it down without choking. Whatever it was, it soon allowed him to slump against the chairback with some degree of calm. Tears or sweat coated his blotchy face below his wild hair.

Sir Mikkael pulled a chair around and sat facing him. "Tell me what happened."

"Agriben didn't come to our sitting room for breakfast, so I went into his bedroom. He was up—dressed—just sitting in his armchair. He was so pale and breathing fast. I went to him to ask what was wrong. He didn't answer, but his hand was cold. I ran to the door and sent someone for a medic streamer, then ran back to...to my master." Charlis sniffed. "He said, 'Open the dome. No matter what—open the dome.' Then...then he groaned and fell forward. I caught him—eased him down to the floor as best I could. He said, 'Open' again, and I promised him I would. Then the medic came in and..." Charlis swallowed. "He died within a couple minutes of his last word. The medic tried, but..." Shaking his head, he straightened. "Anyway, I ran here because...well...you know."

"Yes." Sir Mikkael frowned. "First matters. Colrin, send a page to order that the fountain in Jourendia Square be turned off. Do not admit anyone to Dirklan House until we have announced the death." He stood as Bella brought Charlis a cup of tea. "We will go out onto the balcony. Lady Fanteal, I request that you lift my voice."

"Certainly, sir."

"Jaikon and Charlis, you will join us. You need not speak, but I want you present."

Charlis gulped down the tea. "Thank you, sir, but I'm not important enough for that."

"You are mistaken. You will join us."

"Of course you are," Bella murmured, smoothing Charlis's disheveled hair. She swept Fanteal with a look of careful scrutiny, then nodded.

They all filed out from the dining room and up to the second-floor balcony. Colrin opened the door, and the four designated passed through it into the bright, airy expanse. How discordant with Fanteal's heart.

The square was filling with people. No hint of a party atmosphere now. Some must know. Others might be questioning the rumor. The spurting fountain suddenly choked. The final droplets peaked, then plummeted. The abrupt cessation turned heads. A few people spotted their group on the balcony and pointed.

Between Sir Mikkael and Jaikon, Fanteal gripped the cold railing. This must be formal. A prelude to bring silence. She reached far and took command of the air, stilling the vibrations of sound for a brief pause. "Jourendia...and visitors..." Her words resonated as she pushed them across the city cavern and down toward the settlement cavern. "Hear the voice of Prime Minister Sened Mikkael."

Every eye in the square and streets fixed on them. He spoke into eerie silence. "People of Dirklan..." His slow words sent a somber vibration through the air. "It grieves me deeply that I must share a great loss with you. Our highly esteemed Provincial Chief Former, Agriben, has served us for decades with unparalleled wisdom and integrity. His lifetime gift to us is now complete. He has passed from our midst into the peace of Ellincreo."

He gestured to her, and Fanteal released the air to its own wanderings. The crowd's voices returned slowly. A strange uneven keening of sobbed words. The cavern itself returned the soft wail as though ipenrock mourned the old friend who knew it so well.

Sir Mikkael inclined his head to the crowd in respectful parting, then led his attendants inside. They all followed him to his study, not speaking until Colrin had closed the door. "Despite our grief, we must remember our responsibilities to Dirklan." He focused on Charlis. "Are you up to it?"

Charlis tucked his shoulders back. "Agriben was the finest master any apprentice could ask for. He assigned me a duty this morning, and I promised to fulfill it. I shall."

"All right. Possibilities." Sir Mikkael sat against his desk rather than in the chair behind it. "The Formers' Guild. What will they do, Charlis?"

"They would normally wait until after the funeral, but with the low tides so near, I believe they will meet today or tomorrow. There are plenty of us here to select a new provincial chief former. If anything that I believe about Creflon is true, he will insist that we convene at once."

"You are likely right, but if they don't, what will happen with the dome at low tides? The guild knows I've requested opening it. Will they honor that, and who will do it?"

Fanteal sank into a chair, as Charlis looked thoughtfully aside. "It *can* be opened," he said. "Agriben and I checked it a couple days ago. It *should* be opened, for the guild is bound to honor any reasonable request. I am capable and willing to open it. Creflon is capable too. I don't know if he's willing, but he must have a reason if he refuses."

"Aren't streamers needed too?" Fanteal asked.

"Yes, but they are always standing ready, for—well, you of all people know how the lifting starts from above. Even if a former didn't call or nudge from below, seepage is possible."

Jaikon paused his slow pacing. "What would happen if you tried to open it and Creflon tried to hold it closed?"

Charlis uttered a shuddering grunt. "I cannot say exactly, but that would be very, *very* bad!"

"Unacceptable risk," Sir Mikkael declared. "Any chief former can convene the Guild, but I can also summon them. If they fail to select a provincial chief, Charlis, I will order you to open the dome."

"That would make things easy, but I'm sure they will choose, and it will be Creflon."

"Is that certain?" Fanteal asked.

"We are the only candidates. We have similar skills, but he has years more experience than I. The only way he will fail is if someone can prove a fault in him."

The faults Fanteal saw were not provable. She could claim that he'd interfered with the Wind Weavers' Guild, but if she showed up at a Formers' Guild meeting, they could say the same thing of her.

Sir Mikkael crossed his arms over his chest. "We assume, then, that Creflon will become the provincial chief. I have two options. Either tell him about the plans, or not. If informed, he has two options. Either send the plans aboveground, or not. If he knew about them, what might he do? Opinions?"

"I think," Fanteal said, "that the Armeens will do whatever is necessary to prevent the tunnel."

"Jaikon?" his father asked.

"Creflon does not trust my forming sense to any degree. Even without his Armeen biases, he will not accept a plan that I had anything to do with."

"Charlis?"

"Exactly what Jaikon described. Also, my confirmation counts for nothing in Creflon's opinion."

Sir Mikkael turned to Bella, who sat slightly beyond the group. "I know full well how you quietly observe. What do you think of the Armeens?"

"They are suspicious of Lady Fanteal, or perhaps worried about what she may do. They ignore Charlis and me. Jaikon..." She glanced his way. "Sorry, but he asked me. They *really* don't like you."

"I know."

To Sir Mikkael, she said, "I think they would be livid if Jaikon solved the food problem, but I don't know if that would make Creflon prevent the tunnel. I admit, I've never heard him badmouth people behind their backs, like some of the others do."

Rubbing his chin, Sir Mikkael offered his own opinion. "My experience of them comes from their governor and representatives during the council session. Different forum, but their attitude is apparent in Government House. So…if I believe that Creflon will stop the tunnel, I must decide whether I should tell him about the plans."

Jaikon halted and clutched a chairback. "If you tell only him, the whole thing is over. He will discredit it before anyone else has a chance to even think about it."

"I will not risk that. I can tell the entire Formers' Guild before the vote, after the vote, or not at all."

Fanteal felt their exhalations rifle the air. She studied Sir Mikkael. "If you send the maps and plans aboveground *without* telling the new provincial chief, you could be accused of usurping the rights and authority of the Formers' Guild."

"I am aware. A serious charge that would cost me my office and much more. My defense would be tied to Dirklan's need for food, and all of Welcia's need for trade. I can also claim my belief that separation from the crown is near to destroying the foundation of our constitution, though that argument will get little support. I must prove that the Armeens threaten all of this." He sighed. "A defense which may or may not work, but I'm here for Dirklan, not for the office. I believe I am morally bound to try."

"As ambassador of the crown, I support you. But why wouldn't you tell the entire guild?"

He turned to Charlis. "What happens if I tell them before the vote, after, or neither?"

Charlis groaned and sat down. "If you reveal the tunnel plan before the vote, they will want time to review, which will delay the vote until after the low tides. The plans will not be sent above for at least six months. If you reveal after the vote…Creflon will also claim that he—they—need time to review. Again, they will not be sent up for at least six months.”

“That’s what I thought. Time is of the essence. The import cataract could fail in one moment. If the plans are not sent up, the aboveground formers will have no voice in the matter. They cannot consider their end of the tunnel route as shown in the vision wall.”

“Also,” Charlis said, “they won’t be able to prove whether Jaikon’s range is accurate to the surface. Agriben wanted their confirmation to validate Jaikon’s range. Once proven, his range would become the standard against which newly trained formers could be tested. Dirklan’s entire Formers’ Guild could recover the ranges that we once had.”

“Are you certain,” Fanteal asked, “that Agriben wasn’t going to tell any formers here until we had some answer from aboveground?”

“That was his intention.”

“Well then...” Fanteal turned to Sir Mikkael. “I suggest another defense. You are acting on the plans of Provincial Chief Former Agriben, who was concerned that the Armeens would soon seize control of the Formers’ Guild. Also, you are trying to prevent a belowground provincial chief former from usurping the rights of the aboveground Formers’ Guild.” She cocked her head. “You could bring in something about him robbing Welcia above of much needed resources.”

“Valid points, but they won’t help me much in Dirklan.”

“No, but they will help you with the king. He won’t approve of you hiding a tunnel from the Formers’ Guild.”

He closed his eyes. “More complications. I have enough.”

“You’ll need to send up a notification of Agriben’s death, anyway. You might want to cover some of these points.”

“Be careful with letters,” Jaikon warned. “We have to pack everything into the vessel ahead of time. Even if we delay, Creflon could get a chance to open the thing.”

Fanteal rested her forehead against stiff fingers. “Oh, dear! My letter to my parents—it is quite blunt about the Armeens.” Silence greeted her words. Doubtless the others were thinking of what had been written and whose eyes might see it.

"I will merely write that I am sending the plans of our recently deceased provincial chief," Sir Mikkael said, "who considered them extremely critical. Where necessary, we will replace letters with a vague version. Those will be sent in the first opening of the dome. If Creflon acts in good faith, fine. If he does not..."

Sir Mikkael looked long at Charlis. "We will be forced into an alternate strategy for the nighttime opening. Get your things from the inn. You will be staying in Dirklan House. Lock the doors of Agriben's suite and tell the inn's host that no one is allowed to enter it. Bring the keys to me."

CHAPTER 35

"What's with all the cloaks?" Fanteal asked Bella, drawing her head in from the window. How would she see Jaikon and Charlis returning when everyone's head was covered?

"They are commonly worn in the early days of mourning."

"You have special garments just for the rare occasion of a death? Why?"

"Not just for that. Everyone has a cloak." Bella lightened her tone. "I've heard that winter breezes used to be chilly." The quip fell flat.

"Another complaint heading my way," Fanteal griped. "What does that have to do with mourning?"

Bella went back to copying Fanteal's revised letter. "I suppose because one can pull the hood low. Hide tears or avoid chatter." She looked up again. "You don't have one, do you? I'll go down to the emporium when I'm done with this. Would you prefer green or white?"

"Black. Mourning color."

Bella blinked at her. "In Welcia above? Here it's a former color."

"They don't have exclusive rights to black, gray, and brown."

Bella lowered her gaze to the letter. "True."

Fanteal rolled her lips. Not her best moment. Completely unfair to Bella, who had also lost a friend and mentor. "Sorry I snarled at you. I'm just anxious to hear what is happening at the guild meeting. Poor excuse, I know."

"Understandable, though."

At least Bella hadn't stated the obvious—that fretting wouldn't help. Fanteal had already tried reading. No good. She wandered to the tiancient tree, which now lived in the salon where it could be cared for during Fanteal's long absences.

It was so cute that she always tried to forget who gave it to her. Grellin. He'd arrived in Jourendia and had come with Governor Armeen to utter condolences. Well enough, until he'd made a subtle, questioning reference to Agriben's latter days. Fanteal got past it by speaking of Agriben's support of unexpected gifts. What had Grellin been trying to pry out?

"Finished." Bella stood up from the table.

Fanteal scanned the short missive and initialed it, then Bella took both copies to the library, leaving Fanteal to stare out the window. Soon, she saw Bella walking away from the house, also clad in a cloak with its loose hood spread over her shoulders. She headed across the square toward the emporium, stopped and talked with someone, then continued on her way. One of the prime minister's pages exited the Tea House.

Pathetic. Fanteal had nothing better to do than stare at employees and strangers walking around.

A cluster of people cloaked in somber hues came up Fountain Avenue. The Formers' Guild held their meetings down that way in historic Settlement Hall, not far from Passage Lake. Maybe these were formers, which would mean the meeting was over. Two of them split from the group and strode to the door of Dirklan House.

Soon, Jaikon entered the salon with his cloak over one arm.

Fanteal twined her fingers. "Well?"

"About what we expected. Creflon is now provincial chief former."

Charlis came in a few steps behind Jaikon. Neither of them looked upset by the outcome. "Why did it take so long?" Fanteal asked.

Jaikon tossed his cloak onto a side chair. "He didn't have it all his way. Some of the domain chief formers don't like how the Armeens make sure their local guilds are led by one of their own. It smells like outside control."

"So, others do know about that?"

Charlis untied his cloak. "Agriben mentioned it sometimes when I traveled with him."

"Creflon stresses that his name is Lawfertee and claims that he is not a cropland owner." Jaikon quirked his mouth, shrugging. "Apparently, he transferred his inherited land to a sister, but I doubt that changes anything. Regardless, he was prepared with a glib answer. Knows how to talk about the good of Dirklan, the priority of creating food-producing areas, his willingness to excavate for more cropland in other domains—*if* the areas are suitable—and the importance of dual assessments. All smoothly stated, with quite reasonable caveats."

"What did he say about opening the dome?"

"That he would assess it soon."

That grabbed her attention. "Then he didn't say yes or no."

Jaikon gave her a firm look. "True, but that is sensible. Charlis has already assessed, but it needs two."

"Agriben assessed it also, so that already is two."

His gaze held steady. "Sorry, Fanteal, but I'm going to speak as a former. When Creflon said, 'I must assess it before I open it,' *everyone* in the room agreed. Including me. If he relied on someone else's word, secondhand, and that of a former who is not alive to confirm it…" Jaikon angled his head. "They probably would have instantly called for another vote and barred him from any and all chief former positions for life."

"I get it," she grumbled.

"I'm not sure you do. Belowground, a former's actions can kill."

"It's no different above. Wind and water can kill too." She looked from Jaikon to Charlis, whose brow was furrowed. "Doesn't make decisions easier, though, does it? Inaction can also kill."

Charlis nodded. "If Creflon doesn't open the dome on the first opportunity, I'm going to *hate* him." He raked his hair back. "Not just for refusing. For pushing me into the impossible choice."

She ached for him. Expected to make decisions that could affect multitudes. What she would ask of him would be an enormous burden. Maybe Creflon would step up to his duties, and she wouldn't have to ask. She squelched her inner cringe and tried moving on. "It still seems like it took a long time to get through all of that."

"They argued over funeral arrangements too." Jaikon squeezed Charlis's shoulder. "It will be held in Jourendia Square first thing in the morning—after the half-year celebration."

She opened her eyes wide.

Jaikon answered her obvious thought. "I know. It's awfully close to the first low tide. Charlis is chief mourner. He and Creflon will lead the procession. The domain chiefs insisted that Charlis must also be in the lake cavern for the opening. That is wise, because Creflon hasn't opened the dome in years."

Jaikon gave Charlis a sympathetic look before continuing. "That's what caused the long argument. There will be a massive crowd. Creflon says that peace officers can keep a path clear, so he and Charlis can easily reach the lake cavern."

Fanteal snorted. "*Or* he could make it look like it's not his fault if the dome isn't opened."

"We are all biased, you know," Charlis reminded them. "There is enough time."

"It is still horribly insensitive to force you to rush away early from the funeral."

"Yes, but he is ignorantly giving me exactly what I want. I promised Agriben that the dome would open. Nothing will please me more than to make certain of that in the middle of his funeral."

"Ah." She thought for a moment. "I don't think we can wait to pack the vessel. There's no saying how early the funeral crowd will gather."

"Long before the light shafts brighten," Jaikon said. "The trains are running continuously from Crysalan. Agriben never married, but he had family and friends aplenty. When there are more people than the inns and flats can hold, they sleep in Jourendia Square."

"Oh, dear. And I was already wondering what the half-year celebration would be like."

"Different! Everyone knew *of* Agriben, but many didn't know him personally. We cannot cancel such a significant event, but the crowd will change it. Traditionally, everyone brings a dish to share. That won't be enough with so many visitors. Fortunately, Colrin got ahead of that problem. He sent an express order to Alluthin right after Agriben died. It should be here in time, if it isn't already. We'll have music and try to keep an area clear for those who wish to dance."

Dancing? The same old problem of not showing favoritism. Added to that, the possibility that some might consider it disrespectful of Agriben. "It may be best if I dance only once, and with the prime minister."

"I'm sure he will accommodate you with the opening dance." Jaikon turned to Charlis. "She's right about packing the vessel. I think we should do it when everyone else is going to sleep."

Fanteal acted her part in the opening dance. Though she declined all others, that didn't excuse her from mingling and conversation. Jaikon was right about the crowds—but not about the food. The shipment didn't arrive in time. Late in the event, when the shortage was painfully obvious to everyone, Governor Armeen stepped onto the platform, rang the gong, and announced that Alluthin had sent food. Cartloads were rushed up Fountain Avenue from the train station.

Oh, how blatant! Alluthin to the rescue when Sir Mikkael had failed to feed the crowd. Obvious to Fanteal, but not to the masses. Their plans had better work.

With the festivities over, Fanteal joined Jaikon and Charlis in the library to pack the documents, then watched from the gallery as they slipped out into the night. She uttered a silent prayer in her heart. *Please see it all arrive safely aboveground.*

"I will not be hampered by that crowd," Sir Mikkael said. "Colrin, notify the ceremony master that I will make my remarks from the balcony."

Startled, Fanteal looked at Jaikon and Bella. Their surprised expressions turned thoughtful. Small wonder. It would be a relief.

Colrin headed for the door. "I will have chairs set out."

At least Fanteal was spared the attention that often sparked during her public appearances—so unsuitable at a funeral—but they still had a long wait on the balcony. The solemn procession ascended Fountain Avenue. Charlis and Creflon led it, followed by the bier, Agriben's family, and a couple hundred formers, all cloaked with their hoods drawn up. When the procession reached the square, she, too, lifted her hood and stood with her companions at the railing. It seemed to take forever to get all the official mourners seated. The throng following them shuffled into every empty space.

Sir Mikkael's brief words were among the first. As a rather monotonous speaker droned through a long eulogy, Fanteal's gaze wandered, then caught movement along Fountain Avenue. What? Why was space filling in?

She gripped Sir Mikkael's arm and pointed.

He stiffened, then turned to Colrin, who stood against the back wall. "They are allowing the avenue to fill in. Go down and make sure it is kept clear."

She watched. Colrin would need time to get to the peace officers, who would need more time to separate the crowd. How long? She was still waiting when Colrin returned.

His face showed how bad the news would be. "It was Creflon, sir, who told the peace officers they needn't keep the avenue clear. He told them that the dome is flawed and he will not be opening it."

Never had she seen such anger on Sir Mikkael's face. Jaikon's was no surprise. She probably looked just as bad. Bella jerked her hood low. All they could do was wait through the entire service.

What must Charlis be feeling? Held in place by a vast crowd and the decision of Provincial Chief Former Creflon. Did Grellin have anything to do with this? Fanteal would gladly have slapped either of them. Except ambassadors didn't have that luxury.

Hours later, they still had no answers. The prime minister had sent three pages out, trying to deliver a summons to Creflon. He did not come.

Fanteal waited in the study, where Sir Mikkael wrote one note after another. Jaikon paced. She tried to devise ways to use royal ambassador authority to get that dome opened. There were still two opportunities. One tonight, another tomorrow morning. If only she could believe her arguments would prevail.

Charlis finally walked into the room. Gray shadows lurked beneath his eyes. He looked at each of their faces, then dropped onto the couch.

"Did Creflon give a reason for not opening the dome?" Sir Mikkael asked.

"Said he detected a flaw in one of the panels. It wasn't there when Agriben and I assessed it a few days ago. Nor last night."

Bella carried in a tray of tea, sweet cakes, and some berries that grew in the roof garden. She ignored protocol and served Charlis first, quietly gripping his hand for a few seconds.

Sir Mikkael asked, "Could he have created a flaw?"

Charlis stared at his tea. "Why bother? Creflon only needs to *claim* there is one." He took a sip. "Now what?"

"I have sent for Creflon, though he has yet to respond," Sir Mikkael said. "In the meantime, please confirm again that the dome can be opened. After you've eaten, of course."

"I suppose," Fanteal murmured, "I should write an addendum letter to my parents."

"Stick to bare facts." Sir Mikkael handed Bella a quartz sheet and pen, and she laid it on the table beside Fanteal.

Fanteal picked up the pen. "Charlis, I'll walk down to the chamber with you to put this in the vessel. Give you an extra reason to be there, just in case you need one."

With her letter complete, Fanteal and Charlis left the Mikkaels and followed Fountain Avenue to the settlement cavern. The cloaks proved useful for avoiding attention. No one bothered them until two peace officers stopped them several yards from the lake cavern.

"No one's allowed beyond this point."

Charlis pushed his hood back. "I am."

They clearly recognized him. "Oh. Uh, the new chief former told us no one's allowed."

Fanteal slid her hood so they could see her face. "He couldn't have meant Charlis. Besides, I need him to open the vessel so I may add a letter to Ambassador Trissina."

That worked. As they approached the tunnel, Fanteal whispered, "Was that normal?"

"Never."

She slowed, for the tunnel was dim. Would she ever stride through darkness like a Dirklian? After a couple steps, Charlis matched her pace without comment. Courteous man.

A muffled voice demanded, "Will you never finish?"

She darted her gaze to the source, oddly high on the tunnel wall.

Charlis murmured, "Did you hear a voice?" She nodded, and he pointed to the faintly glowing source. "Those are vents into the equipment room."

She pressed a finger to her lips and concentrated, emphasizing the vibrations that came through the vents and focusing them near her and Charlis. Someone had hushed the first speaker.

After a moment, another voice spoke. "Carefully worded, but these letters are *not* commending us."

"Far from it," Grellin's voice said.

"Would you hush?" That demand came from Creflon.

"Would you finish?" Grellin snapped. "How can you still not know what it is?"

"It's a tunnel route."

"Idiots. Where does it start?"

"Jourendia." Creflon snarled it like Grellin was the idiot.

"Then, what are we waiting for? Just destroy it."

Fanteal went hot and cold.

"Are you out of your mind? There has to be at least one other copy. And far more important—it may be viable!" Creflon might be a snake, but he was a former too.

Someone shuffled. Hissed words escaped Fanteal's hearing. Who was the third person?

A moment later, Grellin whispered, "I have no surety of her. If these get aboveground, food shortages will persuade no one. Her, least of all. Alluthin can feed many, but a tunnel could feed everyone. Provide trade too. Don't you dare call these viable, or we will lose *all* negotiating power."

"Think, Grellin!" Ah, that was Governor Armeen. "Those maps are a far greater negotiating tool."

Silence—too much of it. Shuffling. The slide of quartz sheets.

Fanteal breathed her words. "I think they are packing up. How do we stay out of sight?"

"There's a door at either end of the equipment room. When you hear one open, go the opposite way through the tunnel." Scrapes and clicks came through the vent. "That's the vessel cover," he whispered.

A moment later, the door opened beyond the tunnel entry. Fanteal hurried toward the lake, and Charlis gripped her arm to guide her.

The cavern glowed with partial daylight from two light shafts. They ducked around the corner. No longer visible from the tunnel, they leaned against the wall. She felt Charlis's forming sense rise toward the dome. That would give her time to listen. She sensed the air back through the tunnel. Would the Armeens talk to the peace officers whom Creflon had ordered to keep people out?

When Charlis ceased working, she whispered, "I heard no voices out there. I didn't even hear the Armeens walk past the tunnel."

"Then, they followed the cavern wall instead of the street. The dome is fine. Come."

She followed him to a door, which he opened by former command, then stepped through. She stared at massive gears and chains. More imposing than she'd imagined from her childhood history book.

He spared them little attention, saying, "These operate the gates that are closed during the low tides. The vessel is over here." He entered a side room.

She recognized one of the two-person vessels that were exchanged between Welcia above and below. Used mostly for communication, or most recently, her luggage. The large vessel stood in shadow beyond—too heavy for the half year. Only the new year vortexes could be trusted to lift it. She followed Charlis.

"Watch your step. There are rails."

They seemed to lead to a stone wall, but it must be moveable. Already, Charlis was walking around the vessel, releasing clips. She slipped her hand into her cloak's pocket, the sealed quartz rigid under her fingertips. Fairly safe to add it, since the Armeens would think they had read everything. If...

Charlis slid the cover off. They leaned forward to peer inside.

Empty.

She pressed a shaking fist to her mouth, her teeth denting her finger. She met Charlis's pained eyes over the top of the vessel. Oh, how she hated the heaviness of their breaths in the still air. What were they going to do?

Charlis slid the cover back into place, then rounded it again to close each clip. He gripped her arm. "We need to tell the prime minister."

CHAPTER 36

Fanteal and Charlis stood before Sir Mikkael's desk, cloaks still hanging from their shoulders. How was he so good at guarding his expressions? Only the silence revealed how gravely he took the news that the vessel was empty.

He pulled a drawer open. "I should have gotten Agriben's copy brought here the moment he died. Legal or not." He took out keys and tossed them to Colrin. "Go under my orders and get Agriben's copy of the map and plans. Try for subtlety, but you are free to say I have ordered your actions for the protection of Dirklan. Call for peace officers if you need them."

Colrin gripped the keys tight in his fist. He closed his open lips, swallowed, then nodded and left.

Sir Mikkael braced his forehead against his peaked fingertips. "Ordering my employees to commit crimes now," he muttered.

Jaikon's mouth moved like he was fighting some unseen force to keep it closed.

Sir Mikkael focused on Fanteal. "You heard three men talking and then found the vessel empty. How certain are you that you recognized the voices correctly?"

How like him to want every fact confirmed. "Grellin's voice, I know far better than I'd like. Creflon followed us around Alluthin the first time we visited, so I know his too, and according to the conversation, that person was studying the map while the others were reading our letters. The governor was the hardest to identify, but I occasionally converse with him."

Of Charlis, he asked, "You could hear them too?"

"Yes, once she drew the sound to us."

"Fanteal, relate everything they said. Jaikon, stop pacing and write this down. Charlis, you will confirm or correct as needed."

Fanteal forced herself through all of it. Reasonable that he wanted a record, but it brought them no nearer a solution. They couldn't decide on anything until Colrin returned with the copy of the maps, and even then, they needed to get Creflon to open the dome. The way he was disregarding a summons from the prime minister, that didn't look likely.

Fanteal jumped when the door opened, but it was only Bella.

"Did you hear anything significant at the Tea House?" Sir Mikkael asked her.

"No. Business was slow, and talk was dull." She looked from Charlis to Fanteal. "What's going on?"

They repeated their discovery. Sir Mikkael sent Bella to the library to recopy all the letters and the transcript Jaikon had written.

The door opened again. Colrin. With empty hands.

He closed the door behind him. "I was too late, sir."

"Caverns and skies!" Jaikon snarled.

Fanteal took several steps from the group around the desk. This only got worse and worse. She pressed her hands to her face. Nothing Lord Yaeger or her mother had taught her prepared her for this mess. She tried to focus on Colrin's answer to Sir Mikkael.

"When I reached the inn's lobby, there was already an uproar. A few of Agriben's kin had come to collect his belongings and were upset. Creflon had come shortly before. Without so much as a word to the staff, he walked right up to the suite, opened the lock with a forming command, and went in. Someone saw him and alerted the host, who went to object, but in short, Creflon took two portfolios, one large enough for maps. According to the host, Creflon only deigned to speak once, declaring, 'Former records are property of the Formers' Guild.' The next of kin demanded to see the documents to confirm what he was taking, but he ignored everyone and strode right out of the inn."

"Illegally collected," Sir Mikkael murmured, "but his statement was true. We won't be able to recover them." He stared at the stack of notes he had written earlier. "Let's focus on what we have. There is still a set of maps in the library."

"We need two sets," Charlis said. "One for the aboveground formers and one for below."

"How long will it take you to make another set?"

Charlis sank into a chair, rubbing his brow. "It's a lot of sections in the full map. I cannot finish by tonight's opening. Tomorrow's, yes, if I work all night." He sounded as exhausted as he looked.

Jaikon's pacing had morphed into a thoughtful stroll. "We have the set that Charlis and I made by the vision wall. They're a hurried version. Not signed by Agriben, either, but they cover the basics."

"If we wait for the third opening..." Sir Mikkael drummed his fingers before continuing. "That would allow no confirmation from above that your assessment of the peninsula is correct. Agriben considered that critical. It was explained in his letter."

"I will copy that too," Charlis said, "or Bella can. Witness signatures and so forth. But none of this will work if we cannot get the dome open."

Sir Mikkael folded his hands on the desk, his earnest gaze on Charlis. "Prepare yourself to open it, for I may need to ask it of you. I know that would be a heavy burden. I have plans to protect you, but they depend on our success. If the Armeens succeed in their goals, your career is ruined, and you'll be dragged into court, besides."

"I know. You too, in fact." Charlis shrugged. "At least I'm in good company." His attempted quip fell flat. "The way I see it, I'm a former and have a duty to Dirklan. I believe we all desperately require a tunnel, so I must enable it. I also made a promise to my master, Provincial Chief Former Agriben." Enunciating the title seemed to give Charlis strength. "I will open the dome if Creflon refuses. But understand, I can only open it once. They will arrest me immediately afterward."

"We have friends in the right places," Sir Mikkael said. "Colrin will get you to the flat, and none will see." He scowled. "I begin to think our oily provincial chief will refuse to answer the question of whether he is going to open the dome."

Colrin cleared his throat. "The host of Fountain Inn had called for a peace officer. Two came, and they were within a hairsbreadth of arresting Creflon for theft. One of them followed him, and I told the other to maintain surveillance—to report on everywhere he went and what he carried in and out. We will always know exactly where he is."

Sir Mikkael smiled. "Then I shall have him escorted here if he doesn't come on his own."

How long would he wait? Fanteal looked at her watch. It was dinnertime. Like with lunch, no one mentioned the meal. She poured herself a glass of water from the pitcher beside a tray of finger food, which had gotten them through the afternoon. She still didn't feel like eating but took a nut biscuit to appease her stomach.

Footsteps again. Would this be Creflon?

A page entered, and his gaze settled on her. "Lady Fanteal, Grellin Armeen is requesting to see you." He lifted his nose. "He specifically requested to see you alone."

Alone. The man who read and stole her letters. And maps. "Tell him I shall come in a few minutes if he would like to wait in the salon."

The instant the door shut behind the page, Jaikon insisted, "Not alone!"

She looked at him, considering. What might she be able to learn. Or do?

He rested his hands on her shoulders. "I do not want you alone with him. One of us must go with you."

His concern, his expression, were so endearing that she was tempted to step into an embrace. Not the time for that. "It's not as though he can harm me in Dirklan House."

"But he's a snake. The kind that spits venom to blind its enemies. Grellin's words are more dangerous than physical harm."

"Yes, but he doesn't know that I heard him from the tunnel. Or that I know they emptied the vessel. I would like to learn what he intends to do with his stolen information."

"He won't tell you the truth, you know."

"We may be able to discern it from his lies. What do you think, Sir Mikkael?"

"As your guardian, I would go with you, or at least send Bella. As prime minister to ambassador, I would let you go alone. I will leave the choice with you. Do not underrate the danger or let him draw out *your* information or intentions."

Interesting thought. Might Grellin seek that? "I will see him alone."

She entered the salon with outward calm. "What brings you on a funeral day?"

"It is always a pleasure to see you, but this day is unique. More than a funeral, it's also the day of half-year tides."

"True."

"You know that I like to be of service to you, and I was wondering if you were disappointed that the dome was not opened this morning."

"Disappointed?" She gave the word an incredulous twist. "I have an ambassador's duty to King Darrineth and Queen Ambassador Trissina. I have also written to the Wind Weavers' Guild about air channels and about my temporary role as Chief Wind Weaver. And though Creflon may not care about my affection for family, I do."

"Ah yes, I'm sure that—"

"Do you know whether Creflon has repaired the flaw? Will he open the dome tonight?"

"I have not heard. I've known him most of my life, though. Would you like me to stress to him the importance of sending your letters?"

"My letters? Why mention them specifically? The current prime minister always exchanges letters with the king and ambassador. Import and export records are sent. I believe there were packets from the Schools of Invention and Health. A provincial chief former should know that all communication should be sent without question. Why does he need urging from you? Do you have any idea what this looks like?"

"I only mentioned yours because you did—just the flow of conversation. My dear..." He stepped closer. "I have tried to court you in the traditional manner, but that has been rather difficult. And while my affection for you prompts me to give you time to grow comfortable with a union between us, other matters are more pressing."

"What matters?"

"There are whispers of a tunnel."

"Are there? Odd that I have not heard of these whispers."

"Oh, but I think you have. In a household such as this..." He spread his hands. "So many pages going here and there with messages. Even staff that you might trust implicitly can, shall we say, serve multiple interests."

Was he implying Bella had told him? Colrin? Yesterday's image of the square intruded. Bella chatting with someone. The page leaving the Tea House. More likely Grellin was trying to hide that he had seen the maps and letters. Let him interpret her pause how he chose.

"I know the plans discussed in this house quite well," he said. "A tunnel originating from Jourendia."

"Interesting. That would solve a lot of problems, wouldn't it?"

"And create as many as it would solve."

For him, maybe. "Oh?

"Change is chaotic and difficult to manage. I know you believe that you understand Dirklan well, but there is much you do not realize. I would be greatly honored to assist you. As husband."

"So, this is actually a marriage proposal?"

"Yes."

"On a day of mourning. Unique. Also, the day that the Armeen chief former refuses to open the dome. While my heart flutters at the depth of your love, I have made it clear that I will not resume courtship until after the half-year."

"Forgive me. I was afraid you might misunderstand."

"Then you shouldn't have asked today."

"I do truly admire you greatly and wish to marry you, for the sake of us alone. Unfortunately, as royal ambassador, your decisions affect all of Dirklan. Including your choice of husband."

Like she hadn't heard that all her life. "What does that have to do with a tunnel, Grellin?"

"Do you really want a tunnel?"

"Everyone wants a tunnel."

"One of your misconceptions about Dirklan. I have no need of a tunnel, but I would support it if my wife wanted it."

"Why are we having this conversation *today*?"

"Please stop pretending that I haven't heard about your plans."

"How exactly did you hear?"

"A tunnel cannot be excavated without much help from above. I have no doubt that tunnel plans are in that vessel and—"

"How do you know that?"

"Let's just say, the likelihood is so strong that I find your supposed doubts quite pointless. Do you want those plans aboveground or not?"

"This is all so strange. If I wrote, or drew, or whatever, tunnel plans, no one aboveground would do a thing with them."

He half-closed his eyes and let a silent breath out his nose. "I know that Agriben was in on this. Can we *please* stop pretending?"

"Will you be a little more forthright?"

"I already am, but I will be clearer. The dome will not open unless we are married. You have less than a day to decide. About three hours, if you want the night opening. Fifteen if you can wait for morning."

"Skies above! Do you think there will never be another chance?"

He shrugged. "How can we be sure? Apparently, a crack formed in a dome panel after Agriben assessed it. That means it's unstable. How can we know if it will ever be safe again?"

Definitely a snake.

"Ah, you needn't look so shocked," he said in his loathsome kind voice again. "We don't really need the dome. It hasn't provided any benefit in decades, so no one would be harmed if the panels were permanently sealed. The trade cataracts are still failing, and Alluthin is feeding most of Dirklan. If the Mikkaels tell you otherwise, they are lying. We will continue to care for our province."

She longed to tell him just what she thought of him. No, diverting would be a better strategy. "You mentioned that a tunnel would cause problems. Only to Alluthin, I think, which would no longer control food."

He smiled. "Or textiles, or the many other products we provide Dirklan. For none of them, do we need an ambassador. But if you want a tunnel in Jourendia, the ambassador must be married to an Armeen."

"What a lovely foundation for marriage."

"Don't worry, my dear. I will be kind to you. Arranged marriages are as common in my family as they are in the royal family. They are often happier than a marriage that starts with young passions." He tried a gentle, though ironic smile. "But I do need an answer if we are to be married in three hours."

"Three hours?" She splayed her fingers and, turning away, pressed them to her head. Buying time, when there was none to be bought.

Her heart rushed. A lover's delight, this was not! It didn't matter how he knew about the plans. He did know. It didn't matter that Grellin controlled Creflon illegally. He did control him. And that meant no tunnel without marriage. Her hands were shaking. She mustn't let him see.

She walked to the little table that held the tiancient tree. "Three hours! Couldn't you at least have come when the funeral first ended?"

"Forgive me, my dear. Take your time now. I will wait." A chair cushion behind her made a soft whoosh as he sat down.

Food. Always the food problem that she couldn't solve. A thought crept in, trying to edge her anger aside. She could provide food through a tunnel—*if* she married him. Hateful thought. She made a vile face since she couldn't speak the nasty words that wanted out.

The thought persisted. Sudden realization almost overwhelmed her. Dirklan had always been her duty, but somewhere in the last six months the strangers had become friends. She couldn't let them go hungry. They would, too. She was privy to the import and apportionment records. Alluthin couldn't feed everyone. It was Grellin who lied. Some would starve. She could prevent that.

What would marriage to him be like? One coercive lie after another? Could Creflon keep the tunnel down to a narrow, freight-only dimension? Probably. Letters could be sent, but what good would they do a year or more from now? Oh, skies, what if Grellin could control what letters she sent and received? Letters from Ambassador Melthindi to her father had stopped. Melthindi had lived in Alluthin. Her stomach writhed, and not from hunger.

Was her own misery the only way to feed Dirklan? She wanted to run out onto the balcony and shout that she was being coerced. Defame Grellin and all the Armeens. They would deny everything. Or she could tell Sir Mikkael and drag Grellin and Creflon into court, maybe the governor too. Neither option would open the dome. Certainly not in a day. Maybe forever. Even if everyone knew of a tunnel route, that did no good until abovegrounders knew. This was a disaster, and there wasn't time to fix it.

Focus on what you have.

Calm hope suffused that silent inner voice—a sweeter thought than the bitter idea of providing food by marriage. Sir Mikkael had said much the same earlier today. What did she have?

Time. Ticking away on her wrist. Three hours or fifteen. She had drawings, though there wouldn't be two sets until morning. She had a former who could open the dome. She had friends in this house. She practically moaned. Could any of them be false?

In truth, Grellin was a venom-spraying snake to plant that poison in her mind. If anyone could not be trusted, it was he. Suddenly, that knowledge was an advantage. He'd revealed the core of his motivation, which meant she could negotiate *at that level*. What would he believe she wanted that she was willing to give up? Ah.

She turned around swiftly enough that she caught a satisfied smile on his face.

He didn't try to hide it. "It's interesting how much one can discern from changing posture."

Oh, could he? "What, did I slump at first? You should already know that I'm not thrilled to be married for political ends. If I agree, and that is still an *if*, certain conditions must be met."

He inclined his head. "I'll accommodate anything I'm able to."

"Which is not a commitment to anything. Something you are quite prone to, so I must have certainty. First, since the Armeens have control of the Formers' Guild, I want to retain control of the Wind Weavers' Guild."

He smiled. "I imagine we'll need to use a delay strategy until we can change the law. I'm sure Governor Armeen will support you, particularly when he is prime minister. We can count on Governor Nirundale's support too."

He fell for that one easily. "Second, we will be married in the lake cavern immediately before it is opened in the morning."

He raised his brows. "As you wish."

"Third, Charlis must be on hand to open it since I have little faith in Creflon."

"No problem at all. Creflon wants him there anyway."

"Actually, it was the domain chief formers who insisted on Charlis's presence. There will be no vows if he is not there."

"Understood, my dear."

She wanted to puke every time he called her *dear*. "Fourth, the ceremony will be conducted as follows. The vessel will be on the tracks, at the shore. It will be open, and I will review the contents. I will write our marriage announcement in advance, ready to add to the vessel." He was still smiling. Good. She continued. "We will go into the equipment room and watch the vessel ascend the vortex, then exchange our vows. Agreed?"

"I fear the equipment room will be too crowded. It holds massive gears, plus formers and streamers must be inside to perform critical work. It's true that the lake cavern is a charming place for a wedding. Let's finish it there before the dome is opened. We can invite more guests that way."

"Hmm. The vessel will be pushed out of the equipment room, so that space is available. We only need the Keeper of the Writ and two witnesses, so we will fit." He started shaking his head, so she said, "However, I agree, it would be easier in the lake cavern. In that case, we will exchange vows after the vessel ascends."

"Ah, dear Fanteal, you do not trust me yet, but your fears are unfounded. I have no objection to a tunnel as long as it does not create unfair competition beyond Armeen influence. That is why marriage is necessary. You may trust that I have every intention of sending the vessel up."

She pressed her palm to her heart. "*Dear* Grellin, I find it difficult to trust a man who is forcing me into marriage. I trust Creflon, who lies about the dome, even less." She dropped her hand and sarcastic tone. "A compromise, then. We will begin the ceremony on the shore of Passage Lake. At some point, perhaps right after your vows, I will place the announcement in the vessel, which will then be sealed and released into the lake. We will go into the equipment room, and I will pronounce my vows as the vessel rises through the vortex. Agreed?"

"You are putting far too much emphasis on delaying your vows. I can give you no more trust than you give me."

"I also have a reason to go through with the marriage," she said, "or we wouldn't be having this conversation. I do not trust the import cataract *at all*. I want those tunnel plans sent up now, not in six months. I am already making an enormous concession in marrying you. Many will know the ceremony is happening anyway. And besides all that, you can always tell Creflon to close the dome before the vessel clears it."

"I'm...not sure it works that way."

"I imagine it would ruin the vessel, but that would suit you just fine. I'm not asking for a big concession. You promised you'd accommodate anything you're able to. Was it true?"

He made a sound she didn't like through his nose. "Marriage with you will be interesting." He stood. "I agree to your stipulations."

CHAPTER 37

F anteal once again entered the study. The Mikkaels sat alone beside the tray of snacks.

Sir Mikkael frowned at her. "That took a long time."

"Yes, well..." She drank some water. "I had to negotiate. Enough to make him believe I would go through with it."

"Go through with what?" Sir Mikkael asked.

"Marrying him."

Jaikon leapt to his feet. "What? No!"

"I don't want to!"

"Exactly. And you're not going to."

"Jaikon!" His father turned a stern glare on him. "Some days I think you've conquered your impulsive reactions. Obviously not."

"This is Fanteal we're talking about."

"I am aware. For the record, I also disapprove of the suggested marriage, but you will notice I am still sitting."

Fanteal laughed, then gripped Jaikon's arm. "Thanks for caring, but I said I had to make *him* believe it."

"What's the plan to get out of it?"

"Haven't devised that yet. He's got me—us—in a tight spot, so I need all the help I can get. Might Charlis and Bella be far enough along to join us?"

Jaikon went to get them, and Fanteal plopped into a chair and waved away Sir Mikkael's offer of food. "Has Creflon answered your summons?"

"No."

Not a surprise. She took the moment to shape a concise summary, so when the others returned, relating it didn't take nearly as long as it had to argue her way through it with Grellin.

At the end, she asked Charlis, "Would that last bit about closing the dome early work?"

"Not while the vortex is active."

"I didn't think so, but good to know."

"Why did you opt for the morning?" Bella asked. "That is the last opportunity."

"Allows more time for us to do something. It may be unlikely, but if Creflon destroyed the maps, we would need Charlis's new copy. If Sir Mikkael wants to take some other action I haven't thought of, I wanted time for that too. It would also keep Grellin from trying to pressure me again if I backed out."

"Don't like the word *if*," Jaikon growled.

Fanteal would have answered, but Sir Mikkael said, "Focus. Grellin is on his way to tell Creflon, and maybe Governor Armeen, what he agreed to. Creflon will probably answer my summons after that. I want our plan finished before he arrives."

"Last ditch," Fanteal said, "I can always refuse to say my vows. If the vessel gets through the dome, I'll tell the Keeper of the Writ that Grellin is coercing me into marriage and leave."

"Too many flaws," Sir Mikkael objected. "He could bring a keeper as dishonest as he. I would try to be one of the witnesses, but he will want Armeens. He could change the order of things at the last minute and refuse to send the vessel until you've pronounced vows. Even if I wanted to challenge afterward, he will insist on *protecting* his wife, and I won't be able to get you away from him. He is certain to consummate on the first night."

Jaikon slammed a fist on the table.

"Calm yourself, Jaikon. I'm giving reasons why we *won't* do it this way."

"Then I don't see how any of it will work." Bella raised her chin. "Don't forget, I am her maid, and I will stick to her like tar."

Charlis looked almost as appalled as Jaikon, who said, "Grellin is a big man, and you are not fighters. That isn't the solution, no matter how plucky either of you are."

Despite the awful situation, Fanteal laughed. "No one has ever called me *plucky*. What does it mean?"

"Having plenty of spirit." Bella grew mournful. "Agriben used to say it of me."

"I'll accept it, then, but I'd rather use wits than *pluck* against Grellin. Is there any way to bring some legal action against him and Creflon before ten tomorrow morning?"

"I've been thinking on it all day." Sir Mikkael gestured to the desk. "I've even written summonses to call in the governors and the local judge for an emergency meeting, which I cannot do until Creflon refuses to open the dome. By the way, I sent Colrin with some peace officers to bring him in. But even if I can persuade the judge or governors to take any action, I cannot order the dome opened."

"For that," Charlis said, "we'd have to convince all the domain chief formers that I should go ahead with it, when they haven't reviewed the plans we wish to send. It just won't happen."

"I see now," Fanteal murmured, "why various delays have occurred. The Armeens wanted them. Trying to keep our options limited. Everything we discuss proves that we cannot do this publicly—legally." She drew a deep breath. "We should be talking about tonight." She glanced at her watch. "It's almost seven. When do they close the tunnel gates?"

"Around nine," Charlis replied. "Everything needs to be locked down. I cannot get the maps copied that fast, so we'd have to send either the copy Agriben signed or the rough set. Both are a bad choice, and we cannot prove Jaikon's accurate range."

They'd been through all of that. Fanteal wished Jaikon would say something. He just stared at the floor, frowning like he had sensed all the way to the planet's core and found—She gasped. "Jaikon!"

He startled. "What?"

"If you go up, can't you prove your range aboveground?" He stared at her like she was mad, so she hurried on. "Like, search through Mount Estelle and tell the formers what's on the other side. Or through the peninsula, or whatever convinces them."

"Let me get this straight. I—an unvetted former—am supposed to go to Welcia above—where I made a terrible impression—with a shoddy set of sketches that aren't signed because our provincial chief won't approve them. Somehow, I don't think they're going to jump at the chance to excavate. And, by the way, I will be traveling through a dome opened against the chief former's orders. The prime minister—your guardian—may very likely get arrested for usurping Formers' Guild authority. I'm the only one who might be able to protect you if he is arrested, but I'll be up there!" He jerked his thumb at the ceiling, then rubbed his brow. "Grellin will still be after you in case I can convince anyone to start a tunnel. No. I'm not doing it."

"Oh, my," Bella murmured. "I hadn't thought of that part. Sir Mikkael, where should we take her if you are arrested?"

"Northeshur." He frowned.

"Will that keep me safe?"

"For a while. There are so many unknowns that I cannot say how long."

Fanteal drew another deep breath. "It's a two-person vessel." They all stared at her this time. "I could go with Jaikon. Explain what's going on. They will listen to me."

After a stunned moment, Jaikon murmured, "That does fix...a few problems."

Fanteal watched Sir Mikkael's reactions, then stated the flaw. "It also creates another. Your royal ambassador will not be here to back you up. You won't be able to accuse Grellin of coercion, for the only witness will be gone. You won't have your son, either. Charlis will be in hiding, arrested if he's found. Explanations will be demanded."

"I will complete my strategy for that before Jourendia awakens in the morning."

"Um..." Bella gave Fanteal a strained look. "Are you coming back?"

"Absolutely. If not through Passage Lake in six months, then definitely through the tunnel."

Charlis shifted in his chair. "Sorry to be the naysayer, but there's a problem. Creflon will go to the lake cavern this evening."

So frustrating! "But *why*," Fanteal demanded, "if he's not going to open it?"

"The streamers above swirl the water in expectation that a former will call to have it opened. If there really were a flaw, he should be there monitoring the dome. So should I, actually."

"Convenient that you will have a reason." Sir Mikkael paused for a thoughtful moment. "It so happens that Creflon is going to have a very long meeting with me this evening." He stood, walked to his desk, and started sorting through the notes he had written earlier. "I don't want any of you here when I meet with him. Use the library for the rest of your planning."

Apparently, they were dismissed. They looked at each other and were just standing up as Colrin returned.

"Creflon is here, sir," he said. "In the salon. He seemed annoyed by our escort, claiming that he was on his way to see you."

"Let him wait some more. We have changed plans, and I will need pages to carry notes to several governors." Sir Mikkael handed the notes to Colrin. "Lady Fanteal."

"Sir?" She turned back from following Bella and Charlis through the door.

He spoke softly. "I shall not see you again for some time. Give my greetings to the king and tell Ambassador Trissina that I appreciate all the trouble you have stirred up in Dirklan."

Her shoulders shook as her smile bloomed. "I shall tell them. And I look forward to coming back to stir up some more." She started to turn away, then swung back again. "Oh, I told Audrea that I wanted her to lead the next tour of Wind Weavers. They will be fine with her. Tell them I will return, but they are free to select a new chief wind weaver. I cannot do it forever, anyway."

"Safe travels." He rested his hand on his son's shoulder, making Jaikon linger.

They would need a moment. Fanteal dashed up to her bedroom and stuffed a few things into a bag that would fit under her cloak. The dark emerald dress and black leggings she wore would work for the trip. She draped her cloak over her arm and bag, then headed down the stairs toward the library.

The front door's bell rang. Oh, no. Who? Would they see her?

The page in the hall scanned the galleries as he moved toward the door. He paused when he spotted her and didn't move again until she reached the library. Colrin must have told them enough to keep her out of sight. If only Grellin hadn't sown doubt in her mind. She whisked herself through the door so quick, she surprised Bella and Charlis in a kiss.

"Oh! So sorry!" She almost backed out the door, but she couldn't with some unknown person entering the hall.

"It's all right," Bella said. "You already know we're close, don't you?"

She couldn't prevent a smile. "Well...yes."

Bella, who now seemed strangely calm, pulled a box from a shelf. "These are the letters written before Agriben's death threw everything into disarray." She set it on the table. "Do you want to take any of them with you?"

Interesting way to diffuse tension. Fanteal began looking through the box, and Jaikon soon joined them.

"Governors Brakentel and Yaldeeth arrived together," he told them. "They wouldn't have had time to get the summons, so they likely have their own concerns about the questionable dome."

"Did they see you?" Fanteal asked.

He lifted an eyebrow. "Yes, though I only gave them a nod from the gallery. It doesn't matter, you know. I live here."

"Yes, but you've changed clothes, which could attract attention. Make a person wonder."

"I was on my way to change when I saw them. My father thinks I should go above in Formers' Guild attire."

"Yes, you should," Charlis said. "I think Lady Fanteal is right. We'll keep you out of sight." He reached into an unlabeled box and withdrew the stack of small plates they had used at the vision wall. "Let's figure out plans for the rest of tonight."

They were still discussing the details when Colrin slipped into the library.

They all turned to see who entered, and Jaikon asked, "What are you smiling over?"

Colrin let his tiny smile stretch. "I was in the salon briefly, where Sir Mikkael and Governors Yaldeeth and Brakentel are grilling Creflon. I found it refreshing to watch him squirm." He neared the table. "Charlis, we'll have to give thought to provisions while you're in hiding. If that lasts very long, you won't be able to stay in one place. But first, is there anything you need from me for tonight?"

"Actually," Charlis said, "I do need to stay in the flat, for it's near the tunnel's future opening. For tonight, we need a discreet Keeper of the Writ."

"What?"

Charlis's smile didn't fit their dire situation at all. "Bella and I have been hoping to find a week or two that didn't include constant travel so we could get married. *I* definitely won't be traveling. With the ambassador away, Bella has no need to live here, so her living in the flat would be normal. So would coming and going to Dirklan House if she were still employed here, which also seems likely. And, of course, she would bring food to her own flat. Problems solved."

Colrin frowned. "That does seem unusually free of difficulties." He sounded a little disappointed, then brightened. "It may be challenging to hide the arrival of the Keeper of the Writ, but I do know of an appropriate individual." He half-closed his eyes. "Should anyone inquire why he came, he may say that two of the staff had planned a wedding that was delayed because of the recent sad event." He left them with a spring in his step.

Fanteal laughed. "He is perfect for his position. Bella and Charlis, I am *so* happy for you!"

Both of their smiles burst out, and Jaikon said, "You could have just told us you needed some time off. No need to arrange for a forced hideout."

Charlis shrugged. "I wanted a long honeymoon."

Bella smirked in mock reproof, then gave Fanteal and Jaikon a disappointed look. "We really wanted you to be our witnesses, but I don't think we should."

Fanteal sighed and nodded. Much as she wanted to see their wedding, it made better sense to stay away from all eyes—even those that Colrin trusted. If Grellin got wind that she and Jaikon had been with a Keeper of the Writ, she and all of Dirklan were in trouble.

CHAPTER 38

Jaikon's fury at Grellin grew with every one of Fanteal's jittery movements. She overreacted to the sounds of arrivals at Dirklan House and jumped when footsteps followed the gallery. She even stayed out of the line of sight from the door. He'd never seen her so nervous. Grellin's threats—forcing her to choose between Dirklan and her own future—they must have been convincing.

When Colrin returned to fetch Bella and Charlis, Jaikon went to Fanteal. "Our plans are solid. We will make it. In a few hours, we'll provide for Dirklan's future, and you will be far beyond Grellin's reach."

She sniffed and scowled. "He has already ruined so much. Even outside of Alluthin." She gestured in the direction that Bella and Charlis had gone. "Two of my finest friends have been pushed into a ten-minute wedding ceremony without family or friends to share their joy. Even we cannot join it after spending months with them. How many other people's happiness has been stepped on in the name of Armeen power? I can hardly believe he has me second-guessing the loyalty of people like Bella and Colrin—even though I know for certain that he lied about the source of his information. Where else has trust been broken or died unborn?"

He captured her fluttering hands and held them gently. "I suppose corruption can sprout anywhere. The important thing is, *you* are fighting it with the gifts you possess."

Her gorgeous blue eyes stared into his. "*We* are fighting it with the gifts we possess."

We. Pressure surged through his chest. She'd said *we*. His heart shouted *Now!* His mind warned him not to be impetuous. Seriously, this was the worst possible moment. He allowed himself one brusquely uttered word of confirmation. "We." Now what? "Let's make sure we can wear these packs without them bulging beneath our cloaks."

They were doing so when the newlyweds returned with a strange mixture of happiness and hurry. Fanteal hugged them both, despite looking at her bracelet.

Bella quickly checked their cloaked and hooded appearance, and Colrin took them through a back stairway that Jaikon hadn't known existed. Charlis, who was expected to be on his way to Passage Lake, would take the direct route.

Jaikon and Fanteal had no such luxury. He guided her through back streets. Other cloaked figures still milled about, so they didn't stand out. The light shafts cast ruddy reflections from the house markings, and magnery lamps glowed. He chose one of the side arches to pass into the settlement cavern, then hurried her through alleys behind the first houses of Jourendia.

The steady murmur that always emanated from the lake cavern was missing. That meant the gates were closed. Charlis had planned to shut them as soon as he was sure that at least two streamers were inside. Then he'd unlock the equipment room door. As long as Creflon hadn't escaped from the prime minister's snare, all should be well.

Now, to get through the sheltered walkway that led to the door. They would have to step into Passage Avenue, where peace officers would be on duty.

Keeping his hood forward, Jaikon pushed his cloak back over his shoulders, revealing his slate-gray tunic. "Keep walking," he whispered, "like we belong." They could fall back on her ambassador rank if they must, but he'd rather neither of them were recognized.

An officer challenged them as they drew near the tunnel gate. "No one's allowed here."

Jaikon altered his voice. "Assigned formers." Without breaking stride, he guided Fanteal into the walkway. If the door to the equipment room wasn't open, he'd be proven a fraud, for only a former—a real one—could work the lock.

He pushed the door. It swung inward. His tense stomach muscles got a brief rest.

Charlis approached without a word and locked the door. He let out a long breath as they lowered their hoods. "Took you long enough."

Nerves. No point in answering. Jaikon untied his cloak. "Have you hit any snags?"

"Not exactly. I don't recognize the streamers. One says she's from Jourendia. The man didn't say. They think it's odd that I'm keeping them out of the equipment room. I've only told them that the dome was repaired. I'll have to tell them soon that I'm opening it. They need time to protect the oysters."

Fanteal asked, "Is there anything in the vessel?"

"Still empty. We usually load passengers on the shore, but I don't want you seen. The streamers asked where Creflon was, and they do a lot of whispering."

Jaikon's stomach muscles clamped again. "Let's get inside now."

They helped Fanteal up and over the vessel wall. When she'd adjusted her cloak and sat down inside, he tossed his cloak onto the seat and climbed in. Hard to avoid her in the tiny space. All he needed was to kick the princess on their way to visit her parents. She was so dainty, she could fit her feet between the two padded seats. He found room for his legs on either side of her. How long were they going to be packed in like canned carrots?

Fanteal looked up at Charlis. "Have you called to my father yet to let him know that you are opening the dome?"

"Didn't want to risk it yet. Not with streamers out there that I don't know."

"What could they do about it?" Jaikon asked.

"Not much," he grumbled. "Might try to raise an alarm, I suppose. I'm going to manually lock down the gears so no one can open the gates. Strap yourselves in."

Fanteal's hands shook as she fiddled with the straps. "I'm so nervous."

Metal clanked and scraped near the gears.

"Take your pack off first and anchor it to the side," Jaikon said. He did the same, made sure she was secure, then buckled his own straps.

Charlis returned. "All right. Time to commit. As soon as I seal the vessel, I'm telling the streamers. I'll call to the king and send you down the rails into the lake."

Fanteal raised her chin. "Do it."

The cover slid over the opening, plunging them into darkness. Jaikon felt along the top and found the vent cover. Rotating it open allowed a bit of magnery light inside. The sound of lapping wavelets too.

"I'm sensing," Fanteal whispered. "Charlis left the inner door open."

Jaikon kept quiet.

"I can hear them...one streamer is arguing...he wants Creflon. I'd wager my mother's jewels that he's acting on Armeen orders. Running footsteps." She snickered. "Charlis just said, 'It's locked for the night, and the dome is opening. Now do your job!' The other streamer is talking about covering oysters. There! Charlis has called to my father."

Her smile snapped into a frown. "One of those streamers must have felt it. He's calling, too, with alarm. My father is certain to sense it."

No! Who would the king heed? A former he didn't know or a frantic streamer. Opening the dome was too great a risk—never done unless everyone was certain it could be closed.

Fanteal tilted her face upward and spread her hands wide. An unneeded motion, but he knew what it meant. She was calling to her father. Trying, anyway. How could that work when they were locked away beneath layers of stone?

The scrape of sliding rock meant Charlis was opening the door to the vessel's chamber. Then the jolt of a releasing lock. "Here we go." The vessel tilted, and movement tugged them sideways. They halted abruptly and rocked. In the lake. Air whipped through the vessel.

"There!" Fanteal whispered. "I reached my father. He recognizes me, but I feel his concern. Can you call as a former? Convey confidence?"

Another bit of training he'd never received. He'd never even imagined communicating that way. Could he fake confidence? Maybe focus on his confidence in his long range? He swept his forming sense through the dome. A creased structure, to him. He swept beyond, up the cliff wall that ringed much of the harbor. "That's the best I can do. By the way, there are formers scattered along the cliff." He didn't want to tell her, but he'd better. So much for confidence. "They, uh, noticed me."

"Positive? Affirming?"

"I'd...call it shock."

"Oh!" Too dark to see it, but a frown lurked behind that word. "Well, I suppose they've never gotten a dual call."

"They're always shocked when they feel me."

"You've never told me you connect with formers above."

"Connecting, it was not. Sometimes, above the cataracts or when we searched out air channels—" A sudden sharp tilt interrupted. He snapped the vent closed and groaned. "Wish we hadn't eaten."

"Why is it rocking now? The dome hasn't started opening, has it?"

"No. It must be that streamer. Could he sink us?"

"I don't…" She paused to sense. "We're airtight. We'll float, no matter what."

Why did she still sound worried? The darkness? The rocking? "What's wrong?"

"Not much air between us. If we need to float out here for a long time, we could run short. Ow!"

She must have banged into something. He'd grazed his knuckles already. He groped to the sides and found something to grip. "Feel the vessel wall. There are handholds."

She gasped at another wild pitch. "Something chaotic is going on with the streamers. Maybe they're fighting each other."

"One thing is certain," Jaikon said. "No matter what's threatened or promised, a Jourendian streamer will never forsake their duty beneath an open dome."

"Many help from above. One down here is enough, right?"

"Correct."

"Charlis is calling again."

"I can feel him in the dome. It hasn't moved, but he's trying the nudge. When Agriben did that, it opened right away. The whirlpool must not be ready."

"Whoa!" Fanteal exclaimed. "One of the streamers is just—gone." The rocking slowed. "I think only the Jourendian is left. I wonder what happened."

"Maybe he realized people were in the vessel. If so, he was attempting murder. Ellincreo would have withdrawn his streaming gift. Or maybe Charlis took matters into his own hands. There are some pretty big wrenches in the equipment room."

"Sure hope it wasn't that. He's got enough trouble to deal with already."

Silence was so much worse in the dark. They still moved, but steadily. Jaikon rotated the vent. "The vessel should be exactly in the center when the dome opens. Can you tell our position?" This time, he felt her activity, for air tickled his cheek.

"Near it, I think."

Rock groaned, and Fanteal shrieked. Droplets sprayed through the vent as Jaikon closed it. "Are we airtight?" He demanded.

She panted. "Yes." Then whimpered.

The vessel flung them around with wild shaking. His head slammed backward. Were they even right side up? At least it was brief. The vessel stabilized, its rotation pressing their backs into the seats. If only the vibration would settle, but he was helpless to change anything.

The vortex had them.

Endurance. They had nothing else. Not even time. Did Fanteal's watch stop in the vortex? Stupid thought. Was he unconscious—dreaming? Probably not, because he was worried about her. "Fanteal?" No answer, but he could hardly hear his own voice, much less hers. "Fanteal, are you all right?"

Still no answer. Everything ached. This eternity had better be a dream.

Was the spin lessening? It must be, for he could move his arms now. The blackness was so intense, he touched his face to verify that his eyes were open. Definitely awake. "Fanteal!"

He groped high. The vent didn't seem to be in the right place, but he found it. So little spin remained, they must be floating on the harbor's surface. He dared a slight twist, then rotated the vent to its widest position. The moon's silvery light etched the interior. And Fanteal's hair. Why did it hang toward him?

Finally, he understood. The vessel was off-balance. He was heavier, leaning back while she sagged forward against the straps. Could her neck be injured? Broken? "No," he groaned.

He wanted to shake her awake. *Stay calm. Think.* He slid a hand under her hair and cupped her chin. Air passed between his fingers. She was alive. Relief forced a quiver through his lungs.

Supporting her head, he slid his other fingers along her spine. What was it supposed to feel like? He dared not press. He even searched the bones with forming sense. They seemed regular. But such tiny structures—a medic former, he was not. All he could do was hold her steady as the vessel gently rocked.

He pushed her hair back from her forehead. Her lashes traced silver crescents along her cheeks. "Fanteal. Darling Fanteal. *Please* wake up."

Was that a moan? Her eyelids didn't twitch. How could he awaken a person he couldn't move? In desperation, he blew in her face.

She blinked and gasped. Her hands flailed, then clutched his wrist. "I'm falling."

"No, love. We are tilted. Floating in the harbor. Are you hurt?" He'd said *love*. Out loud. *Control your words*, he chided himself.

She straightened her back and lifted her chin from his palm. Immense relief dizzied him as she looked around and up at the vents.

"Open sky!" Her breathy words ended in a teary laugh. "Oh, it's wonderful! No, I'm not hurt."

"Are you sure you didn't hit your head?"

"No, I was pressed against the seat back. Just a faint. I felt it coming on. I guess I couldn't hold out." She seemed to take him in. "Really, Jaikon, I'm fine." She groped for a grip within the vessel. "Thank you for supporting me, but this is terribly uncomfortable." She let go of his arm and found the other grip.

How long would she be able to shove herself back like that? He unbuckled his straps and shifted forward. "I'll try centering my weight." It worked. Except he sat so close to her now, he only wanted to kiss her. She was so incredibly beautiful—and precious. "Your eyes are silver in the moonlight."

Surely that was a smile on her shadowed mouth. "Yours are dark as a cavern," she teased. "We're moving. They are bringing us to shore." She laughed.

She wasn't thinking about a kiss.

"You were telling me something," she said. "About the formers you contacted when we searched along the surface. What did you mean?"

He struggled for that distant memory. "Oh...just that...contact was no joy. Not like what you felt. More like shock or anger. I thought maybe I was interfering with something and always tried to avoid them. Problem was, I couldn't tell they were present until *after* I irritated them."

"Why didn't you tell me?"

He huffed. "Like at Northeshur, you mean? Right there with everyone listening to the incompetent fellow who dared to call himself a former?"

"Oh." She looked sideways at the pack of priceless cargo. "Do you think the maps survived that hellish trip?"

"Charlis packed them well. Don't worry."

"I suppose I can quit worrying about everything. We made it!"

The instant she relaxed, worry flooded him. In a moment, he would be explaining to the kingdom's chief former. *I had to come myself because no one in Dirklan trusts me or my design. Here are my rough-drawn level maps. Start digging.* Why had he ever believed this would work?

CHAPTER 39

The vessel *thunked* against wood. Voices of the palace dockhands drifted through the vent. Thick, wet ropes slapped and creaked. The sounds of Fanteal's first home. The vessel stopped rocking, held rigid in its dock. She smiled at Jaikon, but it went all aquiver.

He untied the packs from the walls.

The cover scraped and slid aside. The full rush of moist, salty air and moonlight stopped her fingers on the buckles. She simply must savor her element.

Jaikon stood up, his head and shoulders rising through the opening. Someone exclaimed, "The prime minister's son!" Fanteal finished unbuckling as he passed the packs and his cloak to whomever was out there.

Jaikon hefted himself up to sit on the vessel's edge and reached down. "Ready to get out?"

"Ever so." She grabbed his hand and pulled herself up. At last able to see more than sky, she spotted her father, waiting on shore, and sent him a smile. Then Jaikon lifted her straight up to sit across from him. He kept an arm snug around her as she twisted to draw her feet out, then he released her to the hands that waited to assist her onto the dock.

People clustered around. Not unusual, for those who rode the vortex often arrived dizzy.

She took a few steps, then waited until Jaikon jumped to the dock. A man gripped his arm for a second then handed him his cloak.

Fanteal extended her hand to Jaikon. "Your escort, please." He slipped his beneath hers, palm down. There was no room on the dock for the full extension, but she preferred being nearer his side. Like the closer escort of Dirklan. What made this walk between dock lanterns so special? Was it the muted stars, determined to shine despite two full moons? Or the heady scents from the palace garden? Maybe the ocean breeze?

No, not the breeze. It gusted as they stepped onto shore, sending a shiver through Jaikon.

"Chilly," he whispered, then bowed to the king. As Fanteal received a daughter's welcome, Jaikon swung his cloak around his shoulders.

The king's gaze encompassed both of them. "How did you fare through that very strange opening of the dome?"

"It was awful!" she said.

"Worst method of transportation ever devised," Jaikon added. Then he touched the shoulder of a dockhand about to pass them. "That pack stays in my sight."

The man halted, cleared surprise from his face, and assumed a respectful stance a few feet away, with the pack clutched to his chest rather than dangling from his shoulder.

"What was going on below?" her father asked. "And why did you risk it?"

"Oh..." Fanteal half-moaned the word. "I have much to tell you, but the last few days have been unbelievable. We didn't decide to come up until a few hours ago, and of course, we didn't know that a corrupt streamer had been assigned to the opening. It was he who raised the false alarm and kept us from the center of the lake. That gave us a terribly rough start, but there was nothing wrong with the dome."

"What, exactly, do you mean by *corrupt streamer*?"

Fanteal found herself straightening at his stern voice. "I don't think he is anymore—a streamer, I mean. I could feel his gift reaching through the lake and tilting our vessel. Then suddenly, he was gone, and only Jourendia's streamer remained."

"The other was not from Jourendia? From where, then?"

"Charlis wasn't sure where, but I suspect from Alluthin. The Armeens control the gifted guilds of their domain, though they deny it."

He was looking more confused by the moment. "What have the Armeens to do with Jourendia or Passage Lake?"

"They want control of it."

"The domain or the passage?"

"Both. And me. Grellin Armeen tried to coerce me into marriage. Just today."

Ominous silence preceded the king's response. "He has made a grave error."

His dry pitch reminded Fanteal of the day he'd used it on Jaikon on this very shore. How satisfying to hear the same tone directed at Grellin instead of at him.

"In what manner did he coerce you?" her father asked.

"He discovered that Jaikon has found a tunnel route from Jourendia to Welcia above. That means Dirklan will be able to get food without those troublesome trade cataracts. Alluthin would no longer be a critical food source belowground, so the Armeens want control of the tunnel. We had planned to simply send the maps up, but Grellin found out. He threatened to keep the passage closed permanently and not allow the tunnel to be built unless I married him."

Despite the king's obvious need for more answers, they could no longer ignore the approach of running footsteps and labored breathing. A dark figure hurried down the torchlit steps from the cliffside colonnade and dashed toward them.

"Sire! Ambassador?" He panted and got no further. She recognized him now—Wuldour.

"Is something wrong with the dome?" the king demanded.

"Wh—? No!" More gasping. "It closed normally." He clutched his side. "But sire, the renegade. We felt him in the cliffs. Many of us did...from all around the harbor."

"I do not have time for that now."

"Wait a minute," Fanteal said. "What renegade?"

"Some former..." Wuldour tried for steadier breath. "One that no guild member recognizes...has been detected near assets critical to Dirklan. We've been greatly concerned for the province."

"Has he actually changed anything within the rock?"

"No, lady, only been present. But it is still most concerning that such a one—and so active these last few months—should be unknown to any of the local formers."

"Then, I will introduce him to you. Former Jaikon Mikkael, this is Welcia's Chief Former, Wuldour. As I imagine you realize, he ranks above the provincial chief formers."

Jaikon inclined his torso respectfully, and Wuldour gave him a gaping stare. "But aren't you the son of the prime minister?"

"I am."

"Wh—? I had no idea you were a former. I would have made a point of meeting you on your first visit. But, Ambassador, you have misunderstood me. The former I speak of is an abovegrounder."

Jaikon cleared his throat. "May I give you a report, sir?"

"Yes, but—"

"First of all, Dirklan's Provincial Chief Former Agriben died two days ago."

"Oh, no. My condolences, of course. Has a replacement been selected? Who is capable of opening the dome?"

"Only Charlis Torgan, Agriben's apprentice, and Creflon Lawfertee of Alluthin possess that skill. The latter was chosen as provincial chief former. However, he has refused to open the dome, claiming a nonexistent flaw. He was also with Grellin Armeen and Governor

Armeen when maps and letters to the king and queen ambassador were stolen from the vessel, which should have been sent through the dome this morning."

"Wh— Caverns below! That charge must be investigated before he is confirmed as provincial chief. But, *please*, will you all listen to me. The renegade is the most immediate concern."

Fanteal touched Jaikon's arm. "Can you just reach into the rock so he'll recognize you?"

Lovely. Now Jaikon could add *renegade* to his list of disparaging titles. May as well prove more.

"I hope there are still formers along the cliffs, for I will reach past them to the peninsula." Jaikon dipped his sensing gift into the rock at their feet, swept it up the staircase enclosure to the cliff-top colonnade, raced along the cliffs, then reached past into the peninsula as far as the tunnel opening he would one day see excavated. He wanted a moment to savor it, but Wuldour was practically vibrating.

"It *is* you. But to be reaching all that way. You've been sensed at the cataracts! Far beyond the Dirklian caverns!"

"Yes, I know."

"Have you sensed their entirety?" the king asked.

"The food import cataract, yes. The export cataracts, almost. They are failing. And, no, I cannot repair them. My gift is unique and does not include that skill." He may as well get everything out, up front. "Belowground, many formers do not believe I can sense through the full import cataract."

"Well, of course not," Wuldour said. "I wouldn't have believed it either if I hadn't already sensed you from up here. Extraordinary range.

Quite extraordinary, indeed. The maps you mentioned. What were they of?"

Did the man ever stop? "A tunnel route from Jourendia's city cavern, eastern wall, emerging atop the peninsula." Wuldour gaped, and Jaikon continued while he could. "Agriben approved three copies of the official map. Two are in the possession of Creflon. One is safe in the prime minister's library. I have brought the initial rough sketch with me." He pointed to the pack the dockhand still held.

The man stood straighter when he realized what he held.

"Did you make that one?" Wuldour asked.

"Charlis etched it under my direction." Jaikon cringed, but yes, he'd better say it. "We did so before the vision wall in the sacred chamber."

"The vision wall?" The king murmured.

"Could I have a moment," Jaikon asked, "to reach down to friends in Jourendia who do not yet know we arrived safely?"

"Certainly," the king said.

This would be easy. Jaikon reached out.

In the flat near the eastern wall, Charlis hunched on the bed, hands hanging limp between his knees. Suddenly, he jerked upright. There was no mistaking the presence that filled the rock so near at hand. Wait—ha! Filled the whole cavern structure, reaching down from above.

Charlis flopped backwards on the bed with arms spread wide, laughing.

In the study at Dirklan House, the meeting had devolved almost to an interrogation of Creflon.

Sir Mikkael had little to do, for the governors he had invited demanded answers as many times as Creflon skirted their questions. Quite suddenly, Creflon stopped mid-sentence and began turning this way and that, his eyes raised ceilingward.

"What is all this about?" Governor Yaldeeth snapped.

"Jaikon!" Creflon spun to Sir Mikkael. "Where is he?"

"Do you sense him?"

"Of course, I sense him. He's reaching through the entire cavern."

"He's a *former*," Governor Brakentel snarled. "What of it?"

"He's reaching down from *above!*"

The tension fled from Sir Mikkael's neck. "Thank you for confirming that he and Lady Fanteal made it to King Darinneth and Ambassador Trissina." He enjoyed a few seconds of Creflon's appalled stare. "You may leave."

"Indeed?" Governor Yaldeeth uttered on a long exhale. "How?"

"Charlis," Creflon hissed between his teeth, nearly spitting at Sir Mikkael. "Where is he?"

Sir Mikkael shrugged. "I assume he knows that you have no intention of opening the dome again. The trains have been running nonstop, so perhaps he has gone home to Crysalan. As I said, you are dismissed."

On the shore far above, Jaikon laughed deep in his chest.

Fanteal grabbed his hand. "What?"

"Two formers reached out. Charlis seems quite happy." With mock puzzlement, he added, "Creflon seems rather angry about something."

She threw her head back and laughed. Good thing he still held her hand, for she staggered.

In an instant, he clutched her waist. "Are you still feeling the effects of that ride?"

"Just giddy with joy. We did it."

"We've *started*. We still have much to do." He closed his weary eyes. "But I'm not doing any more of it today."

CHAPTER 40

The queen laid down the last sheet upon the stack of letters. She wore her ambassador sash, making it clear which title she preferred today—Ambassador Trissina. "You have been busy, Fanteal."

"Rather."

Her mother folded her hands on her elegant table desk. "Children, it's past time to start your lessons."

Fanteal's youngest sister, leaning against her on the couch, whined, "But she just got here."

"I will be here many days." Fanteal shifted and urged her sister to stand. She had just heard her father's voice in the distance, returning from the shore. Jaikon and Telamien would be with him.

The men reached her mother's salon as the children trailed from the room at a snail's pace.

"Did they open?" Fanteal asked.

"No," her father replied. "We made it clear we were ready, and I swirled the vortex down to the dome even though no one called for an opening. A former was holding it closed. Jaikon tells me it was Creflon."

"Did Wuldour detect any issue with the dome?"

"He did not." Royal displeasure deepened his voice. "It appears that a letter from their king or ambassador is unwelcome to certain persons."

"Considering what has happened," her mother said, "that may be probable. However, the decision to open the dome is the purview of the belowground former."

A servant asked from the doorway, "Ambassador, would you like tea served?"

Fanteal and her mother said *yes* in unison, and the king chuckled.

The man wheeled a tea cart in and began to lift the teapot, but her mother waved him away. "Telamien, pour the tea." The servant exited, closing the door.

Fanteal's brother looked shocked, and her mother told him, "In Dirklan, anyone at all pours tea. We shall also omit our titles, now, in the Dirklian manner."

Fanteal hid her amusement that the heir to the throne was about to serve Jaikon. Telamien followed protocol in serving first the king, then queen ambassador, then poured two cups and brought them to the couch where Jaikon had sat next to her.

"Do you even know whom you're supposed to serve next?" she teased.

"I am too clever for your tricks, sister dear." He handed the cups to them simultaneously.

She whispered loudly, "You forgot to serve the lemon and sugar along with the teacups."

Her mother shook her head and addressed the king. "I believe we all know that several crimes can be alleged. The prime minister, his son, my own daughter, and a belowground former are all party to opening the dome in defiance of Dirklan's provincial chief former."

She gave Fanteal and Jaikon an ironic smile. "I will write a declamation that I am not charging you with those crimes because of the extenuating circumstances. Unfortunately, I cannot do that belowground. Nor can I file charges against any of the Armeens, who will likely take every possible action to remove Sened Mikkael from office. Charlis may succeed in hiding, but the prime minister cannot."

Her father lowered his teacup to his saucer. "Jaikon, do you know what the prime minister intends?"

"He will file at least the two primary charges against Creflon first thing this morning, although Creflon will not know of them until—well, right about now. As soon as Creflon's rooms have been searched, my father will initiate an investigation of the Armeens, particularly naming the governor and Grellin." He glanced at Fanteal's mother. "He expects the same that you do, lady, and plans to stretch the legal battle as long as possible, in order to allow time for the tunnel to be completed. His primary concern is adequate food for Dirklan. Second to that, he wants to keep the control of food out of the Armeens' greedy hands."

"I'm sure the dual cases will be heard by the high judge," the king said. "He will have a dilemma. Civil government may not usurp substance guild authority, but neither may a guild use their gift to achieve political goals. It is dangerous to set a precedent that either of them can commit a crime if they have a good enough reason."

A cold sensation filtered through Fanteal. His words were true, but she hadn't thought of their actions in that way. Had her desperation to escape Grellin blinded her to this ramification? But the tunnel!

She tried to overcome the strangling sensation in her throat. To sound confident. "The tunnel is not only needed for food. The people of Dirklan are too isolated. They have no recourse. I shudder to think what would happen if the high judge ever came under the control of anyone as power-hungry as the Armeens." She licked her lips. "I could not deny Dirklan that tunnel. I suppose I did have another method—a legal one—of providing it, but—"

"No, you did not!" her father said. "A man who would force you into marriage, will force you into anything. Beyond my personal concern for you, the royal ambassador of the crown must never fall under the control of a despotic family."

"He is very smooth and persuasive, though. I can imagine him before a judge." She altered her voice to mimic his. "I've always felt a tunnel would be an excellent idea—as long as it can be excavated safely, and we have stable leadership to oversee it."

"Good imitation," Jaikon murmured.

"And yet," her father pointed out, "four people, with much to lose, were willing to break the law in order to prevent a marriage that would allow Grellin to gain control. Much harder to sound good under those circumstances."

True, but technically, she had committed a crime. She must be realistic about this. "There is no proof of his manipulation, and a judge must have proof."

"Fortunately," her father said, "a king can pardon. I know the integrity of the person I appointed as Ambassador of the Crown. Her words are adequate to justify the pardon, should it be needed."

Tension left her shoulders. "That is good enough for us, but it won't help Sir Mikkael or Charlis."

"It will—once a tunnel is opened." He gestured toward the door. "Telamien, Wuldour is waiting for my summons. Call him in."

Fanteal wasn't in the palace. Or the gardens, or here in the clifftop colonnade. Could she be at the tunnel mouth on the peninsula?

Jaikon doubted it. She hadn't gone there in days. That made him lonely, despite being surrounded by formers who treated him like someone special. Seeing Fanteal only at breakfast and dinner was far from what he'd expected. Or would have expected if they'd had time to think beyond their escape.

He turned his back on the harbor, followed the colonnade in the opposite direction, and bypassed the turn toward the palace. A route he'd taken only once, on their first Savoring Day in Welcia above. She'd strolled at his side with her hand tucked in his arm. He would have savored that all the more if he'd realized how rare it would become.

The lords and ladies of the provinces had been summoned, though not like the crowd of his first meeting. Two or three at a time, often with their families, for a mixture of civil discussions and entertainments. How pleasant it was to be free of the contention below. But he would have preferred that no one else demanded Fanteal's attention.

And now...now the formers had a demand for her.

The colonnade stepped down a few levels, then ended where stairs descended a hillside. He paused, resting his hand against the last column, the stone cool beneath his fingers. In the distance, a ruined pediment jutted above a hilltop. Brown grass on the slope below looked too stiff and tired to dance in a breeze. Was she on the hill? Perhaps weaving the wind through the vast spaces she missed?

The hill was usually deserted, so if he could sense a person atop it, there was a decent chance it would be her. He reached with his gift. A lone person, yes. If it was Fanteal, she would know who reached. He wished he had that sensitivity to recognize her.

A gust of wind swept over him. He laughed. Definitely Fanteal. He trotted down the steps, his heart lightened by her answer. It took some time to descend one hill and climb the next. He half expected her to be waiting for him between the—he snickered—*giant chipmunks*. No, she made him look for her. There, sitting on the wide railing with her back against a column, enjoying the view of plains, hills, and Mount Estelle.

He paused to enjoy the more beautiful view. Fanteal's profile and flowing golden hair.

She turned to look at him, and he didn't care that she'd caught him staring appreciatively. Except that the smile she gave him seemed a little sad. *That* he cared about a great deal. But he was here to ask for her help. Caverns and skies, everyone could wait this time.

He crossed the uneven pavers and joined her on the flat top of the railing, as close as possible, considering that she sat sideways. "This is absolutely shocking, Fanteal! We are alone together."

"It has become rare, hasn't it? What brings you in search of the missing ambassador—or wind weaver—or whatever I am today?"

He wished he could claim it was nothing but his own desire. But then he would sound false when he told her. "There is something." He sighed. "There always is, isn't there? Every time I think I will see *Fanteal* at this, or at that, or soon...well, I do *see* you—in between everyone else."

She skewed the corners of her mouth, giving him an ironic nod.

"Our travels in Dirklan," he said, "seemed so busy at the time. Now when I remember those endless train rides that made me long for a brisk walk, I wish I could sit beside you for hours again. Especially with our luggage taking up the extra seat."

Fanteal chuckled. "I never knew why Bella started directing that the luggage be split between two carriages. Did she want to be alone with Charlis, or was she pushing us together?"

"Huh. That never dawned on me. Even after you pointed out Charlis's interest in her."

She smiled, but again, remained silent.

What was wrong? "Life got easier when I stopped being jealous of him. I suppose, in a way, I was just focusing my jealousy of every one of your suitors onto him." What had happened to his jealousy? He hadn't noticed it evaporate. Protecting her had just started to matter more. "Now, it's visitors and events that get in the way." He huffed. "And all of them favorable, so I cannot object. But they are far more in-the-way than all the disruptions belowground." He reached over and clasped the fingers she rested on one knee. "I miss you."

"Good to know, for I'm feeling quite useless and...not missed at all. Frankly, it's that tunnel *I'm* jealous of." She tilted her head. "Which makes me feel guilty, but it's true. You, at least, have something to do."

She crimped her lips and lightened her tone. "Sorry to gripe. I am glad, of course, that you have broad enough experience to help abovegrounders understand tunneling. And explain the needed equipment designs too. Your presence is far better than simply sending the plans. I do understand that you must focus on the tunnel."

"Ah, the tunnel." His attempted smile went awry. "I can help you with something to do."

She knitted her brow over those lovely blue eyes. "What?"

"Water collected in it after last night's rain. We asked for a streamer to pull it out, which was fine, but now the chief streamer wants to know how I'm handling drainage." He grimaced. "Hadn't thought of that."

"Oh. Did Agriben or Wuldour ever bring it up?"

"No. At least I don't have to be embarrassed alone. The chief streamer let us off with a head shake and one remark of 'planning like a bunch of formers.' The problem is, she can't interpret a level map well enough to identify where we should form drainage channels. She cannot sense for them, since there is no water in the rock." He grinned. "Fortunately, I know someone who is good at finding channels with me through rock."

"Oh." She angled an innocent look his way. "Who?"

He laughed and squeezed her hand tighter. "Someone I rather like working with. And since she's a princess, maybe she'll have her own carriage and I can ride out to the tunnel site with her, instead of in the wagon."

"I'll try, of course, but I'm not sure how much air I will find in ipenrock."

"People trust me here. I can assign several formers to make small piercings into the areas of less density, then...oh, never mind. You'll understand when we're on-site."

She cocked her head. "Using my wind weaving to find water channels in ipenrock. I never would have believed my gift would be used for forming and streaming. Oh, well—a few months of usefulness, anyway."

This really was bothering her. He knew what it was like to feel worthless, but he wasn't used to seeing *her* in that state. "Our circumstances have flipped."

"What do you mean?"

"I've spent half my life feeling like I didn't have anything to offer. My forming flopped. I tried mechanical things. I do all right with it, but nothing stunning. Politics—ugh, I think my father was elected *despite* my campaign techniques. Then forming again, which only worked for me because of you, Charlis, and Agriben. This past month has been the first time I have ever felt truly useful in a way that completely fits me."

He quirked a corner of his mouth. "And now, you—who have excelled at both your wind weaving and ambassador roles—you speak of being useless."

"Truth be told," she said, "I've often felt that way. I could never see how wind weaving fit into an ambassador's life. For a little while, it did, surprisingly. The chief wind weaver position was always temporary. The weavers below have probably chosen another and realize they don't need me. That's as it should be, and I am happy that they'll be able to step into the fullness of their gifts. As for now, I have precious little to do as an ambassador. I assume we'll eventually return below—where I can again try to convince Dirklians that they *need* an ambassador. Which is also something they've gotten along without for many years."

Her feelings were genuine, yet some were based on fallacies. How could he tell her that without insult? Without sounding dismissive? Caverns, how many of *his* feelings were based on things that seemed to be true but weren't. "These gifts we all have...both substance and life gifts. We all think we understand them—how others should use them, and how we should use our own. That there is only one way for today and for the future."

She narrowed her eyes, and the hint of a contemplative smile tugged at her lips. That was so much better than the earlier version. She shifted, lowering the knee she'd held sideways along the railing. Closer to him—her hand sliding deeper within his. "Every gift is unique, even if it has similarities to another. That, I knew, but I've never thought I was misconstruing my own gift. That it would have unique expressions at different times."

She chuckled a little. "People like Lord Yaeger and my parents talk about seasons of life. I've always thought of it as three seasons. Childhood, then the study and training of adolescence, then adulthood. The doing of everything I prepared for. I never expected much variation in that part."

"It changes a lot, doesn't it?"

"So it does. Some, more sudden than I like. And not all changes look good at the outset." She straightened her shoulders, and the champion spirit he'd often admired returned to her face. "Shall we get to it?"

They stood, but he couldn't stop looking at her.

"What are you grinning at?"

"You are so beautiful when you're ready to take on the world. Other times, too, but I'm rather fond of your determined look. Yes, let's get to it."

CHAPTER 41

Finding channels for drainage had only been a start for Fanteal. It turned out that the fastest method for excavating created fine dust. A hazard to eyes and lungs. No one could get it out of the tunnel and on its way to the sea faster than she.

Her mother first hinted—then stated—that a royal ambassador did not belong on a job site every workday. Fortunately, her father held another view, and the decision came down to Fanteal's choice. Easily made.

What a pleasure to watch Jaikon come into his own. He rarely even used his gift—forming sense, that was. Just once each morning to confirm the tunnel's progress and direction. Instead, he led the project, now that Wuldour only came every few days to talk things over.

This was one such moment. Fanteal sat on one of the wool pelts that padded benches and stools in the tunnel mouth. Canvas panels shielded the broad opening, easily parted but heavy enough to fall closed and trap some heat.

Wuldour pulled a blanket around himself as he spoke with Jaikon. "From belowground, I can see why you thought a narrow tunnel would be the best start. But we need the upper portion widened."

Jaikon's shoulders stiffened. "That will take too much time."

"It will give us room for more workers in the tunnel," one of the formers said.

A miner added, "It's a whole lot easier to get the rock onto the conveyors if we aren't slithering through a rabbit's tunnel."

"I've been down there," Jaikon countered. "It's no rabbit's tunnel."

Judging by the looks on their faces, he wasn't endearing himself to the workers. Would he notice and accommodate?

"It's also no pavilion," Wuldour said. "It's a long tunnel and a long job. People need space to work efficiently, or they wear down."

Jaikon drew his lower lip in and back out. "How much of it needs to be that wide?"

A sharp voice demanded, "Why don't you want *all* of it that wide?"

"We do, eventually, but food and communication are the first priority."

One of the few women formers leaned forward on her stool. "Is Dirklan starving right at this moment?"

Perhaps it was time Fanteal offered support. "Actually, communication is the first priority. Jaikon and I didn't get through the dome on our own. We are safe, but those who helped us—including his father—are fighting a different sort of battle belowground. They are in desperate need of support from the king."

Knowing the reason for haste cleared some disgruntled expressions.

"That doesn't mean," Jaikon assured them, "that we don't care about all of *you*. So, how can we quickly and *sanely* get through to Jourendia?"

"Make the tunnel wide enough to walk two abreast beside the conveyors." The miner spread his arms wide to show a dimension. "We'll be able to work a lot faster."

Jaikon nodded, though it twisted. "Much of it, but when we get near enough to Jourendia for the belowground formers to sense the tunnel, we must narrow it."

"Fine. They'll be pulling the rock down, anyway, so it makes no difference to us."

"Don't count on it," Jaikon said. "They may not move a pebble until we get a message through."

Several people mumbled over that, despite knowing the issue. A former asked, "Uh, how narrow?"

"About a yard in diameter."

They stared at him, and one asked, "You expect a person to go through that?"

"No. A container at first."

"What is beyond the planned opening?" Wuldour asked.

"A road rings the cavern wall—a leftover margin from the last extension of the cavern. That allows some space for the excavated rock, but I am not certain that they…will be expecting it."

Probably thinking *not certain that they would allow it.*

Wuldour shoved himself to his feet. "We'll figure that part out when we get close."

Jaikon stood too. "Let's start widening, then."

The workers returned to their tasks, and Fanteal edged close to Jaikon. Divots lingered between his black eyebrows. When no one remained near, she whispered, "Have you felt anything from Charlis?"

"I haven't reached into Jourendia since that first night. If he reaches out to answer me, it could give his location away."

"Are you worried about your father?"

"Hard not to be. For all I know, he's on trial at this very moment."

She wondered as much as he did. Wondered if Charlis had been found. Wondered if Colrin and Bella might be accused of complicity.

Progress down the long slope stalled as the tunnel was widened, then it surged forward. Workers rode carts down the conveyer now, adding sections to it nearly every day. What little copper Welcia received through the export cataracts was dedicated to the tunnel, and a string of magnery lights dotted a pathway into the deep. Fanteal found air channels as often as drainage. It seemed their only rests were the rides back and forth along the peninsula. The long nights of winter darkened the trips. Jaikon often seemed too tired to talk, but they clasped their gloved hands on the blanket over their legs.

One Savoring Day, Fanteal walked from their local gathering with an old friend, who asked, "What's it like to be miles down that tunnel?"

"I don't know. I haven't been very far down it."

Jaikon overheard from a few yards away and turned to her with an arrested expression. As soon as the midday meal was over, he drew her aside. "Shall we escape from the palace for a few hours? It is high time you had a chance to savor the tunnel that you keep breathable."

She needed no more persuasion. The carriage ride in full daylight wasn't as chilly as usual, but the wide chamber atop the tunnel was more so without the many bodies or the magnery heaters running.

Jaikon grabbed a couple sheepskins to pad a cart, settled her on it, then started the conveyor. He ran a few steps to reach the moving cart and jumped on behind her. He spread his legs to either side, wedging his boots into notches. "These are footholds. You can hold onto the side rails too." They were already descending. "Some of it is steeper than this, but I won't let you pitch over the front."

She giggled nervously the first few times the cart suddenly rocked forward or back. She'd better stop. She sounded like her sisters. Jaikon gripped her waist. He would never let her fall. After quite some time, she bumped against his chest. "Why are we climbing?"

"Because this is where the ipenrock was fragmented. The climb won't last. When you feel it crest, the steepest drop of the conveyor is next."

Even with the warning, she uttered a little shriek as the cart pitched forward. Pointless, for he'd wrapped his arms around her and drew her to his chest as he leaned back. Oh, this was worth the shriek.

They reached a milder descent, but she stayed within his arms. "This feels more like Dirklan." Fanteal pulled her gloves off and stuffed them in a pocket.

"Yes, we're deep enough for a steady temperature."

His hands were bare, too, and it felt so natural to rest hers atop them. She sighed, reaching into her element. "Air's coming through channels, too, with a little salt riding in from the ocean."

"Like Jourendia. We'll be stopping soon."

The cart thumped beneath her, and brakes engaged. They must have run over a switch. "Is this the tunnel's end?"

"No." He helped her over the cart's rail. "We call this the pit. A seventy-foot drop."

The area was well lit. A massive iron hook hung from the ceiling. Rods, pulleys, chains, and more glistened in the magnery light, which the dark gray walls tried to swallow.

Jaikon led her to the side. "This way. There's a lift." He guided her onto it. "Keep your hands inside the rail." He worked the crank, and they descended beside another mechanism.

"What is that?"

"A bucket lift. It brings the rock up from the lower conveyer to the upper one."

"This entire undertaking is amazing!"

"It is. Next time I hear someone say that abovegrounders know nothing of invention, I'm going to have to set them straight."

She laughed. They reached the bottom and boarded another conveyor cart for a shorter ride. This time, the end left them beside a spool of copper and a crate of magnery lamps. She left her fur-lined wrap on the cart.

He shed his cloak, too, and led her to the blank wall.

"It looks so...impenetrable."

He smiled at her quip. "I know it all looks the same, but over there..." He pointed beyond the conveyor. "The miniscule grains within the rock are aligned so they fit snug. Here…" He placed his palm against the tunnel's end. "Some are aligned, and some are not, which leaves tiny gaps. This is the rock that feels less dense to me. Sometimes, there are faults, too, like back at the pit, but they are unusual in ipenrock." His expression turned apologetic. "So, now you have seen it, my dear. I should have thought to bring you along on one of my trips down."

"Better on Savoring Day." She stepped closer, which she couldn't have done surrounded by workmen. Would he notice the opportunity or just keep thinking about what needed doing? She glimpsed the answer as a crease deepened between his eyebrows and he half turned toward the blank wall. Frustrating! "You don't have to work every single day."

"I don't. But something is different."

"What is?"

"The part where the tunnel belongs." His voice had softened as he concentrated on sending his senses deeper. "Wow!"

"What?"

"It has been fragmented into small pieces. Still in place, but separated."

"All of it?"

"The near part is. I'm extending slowly, finding out how far. I don't want to search wide and let every former in Jourendia notice me."

"Do you suppose Charlis did it?"

"I cannot imagine who else. But no one has ever sensed him working. I asked the formers to let me know if they detected anyone."

She sensed something unusual in his gift. Holding back, perhaps, when she was used to him flinging it wide. She'd better let him focus.

His smile flashed wide. "Charlis!" The whispered name only emphasized his excitement amid deep concentration. His eyes narrowed, then he withdrew, and his rigid shoulders sank back.

Jaikon uttered an amazed sort of laugh. "He's done a *lot*. He must have worked every night and weekend." Jaikon pressed his palms against the wall as though that helped him sense. "It will take a day—or two, maximum—of our normal procedure. Then, we can pierce a narrow tunnel through the space he's prepared." The words tumbled from him. Was he thinking aloud? "Might be able to pull some back…he'll feel our effort…can pull as much into the street below as he sees fit. I need Wuldour down here for another assessment…We need a container…letters."

He swung away from the wall and grabbed her hands. "Are the letters written yet? We'll be through in a few days. Two, with an all-out push."

He seemed ready to run through the tunnel. Fanteal held tight to him. Were his hands trembling with the excitement or were hers? Both? "Did you get a sense of how Charlis is faring?"

"He's worried. Some relief when he sensed me, then right back to worry before he stopped using his gift. I got five or ten seconds with him at the most. That must mean he hasn't been discovered and doesn't want either of us noticed, so I withdrew. We need to let the king and ambassador know, so they have time to prepare their letters. And Wuldour."

Every ounce of his excitement had bled into her, and she darted with him back to the conveyor cart.

"Ugh, no! Fanteal, wait!"

She'd gathered her skirt to climb on, but he drew her away. "What's wrong?"

"Us. We're always the ones wrapped up in solving problems for others. I thought I'd have more notice…was going to make sure we got our day. And now we won't. But I'm not waiting any longer, no matter who needs me…or you."

Was this finally happening? She kept her lips closed, trying not to give everything away with her expression as she gazed into his brown eyes.

He closed them, tilting his head back. "I've been thinking of ways to ask you for months, and I cannot remember one of them."

Her shoulders shook, but she kept her laugh locked inside. Sure, he would choose that moment to slide his hands up her arms.

"Oh, that's funny, is it?"

He wasn't getting a word out of her until he asked, but she granted him an innocent smile.

"Dearest Fanteal, I must know before the tunnel is opened. Will you marry me?"

"Yes!" It came out louder than expected, and she giggled at the echo. "I've been waiting such a long time to say that. You had me worried we were destined to stay friends forever and nothing more."

He whispered into her ear, "I prefer friends forever and a great deal more."

His embrace was all she had hoped it would be. He slid his lips along her cheek until they found hers. Oh! Ooh...this was why lovers kissed for so long. She slid her hands up his back, holding him near.

When time started again, she nestled into his arms, and he settled for kissing her hair. He must have regained awareness of their surroundings. "I guess I didn't pick the most romantic setting, did I?"

"This little spot here in your embrace is quite romantic."

"Ah, convenient, for I take my arms with me everywhere I go."

She chuckled deep inside. "Oh, I am so happy!"

He tilted his head back, to laugh this time. "Well, that's good."

"Let's go tell my parents."

"Ah, parents." He helped her onto the cart, pushed a few levers, then again ran to hop on. "We travel backwards this time, for our feet must stay downhill." He settled into position. "This time, I can hold you close the entire way."

She leaned her head against one of his shoulders and swept her fingertips along his opposite cheek, slightly rough this late in the afternoon. Uh-oh. "Are we going to be late for dinner?"

"You're the one with the watch."

She angled her wrist to catch the glow of a magnery light. "Hm, probably just make it in time to tell my parents before we go into the dining room."

"I've been assuming that I have permission to ask you, since I could have married you in Dirklan. That's true, isn't it?"

"Yes. They've been expecting it and approve, so no worries there." She thought for a few minutes. "Now I don't know if we should be married aboveground or below. Wouldn't it be wonderful if all three of our parents could be present?"

"Ah, that would be a nice touch. A festive event, with at least some of us coming and going through the tunnel. Have to widen it after the initial messages get through, but with cooperation above and below, it won't take all that long."

His muscles hardened behind her back. "What's wrong?" she asked.

"Just remembering Charlis's worry. I hope my father is still all right."

CHAPTER 42

Sir Mikkael lowered himself into the hard chair designated for the accused. Only Bella's words gave him any hope that he might be spared a guilty verdict for a crime that was only one step down from murder.

He was tired of this courtroom. Somewhat his fault, for he'd ensured that Creflon's trial had taken as long as possible, belaboring the significance of every scrap of evidence.

The one and only thing that saved Creflon from a guilty verdict was the fact that he was, indeed, provincial chief former and possessed final authority over the dome. Despite the high judge's stern words to Creflon, an ominous precedent had been set. A guild chief could stop communication between the Prime Minister of Dirklan and the King of Welcia. If Charlis could have testified, things might have gone differently, but Sir Mikkael couldn't risk bringing him out of hiding. For only a tunnel could reverse the weakening of Dirklan's government.

The stolen letters and maps got him nowhere. All that had been found in the rooms of those accused were piles of quartz sand. Merely routine discarding of old documents, according to Governor Armeen. Again, the key witnesses, Fanteal and Charlis, could not testify.

The inquiry Sir Mikkael started into Armeen influence over the substance guilds of Alluthin, stretched even longer than the trials. Most of the hearings were held in Alluthin, leaving only the conclusional arguments to be heard in this courtroom. Unfortunately, the Alluthin guild members wouldn't speak against the Armeens.

That delay tactic had seeped away, and Sir Mikkael could no longer avoid the case that Creflon raised against him, alleging that he had usurped the authority of the Formers' Guild by ordering the opening of the dome.

He hadn't, exactly, but he'd knowingly allowed it. Almost the same as ordering it, so in the end, he would accept the full responsibility to spare others. After he stretched this trial out as well.

Bella's report that Charlis had felt Jaikon along the tunnel route provided his one hope. It was only a matter of time. He just had no idea how long that time was, and whether he could stretch this trial longer.

Creflon wanted it short. That, he'd made clear at the beginning. Wouldn't he be disappointed?

The day rolled slowly, drawing yawns throughout the crowd. Governors, representatives, guild chiefs, Keepers of the Writ, and every variety of leader had come to Jourendia to see how this pivotal case would unfold. So had many locals, and the courtroom overflowed. How many stood outside the broad windows, listening by a wind weaver's gift?

Halfway through the afternoon, Sir Mikkael suggested recessing until tomorrow. The high judge refused. "We will continue through the entirety of each workday."

Tedium, he was used to. Worry made it much harder to endure. His stomach rumbled, and a glance at the hour markers told him they had one more to go.

A sudden breeze gushed through the chamber. Creflon's words flitted away as the wind weaver looked around with widened eyes.

"What is it?" the judge asked her.

She blinked, still apparently following something beyond the chamber. "Lady Fanteal is sending her gift throughout Jourendia."

"As though we need another refreshing," Creflon said flatly. "Now, resume lifting my—"

"This isn't a simple refresh, sir," she explained to the judge. "It's not flowing through the air channels, but from somewhere else."

Creflon sneered. "Another unnecessary channel, announced with a rude interruption."

Sir Mikkael watched the wind weaver. She moved like she was trying to get her bearings and locate something. She faced the eastern wall, turning to follow it back through the farther reaches of the cavern. Her gaze had started high, but it sank. "How very strange." She curled her fingers into a tight circle. "It's a narrow flow coming in down by the cavern floor."

Creflon lost his sneer and paled. He stood rooted, facing the same way as she. Several other formers in the crowd gaped in that same direction. Creflon's lips spasmed.

"I assume..." The judge's voice turned acidic. "...that you've lost interest in your latest argument. Would you like to tell me what is going on?"

"Unassessed forming," Creflon snarled. "Unapproved. By Charlis Torgan. He must be arrest—"

A rumble echoed through the cavern. The non-formers trembled, but Creflon pulled his lips back from clenched teeth.

"Are we in imminent danger?" the judge asked. By his slow delivery, he must have looked at the formers in the room and drawn his own conclusion from their demeanor. Surprised, certainly, but not fearful.

"Yes!" Creflon shouted. "Unassessed forming is a danger to all."

Sir Mikkael blinked dust from his eyes, as did several others. The wind weaver lifted her voice and sent it through the cavern. "Wind weavers, follow Lady Fanteal's lead and sweep the dust out the ocean channel."

The judge snapped the gong at his desk to gain silence. "Could I get an answer to my question from a Jourendian former?"

A man in the crowd stood. "There is *no* danger of collapse, sir. The caverns are stable. A tunnel has opened in the eastern wall of the city cavern. It is quite small but widening as we speak." He tilted his head. "Former Jaikon's presence is unmistakable, although he is not forming. I can feel Charlis as well, though I cannot tell if he is forming or just sensing. There is another former—one strongly gifted, whom I do not recognize. I believe that former is working on the tunnel."

Creflon shouted, perhaps because the wind weaver no longer aided voices, "This is unassessed forming and must be stopped. Peace officers, come with me." He stomped through the aisle.

"Creflon Lawfertee, return to the bench." The judge's words stopped him midstride.

Sir Mikkael used the moment of Creflon retracing his steps. "It is likely that the tunnel formation was duly assessed and approved by aboveground formers, including the one who is currently doing the work. The belowground portion was assessed months ago by three formers and approved by Provincial Chief Former Agriben. Again, I must state that Creflon's appointment to provincial chief has not yet been confirmed at the highest level."

Creflon made another try. "I currently possess the authority to—"

"Be silent." The judge then addressed the local former who still stood. "Go with peace officers to the location of the tunnel. If you find Charlis, tell him I summon him to give evidence as a...*witness*. Monitor developments and return when the situation is stable." He watched them depart, clearing his throat a few times. "The air seems to be mostly clean," he said to the wind weaver. "Can you lift voices again?"

"Yes, sir." She went back to her place.

The judge proceeded to launch one question after another at Creflon. Fortunately for the chief former, it didn't last very long.

The peace officers returned with Charlis, Bella, and a glistening sphere, which Charlis rolled through the aisle toward the judge's bench.

He stopped it and bowed to the high judge. "This has just arrived, sir, via a tunnel created by aboveground formers."

The judge leaned forward to peer over his elevated desk. His impassive expression gave way to anticipation. "Never did I expect to feel I was reliving the days when the first ambassador came to Dirklan. Have you opened it?"

"No, sir. The engraving states it is from King Darinneth and Queen Ambassador Trissina to you and to Prime Minister Sened Mikkael."

Creflon stepped forward. "I shall open it."

"You?" The judge demanded. "Who has been accused of stealing and destroying official documents? It is only for lack of a witness that you are still free. Do not speak again until I address you."

"I wondered," Charlis said, "whether that might be why you called me as witness. I did hear Creflon, Grellin, and Governor Armeen in the equipment room talking about documents they'd taken from the vessel and were clearly reading. After they left, Lady Fanteal and I looked into the vessel and found it empty. I don't know what happened to the documents after they were taken."

Governor Armeen stood. "I assert that he is lying and claim the right to test him. Did you, Charlis, open the dome at the order of Sened Mikkael?"

"That is not a valid test," Sir Mikkael objected, "but an obvious attempt to incriminate another."

The judge flicked a finger toward Sir Mikkael. "Agreed."

"Nonetheless," Charlis said, "I wish to respond as I see fit."

The judge looked at him curiously. "You do not have to, but you may."

Charlis linked his hands behind his back. "I was faced with two laws. One requires me to use my gift in compliance with civil law, and the other requires me to follow the decisions of the chief former. In this case, each of those laws demanded that I break the other. At least, they did after Creflon was elected, but they did not contradict while Agriben was alive. I was with Agriben when he passed. His final words to me were to open the dome, no matter what happened. I promised him I would. Sir Mikkael never ordered me to open it. I opened the dome in response to my own conscience and Provincial Chief Former Agriben's order."

The judge looked over at his recorder, who was rapidly writing, and waited for her to finish. Then he leaned forward with as much of a smile as his sternness allowed. "Open the vessel."

Charlis knelt beside the sphere, about two feet in diameter, and quickly deciphered the locking mechanism. The halves split apart. A package nestled on one side, portfolios on the other. Charlis lifted them out, reading the inscriptions. He handed one to the judge, one to Sir Mikkael, and held the other.

The judge opened his but nodded to the one Charlis still held. "What have you there?"

"It is addressed to the Formers' Guild, to be delivered after you have read yours."

Sir Mikkael calmly read his first sheet of paper, then leaned back in his uncomfortable chair like it was a cushy armchair. He made no effort to hide his smile, which the judge soon noticed, though he had not yet finished the several documents in his stack.

"Your news looks pleasing," the judge said. "Feel free to share what you wish."

"I am delighted to announce the engagement of my son to Royal Ambassador Fanteal de Noviam. They expect the tunnel to soon be wide enough for me and a few guests from Dirklan to attend their wedding. Afterward, they will return to live in Dirklan." He could have made pointed eye contact with Grellin...but why taint his delight?

"Pleasant news, indeed," the judge commented, once again looking to the opened sphere. "Please hand me that package, which Ambassador Trissina sent to us."

Bella lifted it up to his desk.

"Thank you. I assume you came here for a reason. Who are you?"

"I am Bella Karabeth, aide to Lady Fanteal, so I attend functions pertaining to her. Also, I am the wife of Charlis." A sudden murmur swept through the crowd, and the judge lifted his gaze then focused on her. Bella flashed a mischievous smile. "We were wed a few hours before he opened the dome."

"Ah." The judge unstrapped the package and addressed the crowd. "Ambassador Trissina has sent a token of food to us, reminiscent of the food sent to Devron long ago. This rather curious fruit..." He lifted it, the skin mottled shades of yellow, red, and orange. "...is called pinnpear. It is fragile and unsuitable to send through our import cataract. However, they will be able to ship this and much more through the tunnel when it is completed." He turned it this way and that. "If only I knew how to open it."

"They served it to us at the palace," Sir Mikkael said. "May I assist?"

"Oh, yes." He rang the gong and declared, "I am dismissing the case against Sir Sened Mikkael, for the statement sent by Ambassador Fanteal is quite enlightening."

Sir Mikkael left all his discomfort behind and approached the judge's high desk. He split the fruit into sections, revealing the pods behind thin membranes. "There is nothing like it in Dirklan. Will you try a piece?"

The judge pursed his lips. "I'll have to wait, for I cannot accept anything while I judge. You decide whom to share it with."

Sir Mikkael handed one section to the wind weaver who was serving them, another to Charlis, who certainly deserved something extra for months of hiding, then walked past all the dignitaries in the front and randomly handed the other sections to the local people.

Behind him, the judge promised public reading and posting of the king's and ambassador's letters. "In the meantime," he said, "I must announce that Kingdom Chief Former Wuldour rejects the appointment of Creflon Lawfertee to any chief former position. The high judge of Regissa has issued arrest warrants for Governor Armeen, Grellin Armeen, Creflon Lawfertee, and Governor Nirundale. Trials will be held in the king's court—aboveground." He focused on the men named. "I am assuming you wish to be civil, so you may proceed to the rear and give yourselves into the custody of the peace officers at the exits."

Sir Mikkael had reached the front again, and the judge asked him, "Two empty governors' seats—is that a problem?"

"I will let their representatives choose one of their own to temporarily fill the seats, and I will hold interim elections within a month."

The judge inclined his head, then watched the return of the former he had sent to the tunnel. "What news do you bring?"

"The formers above have lowered a rotating chain system, and I have stabilized our end." When no one reacted, he grinned. "We can send messages up and down. Dozens of them." He began to laugh. "Every day!"

Sir Mikkael joined his laughter. "This, I must see at once."

In the palace, a late elaborate dinner neared its end. Since it honored an engagement announcement, couples were seated together. A servant hurried into the room. He presented a small plate of quartz to the king and queen, and another to the engaged couple.

Fanteal and Jaikon leaned close to read theirs as the king read his note and announced, "The first container has reached Dirklan. Prime Minister Mikkael sends his greetings and thanks to all who helped construct it."

Cheers and clinking glasses erupted for a second time that evening. But Fanteal liked her note the best.

> *I wish you could hear the celebration in Jourendia Square.*
> *The news of your engagement gladdens Dirklan as much as*

*news of the tunnel. Yet that is nothing compared to the joy
you bring to my heart. Savor these days, my children.*

"Aw!" Fanteal murmured. "I love your father."

"That's good," Jaikon said, "because I'm not trading him for any other. Wait a minute. Are you trying to make me jealous?"

She snickered, then whispered, "You have nothing to ever be jealous of again."

"True. I will have the most perfect wife, after all."

"Perfect is a myth."

He slid an arm around her shoulder. "You are perfect for me."

Her cheeks were beginning to hurt from smiling. "I'll accept that."

"Perfect for Dirklan, too."

"I don't know. What Dirklan needs seems to change rather fast. Ellincreo forbid that anything ever happens to that tunnel."

"It is a *thing*, my dear, and *things* do not last forever." He winked. "But I expect it'll outlast our children."

He had a point. She swirled her drink. "A dome once saved Dirklan, but do you suppose it will ever need to be opened again?"

"I don't know. New problems—new answers."

"That all sounds very technical and changeable. But at the core...the deepest things don't change."

Jaikon narrowed his eyes. "Are you thinking of Devron's writings? How he attributed success to love and hope."

"Yes, but it also seems that we need to *see*. Beyond the ordinary, I mean. Otherwise, we will miss out on loving the one we don't understand. Maybe even miss the gifts in ourselves. We won't glimpse the amazing hopes that we could aspire to."

Jaikon's smile slowly stretched. "Oh yes, love, you are what Dirklan needs." He lifted his glass to touch hers. "May we see and savor every gift, no matter how strange."

SHARE THE ADVENTURE

I hope that you found something in these pages that made your life a little richer. If you liked this story, maybe others would too. You can help them find it by leaving a brief review or even by clicking some stars wherever you like to purchase or review books. Those star ratings and reviews help me, too, and I greatly appreciate all of them.

Would you like to read more stories like this one? If so, I invite you to join my newsletter. I will send you some free short stories, share a little about life, and let you know about new books and an occasional sale. I won't overload your inbox or share your email address with others. You may unsubscribe at any time. Sign up at SharonRoseAuthor.com. I hope to hear from you!

THE NEXT ADVENTURE

TO STREAM AN OCEAN
ARTS OF SUBSTANCE – NOVEL 3

Quakes spread from the ocean floor. A small matter compared to corruption among the gifted, empty royal coffers, and regicide. Long live the new king.

Ambassador Danivid, the deceased king's brother, is recalled from Dirklan Province to take on the role he never wanted. The kingdom's shifting beliefs make it all the harder. Machines have reduced the need for the streaming and forming gifts people once relied on. A new constitution has redefined the role of the monarchy and the guilds. Yet, amid rising prosperity, something is going terribly wrong. What had the previous king discovered before his sudden death?

As the crown is placed on Danivid's head, a quake shakes the capital city—as ominous as the realization that his brother was murdered. An attempt on his life follows. Corruption, theft, and murder plague the kingdom. Quakes continue, and volcanic plumes roil the ocean. Danivid is the only streamer who pays attention. What a kingdom to be saddled with!

A neighboring country has gone silent and now provides a steady flow of a supposedly harmless drug, which is anything but. Danivid sends an ambassador to discover what is happening. She is warmly welcomed, and the neighbor's ambassador, Trellian, is appointed to accompany her home. Yet someone is determined to kill them en route. They survive only because Trellian is no ordinary ambassador.

In Danivid's palace, Trellian discovers a plot more devious than simple murder of the king. As they close in on suspects, the volcano and ocean rise to fulfill their warnings. No former or streamer is prepared—except King Danivid. But how can one man stream an entire ocean and survive? Especially when some don't want him to live.

To Stream an Ocean is the third novel in the ARTS OF SUBSTANCE trilogy. These stories merge the excitement of epic fantasy with the camaraderie of cozy fantasy. Each stand-alone novel explores one of the world's three substance gifts: forming, wind weaving, and streaming. With every ability comes risk. The gifts are neither easy nor safe. Who has the courage and wit to use their gift well? And at what cost?

BOOKS BY SHARON ROSE

Fantasy

Arts of Substance

To Form a Passage – Novel 1
To Weave the Wind – Novel 2
To Stream an Ocean – Novel 3

Castle in the Wilde

A Castle Lost — An Early Days Novella
A Castle Sealed — Prequel Novella
A Castle Awakened — Novel 1
A Castle Contended — Novel 2
A Castle From Ashes — Novel 3

Science Fiction

Diverse Similarity — Novel 1
Diverse Demands — Novel 2
Agents of Rivelt — A Novel in Short Stories

More titles are coming. Find the full list at SharonRoseAuthor.com.

Acknowledgements

There's so much to be grateful for! Where to start?

Small? That would be Sheba, the furball who keeps my lap warm while I write. She occasionally types, also, but that is less helpful.

Difficult? That would be editing (shudder). Bridgett makes it bearable.

Typos? Beastly little things! Michael helped stomp them out.

Art? Once again, Kirk turned my imaginings into a book cover.

The long haul? This heavy work is supported by so many. Realm Makers, Write Now Writers Group, friends who know nothing about writing but still listen to me, and of course, my wonderful family.

Ideas and comfort? Father, Friend, and Spirit. Yes, I'm talking about God, but hey, I'm a writer! A single word is not enough for the one who loves me so deeply.

Readers? That's probably *you*. Whether you read in advance, or you found this book long after I write these words, thank you for imagining with me. I hope you found some treasures to keep.

I appreciate all of you more than I can ever say!

ABOUT THE AUTHOR

I started writing when I was seven years old. Okay, *My Life as a Flying Squirrel* may have had a couple spelling errors, but my classmates loved it.

Plenty of life has happened since that first story, and I've come to realize the things that fascinate me. People. Communication. Culture. Personality. Viewpoints. Beliefs. Anything that makes each of us beautifully unique. Small wonder that my art spills out in story form.

It was only a matter of time before I just had to share my stories. I publish fantasy and science fiction because they allow vast spaces to explore. My stories weave cultures and characters, who are more than they seem to be, into adventures with mystery, romance, and hope.

When I'm not writing or reading, I may be traveling, enjoying gardens, or searching for unique coffee shops with my husband. We live in Minnesota, USA, famed for its mosquitoes—uh, I mean 10,000 lakes and vibrant seasons.

To find out more, visit SharonRoseAuthor.com.
Follow me on:
Amazon, Goodreads, BookBub, Facebook, etc.
Find all of my links at: https://linktr.ee/sharonrose.author

www.ingramcontent.com/pod-product-compliance
Lightning Source LLC
Chambersburg PA
CBHW061541190726
48289CB00004B/1121